MILLS & BOON®

The Chatsfield Collection!

2 BOOKS FREE!

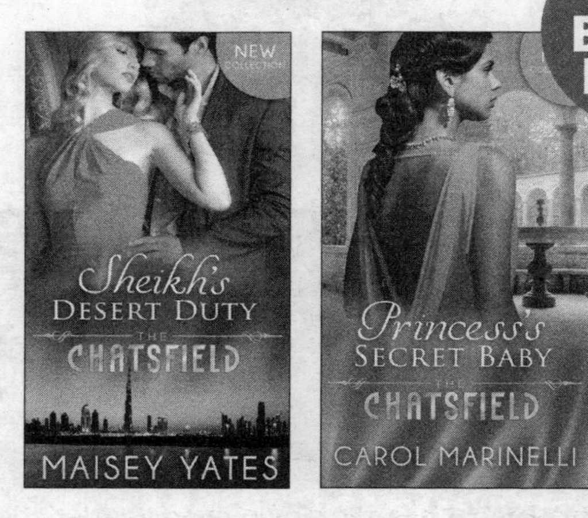

Style, spectacle, scandal...!

With the eight Chatsfield siblings happily married and settling down, it's time for a new generation of Chatsfields to shine, in this brand-new 8-book collection! The prospect of a merger with the Harrington family's boutique hotels will shape the future forever. But who will come out on top?

Find out at
www.millsandboon.co.uk/TheChatsfield2

ATSFIELD_PROMO_BK

BECOMING DR BELLINI'S BRIDE

BY
JOANNA NEIL

When **Joanna Neil** discovered Mills & Boon, her lifelong addiction to reading crystallised into an exciting new career writing Medical Romance™. Her characters are probably the outcome of her varied lifestyle, which includes working as a clerk, typist, nurse and infant teacher. She enjoys dressmaking and cooking at her Leicestershire home. Her family includes a husband, son and daughter, an exuberant yellow Labrador and two slightly crazed cockatiels. She currently works with a team of tutors at her local education centre to provide creative writing workshops for people interested in exploring their own writing ambitions.

CHAPTER ONE

KATIE stood still for a moment, her green eyes slowly scanning the horizon. Her nerves were frayed. Perhaps taking time out to look around her at this part of the sweeping California coastline was just the medicine she needed right now.

She would never have believed she would find herself in such a beautiful place as this small, quiet town, with its charming cottages and quaint shops and general sleepy atmosphere. As for the bay, it was a wide arc of golden sand, backed by rugged cliffs and rocks, a striking contrast to the clear blue of the Pacific Ocean that lapped its shores. Beyond all that was the magnificent range of the Santa Lucia Mountains, lush and green, their slopes forested with redwoods, oaks and pine.

She drank in the view for a moment or two longer, absorbing the tranquillity of her surroundings. Then she pulled in a deep breath and turned away to walk along the road towards a distant building set high on a bluff overlooking the sea.

One way or another, it had been a difficult day so far, and she could see little chance of things improving. She still had to meet with her father, and even though she had become used to seeing him over these last couple of weeks, it was always something of a strain for her to be with him.

'We'll have lunch,' he'd said, as though it was an everyday, natural occurrence.

'Okay.' She'd looked at him and his expression had been relaxed and easygoing. He seemed to genuinely want to meet up with her again. 'I have a half-day on Wednesday,' she told him, 'so that should work out well enough.'

And now he was waiting for her at the restaurant, sitting at a table on the open-air terrace, gazing out over the ocean. Katie guessed he was watching the boats on the horizon. He hadn't noticed her coming towards him, and she was glad of that. It gave her the chance to compose herself, as well as an opportunity to fix his image once more in her mind.

She studied him. He was not as she remembered from all those years ago, neither did he bear any resemblance to the pictures her mother had carefully stored in the photograph album. She guessed at one time he must have been tall and vital, a vigorous man, full of energy and ambition, but at this moment he appeared frail, a shadow of his former self. His body was thin, his face faintly lined, and his brown hair was faded, threaded through with silver strands.

'Hi, there…' Katie hesitated. She was still struggling with the idea of calling this man her dad. It went against the grain to use the word, considering that he was almost a stranger to her. Instead, she asked, 'Have you been waiting long? I'm sorry I'm a bit late. I was held up at work.'

'That's all right. Don't worry about it.' Her father smiled and rose carefully to his feet to pull out a chair for her. 'You look harassed. We can't have that, can we? Sit yourself down and take a minute or two to settle. Life's too short to be getting yourself in a tizzy.'

His breathing was wheezy and laboured, and Katie was concerned. She'd heard that he had been ill for some time, but his health seemed to have taken a downturn even in the few days since she had last seen him.

'Thanks.' She sat down quickly so that he could do the same. Then she gazed around her. 'It's lovely to be able to sit out here and enjoy the fresh air… And it's all so perfect…idyllic, with the tubs of flowers and all the greenery.'

'I thought you'd like it. The food's good, too.'

A waitress approached with menus, and Katie accepted hers with a smile, opening it up to look inside and study the contents. In reality, though, her mind was in a whirl and she was finding it difficult to concentrate, so that the text became a blur.

Her father signalled to the wine waiter and ordered a bottle of Cabernet Sauvignon, before turning back to Katie. 'Why don't you tell me what sort of a day you've had?' he suggested. 'It can't have been too good, by the looks of things. Are you getting on all right at the hospital? You've been there almost a week now, haven't you?'

She nodded. 'I'm really happy to be working there. The people are great…very friendly and helpful. I'm working in Paediatrics most of the time, but I also have a couple of days when I'm on call to deal with general emergencies if they arise locally. Mostly people will ring for an ambulance if there's an accident or medical incident, but if I'm nearer and it's likely to be something serious then I'll go out as a first responder. It's a good opportunity for me to keep up with emergency work, so I was glad with this job came up.'

Her father glanced at his menu. 'It sounds as though it's the kind of work you enjoy. It's what you were doing in England, in Shropshire, isn't it?'

'That's right.'

The wine waiter arrived, pouring a small amount of clear, red wine for her father to taste, before filling two glasses.

Katie took a sip of her drink, savouring the rich, fruity flavour. She sent her father a quick, searching glance. Somehow he always managed to get her to talk about herself. He very rarely revealed anything of his lifestyle, about what had brought him to where he was now.

'What about you?' she asked. 'Did you always have it in mind to come out here—was there something about Carmel Valley that drew you—or was it *someone* who led you to this place?'

'The company I worked for sent me out here, initially,' he answered, placing his menu down on the table. He nodded towards the one she was holding. 'Have you decided what you'd like to eat yet? The filet mignon is always good.'

'Yes, I think I'll go with that. But I'd prefer the cold slices, rather than a steak, I think…with tomato, red onion and blue cheese.'

'And a Caesar salad?'

'That sounds good.'

He nodded. 'I'll grab the waitress's attention.' He studied her once more. 'So what's been happening to get you all flustered today? You've always been calm and collected whenever we've seen one another, up to now. Is it a problem at work?'

She shook her head. 'Not really… I mean, yes, in a way, I suppose.' She gave an inward sigh and braced herself. It didn't look as though he was going to give up on trying to tease it out of her, so she may as well get it off her chest.

'I saw a little boy at the clinic today,' she said. 'He was around four years old, and his mother told me he'd been unwell for some time. She hadn't known what to do because his symptoms were vague, and she put it down to the fact that he'd had a cold and sore throat. Only he took a sudden turn for the worse. When I examined him, his body was swollen with oedema, his blood pressure was high, and his heart was racing.'

Her father frowned. 'Seems that he was in a bad way, poor little chap.'

'Yes, he was. I had him admitted to the renal unit. He was losing protein in his urine, and it looks as though his kidneys are inflamed.'

He winced. 'Definitely bad news. So, what will happen to him now?'

'They'll do tests, and give him supportive treatment. Probably diuretics to bring down the swelling, and he'll be put on a low-sodium, low-protein diet.'

She glanced around once more, looking out over the redwood deck rail to the ocean beyond. The sound of birds calling to one another mingled with the soft whoosh of surf as it dashed against the rocks below.

She looked back at him. 'What about you? You haven't told me much about yourself. Mum said that you worked in the import and export trade years ago—you had to travel a lot, she said.'

'Yes, I did. I suppose that's how I first became interested in the wine business.' He beckoned the waitress and gave their orders. After the girl had left, he said gently, 'This child you treated—he isn't the reason you're not quite yourself, is he? After all, you must have come across that kind of thing many times in the course of your work.'

She nodded, brushing a flyaway tendril of chestnut hair from her cheek. Her hair was long, a mass of unruly natural curls that defied all her attempts to restrain them. 'That's true.' She pressed her lips together, uneasy at having to revisit the source of her discomfort. 'I think he reminded me of a child I treated back in Shropshire... my ex-boyfriend's son, though he was much younger, only two years old. He had the same condition.'

'Ah...' He leaned back in his chair, a thoughtful expression crossing his face. 'So it made you think about the situation back home. I see it now. Your mother told me all about the break-up.'

She sent him a sharp glance. 'You've spoken to my mother?'

'I have.' He gave a faint smile. 'She called me... naturally, when she knew you would be coming out here, she wanted to make sure that you would be all right. A mother's protective instinct at work, I guess.'

Katie frowned, and began to finger her napkin. She wasn't at all pleased with her father knowing everything there was to know about her personal life. In many ways he was an unknown quantity as far as she was concerned, and yet it appeared he knew things about her that she would much rather had remained secret.

She was still trying to take it on board when a man approached their table. He was in his mid-thirties, she guessed, a striking figure of a man with dark, smouldering good looks that sent an immediate frisson of awareness to ripple along her spine. His clothes were superb. He was wearing an immaculate dark suit that had been expertly and, no doubt, expensively tailored, while his shirt was made from a beautiful fabric, finished in a deep shade of blue that perfectly matched his eyes.

Those eyes widened as he looked at Katie, and his gaze drifted appreciatively over her, lingering for a while on the burnished chestnut curls that brushed her shoulders, before moving downwards to lightly stroke her softly feminine curves.

Katie shifted uncomfortably in her seat, trying to shake off the impact of that scorching gaze. She felt warm all over, and the breath caught in her throat. Suddenly, she was all too conscious of the closely-fitting blouse she was wearing, a pintucked design in delicate cotton, teamed with a dove-grey, pencil-slim skirt.

Getting herself together, she looked up, deciding to face him head on and return the scrutiny in full measure. He had a perfectly honed physique, long and lean, undoubtedly firm-muscled beneath all the civilised trappings. His hair was jet black, strong and crisply styled, cut short as though to tame it, but even so there was an errant kink to the strands. He had the dazzling, sensual good looks of an Italian-American.

His glance met hers and a glint of flame sparked in his blue eyes. Then he dragged his gaze from her and turned to her father.

'Jack,' he said, 'this is a pleasant surprise. It's good to see you.' He extended a lightly bronzed hand in greeting. 'I'd thought of dropping by the house in the next day or so, since you've not been looking too well of late. How are things with you?' His voice was evenly modulated, deep and soothing like a creamy liqueur brandy, and Katie's heart began to thump heavily in response. Why on earth was this man having such an effect on her?

'Things are fine, Nick, thanks.' Her father waved a hand towards Katie. 'You haven't met my daughter, Katie, have you?'

Nick looked startled. 'Your daughter? I had no idea...'

'No. Well...' Her father cut him short, his breath rasping slightly with the effort. 'It's a long story. She came over here from the UK just a fortnight ago.' He switched his attention to Katie. 'Let me introduce you,' he said. 'Katie, this is Nick Bellini. He and his family own the vineyard next to mine. He's in partnership with his father and brother.'

Katie frowned. So her father hadn't even told his friends that he had a daughter. Another small part of her closed down inside. Perhaps she had been hoping for too much. Coming out here might turn out to be the biggest mistake of her life so far.

'I'm pleased to meet you,' Katie murmured. She wasn't expecting him to respond with more than a nod, but he reached for her, taking her hand in his and cupping it between his palms.

'And I'm more than delighted to meet you, Katie,' Nick said, his voice taking on a husky, sensual note. 'I'd no idea Jack was hiding such a treasure.'

Katie felt the heat rise in her cheeks. There was nothing casual about his greeting. The way he was holding her felt very much like a caress and it was thoroughly unsettling. Her alarm system had gone into overdrive at his touch and it was way more than she could handle. As if she hadn't had enough problems with men.

As soon as it was polite enough to do so, she carefully extricated her hand. Over the last year she had worked hard to build up a shield around herself, had even begun to believe she was immune, and here, in less than two minutes, Nick Bellini had managed to shoot her defences to smithereens.

'I've a feeling I've heard the name Bellini somewhere before,' she murmured. 'In a newspaper article, I think. I just can't recall exactly what it was that I read.'

He gave her a wry smile. 'Let's hope it was something good.'

He gave his attention back to her father. 'I was hoping we could get together some time in the next week or two to talk about the vineyards. My father has drawn up some papers, and he'd appreciate it if you would look them over.'

Her father nodded. 'Yes, he mentioned them to me.' He waved a hand towards an empty chair. 'Why don't you join us, Nick…unless you have business to attend to right now? We've only just ordered.'

Katie's heart gave a disturbing lurch. She stared at him. What was her father thinking?

'Thank you.' Nick acknowledged the invitation with a nod. 'I'd like that, if you're quite sure I'm not intruding?'

He looked to Katie for an answer, but words stuck in her throat and she had to swallow down the flutter of uncertainty that rose in her. Why on earth had her father made the suggestion? They spent so little time together as it was, and there was so much she wanted to know, so many questions that still had to be answered.

She needed to be alone with him, at least until she knew him better.

But what choice did she have? To refuse after Nick had shown his willingness to accept the invitation would be churlish.

Of course, Nick Bellini must have known all that. She nodded briefly, but sent him a glance through narrowed eyes.

He pulled out a chair and sat down, a half-smile playing around his mouth. She had the feeling he knew something of what she was going on in her mind, but if he had any real notion of her qualms he was choosing to ignore them.

'I came here to see the management about their wine cellar,' he said. 'After all, we might be able to tempt them into adding our new Pinot Noir to their collection—not strictly my job, but I like to keep in touch with all the restaurateurs hereabouts.' He paused as the waitress came to take his order.

'I'll have the teriyaki chicken, please, Theresa...with a side salad.' He gave the girl a careful, assessing look. 'You've done something different with your hair, haven't you?' His expression was thoughtful. 'It looks good. It suits you.'

'Thank you.' The girl dimpled, her cheeks flushed with warm colour.

Nick watched her as she walked away, and Katie observed him in the process. Did he respond like that to every woman who came his way? Were they all treated to a sample of his megawatt charm?

'Pinot Noir is a notoriously difficult wine to get right,' Jack said. 'But your father seems to have the Midas touch.'

Nick gave a fleeting smile. 'The key is to harvest the grapes in the cool of the evening and in the early morning. Then they're cold soaked before fermentation… and we use the whole berries for that process. Then, to reduce the risk of harsh tannins from the seeds and skins, they're pressed early.'

Jack nodded. 'Like I said, your father knows his business. Your vines are looking good again this year. It looks as though you'll have one of the best seasons yet.' He poured wine into a glass and passed it to Nick.

'We're hoping so.' Nick held the glass to his lips. 'Though you don't do too badly yourself. The Logan name is well respected around here…that's why we'd really like to make it part of the Bellini company.'

'It's a big undertaking.' Jack's features were sombre. 'I've worked hard to build up the business over the years. It's been my life's work.'

'Of course.' Nick tasted the wine, savouring it on his tongue before placing his glass down on the table. 'I'm sure my father will have taken all that into account.'

Katie frowned. It sounded as though the Bellinis were offering to buy out her father's company, but as usual Jack Logan was keeping his cards close to his chest. Was he thinking of selling up, or would he try to fend off their attempt at a takeover?

Nick turned towards Katie, as though remembering his manners. 'I'm sorry to talk shop…I expect this discussion of wine and grapes and company business must be quite boring for you.'

'Not at all.' Katie's expression was sincere. 'In fact I was really intrigued to learn that my father owns a vineyard, and I was actually hoping that one day soon I might get a chance to see it.'

'That won't be a problem,' Jack murmured. 'Just as soon as I get over this latest chest infection I'll take you on a tour. In the meantime, I'm sure Nick would be glad to show you around his place.'

'I'd be more than happy to do that,' Nick agreed, his gaze homing in on her. 'Maybe we could make a date for some time next week?'

'I… Possibly.' Katie was reluctant to commit herself to anything. She wasn't ready for Nick's full-on magnetism. Didn't she have enough to contend with right now, without adding to her troubles? 'I'll have to see how things work out at the hospital.'

'The hospital?'

Nick lifted a dark brow and Jack explained helpfully, 'Katie's a doctor…a paediatrician. She came out here to get a taste of California life and she's just settling into a new job.'

'Oh, I see.'

The waitress arrived with the meals just then, and Katie realised that she was hungry, despite her restless, slightly agitated frame of mind. Perhaps food would help to calm her down.

She tasted the thinly sliced beef. It was cooked to perfection, and the blend of tomatoes and cheese was sublime. She savoured the food, washing it down with a sip of red wine, and for a moment she was lost in a sweet oasis of serenity.

'So what was it that prompted you to come out here just now?' Nick asked. 'I mean, I guess you must have decided to come and see your father, but what made you choose to do it at this particular point in time?'

The peaceful moment was shattered in an instant. 'I… It just seemed to be the optimum moment,' she murmured. 'My contract back in Shropshire was coming to an end…and I'd heard that my father was ill. I wanted to see how he was doing.'

Nick studied her thoughtfully. 'There must have been more to it than that, surely? After all, Jack has suffered from lung problems for a number of years, and yet you haven't been over here to see him before this. Why now? Was it the job at the hospital that encouraged you to make the move?'

Katie frowned. Was that remark a faint dig at her because she hadn't visited her father in the last few years? What business was it of his, and who was he to judge? What did he know of their lives, of the torment she'd been through?

She made an effort to calm down. Perhaps she was being oversensitive…after all, the emotional distance between herself and her father was upsetting. It was a sore point that had festered over the years, and no one could really be expected to understand her inner hurt. And Nick was just like her father, wasn't he, probing into things she would sooner were left alone?

She said cautiously, 'The job was a factor, of course, and I suppose the idea of getting to know more of a different country held a certain appeal.'

Nick frowned. 'You could have taken a longish holiday, but instead you chose to come and live and work here. That must have been quite a big decision.'

Katie shrugged. 'Not necessarily.' She took a sip of her wine.

Jack shifted restlessly in his chair, as though he was impatient with the way the conversation was going. 'The truth is, Nick, Katie had a nasty break-up with a fellow back home in the UK. They'd been together for quite some time. Turns out she discovered he wasn't quite what he seemed, and she learned that he had a child by another woman. Katie still hasn't managed to get over it.'

He speared a piece of steak and held his fork aloft. 'So the long and the short of it is, she finished things with him, upped sticks and headed out here. Of course, he tried to stop her. He pleaded with her to stay with him, but she wasn't having any of it. The child was the one obstacle they couldn't overcome.'

He gave Nick a compelling stare, and Nick's eyes widened a fraction. An odd look of comprehension passed between the two men, as though somehow in that brief moment they had cemented some kind of masculine bond of understanding with one another.

Katie drew in a shocked breath. She felt as though she'd had the wind knocked out of her. Why was her father tittle-tattling her private business, especially to a man she'd only just met? Could things possibly get any worse? She was beginning to feel slightly nauseous.

'Well, that would certainly explain things.' Nick rested his fork on his plate. He studied her curiously, a faintly puzzled but sympathetic expression creasing his brow. 'I'm sorry. I imagine it must have come as a great shock to you,' he murmured. 'These things are very upsetting, of course, especially if it came out of the blue. He obviously meant a great deal to you, this man, if his fall from grace caused you to do something as drastic as to leave home and come out here. That must have been really difficult for you.'

He paused, looking at her, taking in the taut line of her jaw, and when Katie didn't respond, he added gently, 'But he was obviously very fond of you, too, and clearly he tried to explain his actions. I find it incredible that any man would do anything to cause you distress... but, in his defence, people do make mistakes, and I suppose all we can do is talk things through and try to understand how the situation came about.'

He hesitated once more, as though waiting for her to say something, but Katie stayed mute. She couldn't speak. Inside, she was a cauldron of seething emotions.

Perhaps her continuing silence had thrown him off balance because he added cautiously, 'It's not necessarily such a bad thing, fathering a child out of the confines of marriage...these things do happen sometimes. It's how people deal with the aftermath that probably matters most—they have to accept responsibility for their actions, and then perhaps we all need to take on board what's happened and move on.'

Katie took a deep breath and finally found her voice. 'So you've studied psychology along with wine production, have you, Mr Bellini?' Her gaze was frosty. 'I do appreciate you trying to help—I'm sure your theory has a good deal of merit, but, you know, I think I handled the situation the very best way I could.'

She stabbed at a slice of green pepper on her plate. 'Since I'd been with my fiancé for some three and a half years and, bearing in mind that his child was just two years old, I wasn't about to deal with his fall from grace lightly. I'm pretty sure we talked it through to the nth degree, and I have a very good idea of how the situation came about. I'm also in no doubt that James accepted full responsibility for his actions. For my part, I acknowledged totally what had happened...and I decided to move on.' Her green glance locked with his. 'That's one of the reasons why I'm here now.'

Nick looked as though he'd been knocked for six. 'It never occurred to me that any man would cheat on you,' he said in a preoccupied tone. 'I'd assumed the child was born before you met.' He held up his hands in a gesture of capitulation. 'Okay… I admit defeat. I was totally out of order. Clearly, it's none of my business and I was wrong to try to intervene.' He frowned. 'And you must call me Nick. I insist.'

Katie gave a crooked semblance of a smile. 'Perhaps it would be for the best if we change the subject?' She glanced at her father. He had started all this, but he seemed altogether indifferent to the havoc he had caused. He simply picked up the wine bottle and began to refill her glass.

'This is an excellent vintage,' he said. 'I'll order another bottle.'

Katie took a sip of wine. 'Tell me more about the vineyards,' she said, shooting a glance towards Nick. 'How much involvement do you have, if you're in partnership with your father and brother? Do you each have separate roles?'

'We do. I deal with the wine-making process rather than the growing side of things, whereas your father is more interested in aspects of cultivation. It's intensely important to get it right, if we're to produce a select variety of wines. You must let me show you the winery—I'm sure you would enjoy a visit. Maybe you could come along for a wine-tasting session?'

'Maybe.' She wasn't about to agree to anything.

'I'll give you a call some time and see if we can arrange a date.' Clearly, he wasn't about to give up, but by now Katie was well and truly on her guard.

From then on, they kept the conversation light. The

meal progressed, and Katie tried to damp down her feelings of antagonism towards this man who had cut in on her time with her father. What did her father care about her sensibilities, anyway? Perhaps she was wasting her time trying to find out why he had left all those long years ago.

And as to Nick Bellini, she had made up her mind that she would steer clear of him…no matter how hard he tried to persuade her into another meeting. He had touched a nerve with his comments, leaving her unusually rattled, and, besides, she knew it was a matter of self-preservation to avoid him. He could turn on the charm as easily as igniting a flame. She had been burned once. She wasn't going to risk body and soul all over again.

CHAPTER TWO

'NO, MUM, I really don't want to go and live with my father.' Katie frowned at the idea. 'He suggested it but, to be honest, it would be like living with a stranger. After all, we barely know one another…even after three weeks I still haven't really managed to fathom him out.'

She glanced around the medical office that she had begun to call her own and leaned back in her seat, beginning to relax. There were still some ten minutes of her coffee break left, more than enough time to sit and chat with her mother.

'These things take time, I suppose…' her mother said, 'but I think it was a wise decision to go over to California to see him. You would never have been comfortable with yourself if you hadn't gone to seek him out. I suppose we all need to discover our roots, if only to find out if there are some genetic characteristics that have been passed on.' Her tone was pensive. 'I know you're like your father in some ways—you know what you want, and once you've made up your mind, you go after it. That's why you've done so well with your medical training.'

Eve Logan was thoughtful for a moment or two, and Katie could imagine her at the other end of the line, mulling things over. 'It's a shame you couldn't find a place to stay that was nearer to the hospital, though,' Eve added. 'A half-hour drive to work every day doesn't sound too good, though I expect it could have been worse.' She hesitated. 'Anyway, how is your father? From what you said last week, it sounds as though he's more ill than we suspected.'

'He has breathing problems—he's suffering from what they call chronic obstructive pulmonary disease.' Katie had spoken to her father about his difficulties, and though he'd been reluctant to dwell on his problems, he'd at least opened up enough to give her a brief outline. 'He's taking a variety of medicines to keep it under control, but I don't think they're having the desired effect. I suspect his condition's deteriorating. He puts on a show of being able to cope, but I can see that it's a struggle for him sometimes.'

She paused. 'Anyway, you're right, it makes me even more glad that I decided to come out here when I did. No matter what I think about him, he's my father, and I feel as though I have to get to know him. Trouble is, every time we meet, he manages to sidestep my questions one way or another, or we're interrupted somehow.'

It still rankled that Nick Bellini had come along to disrupt her lunch with her father, though in truth she couldn't really blame him for that. He was an innocent bystander in all this, wasn't he, and how could he know what kind of relationship they had?

Still, he'd reached her in more ways than she could have imagined. Her father's business associate wasn't someone she would easily forget.

'That must be annoying,' her mother acknowledged. 'Still, you have plenty of time to build up some kind of relationship with him. You've signed a contract for a year, haven't you, so you don't have to rush things... and if, in the end, it doesn't work out, you can always come home. There'll always be a place here for you.'

'Thanks, Mum. That's good to know.' Katie's mouth made a rueful curve. She made it sound so easy, but the truth was, her mother was making a new life for herself back in Shropshire. She was going to marry Simon, a director of the pharmaceutical company where she worked, and they were very much wrapped up in one another right now. Katie wasn't going to do anything to intrude on that.

'Anyway,' she said, 'in the meantime, the scenery around here is fantastic, and with any luck I'll get to see the vineyard before too long. It's not as big as the Bellini vineyard next to it, but by all accounts it's quite impressive.'

'Bellini—I've heard that name,' her mother commented, an inflection of interest in her voice. 'There was an article about them in the Sunday supplement some time ago...all about the different varieties of wine they produce, as I recall. Apparently their land included your father's vineyard at one time—there was something about an Italian migrant seeing the potential for development at the turn of the last century and buying up as much acreage as he could afford. But as the generations went by there were financial problems and part of the land was sold off around 1980. As far as I know, your father didn't get into the business until some twenty or so years ago.'

'Well, he's made a success of it, by all accounts,' Katie murmured. Her mother's comments about the Sunday supplements had triggered a thought process in her mind, but she still couldn't remember what it was that she'd read about Nick Bellini. Some kind of high-society gossip that kept the Sunday papers occupied for a week or two, but annoyingly the gist of it had slipped her mind.

Her pager began to bleep, and she glanced at the small screen, quickly scanning the text message from her boss. 'I'm sorry, Mum,' she said, 'but I'll have to ring you back later. I have to go out on an emergency call. Someone's had a fall at a hotel nearby, and I need to go and see what the damage is.'

'All right, Katie, love. Take care of yourself. Remember I'm always here for you.'

'I will. Bye, Mum.'

Katie grabbed her medical bag and stopped by the reception desk on her way out. 'Divert any patients to Mike O'Brien, will you, Carla? I'm going out on a call to the Pine Vale Hotel.'

'I'll do that. No problem. You'll find the hotel just off the main road out of here.' The clerk gave her a wave as Katie disappeared through the wide front doors of the building.

Pine Vale Hotel was up in the hills, only a short drive from the hospital, and Katie reached it in good time. As she slid out of her car and took a look around, she was stunned by the magnificence of the building. White painted, it was a long, symmetrical edifice with two front extending wings at either end. It stood three storeys high, and there were large, Georgian-styled windows in abundance, with green painted shutters folded back. On the ground floor several sets of French doors were set back in archways, and Katie guessed the hotel must be flooded with light.

She wasn't wrong. Inside, the foyer reflected a quiet elegance, with traditional, comfy sofas that invited people to sit and take their ease. There were low, marble-topped tables and flower arrangements everywhere, adding glorious splashes of colour to delight the eye.

'Hello.' Katie introduced herself to the woman behind the desk. 'I'm Dr Logan. I understand you have a patient for me.'

'Oh, thank goodness you're here.' The woman, around thirty years old, with fair hair cut into a neat, gently curving bob, looked relieved. 'Yes, please come with me and I'll take you to her. The ambulance is on its way...the emergency services said they were sending a doctor out as well, as there might be a head injury, so I'm really glad to see you. I'm Jenny, by the way... Jenny Goldblum. I'm the hotel manager.'

Katie nodded acknowledgement. 'I was told that the lady fell in her room and appears to be semi-conscious—did anyone see the fall? It always helps to know the circumstances.'

Jenny shook her head. She pressed the button for the lift, and frowned as the door swished open. 'It isn't clear what happened. The maid found her when she went to clean the room. We think perhaps it had only just happened because a lady in the room next door had been speaking to Mrs Wyatt just a minute or so before.'

They stepped out of the lift on to the first floor, and Katie was ushered into a large, airy room, furnished in elegant style. There was a double bed with bedside units and an oak dresser to one side of the room, but at the far end, by the window, furniture had been arranged in a seating area. There was an oval oak coffee table and a couple of brocade-covered straight-backed chairs, along with armchairs upholstered in a matching fabric.

The patient, a woman in her fifties, was lying on the floor by the dresser. 'What's her first name?' Katie asked. 'Do you know?'

'It's Laura,' Jenny answered. 'She's staying here with her husband, but he went out earlier for a walk. We haven't been able to contact him yet.'

'Okay, thanks.'

The woman was being tended by one of the hotel staff members, but the girl moved aside as Katie approached. A rug covered the area close by, and it looked as though this had been crumpled when Mrs Wyatt fell.

Katie went to kneel down beside the injured woman. 'Mrs Wyatt...Laura...I'm Dr Logan. Can you hear me? Are you able to answer me?'

Laura Wyatt mumbled something indistinct and Katie tried again. 'Do you feel pain anywhere, Laura?' she asked gently. 'Can you tell me where it hurts?'

Again there was a muffled reply, and Katie came to the conclusion that Mrs Wyatt was too dazed to answer properly. She began a swift initial examination, checking for any obvious injuries and finishing with a neurological check.

'Laura,' she said at last, 'I think you've broken your shoulder—I know that it must be very painful, so I'm going to give you an injection to help with that. Do you understand what I'm saying?'

Laura tried to speak, but whatever she was trying to say didn't come out right, and Katie went ahead and set up an intravenous line. 'We're going to get you to hospital just as soon as possible,' she told the woman. 'In the meantime, I'm going to try to make you more comfortable with a sling that will stop you moving your arm.'

It wasn't clear whether Laura understood or simply couldn't answer, but Katie went on with her examination, checking her patient's blood pressure and listening to her heart.

'What's happened here?' A familiar male voice disturbed Katie's quiet concentration, and she looked up to see with a shock that Nick Bellini had entered the room. 'Katie?' He frowned, studying her for a moment, then turned his attention to her patient. Mrs Wyatt was groaning faintly.

His expression became grim, his eyes an intense, troubled blue.

'Nick?' Katie queried, removing the stethoscope from her ears. What was he doing here? And why had he thought it would be all right to come barging in that way? 'You really shouldn't be in here,' she told him. 'I'm examining a patient.'

'Yes... I see that. I'm sorry for intruding, but you have to understand, I own this hotel... I came as soon as I heard... I'm very concerned that someone has been injured on the premises.' His glance went to the woman once more. 'How is she?'

Katie's eyes widened. He owned this beautiful place? Was there no end to the extent of his empire? She blinked, and then hurriedly dragged her mind back to the business in hand. 'She has a fractured shoulder. I'm sure you must be very worried,' she murmured. 'That's understandable...but this lady has a right to privacy. I think you should leave.'

His head went back, a lock of midnight hair falling across his brow. He seemed stunned by her words, as though it hadn't for an instant occurred to him that anyone would ever try to evict him from where he wanted to be. She waited, bracing herself and expecting an argument, but then he said briefly, 'You'll keep me informed?'

Katie nodded, and without another word he turned and strode out of the room.

She went back to treating her patient. Nick's intrusion had set her emotions in turmoil once more. She had thought she had seen the last of him, and yet here he had turned up when she'd least expected him. His presence had thrown her completely off balance, and now, perhaps because she'd just learned of his association with the hotel, there was a snippet of a newspaper headline running through her head… Something about an heiress…the daughter of a hotel magnate… and Nick Bellini.

She made an effort to push all thoughts of him to one side, and concentrated her attention on her patient, helping the woman to sit up. Then she put the immobiliser sling in place.

'That should keep you fairly pain free until they can take care of you at the hospital,' she said.

The paramedics arrived a few minutes later, and Katie went with them to oversee her patient's transfer to the ambulance. By this time Laura's husband had arrived, and he went along with her, sitting beside his wife and holding her hand.

Katie turned to go back into the hotel, only to find that Nick was right there by her side. She gave a startled jump. He seemed to tower over her, his body firm as a rock. She took a moment to gather herself together and then she gave him a fleeting once-over. He was turned out as faultlessly as ever, dressed in a perfectly tailored dark suit that made him every inch the businessman, a force to be reckoned with.

He looked at her. 'A fractured shoulder, you said. Was she able to tell you what caused her to fall? Was it possible that it could have been the rug in her room—might she have tripped?'

She frowned, walking back with him into the foyer of the hotel. 'Are you worried about liability?' she asked. 'Is that why you rushed over here?'

'First and foremost, I came to see how the lady was doing...but, yes, I have to think about the hotel's liability in this. We take every precaution, but if someone were to be hurt on the premises, it could lead to some very worrying consequences.'

'Well, unfortunately I can't really say what caused the accident. Mrs Wyatt was too dazed to give me any answers, I'm afraid. All I know is that she'll probably need to have shoulder replacement surgery—she fell heavily and it was a nasty injury.'

His mouth flattened as he absorbed that information. Then he said in an even tone, 'Do you have to rush on to another call, or would you have time to stay and have a drink with me?'

She hesitated. Part of her wanted to walk away and avoid getting involved with him any further than need be, but another bit of her recognised his concern. He was anxious for the woman's well-being, and as a hotel proprietor he must be all too conscious of the threat of litigation. Maybe it wouldn't hurt to stay for a while and talk things through with him.

'I don't have to be back at work—my surgery hours are finished for the day, but I'm still on call, so perhaps we should make it coffee rather than anything alcoholic?'

He smiled, his face relaxing for the first time, reminding her all too potently of that sizzling allure that had made her go weak at the knees the first time she'd met him. She had to keep a firm hold on herself. This man could annihilate her sense of security with just one look, and that wouldn't do at all. She'd been down that road, and from her experience it led to heartache...big time. Emotionally, James, her ex, had scarred her for life. She'd been blissfully unaware that he'd been cheating on her, and once his indiscretions had come to light it had torn the heart out of her.

'We'll go out on to the sun terrace,' he said. 'I'll have Jenny send us out a tray of coffee. Just give me a moment to catch up with her.' He lightly cupped Katie's elbow, as though to keep her close, and she stood still for a moment while he beckoned to Jenny. That light touch was like a searing brand on her soft flesh.

The hotel manager was waiting by the desk, talking to the receptionist, but she turned and came over immediately.

'Ask chef to make up a lunch tray, will you, Jenny? Dr Logan will be staying for a while. We'll be out on the terrace by the shrubbery.'

Jenny nodded. 'I'll do that.' She glanced at Katie. 'Is Mrs Wyatt going to be all right?'

'I hope so,' Katie answered. 'The shoulder will give her some problems for quite a while, but those can be dealt with. I'm more concerned about her lack of response. They'll have to do tests at the hospital.'

Jenny nodded and hurried away to find the chef. Nick ushered Katie across the foyer and lounge then out through wide glass doors onto a paved area that was set out with white-painted wrought-iron tables and chairs. The scent of roses filled the air, and Katie was struck by the mass of colour all around, shades of crimson, yellow and pink shrub roses, all vying for attention in the landscaped garden.

'It's really beautiful out here,' Katie murmured as they sat down at one of the tables. 'Everything I've seen so far is overwhelmingly luxurious. I had no idea that you had other interests aside from the vineyard.'

He smiled. 'This place has been in my family's possession for many years—as far back as I can remember. I took it over when my father decided it was time to cut back on his commitments. I bought him out, rather than see it fall to outsiders.'

She gave him a considering look. 'The family name means a lot to you, doesn't it? You're very conscious of your heritage.'

He nodded. 'That's true. Generations of my family have lived in the valley since the end of the nineteenth century, and my great-great-grandfather worked immensely hard to make a go of his enterprise. I feel that we have a duty to secure the results of his labour for generations to come.'

Two waitresses came out on to the terrace just then and placed laden trays down on the table. On one there was a porcelain coffee pot, along with cups and saucers, cream and sugar. The other held an appetising selection of food, as well as plates and cutlery.

Nick began to pour coffee for both of them. 'It isn't just about my own heritage. At the same time I believe we have to give of our best to the local community. That's why what happened this morning concerns me so much. We hold a certain position of trust out here. People look to us to set standards.'

He offered her a plate and napkin. 'Please, help yourself to food.'

'Thank you. It looks delicious.' She gazed at the tempting choices before her. There was *prosciutto*, a dry-cured Italian ham, cut in paper-thin slices, along with sun-dried tomatoes, gnocchi and a crisp salad.

She added a little of each to her plate. 'I wish I could be of more help,' she said quietly, 'but until Mrs Wyatt recovers enough to tell us what happened, we can only wait for the test results to come back from the hospital and hope that they will give us some clue.'

'Was there any head injury?'

'Not that I could see. Of course, that doesn't always mean there's nothing to be concerned about. Any kind of extreme jolting movement within the skull can cause problems that might develop later.'

He tasted a portion of the ham. 'I'll go and see her just as soon as the doctors have had time to treat her shoulder. In the interim I've sent the under-manager along to the hospital to see if we can do anything to make her stay more comfortable.' He frowned. 'It's a dilemma. We generally make sure that the rugs in the rooms are in good condition, not easily rucked. If it was the case that she tripped, I'll have to think about having them removed.'

Katie glanced at him across the table. His concern seemed genuine, and she wondered if there was any comfort she could offer.

'It's always possible that she might have a health problem that caused her to fall—something quite unrelated to the hotel. She might have suffered a dizzy spell, for instance.'

'Or a TIA, perhaps.'

Transient ischaemic attack… Katie gave him a considering look, and slid her fork into succulent, sauce-covered potato gnocchi, giving herself time to think. 'That's a definite possibility. Any restriction of the blood supply to the brain could cause a temporary loss of consciousness.'

'Or stroke-like symptoms.'

She nodded. 'It sounds as though you have some experience of the condition. Has someone in your family had problems with TIAs?'

'No, nothing like that.' His gaze meshed with hers. 'As it happens, I'm a doctor, like yourself. I suppose that's why I didn't think twice about rushing in on you when you were examining Mrs Wyatt. I'm so used to tending these medical emergencies that it didn't cross my mind to steer clear.'

She gave a soft gasp. 'I had no idea.' She studied him afresh, a small frown indenting her brow. 'I can't imagine how you find time to practise medicine when you have a vineyard and a hotel to run.'

He laughed. 'I guess it would be difficult if I tried to do all three…but the fact is, I have managers to do the day to day work for me. They let me know if any problems arise that need my attention—like today, for instance. Jenny called me. Otherwise, I make regular checks to make sure that everything's going smoothly, but for the most part I work in the emergency department at the hospital.'

Her eyes widened. 'That must take some dedication. After all, you could have chosen to stay in the valley and reap the benefits of years of grape cultivation. Your wines are internationally famous, according to my mother.'

'That's true. But I've always wanted to be an emergency physician. When I was a teenager, I saw one of my friends injured in a traffic accident. It was horrific... and for a while it was touch and go as to whether he would survive. Thankfully, he had the best surgical team looking after him, and he made it in the end. It left a huge impression on me. So, you see, I'm passionate about my work, and I can't think of anything else I'd rather do. After all, saving lives is a job that's definitely worthwhile. It gives me more satisfaction than I could ever get from gathering in the grape harvest.'

'I can see how you would feel that way but, then, I'm biased.' She gave a faint smile. 'I have to admit, though, there are times when I'm tempted to swap it all for the kind of life I see out here...lazy days in the sunshine, a trip down to the beach to watch the surfers ride the waves...but then I come back to reality. I couldn't give up medicine. It's part of me.'

He nodded, his glance trailing over her. 'I was surprised to see you here. I remember you said you were a paediatrician...but you did a pretty good job of taking care of Mrs Wyatt, as far as I could see. She didn't appear to be in any pain, there was an IV line already in place, and you had her on oxygen. No one could complain at the standard of treatment she received.'

'Let's hope not, anyway.' She guessed he was still thinking about the repercussions of that morning's accident, and how it might affect him as a proprietor. 'I do work as a paediatrician most of the time, but I'm on call two days a week. During my training, I specialised in both paediatrics and emergency, and I wanted to keep up my skills in both those fields. This job was ideal.'

'I can imagine it would be.' He smiled, his gaze slanting over her, and then he waved a hand towards a platter. 'Won't you try our Burrata cheese? I think you'll find it's out of this world.'

'Thanks.' She helped herself to one of the cheeses, a ball wrapped in mozzarella, giving it a springy, soft texture. As she bit into it, she savoured the buttery texture of the centre, a mixture of cream and shredded mozzarella. 'Mmm,' she murmured. 'It's like a little taste of heaven.'

He chuckled, his gaze moving over her, flame glimmering in the depths of his blue eyes. 'Your expression said it all.' His glance slid to the soft fullness of her mouth and lingered there. 'What I wouldn't give to have savoured that with you,' he said on a husky note. 'You have the lips of an angel...soft, ripe and exquisitely sensual.'

She stared at him, her green eyes widening in confusion. His words took her breath away, and a tide of heat rushed through her body. 'I... Uh...' She didn't know what to say to him. She wasn't prepared for his reaction and his comment was unexpected, disarming, leaving her completely at a loss.

Nervously, she swallowed the rest of her coffee then ran the tip of her tongue over her lips, an involuntary action to make herself feel more secure, to help her to know that all was as it should be, and he made a muffled groan.

'Don't...please...' he said, his tone roughened, his gaze darkening to reflect the deep blue of the ocean. 'That just adds to the torment.'

Katie's pulse began to thump erratically, and a torrent of heat rushed to her head. Panic began to set in. Why was he having this strange effect on her? Hadn't she come all the way out here to start afresh? She didn't want any entanglements, and yet Nick seemed to be constantly in her face, a powerful, authoritative man, someone it was hard to ignore. He wasn't like other men she had met, and she was finding she couldn't trust her instincts around him. At the first foray into dangerous territory she was conscious of the ground sliding out from under her feet. She couldn't let him do this to her.

She straightened, leaning back in her chair. 'Perhaps I should leave,' she said distractedly, her thoughts spiralling out of control. He was altogether too masculine, too hot-blooded for a girl like her. With just a word, a touch he had her senses firing on overdrive.

'Surely not?' he murmured. 'Please, stay a while longer.'

She shook her head. Her bewildered mind searched for options, rocketed from one impossible scenario to the next and collapsed in a panicked heap. 'I've probably spent way too much time here already,' she managed. 'It was good of you to offer me lunch. Thank you for that, but I should be on my way now.'

He reached out to her, laying a hand over hers when she would have drawn back from the table. 'Don't let me frighten you away, Katie. It's just that you shook me to the core the first time I met you, and that feeling hasn't gone away. You're really something special and I'd do anything to see you again.'

She gently pulled her hand out from under his. 'I'm sorry… It's not that I have anything against you, Nick, but I'm not in the market for relationships right now. I just… There are too many things going on in my life, too many changes I have to deal with.'

It was all too much for her. The business with James had hurt her deeply, made her guarded and uncertain, and now she was struggling to build a new life, trying to find her niche in a new job. She couldn't deal with any distractions right now, and she sensed that Nick was way more trouble than she could ever handle.

She pulled in a deep breath and stood up, pushing back her chair. 'Thanks again for lunch,' she said, hating herself for the slight tremor in her voice. 'It was delicious…but I really must go.'

He wasn't going to make it easy for her, though, she discovered. He came to stand beside her, his body so close to hers that she could feel the heat coming from him, could register the heavy thud of his heartbeat as he leaned towards her and slid an arm around her waist. Or was that her own heart that she could feel—that pounding, intense rhythm that warned of imminent danger? His hand splayed out over her rib cage, and her whole body fired up in response.

'That's such a shame,' he murmured. 'There is so much more I want to say to you. I could even show you around the hotel if only you would stay a little longer.'

She shook her head, steeling herself to resist the lure of his embrace. She couldn't allow herself to lean into the warmth of his long, hard body, no matter how great the temptation. 'I can't,' she murmured. 'I… I really ought to go back to the office and type up my notes while everything's fresh in my mind.' It sounded such a weak excuse, even to her ears.

'Such mundane tasks, when life could be so much

more interesting.' He sighed, reluctantly giving in. 'If you're determined to go, you must at least let me walk you to your car.'

She nodded. 'Okay.' At least he was yielding to her decision. Escape was within reach at last, and maybe soon the fog of indecision would lift from her mind... though it didn't help at all that he kept his arm around her as they headed back through the hotel.

Only when they reached her car did he let her go and finally she began to breathe a little more easily.

'I imagine you have to write up a report on Mrs Wyatt's accident,' he said on an even note, 'for the inquiry.'

'Yes.' She nodded. 'There'll more than likely be an official investigation. I gather any kind of accident on public premises causes the wheels to be set in motion.'

'Hmm...do you have any idea what will go in your report?'

She sent him a quick glance. 'I can only state the facts. Anything else would be pure conjecture.'

He considered that for a moment, a line indenting his brow. 'Yes, of course.' He pulled open the car door for her and held it while she slid into the driver's seat. 'I'd be interested in hearing the results of the tests.' He paused. 'Anyway, I expect we'll run into one another again before too long.

She nodded. 'I should think so.' He closed the door and she turned the key in the ignition, starting up the engine.

She frowned as an errant thought dropped into her mind. He'd asked about the report and what she might put in it...and for a good deal of the time while they had been eating he had been asking about the precise details of Mrs Wyatt's medical condition.

Was he worried about the outcome of the investigation and how it would affect the hotel?

Her report could sway things one way or the other. Was that the real reason he was making a play for her? Why would a man such as him be interested in her, after all, when no doubt he could take his pick of beautiful women? The thought disturbed her. She had to tread cautiously, and she couldn't take anything or anyone at face value these days, least of all Nick Bellini.

CHAPTER THREE

'I'M SURE I'd have been all right if we'd stayed at home,' Jack Logan said. His breath was wheezy, coming in short bursts, so that Katie frowned. 'There was no need for you to bring me to the hospital,' he added, struggling to gulp in air as he spoke. 'It's your day off. You shouldn't be tending to me.'

'You're ill,' she said firmly. 'And I'm your daughter, so of course I should be looking after you.' He was a proud man, not one to ask for help, and up to now she had been cautious about stepping in where she might not be wanted. Today, though, he had reached a point where medical intervention was imperative. 'You need to see a doctor right away so that we can get your medication sorted out. You can't go on like this. I won't let you.'

He didn't answer and she suspected his strength was failing fast. She wrapped an arm around him, supporting him as she led him to a chair in the waiting room. The emergency department was busy at this time of the day, just after lunchtime, but she hoped they wouldn't have too long to wait. Her father's breathing was becoming worse by the minute, and it was worrying her.

She paused awkwardly, scanning his features.

'You have your tablets with you, don't you…and your inhaler?'

'Yes.' He eased himself down on to the padded seat, dragging in a few difficult breaths and giving himself a minute or two to recover.

'Perhaps you should have a few puffs on the inhaler now. It might help a bit.' She watched as he fumbled in his pocket for the medication. 'Will you be all right for a minute or two while I go and have a word with the clerk on duty?'

He nodded. 'I'll be fine. I don't need to be here.'

She made a wry face and turned to walk over to the reception desk. He was stubborn and independent, but she wasn't going to let him get away with trying to bamboozle her. He was in a bad way, and he needed help…maybe even to be admitted to hospital.

She gave the clerk her father's details. 'He's gasping for breath and I believe he needs urgent treatment. His medication doesn't seem to be working properly.'

The clerk glanced over to where Katie's father was sitting. 'I'll see if we can have him looked at fairly quickly, Dr Logan. If you'd like to take a seat, I'll have a word with the triage nurse.'

'Thanks.' Katie went back to her father and sat down. 'We shouldn't have to wait too long,' she told him. 'Just try to relax.'

In fact, it was only a matter of minutes before they were called to go into the doctor's room, and Katie was startled to see Nick coming along the corridor to greet them. He looked immaculate, as ever, with dark trousers that moulded his long legs, a crisp linen shirt in a deep shade of blue, and a tie that gave him a businesslike, professional appearance.

She hadn't expected to run into him so soon after their meeting at the hotel. It threw her, coming across him this way, and for a moment or two she wasn't sure how to respond.

'I didn't realise that you worked here,' she said, frowning. 'I'd somehow imagined that you worked at one of the bigger city hospitals.'

He smiled. 'I prefer this one. It has all the up-to-date-facilities, and I've been familiar with it since childhood. It's become like a second home to me.'

He lent her father a supporting shoulder. 'I'm sorry to see that you're having problems, Jack,' he murmured. 'We'll go along to my office where we can be more private.' He turned and called for a nurse. 'Can we get some oxygen here, please?'

'Of course.' The nurse hurried away to find a trolley, while Nick led the way to his office.

Nick waved Katie to a leather-backed chair by the desk, and then turned his attention to Jack.

'Let me help you onto the examination couch,' he said quietly, pumping the bed to an accessible height and assisting Jack into a sitting position, propped up by pillows. 'I see you have your inhaler with you. Is it helping?'

Jack shook his head. 'Not much.' He leaned back against the pillows and tried to gather his breath. His features were drawn, his lips taking on a bluish tinge.

Nick handed him the oxygen mask and carefully fitted it over his nose and mouth. 'Take a few deep breaths,' he said. 'We'll soon have you feeling better, don't worry.'

Katie watched as Nick examined her father. He was very thorough, listening to his chest, taking his blood pressure and pulse and asking questions about the medication he was taking. All the time he was efficient, yet gentle, and she could see that he was a doctor who would put a patient's mind at ease whatever the circumstances. He set up a monitor so that he could check Jack's heart rate and blood oxygen levels. Katie saw that the results were way out of line with what they should be.

'Excuse me for a moment,' Nick murmured. 'I'm going to ask the nurse to bring a nebuliser in here. We'll add a bronchodilator and a steroid to the mix to reduce the inflammation in your airways, and that should soon make you feel a lot more comfortable.'

He went to the door and spoke to the nurse then returned a minute or two later, coming to stand beside the couch once more. 'Your blood pressure is raised,' he said, 'so I think we need to adjust your tablets to bring that down...and also perhaps we should question what's happening to bring that about.'

'I dare say I can give you an answer on that one,' Katie remarked under her breath. Her tone was cynical, and that must have alerted Nick, because he began to walk towards her, obviously conscious that she wouldn't want her father to hear.

'You know what's causing it?' he asked.

'I think so. You and your father have been pushing him to sell the vineyard, and he's worried about making the right decision. It's tearing him apart, thinking about giving up the one thing that has kept him going all these years.'

Nick raised dark brows. 'You're blaming my father and me?' He, too, spoke in a lowered voice.

'I am. Who else would I blame?' She returned his gaze steadily. 'His health is failing, yet you bombarded him with paperwork and tried to persuade him to hand it over. He was looking at the papers this morning when he was taken ill. The vineyard means everything to him, and you've set him a huge dilemma. I don't believe he's in any state to be dealing with matters such as this.'

'I hardly think you can lay the blame at our feet. Jack has been ill for a number of years, and his lung function is way below par. As to causing him any distress, all I can say is that if he didn't want to consider our offer, he only had to say so.' His eyes darkened. 'He's perfectly capable of making his own decisions.'

Katie stiffened. He hadn't added 'without his daughter's interference', but the implication was there, all the same.

The nurse appeared just then with a trolley, and Nick broke off to go and set up the nebuliser. 'Just try to relax and breathe deeply,' he told her father, his manner soothing. 'It'll take a few minutes, but your blood oxygen levels should gradually start to rise. In the meantime, I'm going to go and glance through your medical notes and see where we can make changes to your medication.' He halted as a thought had occurred to him. 'Katie's obviously concerned about you. Do you mind if I discuss your medical history with her, or is it something you would rather I kept private?'

Jack shook his head. 'That's fine. Go ahead. There's nothing to hide.'

'Okay.' Nick checked the monitor once more, before saying quietly, 'I'll also arrange an urgent appointment for you with your respiratory specialist.'

'Thanks,' Jack said. He looked exhausted and seemed relieved to be able to just lie back and let the drugs do their work.

Nick came back to the desk and glanced towards Katie as he sat down.

'He should start to feel better once his airways expand.' He accessed her father's medical notes on the computer, and then said quietly, 'You seem very concerned over this matter of the vineyard. Have you been out to see it?'

She nodded. 'He took me on a tour a few days ago. I was very impressed, completely bowled over by it, in fact. So much work has gone into making it what it is now. It's something to be proud of.' She looked at him through narrowed eyes. 'I can't see any reason why he would want to let it go.'

His mouth made a crooked shape. 'I'd say it was possibly becoming too much for him to handle, but it's probably better if we leave off that discussion for a while. It isn't getting either of us anywhere, is it?'

She clamped her lips shut. Nick glanced at her briefly, and then said, 'Your father's heart is taking a lot of strain—the effect of years of lung disease.' He lowered his voice as he studied her. 'I wonder if you realise just how precarious his situation is becoming.'

She nodded, her mouth making a downward turn. 'I'd guessed. I suppose I just needed to have it confirmed.'

He checked the drug schedule for a moment or two on the computer, and then stood up and went back to her father. 'How are you feeling?' he asked.

'Much better.' Jack managed a smile. 'You've taken good care of me, as always. Thank you for that.'

'You're welcome. It's what I'm here for.' Nick glanced down at his chart. 'I want to prescribe some tablets to ease the workload on your heart, and I think we'll arrange for you to have oxygen at home. If you give me a few minutes, I'll go and see if the respiratory specialist is around. It's possible he might be able to come and see you while you're here, and that way we can finalise the details of your medication in one go.'

'Okay.' Jack nodded. 'I'm not going anywhere for a while.'

Katie could see that he was looking much better. 'The colour is coming back into your face,' she said, going over to him as Nick left the room. 'You had me worried there for a while.'

His glance trailed over her. 'You worry too much. Your mother was the same. I used to say to her, life's too short to be fretting about this and that. Seize the day—as they say. Make the most of it where you can.'

Katie's mouth flattened. 'I suppose that was back in the days when you were getting along with one another...before it all went wrong.'

'I... Yes...' He hesitated, shooting her a quick, cautious glance. 'It hasn't been easy for you, has it, Katie? We tried to make a go of things, you know, your mother and I, but there were problems... For one thing, my job took me away from home so much.'

Katie was unconvinced. 'Your job obviously meant more to you than we did, because one day you went away and never came back.' Even now, her heart lurched at the memory. 'Mum was devastated, and I could never understand why you left us that way. You were living thousands of miles from us. I was eight years old, and suddenly I'd lost my father, and my mother was in pieces. You disappeared from our lives. For a long time I thought I'd done something wrong and it was all my fault that you'd gone away.'

He frowned, his grey eyes troubled. 'I'm sorry, Katie.

I should have handled things differently; I know that now.' He pulled in a deep breath. 'But your mother and I were going through a bad time, and the atmosphere was incredibly tense between us. There were lots of bitter arguments. Back then I thought it would be for the best if I stayed away. I thought it would be easier, less painful.'

She gave a short, harsh laugh. 'You were wrong. It might have been better for you, maybe, but as far as I was concerned a card here and there at birthdays and Christmas was hardly going to make up for the lack of a father. Did you really think it would? And as for presents that you sent—well, they were great but it just made me realise that you didn't even know me. I appreciated the gifts, but I couldn't help thinking that a visit would have been more to the point. But it never happened. I thought perhaps you didn't care.'

It was as though her words had cut into him like a knife. He caught his breath and seemed to slump a little, his features becoming ashen, and Katie looked on in dismay, a rush of guilt running through her. What was she thinking of, having this discussion with him in here, of all places? She had gone too far...way too far. He might have a lot to answer for, but he was ill, after all, and she was layering him with anxiety that could bring on respiratory collapse. She ought to have known better.

'That was thoughtless of me,' she said in an anxious voice. 'I didn't mean to do anything to aggravate your condition.'

'It's all right.' He paused, sucking in another breath. 'It was something I struggled with all the time—leaving you. I kept meaning to come back to see you, but somehow the longer I left it, the harder it became. I thought…if I came back to see you…' he started to gasp, fighting against the constriction in his lungs '…you might be all the more upset if I left you once more. You were very young.'

Katie's expression was bleak. 'Let's not talk about it for the moment. You're ill, and we should concentrate on making you more comfortable. Keep the mask over your face. Take deep breaths and try to relax.'

'What's going on here?' Nick came into the room and hurried over to the bed. 'What happened?' He checked the monitor, and Katie could see that her father's heart rate and respiratory rate had increased to dangerous levels.

'It was… We were just talking. It's my fault,' she said in a halting tone. 'I said some things I shouldn't have said.' She had berated Nick for causing her father stress, and then she had done exactly the same thing, hadn't she?

She pressed her lips together. Wasn't this all part of the problem she had battled with since she had come out here? There was so much resentment locked up inside her, but none of it could gain release…not when her father was so ill. It was frustrating, an ongoing dilemma that could have no end. No matter what he had done, she would have to be inhuman to ignore his condition, wouldn't she?

'No, no…you mustn't blame yourself,' her father said, cutting in on her thoughts. 'It's only right that you should say what's on your mind. I let you down.'

Nick gave her a thoughtful glance. Perhaps he was curious about what was going on between them, but he said nothing. Instead he checked the monitors once more and handed her father a couple of tablets and a drinking cup. 'Take these,' he said. 'They'll bring your blood pressure down and calm your heart rate. Then you need to rest.' He sent Katie a warning glance and her face flushed with heat.

'It isn't Katie's fault,' Jack said, after he had swallowed the tablets. 'The old ticker isn't what it used to be. There isn't much more that you doctors can do for me—you know it, and I know it.'

'I never give up on a patient,' Nick said, his tone firm. 'You'll be fine if you take things easy. Lie back and give the medicine time to take effect.'

They sat with her father for several more minutes, watching as his breathing slowly became easier.

'I feel much better now,' he said, after a while. 'I'll be okay.'

'Maybe, but you can stay where you are for a bit longer,' Nick told him. 'The specialist will be stopping by as soon as he's finished dealing with a patient. He'll sort out your medication and make sure that you're in a good enough condition to go home.'

His pager went off and he turned to Katie. 'I have to go and deal with an emergency that's coming in,' he said. 'Maybe we could meet up some time soon for coffee or dinner? I feel there are things we need to talk about.'

He was probably thinking of her father's illness, and she acknowledged that with a slight inclination of her head. 'Actually, I have the test results on Mrs Wyatt, back in my office—the lady who fell and injured herself at your hotel. She gave me permission to share them with you, although I haven't had time to look at them properly yet. I suppose we should arrange a time to get together to talk about them.'

He nodded. 'Would it be too much of an imposition for you to come over to my beach house with them, say, later this afternoon? I have to be there because I have some people coming to do some work in the courtyard. Just say if it's a problem for you.'

She thought about it and then shook her head. 'It's not a problem. I'm off duty, and you don't live too far from my place.'

'That's great. I'll see you then.' He glanced towards her father. 'I'm glad you're feeling better, Jack. Take care. I'll see you again before too long, I expect.'

He left the room, and Jack sent Katie a questioning look. 'There was a problem at the hotel?'

She nodded and explained what had happened. 'I think he's worried in case the woman or her relatives decide to take it to court. They might try to say her fall was the fault of the hotel proprietor.'

He frowned. 'I can see how he would be worried. It won't simply be the effect this might have on trade at the hotel—the Bellinis have always taken pride in doing the right thing. Nick's father is ultra-traditional in that respect. Everything has to be done the proper way. He's a very private man, and he deplores any negative publicity.'

'I can imagine. But so far they've managed to keep things quiet, and anyway there's a lot riding on the results of various tests that were carried out at the lab.'

'And now he wants you to take the results over to the house?' Jack sent her a thoughtful glance. 'Do I detect more than just a professional collaboration going on here?'

Katie's eyes widened at the question, and she gave a faint shrug of her shoulders. 'You heard what he said. It's just easier this way.'

She wasn't going to say any more on that score. Her father hadn't earned the right to intervene in her private life, had he? Besides, how could she possibly answer him when she didn't know for sure herself what had prompted the invitation? The deed had been accomplished before she'd had time to give it much thought.

Jack was frowning. 'I could see that he was interested in you from the outset…but you should be careful how you go, with him, Katie. I know you're still recovering from what went on back in the UK, and I wouldn't want to see you hurt all over again.'

He halted for a second or two to allow his lungs to recover. 'Nick Bellini's a law unto himself where women are concerned. They seem to fall for him readily enough, but he's never yet settled down with any of them. Don't go getting your heart broken over the likes of him. He's a fine doctor—he's kept an eye on me over the last few years, just because he was concerned for me—and he's a great businessman, a wonderful friend and associate, but he's lethal to the fairer sex.'

Katie frowned. He was only telling her what she'd already guessed. That newspaper headline that had been bugging her for the last few days suddenly swam into her head once more, and this time she could see it with perfect clarity. '*Tearful heiress Shannon Draycott leaves hotel under cover of darkness. Bellini tycoon declines to comment.*' There had been more. The article had said something about a broken engagement, and there had been a lot of conjecture, along with several interviews with friends of the young woman. They all painted a picture of a tragic heiress who had been left in the lurch.

'Well, thanks for warning me. I'll be sure to keep it in mind.'

Was Nick a man who was afraid of commitment, flitting from one woman to another? Katie was determined not to get involved with anyone like that ever again. She had been devastated when her relationship with James had ended. She had trusted him and believed they might have had a future together, but it had all gone terribly wrong, and now she would do everything she could to steer clear of any man who might cause her pain.

She studied her father. He was an enigma. He looked gaunt, with prominent cheekbones and dark shadows under his eyes, and something in her made her want to reach out to him and wrap her arms around him. It was confusing.

All those years he had stayed away, removing himself from her life, and yet now he was acting like a protective father, as though her well-being was suddenly important to him. She couldn't quite work him out. For so long she had tried not to think about him at all. He had walked out on her and her mother and she couldn't forgive him for that…and yet now her emotions were torn.

Little by little, as she came to know him better, he was beginning to tug at her heartstrings. She didn't know how it had happened, but she felt sorry for him and in spite of herself she was worried about him. He looked so thin and wasted, and it occurred to her that he probably wasn't eating as well as he should.

As for Nick Bellini, she'd already learned to be wary of him, and she had to be grateful that her father had let her know what she was up against. Anyway, surely her fears were groundless? Her relationship with Nick was going to be strictly professional, wasn't it?

It didn't surprise her one bit to discover that he had the reputation of a compulsive heartbreaker.

A couple of hours later, Katie dropped her father off at his house and left him in the care of Libby, his housekeeper. 'I'll keep an eye on him, don't you worry,' the woman said, and Katie immediately felt reassured. Libby was kindly and capable looking, and Katie knew she was leaving him in good hands.

Then she set off for Nick's beach house. The scenery was breathtaking as she drove along, with the sun glinting on the blue Pacific Ocean and the rugged length of the coastline stretching out ahead of her.

Living here was like being dropped into a secluded corner of paradise, she reflected as she parked her car in Nick's driveway a few minutes later. She slid out of the car and looked around, gazing out over the bay and watching the surf form lacy white ribbons on the sand. Black oystercatchers moved busily amongst the rocks, seeking out mussels and molluscs with their long orange beaks.

'Katie, I'm glad you could make it,' Nick said, coming out of the house to greet her. 'I was on the upper deck when I saw you arrive.' His arms closed around her in a welcoming hug, and in spite of herself her senses immediately responded in a flurry of excitement. 'How's your father?' he asked.

'Much better.'

'I'm glad.'

His arms were warm and strong, folding her to him, and for a wild moment or two she was tempted to nestle against him and accept the shelter he offered. She could feel the reassuring, steady beat of his heart through the thin cotton of her top.

'It's good to see you,' he murmured, stepping back a little to look at her. 'I hope you didn't mind coming out here to visit me—it's just that I have to be at the house to oversee some work I'm having done out back, as I told you. The workmen are installing a hot tub in the courtyard.'

'That sounds like fun,' she said, easing herself away from him. She ran a hand over her jeans in a defensive gesture, smoothing the denim. This closeness was doing strange things to her heart rate, and it wouldn't do to have him see what effect he was having on her. 'You certainly have the climate for it out here.'

He smiled, his hand slipping to her waist as he gently led her towards the house. 'I'm looking forward to trying it out. All those jets of water are supposed to make you feel really good, like a soothing massage.' He grinned. 'Perhaps you might like to try it with me some time?'

'I...uh...' She gave a soft intake of breath. 'I'd have to think about that.' She blinked. The prospect of sharing a hot tub with him was much more than she could handle right then. In fact, she'd have to know him a whole lot better before anything like that ever happened.

He laughed softly. 'I'll take that as a definite maybe,' he said. 'Let me show you around the house.'

'Thank you. I'd like that.' She gazed at the beautiful building as they walked along the path. It was multi-storeyed, with sloping roofs at varying levels, the tiles a soft sandstone colour that contrasted perfectly with the white-painted walls. There were arched windows and glass doors, and there were steps leading from a balconied terrace on the upper floor, providing external access to the ground below. Behind the whole edifice was a backdrop of green Monterey pines, and in the far distance she could see lush, forested mountain slopes. 'This is fantastic,' she murmured. 'It's a spectacular house.'

She turned to look back at the Pacific. 'I really envy you, living out here by the ocean. It must be lovely to look out over the water every day and gaze at the cliffs that form the bay.'

'It's very relaxing. I know I'm fortunate to be able to enjoy it.' He showed her into the house, and they stepped into a wide entrance hall whose pale-coloured walls reflected the light. The oak floor gleamed faintly.

He led the way into a room just off the hall. 'This is the lounge, as you can see. I tend to sit in here to read the paper or watch TV of an evening. It's a very peaceful room, and it looks out over the patio garden. And, of course, with the French doors it's handy for the courtyard...and, from now on, the hot tub, too,' he added with a grin.

She peered out through the open doors at the courtyard that was closed in on three sides by different wings of the building. The remaining side was made up of a decorative screen wall, providing a glimpse into the garden beyond. 'I can see the men are still working on it. It looks as though you have everything you need out there—a place to relax and enjoy the sunshine, a barbecue area, and all those lovely flowers and shrubs to enjoy. It looks like a little piece of heaven.'

She turned to gaze around the room. 'I like the pale-coloured furnishings in here, too. It just adds to the feeling of light.' Her glance took in glass shelves and a low table, before trailing over the sumptuous sofa and chairs. Pastel-coloured cushions added a delicate touch.

'I'm glad you like it,' he said, claiming her hand and leading her through an open doorway. 'Let me show you the kitchen, and I'll make us a drink. What would you like—coffee, tea? You could have iced tea, if you prefer. Or maybe you'd like something stronger?'

'Iced tea sounds fine, thanks.' She stopped to look around. 'Oh, this is lovely,' she said with a soft gasp. 'And it's such a large room, too.' The cupboards and wall units were all finished in the palest green, verging on white, and marble worktops gleamed palely in the sunlight that poured in through the windows. There were shelves filled with bright copper pans, and corner wall units with attractive ceramics on display.

'Well, it serves as a breakfast kitchen,' Nick explained, going over to the fridge. 'There's a separate dining room through the archway, but I tend to eat in here, mostly…or upstairs on the upper deck. I can look out over the ocean from there.'

'That sounds like bliss.'

He nodded, putting ice into two glasses and adding tea from a jug. 'It is. Would you like lemon and mint with this?' he asked, indicating the iced tea.

'Please. That would be good.'

He placed the two glasses on a tray, along with the jug of tea and a plate of mixed hors d'oeuvres. 'We'll take these upstairs and I'll show you the upper deck. 'It's great up there at this time of day, and you can see over the whole of the bay from the terrace.'

She followed him up the stairs, walking through a second sitting room and out through beautifully embellished glass doors onto the balcony terrace.

He was right. The view from the deck was fantastic, and Katie could even see the wildflowers that grew on the craggy slopes in the distance. He pulled out a chair for her by a wrought-iron table, and she sat down and began to relax.

Out here, there were tubs of yellow and orange California poppies, their silky petals moving gently in the faint breeze, and against the far wall, standing tall alongside a trellis, were spiky blue delphiniums. Hanging baskets provided even more colour, with exuberant displays of petunias.

'Help yourself to food,' he said, sliding a plate across the table towards her. 'I wasn't sure whether you would have eaten or not before you came.'

'Thanks.' She glanced at the food on display. There was pâté with crackers, honey-glazed chicken and a spicy tomato dip with tortilla chips. 'It looks delicious.'

He smiled. 'Not my doing, I'm afraid. I have food sent over from the hotel quite often. I don't always have time to cook.'

'I'm not surprised. You must spend the bulk of your time at the hospital, and even if you don't work on a day-to-day basis at the vineyard or the hotel, there must be a fair amount of organisational work to deal with. I expect you're the one who has to make the most important decisions, aren't you?'

He nodded. 'That's true. Things tend to crop up from time to time that need my attention—like this unfortunate episode with Mrs Wyatt.' He frowned. 'I went to see her, and I'm really pleased that she's looking a lot better than she was a few days ago.'

Katie smiled. 'Yes. I couldn't help noticing that you arranged for her to have a private room—the basket of fruit and the flowers you sent were a lovely touch. I know she appreciated them.'

'It was the least I could do.' He spread pâté onto a cracker and bit into it. 'People come to the hotel expecting to have a good time and live for a while in the lap of luxury. They don't want to find themselves being taken out of there by ambulance.'

'But you weren't obliged to pay anything towards her hospital care, were you?'

He shrugged. 'No, that's true. Her insurance company will pay for that...but I wanted to be certain she had the upgrade to make sure that she's comfortable, and, anyway, I count it as good customer relations.'

'Hmm. I can see that you take your role as hotelier seriously.' She dipped a tortilla chip into the fiery salsa sauce. 'You must be anxious to know what caused Mrs Wyatt to fall and break her shoulder. Would you like to hear the results of the tests?'

'Yes, definitely... I'm glad she said it would be all right for you to discuss them with me. Is it what we thought—a TIA?'

She nodded. 'It looks that way. The doctors monitored her heart and discovered that she has atrial fibrillation—as you know, that kind of abnormal heart rhythm can sometimes cause clots to form in the blood vessels. They did a CT scan, along with blood tests, and found a narrowing of the arteries. The general feeling is that she probably developed a blood clot that temporarily disturbed the flow of blood to the brain. This most likely dissolved of its own accord, but it's possible that more will form as time progresses if she doesn't have treatment.'

'So presumably they have her on anti-thrombotic

therapy? And they'll give her medication to counteract the abnormal heart rhythm?'

'That's right.' She took a sip of iced tea. 'It looks as though you're in the clear—or, should I say, the hotel's in the clear?' She smiled at him. 'That must be a huge relief to you.'

'Yes, it is. I can't tell you how badly I needed to hear that. It's great news. Lucky, too, for Mrs Wyatt, because now she gets to have the treatment she needs to put her back on the road to health.' He rested back in his seat, taking a swallow of iced tea and looking the picture of contentment. 'Thanks for telling me that, Katie. I'm really obliged to you for finding out all this information.'

He set down his glass and looked her over, leaning towards her. 'In fact, if I didn't think you'd take it amiss, I could kiss you for it.' He came closer, as though, having hit on the idea, he was ready to carry it through into immediate action, regardless of the consequences.

Katie flattened herself against the back of her chair, deftly foiling his attempt. 'I think you'd better give that one a miss,' she said, her green gaze meshing with his. 'It wouldn't do if every male doctor tried to kiss me whenever I presented them with good results, would it?'

His eyes narrowed. 'Have any tried?'

'Oh, yes. From time to time.'

'And succeeded?' He was frowning now, his blue eyes darkening.

'Maybe. Once or twice.' His expression crystallised into one of seething frustration, and she laughed softly. 'Sorry about that. I couldn't resist. You looked so put out.'

He gazed at her, totally nonplussed. 'You certainly got me going there,' he said, his mouth twisting. 'My fault. I should have known any number of men would want to try their luck with you. That goes for me, too. Somehow, ever since we first met, I've been hung up on getting to know you better…much better.'

She pulled a face. 'Well, I'm not sure that's such a good idea—not in the way you mean, at least.'

He studied her thoughtfully for a moment or two, his expression serious. 'He hurt you badly, didn't he—this man from back home? You must have been very much in love with him.'

'I thought I was,' she said awkwardly. 'I thought I knew him, but perhaps I was blind to his faults. He had a lot of charisma, and I believed he was saving it all for me. It turned out I was wrong.'

And wasn't Nick so very much like James? He had that scintillating charm that could sweep a woman off her feet, and Katie was no exception. She had to be on her guard. No matter how hard he tried, she wasn't going to succumb to Nick's winning ways. Hadn't her father warned her about him?

'But let's not dwell on any of that,' she murmured. 'I'm here with you now, and we do have two things in common…our work and my father. Maybe it would be safer all round if we simply kept things between us on that level.'

'Hmm…maybe.' He sounded doubtful. His eyes were still dark, and there was a brooding quality to his expression.

Katie decided to plough on with her new diversionary tactic. She helped herself to some food and said quietly, 'Perhaps we should talk about what happened this morning—about your efforts to persuade my father to sell his land, and the effect it's having on him. Maybe we need to clear the air on that score. You know I'd sooner you put an end to any attempt at making a deal. Anyway, I have the feeling he's not at all sure about going ahead with it.'

Nick frowned. 'He hasn't said as much to me...and while there's a chance he'll concede to us, we're bound to keep trying. It would mean a lot to my father to bring the vineyard back into our keeping. My great-great-grandfather bought the land at the turn of the century, but a parcel of it was sold off some years back when the family fell on hard times. It's a matter of pride to my father to restore the vineyards into family ownership once more. He sees it as our inheritance. It's very important to him.'

'That may be so, but I can't say it any clearer—I think you should hold off on those negotiations.'

Nick's steady gaze met hers. 'Jack doesn't need you to hold his hand where business is concerned.'

A glint of steel came into Katie's eyes. 'I have to disagree with you on that one,' she said. 'And this is definitely not the right time to be pursuing it with him.'

Nick frowned. 'That's another matter, of course. We both saw how ill he was today.' He poured more iced tea into her glass. 'You think your father needs to be cosseted but he takes it on himself to take care of business matters, and then it becomes a matter of pride for him to see things through.'

So, no matter what she said, he wasn't giving up on his plan to secure her father's land. She drank her iced tea and studied him over the rim of her glass. Clearly, his family was not going to be satisfied with the empire they had built up. They would go after whatever they wanted. Forewarned was forearmed.

Nick's phone bleeped, and he glanced down at the screen briefly. 'It looks as though the workmen have finished installing the hot tub,' he said. 'Shall we go down and take a look?'

'Yes, of course.'

She followed him down the stairs and out to the courtyard, where the workmen waited, standing by their handiwork.

'We're all done here,' the spokesman said. 'I think you'll find everything's in order. Just turn these controls here to adjust the jets.' He began to point out the various buttons and fittings. 'This is your filter...and here's where you change the heat settings. We've left it set to around midway. Neither too hot nor too cold, but of course it's all a matter of personal preference.'

'That's great,' Nick murmured. 'It looks perfect. Thanks for all your hard work.' He turned to Katie. 'Stay and enjoy the courtyard for a minute or two, will you, while I go and see the men off? There's an ornamental fishpond that you might like to look at, over there in the corner. I'll be back in a few minutes.'

'Okay.' She watched him go, then turned and walked towards the far side of the courtyard, an attractive area, laid out with a trellised arbour and rockery. A gentle waterfall splashed into the pond where koi carp swam amongst the plants and hid beneath white waterlilies.

She gazed down at the green fronds of water plants drifting with the ripple of water from a small fountain and lost herself for a while in a reverie of a past life.

'Sorry to have left you,' Nick said, coming back to her a short time later. 'I think the men did a good job.

They sited the tub perfectly and left the place looking neat and tidy. Didn't take them too long either.'

She nodded. 'I expect you'll appreciate your new tub for a good many years to come.' Turning back to the pond, she added, 'This is beautifully set out. The water's so clear, and the plants are perfect.' Her voice became wistful. 'I remember having one in our garden when I was a child...but it was never as good as this. I suppose you have to keep on top of things—make sure the filter is kept clear, and so on.'

'That's true. I tend to check it every so often. The pond is a hobby of mine. I find it totally relaxing, something you need so that you can wind down after a day in Emergency.' He sent her an oblique glance. 'Did your father set up your pond...or was it something that came with the house, so to speak?'

'It came with the house. My father was interested in it, but he wasn't around for long enough to take care of it, and the work fell to my mother.'

'And she wasn't that keen?'

'She was keen enough when my father was with us, but after he left to go and live here in California she fell apart. She lost interest in everything.'

He frowned. 'I'm sorry. That must have been hard.' He scanned her face thoughtfully. 'I've known Jack for some eighteen years, ever since he pipped us to the post and bought the vineyard from its previous owner. In all that time I had no idea he had a daughter back in the UK.'

'No. It seems he kept it quiet.'

'I suppose you had to take a lot of the burden on your shoulders—how old were you when he left?'

'I was eight. As to any burden, I must say I didn't

really understand what was going on at the time. It was all very confusing. When I realised he wasn't coming back, I was hurt, heartbroken, and then as the years went by I became angry and resentful. There was just my mother and me, no cosy family unit with brothers and sisters to share happy times. I missed that.'

A shadow crossed his eyes. 'And that's why you never came over here until now.' He looked at her with new understanding. 'You were waiting for him to come back to you.'

She lowered her head. 'It wasn't going to happen, was it? So eventually I decided that if I was to make peace with myself, I had to come and find him and sort out my demons once and for all.'

He slid an arm around her shoulders. 'I'm sorry that you had to go through all that,' he said quietly. 'It must have been a terrible time for you.' He drew her close and pressed a light kiss on her forehead. 'It seems almost unforgivable that he should treat you that way, and yet I know Jack is a good man at heart.'

Katie didn't answer. She couldn't. She was too conscious of his nearness, and it brought up all kinds of conflicting emotions within her. Everything in her told her that this man was some kind of adversary. He was a threat to her father, and a danger to her peace of mind, and yet when he touched her like this, she was instantly lost in a cotton-wool world of warmth and comfort.

His arms were around her, his body shielding hers from all that might hurt her, and the searing impact of that tender kiss had ricocheted throughout her whole body. She didn't want to move, or speak. Why couldn't she stay here, locked in his embrace, where the world stood still and she might forget her worries?

'Do you think you can find it in you to forgive him?' Nick murmured. 'He's very ill, and there may not be too much time left.'

'I don't know.' She gave a faint sigh. The spell was broken and she straightened, gazing down into the water of the pond. Fish darted among the green fronds, oblivious to the troubles of the world around them. If only she could find such inner peace.

She took a step backwards. 'I should go,' she said. Nick was the last person she should look to for comfort. He could well turn out to be even more of a heartbreaker than her father.

CHAPTER FOUR

'IS YOUR father really considering selling his vineyard to the Bellini family? That seems very strange to me.' Eve Logan sounded doubtful at the other end of the line. 'I haven't had a lot of contact with him over these last few years, but I did gain the impression that the business meant an awful lot to him. I wouldn't have thought it was something he would give it up lightly.'

'No, probably not,' Katie agreed. 'When I spoke to him the other day he said he hadn't thought it through yet, or words to that effect. I'm wondering if the Bellinis are putting undue pressure on him. He isn't well, and I have the strong feeling that he isn't up to it.'

'Then perhaps it's as well that you're over there and able to look out for him.'

'Yes, maybe.'

Katie cut the call to her mother a few minutes later and gazed around the apartment. She was feeling oddly restless. Ever since her visit to Nick's home several days ago, she had been suffering from what she could only think of as withdrawal symptoms, and it was all Nick's fault.

That kiss had been the lightest, gentlest touch, and it surely had been nothing more than a gesture of comfort and understanding, but the memory of it had stayed with her ever since. Nick had a compelling, magnetic charm that could surely melt the stoniest heart, and she was proving to be no exception.

It wouldn't do at all. She was off men…they could string you along and lead you into thinking that everything was perfect, and then throw it all in your face with the biggest deception of all. No. Every instinct warned her that it would be far better to steer clear of Nick before he could work his magic on her. He spelled trouble and that was something she could definitely do without.

It didn't help that she managed to catch a glimpse of his house every time she headed along the main highway on her way to or from the hospital. Today had been no exception. Nick's home was beautiful, a jewel set in the golden, sand-fringed crown of the California coast.

Annoyingly, against all her better judgement, her thoughts kept straying to him. What was he doing… was he there, sitting outside on the upper deck, watching the seagulls perch on the distant bluffs?

But she wasn't going to waste any more time thinking about him. Enough was enough, and she had work to do. The dishwasher needed emptying and there was a stack of ironing waiting for her…though with any luck she could finish her chores and still have time to wander down to the beach and take in one of the glorious sunsets that were the norm around there.

She set to work, but she was only halfway through her ironing pile when the phone rang.

'There's been a surfing accident just a mile from where you are,' her boss told her. 'Darren Mayfield, a fourteen-year-old, was knocked unconscious and had to be pulled out of the water. The ambulance has been called, but you'll probably reach him before it arrives. A nasty head injury, by all accounts.'

'I'll leave right away,' she told him, unplugging the iron and heading for the door. Her medical bag was in the hall, ready for such emergencies, and the rest of her supplies were in the car.

The boy's level of consciousness was waxing and waning by the time she arrived on the beach. 'Do you know anything about what happened to him?' she asked his mother, who was waiting anxiously by his side.

'He came off his board when one of the big waves hit,' the woman said, her voice shaky. 'The board sort of rose up in the air and then crashed down on him. We had to drag him out of the water. There's a gash on the back of his head and he's bleeding… He hasn't come round properly since we brought him to shore.' Her lips trembled. 'He keeps being sick, and I thought it was just concussion, but it's more than that, isn't it? He should have recovered by now.'

'I'll take a look,' Katie murmured, kneeling down beside the boy. 'How are you doing, Darren?' she asked quietly. 'Can you hear me?' She waited, and when there was no response she added, 'Do you know what happened to you?'

He still didn't answer, and Katie began to make a swift but thorough examination. 'He's unconscious,' she told his mother, after a while. 'I'm going to put a tube down his throat, and give him oxygen, to help with his breathing, and then I need to stabilise his spine to prevent any more damage being done.' She carefully put a cervical collar in place, before checking the boy's heart rate once more. It was worryingly low, and his blood pressure was high, both signs that the pressure within his brain was rising. That didn't bode well.

Suddenly, Darren's whole body began to shake, and Katie reached in her medical bag for a syringe.

'Why's he doing that?' his mother asked in a panicked voice. 'What's happening to him?'

'He's having a seizure,' Katie answered. It was yet another indication that this boy was in trouble. 'I'm going to inject him with medication that will help to stop the fit.'

By the time the paramedics arrived, she had put in place an intravenous line so that fluids and any further drugs could be administered swiftly and easily. 'We need spinal support here,' she told the men, keeping her voice low so as not to worry the boy's mother any further. 'He has a depressed skull fracture, so we need to phone ahead and tell the trauma team what to expect. They'll most likely need to prepare him for Theatre.'

She spoke to the lead paramedic as they wheeled Darren into the ambulance a few minutes later. 'I'll ride along with him in case there are any more complications along the way.'

The paramedic nodded. 'You go ahead with Mrs Mayfield and sit by him. I'll call the emergency department and keep them up to date.'

'Thanks.'

Katie looked at her patient. He was deathly pale and she was deeply concerned for this boy as she sat beside him in the ambulance. She had placed a temporary dressing on the wound at the back of his head, but it was bleeding still, and she was worried about the extent of the damage.

The journey to the hospital seemed to take for ever,

though in reality it was probably only about fifteen minutes, and as soon as they pulled into the ambulance bay, Katie was ready to move. The paramedics wheeled Darren towards the main doors.

'He had another seizure in the ambulance,' she told the doctor who came out to greet them, 'so I've boosted the anti-convulsive therapy. I'm afraid his blood pressure is high and it looks as though the intracranial pressure is rising.' Again, she spoke quietly so that the boy's mother wouldn't be unduly alarmed, but to her relief a nurse stepped forward and gently took the woman to one side.

'We'll get an x-ray just as soon as we've managed to stabilise his blood pressure,' a familiar voice said, and Katie was startled to see Nick appear at the side of the trolley. He was wearing green scrubs that only seemed to emphasise the muscular strength of his long, lean body. Her heart gave a strange little lurch.

He listened attentively to the paramedic's report and was already checking the patient's vital signs, scanning the readings on the portable heart monitor that Katie had set up. Then he looked at Katie and gave her a quick smile. 'Hi,' he said.

'Oh... I...somehow I hadn't expected to see you here.' Katie's response was muted, but she recovered herself enough to acknowledge him, and also the paramedics, who were ready to leave on another callout. She was troubled about her patient's progress, but Nick's sudden appearance had thrown her way off balance. In the heat of the moment it had completely slipped her mind that he might be on duty.

'I'm on the late shift today,' he told her, as if in answer to her unspoken thoughts, as they moved towards the trauma room. His glance ran quickly over her. 'It's great to see you again.'

'Likewise,' she said, and then tacked on hurriedly, 'I'd like to stay with Darren to see how he goes, if that's all right with you?'

'That'll be fine.' By now they had arrived in the resuscitation room and from then on he concentrated his attention on his patient, examining the boy quickly and telling the nurse who was assisting, 'We'll monitor blood glucose, renal function, electrolytes. I'll take blood for testing now and we need to consult urgently with the neurosurgeon. Given the boy's condition, it's quite likely he'll want to put him on mannitol to reduce the intracranial pressure. Ask him to come down to look at him, will you?'

Katie watched him work. He was remarkably efficient, cool, calm, and obviously concerned for this teenager. He didn't hesitate for an instant, but carried out the necessary procedures with effortless skill, delegating other tasks to members of the team. Then, when the neurosurgeon came to the side of the bed, he spent several minutes talking to him about the boy's condition.

'I'll be ready for him in Theatre in about half an hour,' the surgeon remarked as he prepared to leave the room. 'Let me have the CT images as soon as they're available.'

'Of course.' Nick checked Darren's vital signs once more, and only when he was satisfied that he had done everything possible for the boy did he turn back to Katie.

'Okay, we'll take him along to the CT unit. Let's find out exactly what's going on here.'

As soon as Darren had been placed on the CT trolley,

they went into the annexe to watch the images on the computer screen as the technician began the X-ray. 'You're right,' Nick said, after a few minutes. 'It's a depressed fracture, with the bone fragments pushing down on the lining of the brain. There's a large blood clot causing a build-up of pressure. If we don't act soon, there's a risk that the brain will herniate.'

He spoke to the technician. 'Download the films to the computer in Theatre, will you? Dr Kelso will want to see them.'

The technician nodded, but Nick was already striding out of the annexe towards his patient. 'We'll have to get him to Theatre just as soon as we've cleaned the wound,' he told Katie. 'By that time Mr Kelso should be ready for him.'

They went back to the trauma room and Nick began the process of irrigating the wound while Katie looked on.

'Okay, that should be clean enough now,' he said after a while. 'We'll start him on antibiotics to prevent any infection,' he told the nurse, 'and keep on with the anticonvulsant therapy. In the meantime, give Mr Kelso a call and find out if he's ready for him up in Theatre, will you?'

The nurse nodded. 'Right away.'

A few minutes later when they had the go-ahead, Nick took his patient to the lift. 'Will you be here when I come back?' he asked Katie. 'I'm going to stay with Darren until the operation's over, but it would be good to talk to you some more.'

She nodded. 'I want to see how he does in surgery. Perhaps I should go and talk to Mrs Mayfield? I know Mr Kelso has spoken to her already, but she might appreciate having someone with her to answer any questions.'

'That would be brilliant, if you don't mind. I'm sure you and she have already managed to build up rapport and it'll be good for her to have someone familiar to be with her.'

The lift doors closed behind him, and Katie walked away, heading for the waiting room where Mrs Mayfield was sitting anxiously, hoping for news of her son.

'Can I get you anything?' Katie asked, going to sit beside her. 'A cup of coffee, perhaps?'

Mrs Mayfield shook her head. 'A nurse brought me one already, thank you.' She looked near to tears. 'I've been trying to contact my husband. He was at a conference, but he's coming straight back here now.' She looked at Katie. 'Darren's in a bad way, isn't he? He was unconscious for so long. What's going to happen to him?'

'Darren was unconscious because the impact of the surfboard pushed the bones of his skull inward, causing them to break and press down on the lining of his brain. This damaged some of the blood vessels, so that a blood clot built up quickly between the skull and the lining.'

Mrs Mayfield nodded to show that she understood. 'And this operation that he's having—Mr Kelso said they needed to bring down the pressure. How will they do that?'

'The surgeon will lift up the bone fragments that are pressing down, and at the same time he'll suck out the blood clot.'

'But will he be able to stop the bleeding? Won't the clot build up again?'

'He'll use special materials to repair the blood vessels

so that shouldn't happen. You can be sure that he'll do the very best he can for your son, Mrs Mayfield.' Katie used a reassuring tone, her heart going out to this woman who was petrified for her boy's safety. She couldn't bear to think how she would feel if she had children of her own. It must be the worst thing in the world to know that they were in danger.

She stayed with her for some twenty minutes, until the door opened and Mr Mayfield walked into the room. He went over to his wife and held her tight, both of them fearful and anxious about their son.

Katie left them alone. A nurse would come by and see how they were doing in a while, and now Katie went along to the emergency room to find out if there was any news.

She knew quite a few of the doctors and nurses who worked there by now, from her work as a paediatrician and first responder. Sometimes she had to liaise with them over the phone, and occasionally, as today, she would ride along with the patient and make the handover in person.

'No news yet,' the nurse said, 'but Nick's on his way down from Theatre. He wants us to make preparations to send the boy over to the intensive care unit.'

Katie nodded. 'Thanks for letting me know, Abby. I'll wait by the nurses' station, if that's all right. I really want to know how he does.'

'Of course it is.' She smiled. 'The one consolation is that having you there from the outset must have given the boy at least a sporting chance. Too often, time drags on before people with head injuries have expert treatment. Nick reckons you did a great job.'

Katie gave a bleak smile. 'Let's hope we've all done

enough to make a difference. It's such a devastating experience all round. One minute the boy's out there, enjoying the sunshine and the exhilaration of surfing the waves, and the next, in a freak accident, he's out cold and fighting for his life.' She shook her head. 'I've trained for this, but I don't think I'll ever get used to it.'

'Neither will I,' Abby said.

'You get through it by doing the best you can for your patients,' Nick commented, coming to join them. 'That way you get to sleep easier at night.'

Katie turned to face him, while the nurse left them to go and fetch linen from the supply room. 'Maybe you manage to drop off well enough,' she murmured. 'I can't say that it comes that easily to me.'

'That's a shame.' He draped an arm around her. 'Maybe I could help to remedy that?' he ventured on a husky note. 'Perhaps I could find some way to soothe you to sleep.' He lifted a quizzical brow, looking deep into her eyes.

Katie felt her colour rise. 'In your dreams,' she murmured.

He laughed. 'Well, it was worth a try, I thought.'

'Not really...and I have to say, your timing sucks.' She frowned. 'How is Darren? Did he come through the operation all right?'

His expression sobered. 'Mr Kelso managed to finish the procedure without there being any added complications,' he said. 'The boy's intracranial pressure is at a safer level now, but his blood pressure's still alarmingly high. ICU will monitor him closely, of course. All we can do now is wait and see if he can pull through. He's young and previously in good health, so that's in his favour.' He sent her an encouraging smile. 'The young are quite resilient, as you know. It never ceases to amaze me how they bounce back from even the most traumatic of situations.'

'I'll keep my hopes up for him.' She gazed around the emergency department. 'Everything seems very well co-ordinated around here,' she said. 'The staff all seem to work very well together—I expect that has something to do with the way you run things. You're in charge here, aren't you? Everyone speaks very highly of you.'

'I'm glad of that.' He looked at her from under dark lashes. 'A lot of people, the press especially, seem to think that because I come from a wealthy family I don't need to work and I'm not career orientated, but they couldn't be more wrong. I love my job.'

'I think I've seen that for myself. Though you're right…you do tend to get negative publicity from time to time, don't you?'

He sighed, leaning back against the nurses' station, crossing one long leg over the other at the ankles. 'It seems to be an occupational hazard. If you belong to a family with international holdings, I suppose you're bound to find yourself in the news from time to time.'

She nodded. 'There was a short piece about Mrs Wyatt's accident in the local press, but it was quite favourable. The journalist pointed out that you'd acted swiftly in sending for medical treatment, and that you'd helped make her stay in hospital more comfortable.'

'That's something, at least.' He made a wry smile. 'My father employs a spokesman to deal with the press. It helps to dispel any of the more outlandish stories, and gives the public our take on events.'

'Perhaps your spokesman wasn't around when the

Shannon Draycott story broke?' she said softly. 'That must have caused you a few uneasy moments.'

His mouth turned down at the corners. 'I see you've been discovering my lurid past. No wonder you keep fending me off. I expect you're one of these people who believe everything you read in the papers?'

She shrugged lightly. 'Not necessarily. Though I do go along with the principle that there's no smoke without fire.' He hadn't exactly denied the story, had he? According to the papers, they had been engaged to be married—what kind of man was he that could make light of such a thing?

He winced. 'Then I'm obviously doomed.' A glint of amusement came into his eyes. 'Is there anything I can do to restore your confidence in me? I'm really one of the good guys, you know. And when I spoke to Shannon last week she seemed reasonably content with the way her life was going.'

So he was still in touch with her. The thought sounded a death knell in Katie's mind to any hopes that the stories might be a figment of someone's imagination. 'I'm glad to hear it. Perhaps she counts herself lucky to have escaped.'

'Ouch!' He clamped a hand to his chest and pretended to stagger. 'That was a well-aimed blow. I didn't realise Dr Katie Logan had such a cutting edge…though I suppose you've sharpened up your defences this last year or so.'

She nodded. 'You can count on it.' After her experience with James, she was well prepared, and on her guard, for men who had hidden secrets and a good deal of charm.

'Hmm.' He studied her thoughtfully. 'So what am I

to do to persuade you that things are not as they seem? Do you think spending more time with me would help you to get to know me better?'

It was her turn to laugh. 'I have to give you eleven out of ten for trying, anyway. You're irrepressible, aren't you?'

'Where you're concerned, yes, I am.' His gaze meshed with hers. 'So how about coming along to a wine tasting at the vineyard? We're celebrating a new Pinot Noir this year, one of our finest…and you did say you'd like to see around the vineyard, didn't you? Your father's maybe, but ours is right alongside?'

'I… Um…' She thought things through. Ever since she had seen her father's land, she had been caught up in the wonder of vine culture, and now she was fascinated by everything to do with wine and wine making. She was intrigued to take a look over the Bellini land and see if it was anything like her father's. Where was the harm? It wouldn't be like going on a date, would it? After all, there would be other people around.

'A little wine tasting can be good for the soul,' Nick murmured in a coaxing tone. 'It helps you to look on life with a much more mellow attitude.'

'I'm sure that's true.' She smiled, and against all her best intentions heard herself say, 'Thanks, I think I'd enjoy that.'

. 'That's great news. I'll come and pick you up. Will you be free after work on Wednesday? I have a half-day then.'

'I will,' she murmured. 'I'll look forward to it.'

Later, though, as she waved goodbye to the paramedic who gave her a lift back to her car where she had left it on the coast road, she couldn't help wondering if she was making a mistake. Why, when every part of her knew that she should avoid getting involved with Nick, did she keep digging herself in deeper?

CHAPTER FIVE

'KATIE, Dr Bellini wants to know if you will consult with him on a young patient in the emergency department.' Carla popped her head round the door of Katie's office and waited for an answer. 'I could ask Mike to cover for you here, if you like.'

'Okay. Tell him I'll be along in five minutes.' Katie put the last suture into the cut on a small child's lip. 'There you are, young man, all finished. You've been very brave.' She smiled at the six-year-old and reached into her desk drawer for a colouring sheet and a teddy-bear badge. 'I think you deserve these, don't you?'

The boy gave a tentative nod and studied the piece of paper she'd handed him. 'A racing car!' he exclaimed in delight. 'I'm going to colour it red, and put stripes on the wings.' He looked up at her. 'Thank you.'

'My pleasure.'

She saw the boy and his mother out into the corridor, and then readied herself to go along to the emergency unit, smoothing down her pencil-line skirt and making sure that her blouse neatly skimmed the curve of her hips.

She paused, trying to make sense of her actions. Why was she doing this? Was she really so bothered about meeting up with Nick that she needed to fuss about the way she looked? Unhappily, the answer had to be a resounding 'Yes'. It gave her confidence to know that she looked okay.

A final check in the mirror showed her that her hair was the usual mass of chaotic curls, but there wasn't much she could do about that. At least it was clean and shining.

'Thanks for coming along, Katie.' Nick met her at the door of his office. His glance flicked over her, and an appreciative gleam came into his eyes. 'I'd like you to take a look at young Matthew Goren, if you will. I've asked his mother if she wouldn't mind you giving a second opinion.'

'That's okay. I'm happy to do it.'

He introduced her to the boy's mother and then to Matthew, a thin-looking eleven-year-old who looked uncomfortable and deeply troubled.

'Matt's complaining of pain in his thigh,' Nick said, as they went over to the trolley bed. 'It came on three days ago, and now he's unable to walk because of it. He has a low-grade fever, mild hypertension and slight anaemia, and he's been suffering from frequent nosebleeds in the last couple of years. Liver function, lungs and white-cell count are normal. I've done an abdominal ultrasound and an MRI of the thigh as well as X-rays, but I'm waiting on the results of other blood tests to see if they eliminate certain other possibilities.'

Nick had obviously been very thorough. This must be an unusual case or he wouldn't have brought her in on it, and she was glad that he respected her enough to ask for her opinion.

Katie gave the boy a smile. 'Hello, Matt. I'm Dr

Logan. I'm sorry you're having problems with your thigh. That must be really uncomfortable.'

He nodded. 'I had it once before, when I was ten, but it went away. This is a lot worse.'

'Oh, dear.' She sent him a sympathetic glance. 'We'll have to find out what's wrong and put it right, then, won't we?' She studied his chart for a moment or two and then asked, 'Would it be all right if I examine you, Matt?'

'It's okay.'

Katie was as gentle as she could be, taking her time to assess the boy's condition. When she had finished she asked a few general questions about his symptoms.

'Has the swelling in his abdomen come on recently?' she said, looking at his mother.

Mrs Goren shook her head. 'It started just over two years ago. He says it isn't painful. To be honest, we didn't think anything of it at first—we just thought he was putting on a bit of weight around his tum.'

Katie nodded and glanced at the results of the ultrasound scan on the computer monitor. 'The spleen is definitely enlarged,' she said in a low voice, looking at Nick.

'Take a look at the radiographs and MRI films,' he suggested. 'It looks to me as though there's a patchy sclerosis in the left femoral head…and abnormalities in the bone-marrow density.'

Katie studied the films. 'That could suggest replacement of the marrow fat by an infiltrate,' she said thoughtfully.

'That's the conclusion I came to.' Nick frowned. 'This isn't something I've ever come across before, but if my suspicions are correct it could mean subjecting the boy to more invasive tests, like a bone-marrow biopsy. I'm reluctant to do that.'

'That's understandable.' She looked over the boy's notes once more then said quietly, 'You're right—this is very rare, but given the increased erythrocyte sedimentation rate, the history of nosebleeds and two separate incidents of bone pain a year apart, I'd suggest you do a blood test for glucocerebrosidase enzyme in white blood cells.'

He pulled in a deep breath. 'So you've come to the same conclusion as me—thanks for that, Katie. I was reluctant to order specialised tests on an instinctive diagnosis, but you've picked out the associated patterns of disease and helped me to make my decision. I'll go ahead with the enzyme test.'

He turned once more to his patient and spoke to the boy's mother. 'I think we'll admit Matt to hospital overnight so that we can keep him under observation and try to reduce the inflammation in his thigh. I'll arrange for a nurse to wheel him up to the ward—I'll go and organise that now—and then, once he's settled, I'll order another blood test to check for an enzyme deficiency. The sample will have to be sent off to a specialised centre for testing, but as soon as we have the results, in maybe a week's time, I'll be able to tell you more about what's going on.'

He looked at Matt. 'In the meantime, you have to rest…so that means lots of boring things like playing games on your portable computer and watching videos or TV.' He gave an exaggerated wince, and the boy laughed. 'We'll give you some tablets to take away the pain and bring your fever down,' Nick added. 'Once the leg starts to feel more comfortable, you should be up and about again—I'm hoping that will be fairly soon.'

A few minutes later, Katie said goodbye to the boy and his mother and made her way to the door. Nick excused himself and went with her, leaving the two of them to talk about Matt's hospital stay.

'Would you let me know how he goes on?' she asked, and he nodded.

'Of course.' He smiled. 'I knew I could rely on you to pinpoint the essentials,' he said as they went out into the corridor. 'You may not have been here long, but your reputation for being an excellent doctor is already hailed throughout Paediatrics and Emergency.'

'Is it?' Katie was startled. 'I'm pleased about that, of course, but I'm just doing my job, the same as everyone else.' She sent him a fleeting glance. 'Anyway, you do pretty well yourself. I thought you were brilliant with my father the other day. He hates fuss and feeling as though he's putting people out, but you handled him perfectly and you had him feeling better in very quick time. I was impressed.'

He smiled. 'We aim to please.' Then his expression sobered and he asked, 'How is Jack? Is he coping all right with his new medication?'

She nodded. 'On the whole, it's been working well, but I think he had a bit of a setback earlier today. He wasn't feeling too good first thing, apparently.'

Katie recalled the phone conversation she'd had with her father that morning. She'd sensed he'd been holding something back, but, then, he probably kept a good deal of his thoughts hidden from her. He wouldn't want her to know the full extent of his disability, and that saddened her. He was her father, and yet there was so much that they kept hidden from one another. How could she confide her uncertainties, and how could he share his problems with her, if no bond had built up between them over the years?

'He didn't sound quite right, and I could hear the breath rasping in his lungs, but he wouldn't admit to anything more than being a bit under the weather.' She frowned. 'I know he's using his oxygen every night, and sometimes in the daytime, too, and he seems more frail every time I see him. Of course, he never tells me any of his problems. He hates being vulnerable, and it's difficult for me to reach through to him sometimes.'

'Yes, I wondered about that.' Nick sent her an oblique glance. 'Are you and he getting on all right? I know it must be difficult for you. At the hospital the other day it was fairly obvious you and he still had a lot of issues to resolve.'

She wondered how much of their conversation he had overheard. 'That's true enough.' She frowned. 'To be honest, I don't know how I feel. I've made a real effort to break down the barriers between us lately, and I think it's beginning to pay off. I've definitely grown closer to him over these last few weeks.' Even so, doubt clouded her eyes.

'Learning to forgive must be the hardest thing of all.' Nick's gaze trailed over her features, lingering on the vulnerable curve of her mouth. 'You've had to come to terms with two betrayals, haven't you...your ex's and your father's? That's why you have so much trouble contemplating any new relationship.'

'I suppose so.' She pressed her teeth into the fullness of her lower lip. 'I hope I'm succeeding with both of those. At least with James I'm beginning to see that there were already cracks in our relationship. Maybe I was too ambitious, too set on a career path…whereas James was more easygoing, taking life as it came. I'm wondering if he simply wasn't the type to settle down. He had a child, but he didn't have much contact with him.'

'Much like your father.' Nick's expression was sombre. 'No wonder your ex's weakness hit you so hard. Your father had done exactly the same thing…followed his own path and then abandoned you.'

'Yes.' She was silent for a moment, mulling things over. Could any man be trusted? Could Nick? Not according to her father.

She frowned. 'Where my father's concerned, I still don't really understand what goes on in his head. He treats me as though he's very fond of me and has my welfare at heart…but after all those years of little or no contact it takes a bit of getting used to, to believe that he cares.' And yet only yesterday he had told her how proud he was of her, how much it pleased him that his daughter was a doctor, working to save lives. 'I needed to tell you that before I pass on,' he'd said, and she'd put her arms around him and given him a hug.

'Oh, Dad, please don't say that,' she'd implored him, her throat suddenly choked up. 'Please don't talk about passing on. I'm only just getting to know you.'

He'd smiled. 'What'll be will be.'

Nick's brooding gaze rested on her, as though he sensed something of her troubled thoughts. 'I'm sure he cares very deeply for you…but unhappily something went wrong and he didn't feel able to be there for you. Perhaps distance was a problem—living out here in California meant you were so far apart that visits would be infrequent, and he might have thought it would be less painful for you if he didn't visit at all. You would be able to settle to life without him, rather than be hurt all over again every time he went away.'

'Then again,' she pointed out, 'he could have chosen to stay in England. What was more important…his family or the job?'

He seemed to hesitate. 'That's something you must ask him yourself. I can't answer that one for you. But knowing him, I'm sure he had his reasons.'

'Did he? I've no idea what they were. All I know is that he condemned us—me and my mother—to a lonely life.' Her expression was bleak. 'Some people may like being an only child, but I wasn't one of them. I always felt there should be something more.'

He was solemn for a moment, his lips parting as though he was about to say something, but apparently he thought better of it. He laid a hand lightly on her shoulder. 'I'm sure it will all come right for you in the end, Katie. You've taken a huge step, coming out here, and you're making great headway. Just give it a little more time.'

He glanced at his watch. 'I'm off duty in a couple of hours. I'll come and pick you up from the apartment and we'll drive over to the vineyard. Perhaps that will cheer you up.'

She nodded. 'Okay. I'll be waiting.' A day or so had passed since he'd made the suggestion, and already she was beginning to regret agreeing to it. What had happened to her plan to avoid him at all costs, to steer clear of getting involved with him in any way? Working with him was proving to be a hazard in itself. It seemed that he was there at every turn…and it was impossible for her to get him out of her head.

She was beginning to realise that there was so much more to him than she had at first imagined. He was caring and perceptive and even though that made her want to get to know him a whole lot better, she was desperately afraid of the consequences. Little by little, though, he was drawing her into his electric force field and she was powerless to resist.

The vineyard, when they arrived there some time later, was bathed in late-afternoon sunlight. Nick helped her out of the passenger seat of his gleaming silver saloon and waited as she stepped out onto the wide, sweeping drive. Katie looked around. She couldn't explain it, even to herself, but just the simple fact that he was there beside her made the breath catch in her throat and in spite of herself filled her with a kind of delicious expectation. He was wearing casual clothes, a deep navy shirt, open at the neck, teamed with dark trousers, and just looking at him made her heart skip a beat.

'Let me show you round the place,' he said. 'From a high point in the gardens you can see for miles around.' He slipped an arm around her waist, his hand coming to rest on the curve of her hip in a gentle act of possession that brought heat surging throughout her body. 'I'm sure you'll love it out here,' he murmured. 'We have a beautiful day for it…the sun's shining and the vines are heavy with grapes.'

She nodded, and tried not to think about that casual touch that was so much like a caress. It only fogged her brain and left her confused and distracted.

He led the way through the house, a pretty French

château-style building that had steeply pitched roofs and round towers with turrets. Painted white, it was a gem set in the middle of the Carmel Valley, and Katie fell in love with it on sight.

The gardens were exquisitely landscaped, with trees and shrubs in full bloom so that there was a mass of colour all around. Nestled among the various arbours and flowering trees there was an elevated hardwood deck, and Nick started to head towards it.

'From up here on the deck you can see the vineyard in all its glory. It's a great vantage point,' he said, mounting the wooden stairs and walking over to the balustrade.

Katie followed him and turned to gaze at the distant Carmel Valley Mountains. 'I didn't realise that you had so much land,' she murmured. 'Are all those vines yours, or do those slopes belong to another vineyard…my father's, perhaps?'

Nick followed the direction of her gaze. 'They're ours. Your father's land is a little further to the west. We've terraced the slopes here in order to grow certain types of grapes, and then we have more vines spread along the valley floor. We're incredibly lucky in this area because there's such a long season. The grapes ripen slowly and that helps to intensify the flavour.'

She nodded, trying to take it all in. In the far distance, the verdant slopes of the ever-present Santa Lucia range added to the sense of lush, rich farmland all around. 'It looks heavenly,' she murmured, 'like an Eden where everything is in harmony and the fruit is bursting off the vines.'

He smiled. 'At least, that's how we hope it will be. A good year will produce a premium vintage, but we can't rely on that. If we get too much rain at the wrong time it can cause all kinds of problems, like mould, rot or mildew. Then again, the weather one season can be too hot and another too cool. It all helps to produce a variety of flavours and different qualities of wine.'

'So you can't simply sit back and leave things to nature?'

He laughed. 'I wish! But, no, definitely not…we have to take steps to compensate for adverse conditions.' He laid an arm around her, his hand splaying out over her shoulder and sending a thrill of heat to course through her veins. 'Over the years my family has put a huge amount of effort into building up a reputation for producing quality wines…and it all came about because of my great-great-grandfather's drive and ambition.'

She was thoughtful for a moment. 'He certainly managed to pick out a piece of prime land. He must have been an astute man—and I dare say a wealthy one, too.'

Nick shook his head. 'His family were immigrants, dirt poor, and they had to scrape a living for themselves. They came out here hoping for a better life, but it was a struggle, and I think Joseph, my great-great-grandfather, made up his mind that he would carve a path for himself, come what may. He worked at all kinds of jobs, day and night, determined to earn as much money as possible. He was thrifty, too, and put aside a good part of his earnings until, after about fifteen years or so, he had saved enough money to buy this vineyard.'

'That was a huge accomplishment.'

He nodded. 'It was. But the hardest bit was turning the vineyard around. When he first took it over they were producing inexpensive table wines, but Joseph had other ideas. He had a certain vision and he wanted to make big changes. Quality was everything to him and even though people told him he was making a big mistake, he went ahead with his plans to produce grapes that would provide superior wines. Then he had to convince the buyers that this was a product they wanted, and it all took tremendous hard work and a lot of money.'

He frowned. 'Over the years, when wine consumption declined and harvests were poor, the vineyard suffered losses that could have ruined everything for us. That's why my grandfather had to sell off a third of the land… the piece that Jack owns now. He needed the money to go on running things in keeping with Joseph's ideals.'

'And now you want it back,' Katie said flatly. 'That's why you've been asking my father to sign papers that will turn the ownership over to you once more.' She looked at him directly. 'He should have his solicitor look them over before he does anything, shouldn't he? I think I should get in touch with the law firm that deals with his affairs.' It was a subtle warning, designed to let him know that she wasn't going to stand by and see her father put under pressure. 'Only, like I said before, I don't think he's in any fit state to deal with these kinds of problems just now, do you?'

Her expression was faintly belligerent, her jaw tilted, and Nick's gaze flicked over her, taking it all in. 'I was just telling you the history of the place, that's all,' he said in an even tone. 'I don't want to get into an argument with you.'

She backed down a little. After all, she was on his territory, she was a guest here, and this was perhaps the wrong time and place to thrash out their differences.

'I'm just concerned for my father,' she said.

'I know that, and I respect you for it.' He studied

her thoughtfully. 'But if you really care about him, you would probably do well to persuade him that his life would be easier if he were to offload the worries of the business onto us. That way he could relax and enjoy his remaining years.'

She stiffened. 'I think you're mistaken if you believe I'll do your deal for you.' She sent him a flinty stare. 'I haven't had many weeks to get to know him, but it's been long enough for me to begin to care what happens to him. I didn't know what it was to have a father until now, and I've started to realise that it's something precious. I never imagined I would feel this way, about him or his land—so I'm not likely to suggest that he changes anything.'

She threw him a quick glance. 'I expect you're equally protective of your parents—more so, in fact.'

He nodded. 'I'm not criticising you in any way. It's natural that you should want to protect Jack's interests... but I'm sure he's astute enough to recognise a good deal when he sees one, and ours is far above anything he would get on the open market. Instead of trying to shield him, you could show him that it's the sensible route to follow.'

'I don't think so. I think you and your father need to back off.' She hesitated as a thought struck her. 'I don't believe you've ever mentioned your mother...'

'No.' His eyes were briefly troubled. 'She passed away some years ago...it was a virus, a nasty one that attacked her heart. The doctors did everything they could, but it wasn't enough to save her. I think she was already weak from a chest infection that laid her low.' He looked at Katie. 'I loved her dearly. She was a wonderful woman.'

'I'm sorry.' Katie pressed her lips together in a moment of regret. 'That must have been hard for all of you—your brother and your father.'

He nodded. 'Alex—my brother—was in Canada when he heard she was ill, but he came back as soon as he found out. At least we were all able to be with her at the end, and that makes it a little easier for us to bear.'

He moved away from the deck rail, becoming brisk and ready for action as though he wanted to shake off such sombre thoughts. 'Shall we go over to the winery? I said I'd take you on a tour after all.'

'Yes, I think maybe we should.' She followed him down the steps, saying, 'I was expecting some of your family to be here today—your father, maybe, or your brother.'

He shook his head. 'My father had to go into town, and Alex is in Los Angeles on business. I told him all about you, and I know he wants to meet you.'

Katie wasn't sure how to respond to that. Why would he have spoken to his brother about her? Unless, of course, he'd simply confided in his brother that a new girl had wandered in on his horizon…but perhaps she was misjudging him. It could be that her father was the factor in all this. The Bellinis were strongly allied to him through their business dealings, and it was probably only natural that they would be interested in the fact that he had a daughter—one that he had kept secret for a good many years.

They walked along a path leading from the house towards a collection of buildings some five hundred yards away. Nick pointed out a large stone-built complex where the grapes were processed, and then indicated another outbuilding where the offices and labs were housed. 'I'll show you around there later on,' he said, moving on.

She nodded. 'I know next to nothing about wine-making, I'm afraid.'

'You're not alone in that,' he murmured. He paused by a heavy wooden door set into a stone arch. 'Through here is the entrance to the cellar,' he told her. 'It has walls that are some fifteen inches thick, and it's a cool, well-ventilated environment, essential for producing good wine.'

The wine-tasting room was in a building set a little apart from these processing areas. The outer walls were painted in a soft sunshine yellow, and there were tubs of flowers and hanging baskets facing out on to the courtyard, giving it a mellow, cottage-style appearance.

'This is so pretty,' Katie said, glancing at the winery and looking back at the chateau in the distance. 'Your father must be really pleased to live in such an idyllic place.'

'I'm sure he is. I know I loved it. I was brought up here, and it was a wonderful childhood.' He looked around. 'It might be a good idea to sample the wines out here. Perhaps a table in the shade would be best.' He indicated a table in a far corner that was bordered by diamond-patterned trellises on two sides.

'Come and make yourself comfortable,' he said, holding out a seat for her, 'while I go and fetch the wines.'

He returned a moment later, bearing a tray. 'We'll try a Burgundy-style Pinot Noir first of all. It's our pride and joy, the best vintage yet. See what you think of it. It's made from black grapes that grow on the cooler slopes.'

Once she was settled, he handed her a glass filled

with dark red wine, and she took a sip. It was rich and smooth, with a hint of spice and an aftertaste of black cherry plum. Katie savoured it, letting it roll over her tongue before she swallowed it. 'I can see why you're excited about this,' she said. 'I'm not a wine buff, but I do know what I like, and this is delicious.'

Nick said quietly, 'Joseph Bellini would have been proud.' He turned to Katie. 'This is what his hard work was all about, and nowadays we do our level best to live up to his vision. As well as this special wine, we produce our own Cabernet Sauvignon. It's stored in barrels made of French oak and allowed to mature over many years. The oak helps to smooth out the harsh tannins and introduces softer, wood tannins.'

Katie nodded and tasted the wine once more. 'Don't you have a problem if my father's vineyard produces similar wines? Doesn't that put you in direct competition with one another?'

He shook his head. 'Your father concentrates on Chardonnay. He had a really good season last year, and the result should be a superb wine.' He picked out another bottle. 'This is one of his Chardonnays,' he said, pouring white wine into a glass and handing it to her. 'Try it. I think you'll like it. It's full of fruit flavours—like pear, apple and melon.'

Katie sipped the wine and tried to forget for the moment that Nick and his family were doing their level best to pull her father's business out from under his feet. How could she be drawn to a man who would do that? He was the enemy and yet she was calmly sipping wine with him and enjoying the comfort of his home. She felt like a traitor.

She would simply have to be on her guard and watch

out for Jack's interests whenever possible, she decided. Maybe she would carry out her threat and get in touch with the law firm that dealt with his business affairs. The Garcias were in the phone book, and a straightforward call might do the trick. They could advise her what to do and monitor her father's dealings at the same time.

'Mmm.' She nodded. 'This is lovely.' She raised her glass to him and then looked at the tray of wines. 'I see you have at least a dozen bottles on the trolley,' she said quietly. 'At this rate I shall be tipsy before dinner.'

Nick smiled and answered under his breath, 'I think I'd quite like to see that.' Then he pulled a wry face. 'I do have a secret stash of crackers and cheese hidden away, designed to soak up the alcohol, once we've had a taster. It's a pity that we have to eat them,' he added, his voice low and husky. 'With your senses blurred, I might have been able to persuade you that I'm everything you ever wanted in a man.' His expression was mournful, and Katie stifled a laugh.

'Give it up,' she murmured. 'I wouldn't want your hopes to be dashed.'

They tasted several more wines, including the Merlot, which her father seemed to favour most of all. It was another red wine, rich and fruity with notes of currant and cherry.

Katie was glad of the savoury biscuits and the cheese platter that Nick brought out a short time later. She had missed lunch and she was beginning to feel more than a little heady. Alongside the various cheeses, there were pizza slices and *bruschetta*—slices of toasted bread topped with *prosciutto* and tomato. He had provided a selection of nuts, too, served with slices of dried apricot.

'This has been such a great experience,' she told him. 'I've never been to a wine tasting before, and to be here surrounded by greenery and row on row of vineyard slopes has been wonderful.'

'I'm glad you've enjoyed it,' he said, giving her an appreciative smile. 'Perhaps we should go along and have a look at the processing complex, before the wine goes right to your head. You're looking a trifle flushed, and it might help if you were to stretch your legs for a bit.'

'Okay.'

He helped her to her feet, and they strolled slowly over to the stone-built production plant. Nick explained some of the processes involved—the pressing of the grapes, the addition of yeast and the many checks that were done to test each stage of the fermentation process. In each separate room there were photos and clear text descriptions on the walls to enable visitors to understand what went on there. There were photos, too, of Joseph Bellini, his son Sebastian, Nick's grandfather, Thomas, and finally Robert and his two sons. Katie stared at them in wonder. They all had the same rugged good looks, the strong bone structure, and that dark, Italian machismo.

'I had no idea such a lot of effort went into producing a bottle of wine,' she told Nick a while later as they stood by the window in the scrupulously clean barn where the grapes were poured into a giant hopper. The building's double doors were open to allow a cooling drift of air into the room. 'It must be tremendously satisfying to overcome all the hazards of production and finally taste the result—and discover that it's perfection.'

'It is. Wine-making is in our blood. It has become a part of us, much as the hills and valleys all around have become our home. I wouldn't want to be anywhere else than this small corner of the world.' He gave a crooked smile. 'My brother chose to travel, to go from place to place marketing our wines, but that wouldn't do for me. My roots are here. I love this valley and my beach house. I'm very content.'

'I imagine you are.' She gazed out of the window at the surrounding hills and then looked back at him. 'You must be very proud of your ancestors…all the dedication, strength of mind and sheer stamina that has gone into making the business what it is now. No wonder you're such a fit-looking family—what I've seen of it so far. It must be in the genes.'

He leaned against a guard rail, turning to face her full on, his dark eyes glinting. 'Fit is good, isn't it?' He slightly raised dark brows. 'Does this mean you're beginning to alter your opinion of me?' He reached for her in a leisurely fashion, his hands at the base of her spine, drawing her to him and holding her lightly within the circle of his arms. 'Perhaps there's still hope I could persuade you that I'm the sort of man you could go for?'

She laughed softly. 'There's always hope, I suppose.' She looked at him from under her lashes. 'But I wouldn't get too carried away if I were you.'

'A good thing you're not me, then,' he murmured huskily, 'because I have entirely different ideas on that score. Carried away sounds just about right to me.

Carried away is a chink in the armour, and definitely something I'd like to explore a little further.'

He came towards her, his arms tightening around her waist, and as his head lowered she finally began to realise his intention. He was going to kiss her, and even though, way down in the depths of her mind, she knew she really ought to be doing something to stop him, she did nothing at all. And as his lips brushed hers in a touch that was as light as the drift of silk over her skin, she discovered the last thing on earth she wanted was to pull away.

Just the opposite, in fact. Instead, she wanted to lean into him, to revel in his warm embrace, and delight in the strength of those muscular thighs that were pressuring her softly against the cool, steel wall of the hopper. And he must have known what she wanted because he drew her ever closer until her breasts were softly crushed against the wall of his chest and she could feel the heavy thud of his heartbeat marching in time with her own.

He kissed her, tenderly at first and then with rising passion, so that his breathing became ragged and his hands began to smooth over her curves.

Katie was lost in a haze of fevered pleasure. The sun was bright in an azure sky, and for a moment or two time seemed to stand still. There was only the sensual glide of his lips as they slowly explored the contours of her face, her throat and the creamy expanse of her shoulder, laid bare by the thin straps of the cotton top she wore. And with each lingering kiss her senses soared in response.

It was all so exhilarating, so perfect, and nothing like anything she had ever experienced before. What was it about him that made her feel this way? Did he have some kind of magical touch? If so, she wanted more, much more.

Only, as his lips began to slide lower, drifting into unsafe territory, alarm bells started to ring inside her. He gently nudged aside the delicate cotton strap and ventured even further into the danger zone, trailing soft kisses over the rounded swell of her breasts and leading her to a heady, disturbing place where feeling and emotion were all, and logical thought was banished.

Even so, a tiny sliver of common sense began to filter through the mist that spread, unbidden, through her brain. Perhaps it was the swish of sprinklers being started up on the lawns outside that alerted her, or maybe it was the soft flap of a bird's wings that dragged her attention back to the reality of what was happening. What was she thinking? How could she have let this happen?

She struggled to get herself together. Wasn't Nick the man who avoided commitment? Wasn't he the one who was trying to persuade her father to sign away his land?

And here she was, betraying every instinct she possessed by falling into his arms at the first opportunity. She was a fool. She ought to have known better.

'Are you all right?' Nick lifted his head, depriving her of that heavenly, forbidden contact, and she tried to answer, but no words came. 'Have I done something wrong?' His voice was a soft murmur against her cheek.

'No... I... Yes...' She tried to ease herself away from him, her hands flattening against his chest as though she would put an end to his kisses. Why, then, did she feel the urge to stroke the velvet-covered wall of his rib cage and let her fingers explore the broad expanse of his shoulders? His muscles were firm and supple, inviting her to touch him and savour the moment.

Truly, she was a basket case—a woman at the mercy of her hormones and not to be trusted with the slightest task. 'I don't think I'm ready for this,' she said huskily. 'I shouldn't have let things get this far.'

'Are you quite sure about that?' His hands caressed her, and his tone was soft and coaxing, inviting her to drift back into the shelter of his arms once more. 'Life could be so much sweeter if only you'd allow yourself to taste it.'

She pulled in a shaky breath, willing herself to resist temptation. 'I'm sure…absolutely sure.' Even as she said it she wondered if she was trying to convince him or herself. She straightened and took a step away from him. 'I don't know how you manage to do this to me,' she said huskily, her gaze troubled. 'I need to feel good about myself, and none of this is helping. I'm very confused. I need time to think.'

'Okay.' He gave a soft, ragged sigh and moved to lay his forehead gently against hers. 'But I can't help thinking that you'd do better to throw caution to the wind. Life isn't easy. It's full of what-ifs and might-have-beens, and if you thought hard about all of them you might never experience the good side of things. I know you've been hurt, but sometimes you have to get back into the fray if you're to have another chance of happiness. Sometimes you simply have to go with your instinct and trust in people.'

Slowly, he released her, and then stood with his hands

to either side of him on the guard rail, so that she finally began to breathe a little easier.

He straightened. 'I'll walk you back to the courtyard.' He gave a crooked smile. 'You'll be safe there.'

CHAPTER SIX

KATIE placed the consultant's letter back in her tray and tried to steer her thoughts towards work. 'Good news there, at least,' she told Carla, the desk clerk, indicating the sheet of headed notepaper. 'My young patient who was rushed to hospital from here a few weeks ago is back home and on the mend.'

'The child with kidney problems? I remember his mother was so upset.' Carla gave a relieved smile. 'It's good to know he's pulled through all right. I've been worrying about him…about the poor boy with the head injury, too.'

Katie nodded. 'Me, too. Last I heard, they were thinking about moving him from the intensive care unit. I was hoping I might find time to ring and check up on him some time today, but the time has simply rushed by.' She frowned, straightening up and easing the slight ache in her back. Earlier today she had rung her father to find out how he was doing, but things weren't good, and that was playing on her mind. His nurse, Steve, was worried about his condition.

She dragged her mind back to work. 'Do I have any more patients to see this afternoon? There's nothing on my list and the waiting room's empty.'

Carla glanced at her screen once more. 'No, but there was a message from Dr Bellini. He said Matthew Goren was coming in to hospital as an outpatient today. He thought you might like to be in on the consultation with him. His appointment's scheduled for four o'clock—that gives you a quarter of an hour to get over there.'

'Right…thanks, Carla. I'd better run.'

She hurried over to the emergency department. She wasn't at all sure how she was going to cope with seeing Nick again—his scorching kisses had seared a memory into her brain that would last for all time. It made her feel hot and bothered even now, just thinking about it. And she had also been mulling over his words of advice… 'Sometimes you have to go with your instinct and trust in people.' Could she do that? Was she ready to put the past behind her and accept that she might be able to find happiness in his arms?

She went along the corridor in search of his room.

'Katie, I'm glad you could make it.' Nick's voice was deep and warm, smooth like honey drizzled over caramelised pears. He gave her a quick smile and invited her into his office. 'I thought you might like to be in on this one. The lab results are back, and this is the last appointment of the day so there will be time to break the news to the boy and his mother without having to rush things.'

'Break the news—it's what we thought, then?'

He nodded. 'Gaucher's disease. Fortunately, even though it's rare, there are treatments for it, so it isn't as bad as it might have been some years ago. And Matt has the mildest form of the disease, so that's another point in his favour.'

He accessed the boy's notes on his computer, and they

both took time to sift through the various test results and read the letter from the consultant. When the clerk paged them a few minutes later, they were both ready to receive mother and son with smiles of greeting.

'I know you're anxious to hear the results of the tests,' Nick told them after he had made some general enquiries about the boy's state of health. 'As you know, I was concerned because Matt's spleen appeared to be enlarged and because he's been having pain in his joints. We discovered there was also some slight enlargement of the liver.'

Mrs Goren nodded. 'You took some blood for testing, and he had an MRI scan.'

'That's right.' Nick brought up the film of the scan on his computer monitor and turned to Katie. 'Do you want to explain the results?' he asked.

Katie nodded, and looked at the boy. He was a thin child, slightly underweight, with cropped brown hair that gave him an elfin look. He was looking at her now with large eyes and a faintly worried expression.

'What we discovered,' she said, 'was that you have a fatty substance in your liver and spleen. It shouldn't be there, and so we needed to find out what was going on inside you that would have caused it.'

Matt nodded, but looked puzzled and, picking up on that Katie said quickly, 'I want you to feel free to ask me questions at any time, Matt. If there's anything you don't understand, or anything you'd like to say, just go ahead.'

He frowned. 'Have you found out what caused it? Is it something I've done? The boys at school tease me.'

Katie gave him a sympathetic smile. 'No, it's nothing that you've done, and I'm sorry that you're being teased.

Perhaps when you explain to the boys what's wrong, they'll understand a bit better and stop making fun of you.'

She glanced at his mother. 'Matt has a condition called Gaucher's disease. Basically, it means that he was born without an enzyme that breaks down a substance called glucocerebroside.' She turned to Matt. 'Because you don't have this enzyme in your body, the fatty substance isn't broken down and has to find somewhere to go. Unfortunately, when it finds a home in places like your liver, your spleen or even your bones, for example, it stops those parts of you from working properly. That's why you've been having pain in your thigh, and it's the reason for you being tired all the while.'

'You're saying he was born with it?' His mother was frowning. 'Does that mean it's a hereditary disease?'

Mrs Goren's gaze flew in alarm from Katie to Nick, and Nick answered quietly, 'That's right. You and your husband may not suffer from the disease, but it's possible that either one or both of you may be a carrier. It can go back through generations, although there may not be anyone in the family that you know of directly who has the disease.'

All at once Mrs Goren looked close to tears and Katie hurried on to say, 'The *good* news is that we do have treatment for it.' She smiled at Matt. 'There's something called enzyme replacement therapy, which helps to break down this fatty substance and should soon start to improve things for you.'

Matt's brow cleared, and his mother dabbed at her eyes with a tissue and did her best to pull herself together. She looked at Nick. 'Can we start him on this treatment straight away?'

He responded cautiously. 'I can arrange an appointment for him at the hospital. The answer isn't as simple as taking a tablet, I'm afraid, but what happens is that Matt will be given an infusion—it takes about an hour to administer, and the treatment is given once a fortnight. He'll need to stay with the treatment for life, until such time as science comes up with a better answer. It's a rare disease. Of course, he'll be carefully monitored on a regular basis, so that we can check how he's responding.'

Katie was silent, watching as mother and son tried to absorb what he had just told them. Nick waited, too, before gently asking if they had any questions for him. He was unfailingly patient and kind, and her respect for him grew. In fact, every time she saw him at work, she marvelled at his caring, conscientious manner.

Mrs Goren and Matt both remained quiet for a moment or two longer. Perhaps they had all the information they could handle for the time being. It was a lot to take in, but the consolation was that from now on they would receive masses of help from the clinic at the hospital…along with ongoing input from Nick and herself, of course.

'Will the treatment cause the swelling to go down?' Mrs Goren asked, and Nick nodded.

'You should see a great improvement.' He looked at Matt. 'And the pain will go away.'

After answering a few more questions, and doing what he could to put the mother's mind at ease, he said, 'Let me leave you with some reading material that I've printed out for you. I'm sure there will be things that you think of once you leave here, but I'm hoping that these papers will help answer any immediate queries…

and, of course, you can always come and see me again if you want to talk.'

Katie glanced at Nick. That was a thoughtful touch—he had gone that one step further to give his patient everything he could, and she could see that Mrs Goren was pleased.

Nick gave his attention to Matt, and said, 'The nurses and doctors at the clinic will look after you and explain anything you want to know. Next time you come to the hospital for an outpatient appointment, I'm sure you'll be feeling a whole lot better. In the meantime, keep taking the painkillers if you have any more trouble with your thigh, and get plenty of rest. Once you get started on the treatment, I'm certain you'll begin to feel much more energetic.'

Matt nodded. 'Thanks,' he said, and gave a shuddery sigh. 'I thought I had some horrible illness that was going to make me die, but it's not as bad as that, is it?'

'No, it isn't,' Nick told him with a reassuring smile, and Katie's heart went out to this child who had suffered in silence all this time. 'And if you ever have worries of any kind,' Nick added, 'please speak up. Don't keep it to yourself. Often things aren't nearly as bad as you think, and we're here to help you in any way we can.'

After they left, Nick invited Katie to stay awhile and made coffee for both of them. 'I need to write up my notes while they're fresh in my mind—but perhaps we can talk after that?'

'Okay.' She sipped her coffee and leaned back in her chair, thinking about the day's events. From a medical standpoint at work, things had gone well, but she felt uneasy somehow. There was still that niggling worry over her father's health.

She gave a faint sigh, and then stretched. What she needed right now was a complete change of scene, a trip to the beach, perhaps or maybe even a walk through the cobbled streets of the town. But that wasn't likely to happen for a while… Perhaps she ought to go and see her father, see how he was bearing up. There might be something she could do for him.

'Are you okay?' Nick asked.

Caught off guard, Katie quickly tried to collect her thoughts. She hadn't realised he'd been watching her. 'I'm fine, thanks.'

His gaze flicked over her. 'You seem…pensive. If there's something wrong, perhaps I can help?'

She shook her head. 'I was just thinking about my father—I feel that I should go over to his place to see if he's all right. I rang this morning and he was having a bad day, according to the nurse, Steve. It's a bit worrying—apparently he was talking but not making much sense.'

Nick winced. 'That happens sometimes when the blood oxygen levels are low.'

'Yes. Even so, I asked Steve to send for the doctor to see if he would prescribe a different medication. He hasn't called me yet to let me know what happened. I suppose he's been too busy, with one thing and another, or perhaps he didn't want to tie up the phone line if the doctor was likely to call.'

'That's probably the case.' He studied her thoughtfully. 'Would you like me to go with you to see him? It's never easy when someone in the family is ill, is it?'

'No, it isn't.' She might have known Nick would

understand. He had been through difficult times with his mother in the past, and it said a lot about his compassion and perception that he was offering to be by her side. 'Thank you,' she said softly. 'I'd really like it if you would be there with me.'

'We'll go as soon as I've finished up here,' he said, becoming brisk and ready for action. 'Give me five minutes.'

A feeling of relief swept over her. She didn't know why she had involved Nick in any of this, there was no accounting for her actions, and she was working purely on instinct. All at once, though, she felt that with him by her side, she could handle anything.

They went out to his car a short time later, which was in a leafy, private space in the car park. She glanced at him. Even after a day's work, he looked cool and fresh, dressed in dark trousers and crisp linen shirt that perfectly outlined his long, lean figure. His black hair glinted with iridescent lights as they walked in the sunlight, and she gazed at him for a moment or two, wondering what it was about him that stirred her blood and made her want to be with him.

He touched her hand, clasping it within his, and suddenly she felt safe, cherished, as though all was right with the world. 'I'm here for you, Katie,' he said softly. 'Any time you need me.'

Her heart swelled with joy. The truth was, he had never been anything but good towards her. He had treated her with warmth and respect, with care and attention, and he was here now, ready to be by her side at a moment's notice and support her through what promised to be a difficult time. What more could she ask?

She stood in the shade of a cypress tree, watching

him as he paused to unlock the car, and it finally hit her that she was bedazzled by him. He made her heart thump and her thoughts go haywire, and there was no knowing why it was happening. Why was she holding back? She might just as well cast her fears to one side and start living again, mightn't she?

Okay, so she had been hurt once before. Her ex had had a child by another woman and had shocked her to the core with his infidelity, but that didn't have to mean all men were of a similar nature, did it? Was she going to let that experience ruin her life for evermore?

Nick came to stand beside her, his lips curving in a faint smile, and he said softly, 'Are you feeling all right? You look different somehow.'

A faint bubble of laughter rose in her throat. 'I'm fine. I'm just so glad that you're here with me. Whatever happens, I feel as though I'll be able to cope with it, just as long as we're together.'

'That's good to know.' His voice faded on a shuddery sigh. 'I've waited a long while for you to learn to trust me, Katie. I won't let you down, I promise.'

He wrapped his arms around her and kissed her gently on the mouth. His touch was light as the drift of silk, but it sent fiery signals to every nerve ending in her body, and she wanted to cling to him, to savour that moment and make it last for ever.

Her fingers lightly stroked his arms and then moved up to tangle with the silky hair at his nape. She belonged in his arms, it felt right, as though it was the only place to be at that moment.

He kissed her again, trailing kisses over her cheek, her throat, and then with a soft, ragged sound he reluctantly dragged himself away from her.

'Wrong place,' he said in a roughened tone, as though that explained things. 'I can think of better places where I can show you how much I care.'

Katie stared at him, blankly, her lips parting, a tingle of delicious sensation still running through her from head to toe.

He sent her an oblique glance in return, his mouth twisting a little. 'Did I go too far again?' he asked. 'I hope not, because I really wanted to do that. In fact, it's on my mind every time I see you—and even sometimes when we're apart.'

She didn't answer, still lost in that haze of delirious excitement. He'd kissed her…he cared about her… All at once the world was bright and new. Was this love?

Nick pulled in a deep breath, as though to steady himself. He held open the passenger door for her and she slid dazedly into the air-conditioned comfort of his car. Then he went around to the driver's side, coming to sit beside her.

He turned the key in the ignition, starting up the car. 'I need to get my head right,' he said. 'Perhaps we should talk about everyday kind of things for a while—like work, for instance.'

She blinked and closed her mouth, trying her utmost to bring her thoughts back down to a level plane, and he went on cautiously, 'I thought you might like to know—I checked up on Darren Mayfield this afternoon.'

'You did?' She finally found her voice. 'Oh, I'm glad of that. I haven't had time to ring the unit yet today. How's he doing? I know they were thinking of moving him from Intensive Care.'

He nodded. 'That's right. I know you've been keeping tabs on his condition over the last week or so. Anyway, he's on the main ward now and he seems on course to make a full recovery. There's some weakness in his limbs apparently, but the physiotherapist is going to be working with him and he looks set to be back to normal within a few weeks.'

Her face lit up. 'Oh, that's wonderful news…the best.'

He nodded. 'I knew you'd be pleased.' He set the car in motion and turned his attention to the road, leaving her to gaze out at the passing landscape.

'You said you'd been to see your father's vineyard,' Nick remarked as he turned the car on to the valley road. 'Of course, he doesn't live on the property—his manager is the one who stays on the premises. I expect you'll have met him when you went over there.'

Katie nodded. 'Yes, I've been introduced to Toby. He seems a very friendly and approachable man. At least he was willing to answer all my naïve questions. Like I said, I've been fascinated with the whole process of growing vines and turning the fruit into wine ever since I came over here and learned what my father was doing.'

Nick frowned. 'You could always ask me anything you want to know…anytime. I'd be only too glad to tell you. We could even combine it with dinner out or supper at one of the ocean view restaurants around here, if you like. Or a stroll along the beach if that takes your fancy more.'

Her mouth curved. 'I'll definitely think about it. They all sound good to me.'

He relaxed, a look of satisfaction crossing his face. 'Wow! I think I'm actually winning for a change! Wake me up, I think I might be dreaming!'

'I seriously hope not,' she said with a laugh, 'or any minute now you'll be crashing the car into my father's gatepost.'

They had reached her father's property, a stone-built house set in a secluded area some short distance from the coastal stretch where Nick had his home. They approached it along a sweeping drive that cut through well-kept lawns, bordered in part by mature trees and flowering shrubs.

The house was a solid, rectangular building on two storeys, with the ground-floor windows placed symmetrically either side of a wide doorway.

Katie frowned as Nick drew the car to a halt. 'It looks as though my father has a visitor,' she said. 'I don't recognise that four by four, do you?'

'It's the doctor's car. Dr Weissman—I've known him for some years now.'

'Oh, yes.' Katie collected her thoughts. 'I think I've bumped into him once or twice.' Her gaze was troubled. 'I wonder if my father's taken a turn for the worse?'

Nick was already sliding out of the car, and she hurried to join him on the gravelled forecourt. It was a fresh, warm summer's day, but the sun went behind a cloud just then and a sudden sense of foreboding rippled through her. She walked quickly towards the oak front door and rang the bell.

Libby, the housekeeper, came to answer it, looking unusually flustered. 'Oh, Katie, there you are.' She pulled open the door and ushered them inside. 'I was just about to call you,' she said, pulling at a wayward strand of soft brown hair. 'The doctor and Steve are with your father now. Jack's been having a bad time of it all day. It's his heart, I think. At least, that's what the doctor said.'

'I need to go and see him,' Katie said, a thread of unease edging her words. The feeling of dread that clutched at her midriff since she'd arrived at the house was intensifying by the minute.

'I understand how you must be feeling,' Libby answered, worry lines creasing her brow, 'but the doctor said he would come and let us know as soon as there was any news.'

Katie frowned. 'But I'm his daughter. I want to be with him. I want to know what's going on.'

The housekeeper's face seemed to crumple, and she made a helpless, fluttering gesture with her hands, as though this was all getting too much for her, and Katie said quickly, 'It will be all right, Libby, I promise. We made up our differences a while ago, my father and I… he'll want me to be there with him. I know he will.'

Libby was still fraught with indecision. 'I should have rung you earlier, I know I should, but I had to ring for an ambulance and try to contact the others and that took up so much time. It's been such an awful day, one way and another. And the ambulance still hasn't arrived.'

Katie frowned. What others? What was Libby talking about? But perhaps she had tried to phone Jack's friends, the people who knew him best…along with the doctor, of course. Katie might be his daughter, but she had only been in town for a couple of months at most.

Nick took hold of her arm, as though to add a helping hand, and she turned to him in gratitude. 'Thanks for bringing me here. It looks as though things are much more serious than I thought. Otherwise why would Dr Weissman have wanted an ambulance?'

'It does sound as though he's concerned,' Nick admitted, 'but let's wait and hear what he has to say.'

'I must go to my father,' she said again. She knew the way to Jack's room from the first time she had been there, when her father had shown her around, and despite Libby's distressed expression she made an instant decision and began to head in that direction.

Nick went with her, but as they came to the first floor and walked along the corridor, the door of her father's room opened and Steve walked out.

He stopped as soon as he saw them and pulled in a deep, calming breath. 'Katie,' he greeted her. 'I don't think you should go in there just yet. Let me talk to you for a while. Shall we find somewhere to sit down?' He glanced at Nick, and an odd look passed between them. Katie didn't understand it. Hadn't that same mysterious kind of glance occurred when she and her father had had dinner together and she'd met Nick for the first time?

She allowed Nick to lead her away, following Steve along the corridor and back down the stairs to the sitting room.

'Please, sit down, Katie.' Steve indicated a comfortable sofa and then turned to Nick. 'You, too, Nick,' he said.

Katie did as he suggested, feeling for the settee with the back of her legs and not once taking her gaze off Steve. Nick sat down beside her, and the nurse took the armchair opposite.

She was more bewildered than ever. Something was going on here and she had no idea what it could be. Right now, though, she wanted more than anything to know what was happening with her father.

'Katie,' Steve began quietly, 'I'm really sorry to be the

one to tell you this…but I'm afraid your father passed away a few minutes ago. In the end his heart simply gave out.'

'No…' Katie's mind refused to take it in. 'That can't be… I only spoke to him on the phone this morning. How can this be happening?' For all her training as a doctor, coming face to face with the death of a loved one was turning out to be every bit as difficult for her as it was for her patients. She had no idea it could be so hard to accept.

Nick put his arm around her and held her tight. 'I'm so sorry, Katie. It's a shock—in fact, it's a shock for both of us.'

Steve pressed his lips together in a fleeting moment of sadness. 'Dr Weissman did everything he could to try to resuscitate him, but in the end it was impossible. There was nothing more he could do.'

Katie was bewildered. 'I just can't take it in. I came here thinking he was just having one of those bad days. He always seemed so stoical, so determined to get the best out of life.'

'And I'm sure he did, Katie.' Nick leant his cheek against hers. 'He was over the moon because you had come out here to see him. These last few weeks he was always talking about you, saying how well you'd done for yourself.'

'Was he?' Tears began to trickle slowly down her face. 'It seems such a waste. All these years I've waited, wanting to get to know him but always holding back because I was afraid of what I might find. It took me such a long time to forgive him for walking out on my mother and me. It was such a strange sort of life…as if it was somehow off key. And now he's gone.'

He held her close, letting her weep for what might have been, and all the time he stroked her hair, comforting her just by being there for her when she needed him most.

Libby brought in a tray of tea and quietly set it down on the coffee table. 'The doctor's gone into the kitchen to fill in his forms. He's very sad. They were good friends—your father always spoke highly of him.'

Katie glanced up at Libby. The woman was ashen-faced, struggling to keep her emotions in check.

'Perhaps you should sit down and give yourself some time,' Katie suggested softly, still shaken but subdued. 'You must be as upset as the rest of us. More so, perhaps…my father told me you'd been with him for years.'

Libby put a tissue to her face. 'I have, yes, that's true.' She wrung her hands. 'I ought to go and…' She turned distractedly, as though to go out of the door, and then changed her mind and came to sit down on one of the straight-backed chairs by a polished mahogany desk. 'I don't know what to do,' she said in a broken voice.

'Don't do anything. Just sit for a while and I'll get you some tea.' Katie moved as though to go and pour a cup, but Nick gently pressured her back into the sofa.

'I'll do it,' he said. 'You stay there.'

Steve looked towards the sitting-room door while Nick poured tea and handed it around. 'I should go and have a word with the doctor,' he murmured. 'He'll need someone to see him out…and I'd better call the paramedics and tell them what's happened.'

He walked over to the door and opened it, walking out into the hallway. The sound of voices coming from there alerted Katie and made her sit up and take notice. Had the paramedics arrived already?

'We just want to talk to Libby for a minute or two,' a male voice said. 'There will be things to arrange.'

Steve said quietly, 'Perhaps it can wait for a while. Libby's in shock, as we all are. Do you want to go and talk to the doctor instead, in the kitchen?'

'Not just yet.' The sound of the man's voice drew nearer, and Katie looked across the room as the door opened. A young man walked in, followed by a slender girl who looked to be slightly older than him, about twenty-three or twenty-four years old. She was pretty, with auburn hair that fell in bright curls about her shoulders, but right now her features were taut, as though she was doing her best to hold herself together.

Katie stood up, dragging her thoughts away from all that had happened and making an effort to behave in the way that Jack would have expected. He would want her to politely greet his guests and make them welcome, even now.

'Hello,' she said, going over to them. 'I don't think we've met before, have we? I'm Katie. For a moment there I thought you were the paramedics.'

The young man shook his head. 'I think the doctor rang and told them there was no urgency.'

'Yes, that would be the sensible thing to do.' Katie studied him briefly. He had black hair and hazel eyes, and she had the impression he was struggling to keep his emotions under control, his face showing signs of stress, with dark shadows under his eyes and a gaunt, hollowed-out appearance to his cheeks.

'I'm Tom Logan,' he said, 'and this is my sister, Natasha.' He put an arm around the girl's shoulders.

'You've caught us at a bad time. I expect you've heard that our father has just died. Did you know him? Were you a friend of his?'

Katie almost reeled back in shock. She stared at him. *Their father?* Surely there had to be some mistake? She felt as though all the breath had been knocked out of her and for a moment or two she simply stood there and tried to absorb his words.

'I didn't realise…' she began after a while, but broke off. There couldn't be any mistake, could there? *Logan*, he had said. How much clearer could he have made it?

'Are you all right?' Tom was frowning, looking perplexed, and his sister pulled in a shaky breath and tried to show her concern, too.

It wasn't fitting that she should be here, Katie decided suddenly. These were Jack's children, and they had the right to grieve in peace. She had to get out of here. 'Yes, I…' She swallowed hard. 'I have to go… I need to get some air…' This wasn't the time or the place to explain who she was and where she had come from, was it? They'd obviously had no idea that she existed before this.

She swivelled round, desperate to get out of there, away from all these people. All at once she felt as though she was part of a topsy-turvy world where nothing made sense any more. She needed to be alone, to try to take it all in.

'Katie's upset,' she heard Nick saying. 'This has all been a bit too much for her. Excuse us, please. I think I'd better take her home.'

Katie was already out of the front door, standing on the drive, when she realised that she didn't have her own car there. But perhaps that was just as well. She was probably in no state to drive.

Was it too far away for her to walk home? She could always get a taxi, couldn't she? But for now she just needed to keep moving, to get away from there, to get her head straight.

'Katie, wait, please.' Nick dropped into step beside her.

'Why would I do that?' She shot the words at him through gritted teeth. 'I really don't have anything to say to you.' She kept on walking. Hadn't he known all along?

'But we need to talk this through,' he said. 'You've had a shock—a double shock, given what's happened to Jack.'

'Yes, I've had a shock—and whose fault is that, precisely?' The words came out flint sharp. 'Did you really think you could hide it from me for ever? Why would you want to do that?' She clamped her lips together. 'No, don't answer that. I don't want to hear it. You colluded with him, let me go on thinking I was the daughter he loved and cared about, when all the time he…' She couldn't get the words out. Her anger was rising in a tide of blood that rushed to her head. It made her feel dizzy, and it thumped inside her skull like the stroke of a relentless mallet.

'It wasn't the way you think…believe me…'

'Believe you?' She gave a harsh laugh. 'Why should I believe you?' She looked at him, her green eyes glinting with barely suppressed fury. 'Why should I listen to anything you have to say? I was foolish enough to think that you had some integrity, that you were different to the others…that you could be honest with me. Well, I was wrong.' She was still walking, her footsteps taking her out through the large wrought-iron gates, flanked on either side by stone-built gateposts.

'Katie, this is madness. At least stop and talk to me. Let me explain.'

'There's nothing to explain, is there? I know exactly how it went. You knew all along that my father had another family, a family he didn't want me to know about... or my mother, for that matter. How old is Natasha, do you imagine? Twenty-four? That means she was born while he was still married to my mother. How do you think I feel about that? Can you imagine? And yet I still would have wanted to know that they existed. Don't you think I had a right to know?'

'Of course you did. And he would have told you, given time. It's just that he wanted to pick his moment. You were getting along so well together. He didn't want to spoil that.'

He frowned. 'Katie, you've only just discovered that he's passed on. You're bound to be upset and not thinking clearly about things. You're emotional and overwrought, and you should give yourself time to get used to the idea that he's gone before you start dissecting his behaviour and giving yourself grief over it. You'll have a much more balanced outlook in a day or so's time.'

'Will I? I think I have a pretty firm handle on the situation right now. I might even forgive my father for his deception...after all, I've been there before. He left us back in England and eventually I managed to come to terms with what he had done. I know what kind of man he is...' her voice lowered to a whisper. 'Was.'

She stopped walking and faced him head on. 'It's you I have a problem with. You're the one who kept the pretence going. You banded together to keep me in the dark about it, about my family—my brother and sister, for heaven's sake.'

She shook her head as though to throw out all the debris of broken dreams that had gathered there. 'You knew how lonely I was through all those years after he left us,' she said, her eyes blurred with tears. 'You knew how much it hurt me to be rejected and how desperately I needed to know the reason for that. You should have told me the truth…that he had another family out here, one that he was prepared to stand by, to love and protect. It would have helped me to understand. I wouldn't have kept my hopes up that my relationship with my father could have been something more than it was.'

Her gaze locked with his. 'Instead, you let me flounder and lose my way. You made it so that I stumbled across his children at the worst possible moment. You could have stopped all that, and yet you did nothing.'

'Katie, I had to keep it from you. Jack made me promise. He wanted to tell you himself when the time was right.'

'Well, you should never have made that promise,' she told him flatly. 'Because of it, all my illusions are shattered. I thought I knew you. I thought I could trust you…but I was wrong.' She took in a shuddery breath. 'You should go back to the house, Nick. I need to be alone.'

CHAPTER SEVEN

'IF THERE's anything at all that I can do to help you through these next few weeks, Dr Logan, please be sure to give me a call…at any time.' The lawyer handed Katie his embossed card. 'I know this must be a particularly difficult time for you.'

'Thank you.' Katie accepted the card and slipped it into her bag. She was still numb from everything that had happened over the last couple of weeks. Her father had died, the will had been read and now she had to try to pick up the pieces and go on with her life.

How was she to do that? Nick had betrayed her. The one man she'd thought she could trust had let her down, with devastating consequences. He'd once told her that she was special and that she'd shaken him to the core, and yet those had been empty words. It seemed those feelings were fragile, and he was easily diverted.

His duplicity left her feeling utterly lost and alone and she couldn't see how she was ever going to recover from this.

Even now, Nick was watching her from across the room. It was bad enough that he was there at all, but there was nothing she could do about that. She could feel his dark gaze homing in on her, piercing like a laser, but she was determined to ignore him. She wanted to avoid him at all costs. He'd known all along about Tom and Natasha, but he had said nothing. How could he have left her to find out about them that way? If he had cared anything for her, wouldn't he have told her?

'It can't have been easy for you, discovering that you had a family out here in California,' the lawyer commented.

'No,' she confessed. She'd had two long weeks to think about that awful day at her father's house, and now she was here with her half-brother and -sister, gathered together under the same roof once more, and it was every bit as unsettling now as it had been then. 'I'm finding it all a bit of a strain, I must admit. I'm still struggling to take it all in. It hadn't occurred to me that my father would leave the vineyard, the house—everything, in fact—to the three of us.' She frowned. 'I'm not sure what I expected, really...after all, I hadn't been part of his life for some twenty years.'

'The terms of the will were very precise.' His brows drew together in a dark line. 'After his second wife died, he stipulated that the property and the land should go to his children, and he named each one of you specifically. It wasn't an afterthought. He had the will drawn up several years ago. Other bequests were added later—like the monetary gifts to his housekeeper and manager.'

'And the collection of rare books that went to Nick Bellini.' That was the reason for him being there, wasn't it, on a day when she'd thought she would be safe?

He nodded. 'Jack knew that he had a special interest in them, and he wanted to thank him for his help over the years. He said Nick had always been there to advise him about matters to do with the vineyard, and lately he had looked out for him when he was ill.'

'It sounds as though you knew my father very well.' Her mouth softened. 'He must have talked to you quite a bit about these things.'

'That's true. I often had occasion to meet with him, so we got to know one another on a friendly as well as a professional basis. I had a lot of respect for your father.'

Katie's mouth made a faint downward curve. It was a pity she couldn't share that opinion. Her world had been turned upside down when she had discovered her father's secret. Now she would remember him as a weak man who hadn't had the courage to admit to his shortcomings. How much grief would he have spared his family if he had done that? Even her mother had echoed those thoughts at his funeral.

For Katie's part, she wanted to weep. What was it about her that made people treat her this way? As a child, for a long time after her father left she had felt that she was unlovable…worthless…and now those feelings of rejection and isolation were intensified.

Was there anyone she could rely on? Her ex had cheated on her, and her own father had left her so that he could be with his other family. And now Nick had hurt her deeply by keeping her in the dark about her brother and sister. If he'd cared about her at all, wouldn't he have confided in her, tried to smooth her path and let her know about something so significant as a family that was being hidden from her?

'How are you bearing up?' Nick came to join them, and the lawyer discreetly excused himself to go and talk to her new siblings. 'If there's anything I can do—'

'You could stay away,' she said, slanting him a brief, cool stare.

'I'm sorry you feel that way.' His gaze flicked over her, taking in the silky sheen of her chestnut hair, the troubled curve of her mouth, and then shifted downwards over the slender lines of her dove-grey suit. The jacket nipped in at the waist, emphasising the flare of her hips, while the slim skirt finished at the knee, showing off an expanse of silk-smooth legs. 'I was hoping by now you'd have had time to think things through… and maybe come to the conclusion that I'd acted with the best of intentions.'

'Then you'll be disappointed. I won't forgive you for holding back from me. You let me down. You betrayed my trust…my faith in you. I'd begun to think you were someone I could believe in, but it turns out you're no different from any of the other men in my life.'

His head went back at that and sparks flared in his eyes, as though she had slapped him. A moment later, though, he recovered himself and said in an even tone, 'I can see I've a lot of fences to mend. I hoped you would understand that I did what I felt was right. I had to keep my promise to your father.'

She gave an indifferent shrug. 'That's as may be. I'm not disputing that. You made your choice and you stuck by it. That's fine. Just don't expect me to agree with you. If you had any thought for my feelings at all, you would have warned me. Instead, you let me blunder on, thinking I actually had a father who loved me but who had simply made a mistake.' Her jaw clenched. 'But, of course, it turns out that *I* was the mistake. That's laughable, isn't it? The offspring who really mattered to him are standing over there, talking to his lawyer.' Her gaze was steel sharp. 'You colluded with him.' She gave an imitation of a smile. 'I must have thrown the cat among the pigeons, turning up here out of the blue.'

His mouth compressed. 'You know I'm not to blame for any of that, Katie. You're putting the sins of your father onto me. Don't you think you're mixing things up in your head just a little?'

'No, I don't. Not at all.' Her mouth tightened. 'You should have told me, and you could at the very least have persuaded my father to tell me, instead of leaving things until it was too late.'

She started to turn away from him. 'I'm going to talk to Libby for a while,' she said, 'and maybe I'll go and help myself to something from the buffet.' She threw him a warning glance. 'I hope that doesn't mean you'll feel obliged to butt in there as well.'

A muscle flicked in his jaw. 'You're mistaking concern for interference, Katie. I only want what's best for you.'

Katie's mouth twisted. 'Whatever. I don't need your help or your concern. It's way too late for that.' She walked away from him, going over to the buffet table where Libby was standing alone, looking lost. She had to get away from him.

The truth was, she still could not sort out in her mind where everything had gone wrong. He had stolen into her heart and she had glimpsed a snapshot of how wonderful her life might be with him as part of it. She had begun to care for him and those feelings lingered on, in spite of herself. It wrenched her heart to know what a fool she had been to fall for him.

Natasha came to join them a minute or so later. 'I'm just going to grab a quick bite to eat and then I'll go and fetch Sarah down from upstairs.' She bit into a cheese topped cracker, savouring it as though she hadn't eaten for hours.

Katie frowned. 'Who's Sarah?' she asked.

'Oh, of course, you don't know, do you?' Natasha smiled. 'She's my little girl. I laid her down in the cot upstairs before you arrived. Even with the excitement of a house full of people, she was ready for sleep.' She helped herself to a sandwich. 'I thought I heard her stirring a minute ago. She usually naps for a couple of hours in the afternoon, so I take my opportunities while I can.' She waved the sandwich in explanation.

'I'd no idea,' Katie said. 'You look so young, and I'd assumed you were single, like Tom.'

Natasha smiled. 'She's eighteen months old—I've been married for four years, but Greg and I separated a few months ago, so it's just Sarah and me now.' Her mouth flattened briefly. 'Not that she's any trouble. Lately, she just wants to sit quietly and play with her dolls. None of that racketing about that she used to do when she first started to walk.' She frowned, thinking about it. 'Perhaps I ought to take her to the doctor. She's definitely not as lively as she used to be…but, then, I don't want to be labelled as a fussy mother, and it could be that she's fretting over her father.' She crammed another cracker into her mouth, brushed the crumbs from her hands and hurried away. 'Must go and check on her,' she said.

Katie watched her go, feeling a little sad. There were so many things she didn't know about her newfound family. They had at least twenty-four years of catching up to do.

'We ought to get together over the next day or so,'

Tom said, coming to the table to pour himself a cup of coffee from the ceramic pot. 'There's been a lot to take in today, and the land and holdings are all a bit complex, so we really need to iron out what we're going to do.' He looked around. 'There's no use doing it here. I can't think straight in this house…too many memories. I can see Dad in my mind everywhere I go. And if today's anything to go by, there are likely to be interruptions, with visitors stopping by to pay their respects over the next week or so.'

He swallowed his drink. 'Nick has offered us the use of a conference room at his hotel. It's quiet there, and the lawyer, Antony, has said he'll come along and talk us through things in detail. I thought Wednesday would be a good day for it—you have a half-day then, don't you, Katie?'

'Um…yes, that's right.' Katie was looking at Nick, who had somehow managed to appear by Tom's side. The last thing she wanted to do was spend time at Nick's hotel. He must surely be aware of that.

His gaze meshed with hers and in that moment she knew without a doubt that he had set this up. There was a hint of satisfaction in the faint curve of his mouth. She might run, his blue eyes were telling her, but he would always be there, in her wake.

'I ran it by Natasha, and she's okay with that,' Tom said, 'so if it's all right with you, Katie, we could go ahead and make arrangements.'

She could hardly disrupt their plans for her own selfish reasons, could she? Katie flinched inwardly, but heard herself saying, 'Wednesday's fine by me,' and Nick's mouth curved.

'Juice!' A child's voice cut into their conversation,

sounding clear and sharply commanding, and Katie looked round to see Natasha crossing the room. 'Juice, Mummy.' A chubby little hand appeared from out of the blanket-wrapped bundle that Natasha was carrying, the fingers curling and uncurling as the child poked her head above the fleece and spied the jugs of orange juice on the table. Pale faced, she had a mass of auburn curls that quivered around her cheeks with her excitement at seeing the buffet table.

'There's a girl who knows exactly what she wants.' Nick laughed, glancing from the infant to Natasha. 'Would you like me to get it for you? You seem to have your hands full.'

'Would you? Thanks.' Natasha handed him the child's drinking cup. 'She's such a fussy madam, this one…and you're right, she's very clear about what she wants. She'll never settle for second best.'

'Seems to me that's a good enough way to go through life.' Nick filled the cup, pressing the lid into place before handing it to the child.

'Tanka,' Sarah said, giving him a beaming smile and sucking on the spout of the cup as though she hadn't seen a drink in twenty-four hours.

'Um…tanka?' Nick echoed, looking at Natasha for an explanation.

'I'm trying to teach her please and thank you,' Natasha answered. 'She hasn't quite got the hang of thank you yet.'

'Oh, I see.' Nick chuckled. He glanced at Sarah once more and commented softly, 'I see you made short work of that, missie. I guess sleeping made you thirsty.'

'More!' Sarah reached out and waved the cup in front of his nose, and as he gently took it from her, she lunged towards him and planted an open-mouthed kiss on his cheek, letting her face linger there as though she was testing him out for touch and taste.

'Well, that was nice,' Nick murmured with a smile, gently disentangling himself from a mound of blanket as Sarah finally retreated. 'It's good to be appreciated.'

Watching the two of them brought a lump to Katie's throat. Nick seemed perfectly at home with the child's gloriously uninhibited behaviour. Seeing him relate to her, she could almost imagine him as a father—he would be a natural from the looks of things.

Her heart flipped over, even as her mind veered away from that startling thought. Over the last few years she had wondered what it would be like to have a family of her own, but she felt totally ill equipped for the role. Perhaps with the right man by her side, it would be different. She glanced at Nick once more, this time with wistfulness in her gaze. Why did all her hopes and dreams come to nothing? First her ex, and then her relationship with her father, and now Nick had let her down. What was wrong with her that these things kept happening? Why couldn't she be happy?

Nick caught her glance, sending her a thoughtful look in return, and she quickly turned away.

'Do you have any nieces or nephews back in England?' Tom was saying, and she came out of her reverie with a start. 'You haven't told us much about yourself up to now.'

'Uh—no, I don't, I'm afraid.' She smiled briefly. 'I'm an only child—or at least I thought I was until now. I wish I'd known about you and Natasha before this. I would have liked to be part of a family—or to feel that I was, anyway. It makes me regret that I didn't have the confidence to come out here earlier. I feel I've missed out on so much.' What must it be like to know the intimacy and joy that came from having young people around, from sharing a household with siblings?

'Perhaps that's why you chose to work with children,' Nick suggested, his glance moving over her, almost as though he had read her thoughts. 'That way you get to have the contact with youngsters that was missing from your life. It isn't the same, I know, but it must help in some way.'

He was perceptive, she had to give him that…far more perceptive than any man she'd known up to now. 'I expect you're right,' she murmured. 'I hadn't thought about it that way.'

'It must be very fulfilling work, being a paediatrician,' Natasha commented. She set Sarah down on the floor so that she could toddle along to a corner of the room where Libby had set out a box of toys. 'We rely on doctors so much when things go wrong. I know when Sarah had a nasty virus a few weeks ago I was really worried, but it helped to talk things through with my doctor.'

She frowned. 'I don't do anything nearly so grand as you—I work in an office, part time, and Libby looks after Sarah for me while I'm away from home. I don't know what I'd do without her. The job doesn't pay very well, but I didn't want to work full time and lose out on Sarah's young years.' She grimaced. 'I suppose things will be a little easier once we've sorted out the inheritance, though everything's tied up in land and property from the sound of things…and stocks and shares.' She hesitated, thinking through what she had said. 'That sounds awful, doesn't it, thinking about the estate when we've only just lost our father?'

'I know what you mean, though,' Tom said. 'I started up my business a year ago—glass manufacture,' he added, for Katie's benefit, 'but without injecting extra capital I can't see how the company will survive for much longer.'

Katie looked from one to the other. 'Did neither of you want to follow in your father's footsteps?'

Natasha shook her head. 'It was very much his thing, you know. He didn't really involve us in it, and we didn't exactly badger him to let us know the ins and outs of it. We knew when the harvest had been good, or when it had been disastrous, and I suppose that's what put me off. I couldn't give my all to something that relied on the vagaries of the weather or could be destroyed by a disease of some sort. I like to know where I stand.'

Tom nodded agreement. 'I feel much the same way. I suppose we both take after our mother. She was always the practical one, the one who wanted to do something other than work a vineyard…but it was Dad's dream, and so she went along with him.'

Natasha smiled. 'Yes. Do you remember the time when she'd planned a day out and Dad didn't want to leave because he wanted to go out and inspect the crops?'

Their conversation faded into the distance. Katie found it hard to take in this glimpse of family life. It seemed strange to hear them talk about their relationships, the way that they had been at odds with their father. And yet they had loved him, there was no doubting it. That was what her father had denied her for so long. And now Nick was also to blame.

CHAPTER EIGHT

THE hotel's Garden Room was aptly named. Patio doors opened up onto a terrace, enlivened with stone tubs that were filled with bright, trailing begonias in shades of scarlet and yellow. Beyond that was a lawned area, bordered by trees and shrubs, with trellised archways and rustic fences providing support for scrambling clematis in various hues of pink and lilac.

The room was comfortably furnished with soft-cushioned sofas and low, glass-topped occasional tables. It was the perfect setting for a family meeting, but the atmosphere was tense, and Katie was feeling distinctly uncomfortable.

'I can't believe you're doing this.' A faint scowl marred Tom's features as he turned on Katie. 'You're acting on a whim, and your idea of holding onto the vineyard is going to ruin me. My business is failing and selling the vineyard is my way out. It would be different if we could sell our individual assets, but we can't, according to the will. It's all or nothing.'

'And I'm in arrears with my rent,' Natasha put in, 'and there are so many bills to pay I hardly dare open the envelopes when they come through the door. I even tried asking my ex for help, but he's struggling, too.' She hesitated, her gaze clouding momentarily. 'But, then, that's half the reason we split up. He couldn't make a go of his business and the strain was too much for us.'

'I can see why you're both upset,' Katie answered cautiously, 'and it's true I've only just come to know about the vineyard and all it represents...but it has been long enough for me to realize that it's very important to me.' She tilted her chin. 'You're forgetting that Jack was my father, too. I was his firstborn, and that means something to me. It means that I have his genes, and now I have a heritage that I want to safeguard. I'm sorry if that causes problems for you, but it's the way I feel.'

They stared at her in stunned silence, their expressions totally hostile. She didn't want to be at odds with either of them, and a surge of guilt ran through her, but with every fibre of her being she felt she had to stick to her guns.

She had been battling with them for the last hour and at times the argument had been heated and bitter. It left her feeling shaky inside, and it hurt that they had turned on her in such a savage way. It was easy enough to understand how they felt, but this was a once-in-a-lifetime opportunity and everything in her told her that she didn't want to let it go.

Was it selfish of her to want to carry on what her father had started? He might not have been the greatest father in the world. He'd let her down, but the vineyard was his handiwork, something to be proud of, the one solid achievement that she could preserve for posterity.

Her pager began to bleep. She checked the text message and said flatly, 'I have to go. There's been a road traffic accident.' She glanced at her half-brother and -sister. 'I'm sorry…perhaps Antony can help you to come to some arrangement over finances that will help you both out…but I've made my decision. Believe me, it wasn't an easy one…but I've been thinking about it for these last few weeks and I've made up my mind. I'm not prepared to sell.'

She left the room and hurried along to the hotel foyer, but she was taken aback to see Nick standing by the reception desk. He was talking to the manageress, looking through a brochure with her, but as Katie approached he turned away from the desk and let his glance drift over her.

Katie felt her stomach clench. She had been right to push him away, hadn't she? For all his careful attention and sweet-talking ways, he had shown that he was just like everyone else.

And what would he make of her dispute with her brother and sister? Most likely he would side with them and encourage them to pressurise her into selling. It would be in his interests to do that, wouldn't it?

'You're leaving already?' Nick said with a frown. 'I'd expected the meeting to go on for much longer.'

'I have to go out on an emergency.' Her voice was terse. 'There's been an accident on the main highway, with several cars involved, and they're calling for medics to attend.'

Nick's brows drew together, and as he handed the brochure to the manageress his phone began to bleep, signalling a text message. He quickly scanned it and then said, 'Me, too. It must be a bad one.' He turned to the woman once more. 'I have to go,' he murmured. 'Change the layout as we discussed and I'll look over the copy as soon as soon as you have it.'

She nodded. 'That's fine. You go ahead. I'll deal with this.'

'We should go,' Nick said, taking Katie by the arm. 'I can give you a lift—there's no sense in taking two cars, is there?'

'I suppose not.' Katie shrugged. 'I'll get my medical kit from the boot of my car.'

They set off just a few minutes later, driving along the main road from the hotel towards the coastal highway. Katie watched the rolling hills pass by, took in the magnificent cypress trees forming silhouettes against the skyline, and tried not to think about the fact that she was in Nick's car, that her heart was encased in ice, or that her siblings hated her.

'You're very quiet,' Nick said, turning the car on to the highway. 'How were things back there?'

'Not too good. Natasha was a bit edgy—she's worried about her little girl. She said she's tired all the while, but the doctor thinks the child's just a bit run down and it will pass.'

She frowned. From her experience she knew that doctors ought never to ignore a mother's instinct. But the toddler's symptoms were vague, and you could hardly expect the physician to be too worried at this stage. 'Tom seems to think the little girl is a fussy eater, and that might have led to her problems.'

'He could be right,' Nick murmured. 'At least the doctor's given her a check-up.'

'I suppose so.'

'So, how did the meeting go? You seem quite subdued. Was it not as you expected? It's a shame that you didn't get to finish it.'

'Perhaps it's just as well we were interrupted,' she

answered with a faint sigh. 'Things weren't going too well. Tom and Natasha are very upset with me, and I'm sad about that because I want to get on well with them.'

He sent her a sideways glance. 'Why would they be upset with you? You only had to talk over what you were going to do about the estate, didn't you? I would have thought that was a positive thing, albeit tinged with a good deal of sadness. It's not every day you get to decide how to manage an inheritance like that.'

'Well, there's the rub.' She made a face. 'We couldn't agree on how to deal with it.'

He frowned. 'You'll have to explain. I've no idea what could have gone wrong. I know they were very keen on selling to my father and me. It was agreed that Toby would stay on as manager, so there shouldn't be any hitches.'

'No, there shouldn't...but you see, even you believe it's all a foregone conclusion. Except that isn't how it is at all.' She shot him a quick glance. He must have been feeling very satisfied, thinking all was going to plan.

The thought depressed her. How could she have had him so wrong? She had fallen for him, been caught up in a whirlwind of emotion that had threatened to overwhelm her, and life had become bright with the intense colours seen through the eyes of new love. But it had all faded, and she'd realised that she didn't know him at all.

'Katie?' His quiet voice jerked her out of her reverie.

'I told them I don't want to sell.'

His eyes widened. 'Are you quite sure you know what you're doing?' he asked, his tone incredulous. 'How on earth are you going to handle things? You have absolutely no experience of running a vineyard.'

'Then I'll have to learn, won't I?'

'Do you think it's just a matter of harvesting the crop and sitting back while the money rolls in?' He shook his head. 'It doesn't happen that way, Katie. It takes a lot of hard work and dedication.'

Her eyes narrowed on him. 'Do you think I'm not capable of that?'

His mouth twisted. 'That's not what I'm saying. I'm just pointing out that if you go ahead with this, it's quite possible you'll come a cropper.'

'And there wouldn't be just a hint of sour grapes in your reaction, would there?' she challenged him. 'I know how much you wanted the vineyard for yourself.'

'For my family.' The correction was brusque and to the point. 'Yes, we want it.' His eyes darkened. 'And I'm not giving up on that. The offer still stands.'

Her gaze was troubled. 'But I'm not going to accept it. Okay, I'm not at all sure I'm doing the right thing, and I really don't want to upset my family. I know they're going through a difficult time. But instinct tells me I shouldn't be making such a big decision about selling so soon after my father's death. If I let the vineyard go now, I might come to regret it some months or years down the line. I'm really keen on the idea of owning a stretch of land—my father's land—that produces some of the finest wines in California. For me, that's far more important than the money.'

'It's a huge undertaking. I think you're making a big mistake.'

'I know.' She frowned. Clearly, she was on her own in this, and if things went wrong, she would only have herself to blame. He was right. What did she know about owning a vineyard? The enormity of what she was planning to do began to crowd in on her, overwhelming her with all sorts of dire possibilities, and to distract herself she looked out of the window and gave her attention to the road once more.

They were passing through scenic countryside right now, and she could see the ocean in the near distance and she watched as waves crashed on to the rocky shore. It seemed to perfectly echo the way she was feeling right now.

A minute or so later they reached the point in the road where the accident had happened. Police officers had sealed off the area and set up diversionary routes for other drivers.

Katie looked around and then let out a slow breath. 'This is a mess,' she said softly.

Nick's mouth made a grim line. 'It looks as though an SUV turned over. From the skid marks, I'd say he tried to avoid something up ahead and everyone else piled in. You're right, it's a mess.'

'There are a couple of drivers in the cars who look to be in a bad way,' a police officer told them as they went over to the cordoned-off area and introduced themselves. 'The fire department is working to free them right now. We've led the walking wounded away to a place of safety, but there are two women in the SUV who look as though they have serious injuries. Seems the driver had to slam on the brakes when someone pulled out in front of her. She swerved and lost control of the vehicle and then ended up on the embankment at the side of the road. There are some others who are injured, but the paramedics don't seem to be too worried about them at the moment.'

'Thanks for letting us know,' Nick said. 'We'll go and check them out.'

Two ambulances were already on the scene, and the paramedics were doing triage, trying to find out which people needed attention first.

'Glad to have you along, Doc.' The lead paramedic nodded towards Nick and then gave Katie a brief acknowledgement. The two men obviously knew one another.

'The drivers of the cars have fractures of the legs and arms,' he said. 'They're in a lot of pain and discomfort, but we're doing what we can to stabilise them right now. It's the women in the SUV who need looking at. I think one of them is going into shock. My colleague did an initial assessment and we're giving them oxygen.'

'Okay, we'll see to them.'

Nick and Kate hurried over to the SUV. It was partially on its side, having come to rest on the embankment, but at least both women were accessible, albeit with some difficulty. Katie manoeuvred herself into the doorway of the vehicle and assessed the woman in the passenger seat, while Nick attended to the driver.

'Can you tell me your name?' she asked. The woman appeared to be in her early forties, and her companion was of a similar age, she guessed.

'Frances…Frances Delaney.' She struggled to get the words out, and Katie could see that she was having trouble with her breathing.

'Okay, Frances,' she murmured. 'I'm Dr Logan and I'm here to help you. Can you tell me where it hurts?'

'My chest. It's a bad pain.' The woman tried to point

to her upper rib cage, but then she tried to look round and became agitated. 'What's happening to Maria…to my sister?' she asked. 'She's not speaking—is she all right?'

Katie glanced to where Nick was carefully examining the driver. 'She's conscious,' she told Frances. 'Dr Bellini is looking after her.'

'She's hypotensive,' Nick murmured, 'and her heart rate is low. There's a contusion where the steering-wheel must have impacted, so I think we're looking at some kind of abdominal injury.' He looked at his patient. 'As soon as I've finished examining you, Maria, I'll give you something for the pain.'

Maria tried to say something, but couldn't get the words out. Katie's strong guess was that she might be asking for Frances, but the sound was indistinct and faded on her lips. 'Try not to worry, we're going to take good care of you and your sister,' Nick told her. He must have come to the same conclusion as Katie.

He had a soothing way with his patients, Katie reflected. He was gentle and soft spoken, and at the same time very thorough and methodical. Maria was in excellent hands.

She went on with her own examination of Frances. 'It looks as though you have some broken ribs,' she said quietly. 'And as far as I can tell, your forearm is fractured in two places. I'll give you an injection for the pain and immobilise it with a sling, but you're going to need surgery to fix the bones in place.'

Frances was white-faced and it was fairly obvious that her condition was deteriorating by the minute…something that started alarm bells ringing in Katie's head.

'Yes. Thank you for helping me.' The taut lines of

the woman's expression relaxed a little as Katie administered the injection. 'It's my sister I'm worried about,' she said, her voice husky with emotion. 'She's always looked out for me...we look out for each other. I can't bear the thought that...' her voice began to fail '...that something might happen to her.'

'Try not to fret yourself.' Katie frowned. Despite the nature of the arm injuries, it was the rib fractures that concerned her most. Her patient was already experiencing severe pain and breathlessness. As a doctor, Katie knew that first and second rib fractures were often associated with damage to important blood vessels, and if that was happening, time was fast running out. It was imperative that Frances be taken to hospital as soon as possible.

She set up an intravenous line so that she could give her patient fluids, a first stage in defence against shock and blood-pressure problems that stemmed from traumatic injury. Nick was doing the same for Maria, but his expression was serious, and she guessed he was concerned for his patient.

'How is she doing?' Frances whispered the words, straining to summon the energy from a well that was beginning to run dry. 'I can't hear her. I need...to know... she's all right.'

Nick's gaze met Katie's. He made a small shake of his head. Maria had lapsed into unconsciousness and he had secured an artificial airway in place in her throat.

'We're doing everything we can for her,' Katie said softly. 'We'll be taking her to hospital with you, just as soon as we can.'

Nick called for the paramedics to assist with spinal boards for both women, and within a matter of minutes they had stabilised the sisters sufficiently so that they could be transferred to the ambulance.

Katie went to check on the other injured people. She checked vital signs and applied dressings to stem bleeding where necessary, and when she looked around some time later, she saw that Nick was doing the same.

The injured drivers had finally been freed from their cars, and were at that moment being taken into the second ambulance.

As soon as he was certain everyone was secure, Nick started to gather together his medical kit. 'I want to follow them to the hospital and oversee things from there,' he told Katie. 'Is that all right with you? Otherwise I could arrange for someone from the hotel to come and pick you up.'

'No, it's okay. I want to go with you.' She walked with him to his car. 'I'm worried about both of them. I want to make sure that Frances has an angiogram—I'm pretty sure there's some internal bleeding, and if it isn't dealt with quickly she'll be in bad trouble.'

He nodded. 'Same here. Maria's heart rate is way too low, and her abdomen felt full and doughy when I examined her. I'm sure there's some bleeding into the abdominal cavity, and the problems with her lower rib cage make me think there could be damage to her liver or spleen. An ultrasound scan should tell us what's going on there. If we can't find where the bleeding is coming from, we'll have to do a peritoneal lavage…but whatever happens, we need to do it quickly.'

They set off, and Nick drove as fast as was possible towards the hospital, arriving there as the paramedics were unloading their patients from the ambulance.

Both he and Katie made their reports to the emergency

teams, and followed the women into the trauma room. 'Is Dr Wainwright on duty?' Nick asked as a nurse, Abby, hurried to assist.

She nodded.

'That's good.' He turned to Katie. 'He's the best vascular surgeon we have. If there's any damage to your patient's subclavian or innominate artery—or both—he's the man to put it right.'

'That's a relief.' A patient could die from an injury like that if it wasn't picked up in time, or if the surgeon was unable to stem the bleeding.

Nick was talking to the doctor in charge of the emergency room. 'I'd like to oversee my patient's ultrasound scan. I hope that's all right with you?'

'Of course. Any time. You don't need to ask, Nick.'

Katie went to discuss her patient's case with the doctor who was taking care of her, and a few minutes later she watched as Frances was whisked away to the angiography suite. The woman was agitated, distressed at having to leave her sister behind, and, unnacountably, as she saw the lift doors close on the trolley bed, Katie was overcome by a sudden tide of unhappiness.

Perhaps it had come about because this was the end of a long day. She had been hard at work in the paediatric unit this morning, before hurrying to the meeting with her half-brother and -sister, and now, in the aftermath of the traffic accident, she was beginning to register the dreadful impact of tending injured people in the wreckage of vehicles that had been slewn across the highway. She didn't know what had caused these feelings to well up inside her. She couldn't explain it, but her heart was heavy and she felt desperately sad.

'I need to go and get a breath of air,' she told Abby. 'I'll be outside in the courtyard if there's any news.'

'That's all right. I'll come and find you if there are any developments.'

'Thanks.'

Katie went out into the courtyard, a quiet, paved area where hospital staff could sit for a while on wooden benches set at intervals on the perimeter. There were a couple of cherry trees out there, along with tubs of velvet-petalled petunias that provided bright splashes of colour.

She sat down and tried to sort out the bewildering thoughts that were crowding in on her. She was feeling overwhelmed and off balance, and it scared her quite a bit because she wasn't used to feeling that way.

'Are you okay?' Nick came out into the courtyard a few minutes later and sat down on the bench beside her. He handed her a cup of coffee. 'Sorry it's a styrofoam cup—the coffee machine was closest to hand. I doubt you had time to enjoy the coffee and sandwiches I sent round earlier at the hotel...you seemed to come out of the room almost as soon as the waitress took them.'

'No, you're right, I didn't.' She frowned. 'Come to think of it, I haven't had anything to eat or drink since first thing this morning.' She sent him a quick look as she sipped the hot liquid. 'We had a few difficult cases to deal with in the paediatric unit this morning and I had to stay on for a couple of hours after my shift finished to make sure everything was sorted out properly.' She took another swallow of her drink. 'This is good...thanks.' Even the delectable aroma of the coffee teased her taste buds.

He smiled. 'Are you going to tell me what's wrong,

or do I have to prise it out of you? I know there's something, because you were very quiet back there and you had that far-away, hurting kind of look in your eyes.'

She hadn't realised that he'd been watching her. 'And there I thought your mind was all on your patient.' She cradled the cup in her hands and swallowed down the rest of the liquid.

He shook his head. 'You're the one who's always on my mind,' he said quietly. 'Everywhere I go. I think about you, wonder what you're doing or whether you're okay. And I know you're not okay right now, so you should tell me what it is that's bothering you. What's upset you?'

'I don't know,' she said simply. Did he really think about her all the time? She put the empty cup down on the floor. 'I watched Frances being wheeled away and this bleak feeling swept over me. She looked so devastated, so torn, because she was being separated from her sister.'

She looked up at him, her eyes troubled. 'Perhaps that was it. She and her sister seem to be so close to one another, and maybe I wish things could have been like that for me. I never had any siblings until now, and it was all I ever wanted, to share that family feeling with people close to me. Finding out about Tom and Natasha was a shock, but once I got used to the idea I realised that a whole new world had opened up for me. And then I went and ruined it by throwing a spanner in the works. I don't think they'll ever forgive me.'

'But you have to be true to yourself in the end, don't you? And that means sticking by your decision.' He put an arm around her and drew her close and she didn't have it in her to pull away from him. The truth was, she missed that closeness, that feeling of being cherished. A lump formed in her throat. 'Isn't that what your father would have wanted?' Nick asked. 'Either way you choose, you risk losing out in some way.'

'Maybe.' Her eyes clouded. 'I suppose you were just pointing out what I already know when you said I haven't a clue about running a vineyard. And that's perfectly true. Perhaps the enormity of what I'm taking on is just beginning to sink in. It's one thing to do it when you have back-up, but quite another when everyone who matters is against you.'

'And I'm included in that group, aren't I?' His mouth made a crooked shape. 'I don't want to cause you any hurt, Katie...but the vineyard is my heritage, mine and my brother's. Running the family business is in our blood, it flows through our veins as though it's part of our being. You're just beginning to feel something of that with this inheritance from your father.'

'And I'm finding just the thought of it a little overwhelming, as you said I would. But I can't turn my back on it. I just need to find the strength, from somewhere, to go on.'

She pressed her lips together. 'I've had to come to terms all over again with the kind of man my father was. I was hurt when I found he had another family who had been kept from me, and perhaps I overreacted.' She gazed up at him. 'It was like a betrayal, and I thought I'd done with all that. I thought I had this tough outer shell that couldn't be broken, but it wasn't so. I crumbled at the first blow. I'm every bit as weak as he was. I can't even hold it together in the emergency room.'

'You know that isn't true, Katie.' He wrapped both arms around her and folded her to him. 'You're forgetting that you've only just lost your father in these past few weeks. You can't make decisions—any kind of decisions—when you're still grieving. And you *are* grieving, even though you feel he let you down.'

His lips lightly brushed her temple and Katie realised that more than anything she wanted to nestle against him and accept the comfort he offered. 'You'd grown to love him,' he murmured. 'That's why you want to hold on to what he left behind. You see his touch in every row of vines, in every grape that ripens. That's how I feel, too, when I think about how my ancestors carved out this valley and planted their crops. We can't let it go, Katie. We're no different from one another, you and I.'

'Aren't we?' She gazed up at him, her features troubled. 'You seem to be so confident, in everything you do. I'm still struggling to find my way.'

'Then let me help you,' he said softly, bending his head to gently trace her lips with his own. 'Let me help you to forget your worries for a while.'

He kissed her again, a lingering, wonderful kiss that filled her with aching need and made her want to run her hands through the silk of his hair. She ought to have been wary of him, because she knew that he would never stop trying to make her change her mind and relinquish her inheritance. Wasn't that what he'd meant when he'd said it was the wrong time to be making decisions?

She was at war with herself. On the one hand she felt he had the power to destroy everything that mattered to her...what was there to stop him from piling on the pressure until she gave in and sold out to him? And on the other, she wanted to drink him in, as though he was the water of life, a fount of everything that could save her from herself and make her whole again.

But the moment was short-lived. He eased back from her, reluctantly dragging his mouth from hers, and she stared at him, her senses befuddled, until she gradually began to realise that she could hear the rustle of someone approaching.

'I thought you'd like to know that your patient is back from her angiography,' the nurse said. 'Mr Wainright is going to operate. And the other lady is in a bad way, too, by the looks of things. They've called for someone from the surgical team to come and look at her.'

'Thanks, Abby,' Katie managed in a low voice. 'I'll come back in and take a look at the films.' Reality began to set in once more. She felt as though she'd had a near miss…a brush with danger…but she didn't think she'd come away unscathed. She felt as though the life was being sucked out of her.

Nick stooped to pick up her abandoned coffee cup then straightened and waited for her to come and stand beside him. 'Ready?' he said.

She nodded, but she wasn't ready at all. Far from it. After that kiss, she was more bewildered than ever.

CHAPTER NINE

THE doorbell pealed, and Katie checked her watch as she went out into the hallway. It was mid-afternoon and she wasn't expecting anyone—though there was always the slim chance that Tom or Natasha might drop by to talk things through with her. It would be a relief if they did. She desperately wanted to try to clear the air between them.

It was neither of them. Instead, she opened the door to discover that Nick was standing there, casually waiting, one hand planted flat against the wall as he gazed around the vestibule.

'Katie,' he said, straightening up. 'I'm glad I've found you at home.'

His gaze travelled over her and already her body was on full alert. He looked good, too good for her peace of mind, dressed in dark trousers that moulded his hips and thighs and emphasised the taut line of his stomach and a loose cotton shirt that sat easily on his broad shoulders.

She pulled the door open wider and waved him into the hallway. 'Come in,' she said. 'This is unexpected. Is everything all right? Is there a problem at the hospital?' She led the way to the living room and tried not to think about the way he'd held her just the day before or the way his kisses had melted the ice around her heart.

'It's nothing like that. Everything's fine. I just thought you might want an update on the Delaneys. I know you've been asking about them.'

She nodded. 'No one was very forthcoming. I know Frances had arterial grafts to repair her damaged blood vessels, and her forearm fracture was so bad that both bones had to be fixed with metal plates and screws. She was still in a fragile condition this morning when I rang. But no one seems to be able to give me much information on Maria.'

'I think that's because the situation was complicated,' Nick explained. 'Both her liver and spleen were lacerated, but the surgeon managed to repair the damage. The biggest problem was that while he was operating he discovered damage to the pancreas. He did what he could to preserve the organ, but it's touch and go from here on.'

Katie sucked in her breath. 'Poor Maria.' Pancreatic trauma was often not detected until it was too late. Sometimes, if it was a simple contusion, it could be cleaned up and drained, but in Maria's case it sounded as though the damage was extensive. All they could do now was wait and see what happened.

'Thanks for coming here and telling me,' she said. 'I was hoping you'd follow up on them and let me know how they were doing.'

His glance touched her, moving over her features in a lingering, thoughtful manner. 'That's one of the things I love so much about you...that you care about people. They're not just patients to you, but people with families and lives outside the hospital.' His mouth flattened.

'Of course, that can be a hazard in itself. Getting too involved isn't always a good thing—not if you want to feel easy in yourself.'

Katie's gaze met his briefly. There were things he loved about her? She looked away. She'd been through too much heartache to start hoping all over again… hadn't she? How many times was she going to get up on to her feet, only to have life knock her down again?

If Nick wondered what she was thinking, he made no mention of it. Instead, he cast an appreciative glance around the room, his gaze lingering on the shelves that decorated one wall. 'It looks as though you've picked up one or two pieces from the fine-art shops around here,' he murmured.

'Yes.' She pulled herself together. 'I wasn't able to bring much with me from England, so I thought it would be good to brighten up the apartment with a few colourful touches here and there.'

He nodded, and turned his attention to the glassware on display. 'I like these bowls…the etchings on the glass make me think of sea life, with all those fronds and water plants.'

'They're similar to some my mother has at home.' Her mouth made a straight line. 'She and my father brought quite a bit of glassware from Murano. She likes to collect special pieces, paperweights and so on.'

Nick's gaze flicked over her. 'Have you forgiven him yet?'

The breath left her lungs in a sudden rush. 'I don't know. Perhaps.' After all, she'd been living with her father's imperfections for some twenty years. In the end, maybe she simply had to accept that he'd had genuine feelings for her. He'd told her he was proud of her, and he'd taken the trouble to warn her against falling for Nick. Though that was probably a warning that had come too late. Wasn't she already living with the consequences?

'And me?'

Her gaze faltered. 'Where you're concerned, I just think it's safer if I try to keep my wits about me.'

His mouth twisted. 'There must be some way I can get back into your good books,' he said softly. 'Maybe I could drive you over to Jack's vineyard so that you could have another look at the place? I know you've been so busy lately that you haven't been able to go over there.'

'And you think when I do I'll perhaps decide that I've made the wrong decision about keeping it?'

He laughed. 'Well, maybe that, too.' His expression became thoughtful. 'Actually, I heard Natasha was thinking of going over there this afternoon, and I guessed it might be a good opportunity for you to talk to her again—to the manager, Toby, as well, of course. He's usually up at the house at this time of day.'

She hesitated. Why was he doing this? Was it really as he said, to try to win her over, or did he have an ulterior motive? Did he think that when she saw the vast extent of the place once more she would realise she had taken on too much?

'It sounds like a great idea,' she murmured. 'Though I don't know how Natasha is going to react to me. I'm not altogether sure that there's anything I can say to her that will put things right.'

'I wouldn't worry too much about that. At least you'll have made the effort.'

'I suppose so.' She sent him a quick glance. 'Won't I be putting you out, though?'

'Not at all. I've been meaning to see Toby about a planting programme we were talking about last month. Your father and he were thinking about trying a new variety of grape, and my father wants to try it out, too.'

'Okay, then.' She hesitated. 'Are we ready to go now? I'll fetch my jacket.'

The approach to her father's vineyard took them through a glorious green valley, with pine-clad hills that soon gave way to row upon row of vines. The fruit was lush, soft hued as it began to ripen, and Katie felt an overwhelming sense that all was right with the natural world as she gazed at the sun-dappled slopes. If only her own life could be so serene.

Toby was at the front of the house, talking to Natasha, when they arrived, but they both turned to look in their direction as Nick drove on to the forecourt.

Natasha was holding Sarah in her arms, but she set the infant down on the ground once Nick had parked the car. A black Labrador had been padding about, sniffing amongst the flower-beds, but he came to greet them, tail wagging, as they stepped out of the car.

'Hi, there, Benjy.' Nick patted the dog on the head and received a boisterous welcome in return, the Labrador's whole body moving in excited recognition. Then it was Katie's turn, and she gently stroked the dog, tickling him behind the ears.

She smiled at Natasha but received a blank stare in return. Toby, on the other hand, nodded to both of them.

'Hi, there,' he said. 'I wondered if you might drive over today.' He was a tall man in his early forties, with brown hair and a face that was bronzed from many hours spent out in the sun. 'My wife had to go out, but she made some oatmeal cookies before she left, so we can enjoy them with a pot of tea. I'll put the kettle on and we can sit outside on the patio for a while, if you like. Then I'll show you around.'

Satisfied he had made his presence known, the dog went to lie down at his feet, regarding them all in a slightly curious fashion, raising an eyelid every now and again in case he was missing something.

'Thanks,' Katie said. 'That sounds good. I wanted to talk to you for a while, about the vineyard and so on.'

His expression was serious. 'I thought you might.'

'We were just going to take a look around the house,' Natasha said, glancing at Nick. 'There are one or two maintenance problems that have cropped up—like a couple of broken fences and some roof tiles that need to be replaced. Toby said he didn't mind fixing them, but I think he probably has enough to do already.' She looked at Katie, her expression cool and vaguely antagonistic. 'I suppose the ball's in your court. You were keen to take this on, so I dare say we can leave the decisions to you. Tom and I never wanted the stress of running the business and everything associated with it.'

Katie pulled in a deep breath. 'If that's what you want, then of course I'll deal with everything that comes along. I'll keep you up to date with what's happening.' She was disappointed by her cool reception, but she could hardly have expected anything else in the circumstances. Natasha was still annoyed with her, from the looks of things, but there was no point in getting into a state about it, was there?

Sarah toddled over to Katie and stood, gazing up at

her. Her bright curls quivered and shone in the sunlight. 'Pwetty,' she said, and for a moment or two Katie was taken aback, until the little girl pointed to her necklace. 'Pwetty,' she said again, and Katie smiled.

'You like it? It is pretty, isn't it?' She fingered the silver filigree necklace and crouched down so that the infant could take a better look. 'My mother gave it to me, so it's very special.'

'Best not let Sarah get her fingers round it, then,' Natasha said flatly. 'She doesn't distinguish between special or worthless. She grabs everything. One tug and it's ruined.'

'Oh, dear. Well, I'd best protect it, then, hadn't I?' Katie placed her fingers over the necklace and glanced towards Nick, wondering what she could do to distract the child.

'You can play with my keys for a while, if you like, Sarah,' he said, coming to the rescue by jangling them temptingly in front of the child's face. Her eyes widened and she turned her attention to Nick, the pink tip of her tongue coming out to touch her bottom lip as she gazed up at him. The keys were irresistible, it seemed, and she held up her hands, trying to grasp them as he gently teased her, darting them about in a catch-me-if-you-can kind of game.

It didn't have quite the effect he was looking for, though, because being thwarted proved altogether too much for her, and the toddler burst into tears.

Nick's jaw dropped, and Katie looked on in consternation. 'I was just playing with her,' Nick said. 'I didn't mean to upset her.' He turned to Natasha. 'Do you think she'll let me pick her up and comfort her?'

'You can try,' Natasha said. 'It isn't your fault, mind.

She's been like this for some time now, fretful and tearful, on and off. I just haven't been able to work out what's wrong with her. I've put it down to tiredness. She's been sleeping an awful lot lately, so perhaps the doctor was right when he said she was run down. I've just been letting her rest as and when she needs it.'

Nick picked up the little girl and cradled her in his arms, offering her the keys, but by now she had lost interest in them. She sobbed, large hiccuping sobs that racked her body, and tears trickled down her face, giving her a woeful expression.

'I'm sorry, cherub,' Nick said in a soothing tone. 'I was only teasing. I didn't mean to upset you.' He was thoughtful for a moment or two, and then asked quietly, 'How about I give you a rock-a-bye swing—would you like that, hmm?' He began to rock her gently to and fro in his arms, and after a while she stopped crying and stared up at him, her face pale.

Katie watched him with the little girl and felt a pang of emotion well up inside her. He was so natural with her, so caring and gentle, so obviously concerned for her well-being.

'You definitely have the knack,' Toby said with a laugh. 'I expect Natasha will be calling on you for babysitting duties from now on.'

'Heaven forbid!' Nick looked aghast. 'I'd need a bit more practice before I took up that kind of challenge.' He looked at Katie, a questioning, odd kind of look, and an unbidden thrill of expectation ran through her. What would it be like to have his children?

Toby showed them the way through the house to the kitchen, the dog following at his heels. It was a large breakfast kitchen with glass doors to one side leading out on to a terrace. 'Make yourselves at home out there,' Toby said, waving them out towards a teak wood table and chairs. 'I'll make the tea and bring it out to you.'

Nick was still holding his precious bundle, but now he looked over at Natasha. 'Do you want to take her?' he asked. 'She looks as though she's settled now.'

'Okay. I'll put her in her buggy,' Natasha murmured. 'She can sit and watch us while we talk.'

Katie glanced at the child as she lay back in her buggy a short time later. She was white faced, her curls slightly damp against her forehead as though she was a little feverish. Her breathing was rapid, and it occurred to her that the child looked exhausted.

Toby arrived with the tea, and once he had seated himself and they had chatted for a while, Katie brought up the subject of the management of the vineyard.

'I hope you'll stay on here and run things for us as you've always done,' she said. 'I know how much my father valued your work here.'

'Thank you. I'd like that.' Toby looked relieved. 'Does that mean my family can go on living here at the house?'

'Of course. I've asked Antony to draw up the paperwork to give you a more secure tenancy.'

Natasha sent her a quick look, but said nothing, and Katie said evenly, 'I'm assuming that will be all right with you and Tom?'

Her sister nodded, and soon after that Nick began to talk to Toby about the new planting programme. Benjy, who had been supposedly dozing at Toby's feet, was disturbed by a butterfly and decided he needed to go and check things out. As the butterfly flitted away to the flower border, he got to his feet and went after it.

'Up, Mummy!' Sarah suddenly exclaimed, looking at Natasha. 'Up.' She stretched out her arms to her mother, and Natasha frowned.

'If I lift you up, what then?' she said, giving her daughter a quizzical look. 'You'll be demanding to be set down, then, won't you?' She frowned. 'You want to play with Benjy, don't you?'

Sarah's expression was gleeful. 'Up...play Benjy,' she said, and by now her fingers were doing their familiar clasping and unclasping as if she was clutching at the air.

'Okay, then, young madam,' Natasha murmured, lifting the child out of the buggy. 'But try and stay out of trouble. No pulling at the flowers.'

'F'owers,' Sarah echoed happily. 'Benjy f'owers.'

Benjy was indeed exploring the flowers, Katie noticed. His nose was pressed up against them as he drank deeply of their scent, and a moment later he drew his head back and gave an enormous sneeze. Sarah giggled.

The dog's nose was covered with pollen, and Katie smiled. She looked at Nick and saw that he was chuckling, too. Their glances met in a shared moment of amusement.

Sarah toddled off to where Benjy was getting ready for another sneeze. She patted him vigorously in sympathy and then wandered away to inspect the scarlet begonias.

Katie watched her go, and saw how the little girl seemed to slow down and come to a standstill. It seemed that she had stopped to look at a ladybird or some such, but there was something about the way she was standing that had Katie's instincts on alert all of a sudden. Then the child's legs seemed to crumple under her and in an instant Katie was out of her seat. She hurried over to her, catching her as she would have fallen.

'What's wrong with her? What's happened?' Natasha was beside herself with worry. She rushed over and began to stroke her little girl's hair as though by touch alone she would bring her back to normal.

'She just collapsed,' Katie said softly. She used the second hand on her watch to carefully check the infant's pulse. Then she glanced at Nick, who had come to kneel down beside her. 'Her heart rate is very fast, and she's much too pale. I think perhaps she ought to have a proper check-up at the hospital.'

He nodded. 'I agree with you.' The dog came to find out what was going on, and Nick said softly, 'We should take her into the house.' He glanced at Natasha and she nodded.

'You could lay her down on the sofa in the living room,' Toby suggested. 'It's cooler in there. Maybe she had a touch too much sun.'

'It's possible,' Katie said, gently handing the child over to Nick, who lifted her into his arms and carried her into the house. 'We'll give her a few minutes to see if she comes round, but I think it's something more than that.'

'You thought she was ill earlier, didn't you?' Natasha glanced sharply at Katie as they gathered in the living room a moment or two later. 'I saw you looking at her when she was in her buggy.'

Katie nodded. 'If I'm right, I don't think it's anything too serious.'

'Tell me.' Natasha crouched down beside the sofa,

holding her child's hand, letting her know that she was there with her the whole time.

'Her main symptoms seem to be the tiredness and her pallor,' Katie murmured. 'You haven't mentioned anything else that's bothering you, apart from the fact that she's been quite fretful lately.'

'That's right.'

'And you mentioned some time ago that she had suffered from a viral infection—I'm guessing that this has been going on since then?'

'Yes… I think so.' Natasha's brows drew together. 'It's hard to know exactly when it started. It's been coming on gradually. What do you think is wrong with her?'

Sarah began to stir, rubbing her eyes and shifting to a more comfortable position.

Katie glanced at Nick. 'I'm thinking some kind of transient anaemia.'

'Yes.' He nodded. 'That sounds about right. Of course, we would need to confirm it with tests.'

'Anaemia?' Natasha's voice was filled with stress. 'Is that because of something I've been doing wrong? Haven't I been feeding her properly?'

Katie recognised the guilt in her voice. Parents often blamed themselves where no blame was due.

'No, it's nothing at all like that,' Nick said quietly. 'You don't often see this, but sometimes, after certain types of viral illness in young children, their bodies stop making red blood cells for a while. That would account for Sarah's tiredness and pale appearance.'

Natasha was horrified. 'That sounds awful,' she said. 'Can something be done? Is there a cure?'

He nodded. 'Usually it sorts itself out after two or three months.'

'But she collapsed. She can't go on like that, surely? That can't be right.'

Katie laid a hand gently on her arm. 'I know this is really worrying for you, Natasha, but Nick's right. Usually this type of illness clears up of its own accord. When a child collapses, though, as Sarah just did, it's best to get things checked out. She might need a transfusion. If this is what we think it is, that will help a lot and she'll soon start to feel better…though it's possible she'll need another transfusion before she recovers completely. At some point her bone marrow will start manufacturing the cells once more.'

Natasha had a panicked look about her. 'But I need to go and get help now. I want to take her to the emergency room.' She looked around distractedly. 'I shan't rest until I find out exactly what's happening.'

'I could take you to the hospital,' Toby offered, but Nick intervened.

'I'll go with her,' he said quietly. 'You stay and show Katie around the vineyard. I'm sure you must have a lot to talk about. Natasha and Sarah will be fine with me.'

'You don't mind?' Natasha asked. 'Are you sure? I don't mean to break things up, but I'm really worried about her.'

'Of course you are,' Nick said. 'I would have suggested it anyway. Sarah needs to be checked out.' He turned to look at Katie. 'Here, take my car keys. I'll take Natasha's car, and if we're delayed at the hospital for any reason, you can drive yourself home in mine. I'll pick it up later. Don't worry if you're not around when I come to collect it, I'll use my spare set of keys.'

'Okay.' Katie wasn't at all sure how she felt about driving his beautiful, streamlined car, but she judged that now wasn't the moment to dither or argue. It said a lot about him that he'd thought of her in this moment of crisis.

Natasha hurried away to gather together everything she needed to take with her while Nick secured Sarah in her car seat. The child was still drowsy, not really taking any notice of what was going on around her.

'Will she be all right?' Toby asked as he and Katie watched them drive away a few minutes later. 'I know you said it would clear up on its own, but it sounded pretty horrific to me. Anything to do with bone marrow not working properly is pretty scary, isn't it?'

'You're right,' Katie answered. 'Normally, it would be very worrying, but I'm hoping that this is one of those instances where she'll make a full recovery. We won't really know until we have the results of the tests.'

'It's a difficult situation—a worrying time all round.'

Katie nodded. 'Yes, it is.' She was glad Nick had gone with Natasha. He would be a comfort to her, and he would be able to explain anything that she didn't understand. He was a man to be relied on, a good man to have by your side in times of trouble. Or at any time, come to think of it.

She sighed inwardly. Her feelings for Nick were complex and very unsettling. Could it be that she was falling in love with him? In fact, the more she thought about it, the more certain she became that he was the one man who could make her happy…if only she could be sure that she could put her faith in him.

'Perhaps you'd like to look around the parts of vineyard you haven't already seen while we're waiting to hear what's happening?' Toby suggested. 'I know you were interested in the vines and the type of grapes that produce the Chardonnay. We have a separate area for the new planting on the west side.'

'Thanks. That would be great.'

The hills were bathed in sunshine at this time of day, and as they walked around, Katie was glad that she was wearing a simple, sleeveless cotton dress that kept her relatively cool and fresh. Even so, she was thankful for the occasional ocean breeze that fanned her hot cheeks.

Row upon row of glorious vines stretched out ahead of her, all of them in full leaf and heavy with fruit. 'You're doing a great job here, Toby,' she said.

'I do my best.' He sent her a quick look. 'These two vineyards, the Logans' and the Bellinis', have always been interconnected and run in a harmonious fashion. That might be under threat now that Tom and Natasha have shown that they're not interested.'

She frowned. 'You're afraid it will affect the smooth running of the place?'

'I think it might. At the moment they're happy for you to make the decisions, but that might not always be the case. There could be problems.'

She thought it over. 'I can see how that's a possibility—but right now I don't see any way round the situation. I can't afford to buy them out.'

'No.' Toby was quiet for a moment or two then added,

'I know Nick has an idea for smoothing things out. I expect he's spoken to you about it?'

She shook her head. 'No, he hasn't—except to say that he'd like to buy us out? Is that what he meant?'

Toby put up his hands as though to ward off any more questions. 'I'd better leave it to him to tell you his thoughts on that subject. Anyway, he wasn't specific, and I'm only concerned for the smooth operation of the vineyard.' He gave a wry smile. 'I don't want to get involved in sibling rivalry and multi-million-dollar takeovers.'

Katie stayed silent for a while after that. Toby's words had set up a welter of turbulent emotions inside her. Was Nick intending to increase his offer for the vineyard? How could he go on with his bid when he knew how much her father's legacy meant to her? She had begun to think he might have deep feelings for her, might actually come to love her, but now all her dreams were dashed once more. Her hopes had been reduced to ashes.

CHAPTER TEN

KATIE wandered barefoot along the beach, picking her way over craggy rocks and alternately feeling the warm sand glide between her toes.

There was so much to think about, so many questions that niggled at the back of her mind. What could Nick be planning? Would he really do anything to upset her? Why hadn't he rung to let her know what had happened at the hospital yesterday?

She missed him, she wanted to hear his voice, but instead there had just been a brief note pushed into her mailbox that morning to tell her that he had come along and collected his car while she was out—and to say that Sarah was being admitted to the paediatric ward so that the doctors could do tests. When Katie had tried to phone him, there had been no answer and the service had cut straight away to voice mail.

She stopped for a moment to listen to the calls of gulls overhead and to look around at the rugged, coastal bluffs. Out in the ocean, sea stacks rose majestically, carved out of ancient volcanic rock, a playground for sea otters that played offshore, feeding off the underwater kelp.

It was somehow soothing to be at one with nature…

but in the end it didn't take away her inner torment. How could it? Her life had changed so much in these last few months, and she'd had no choice but to confront her demons. Where had that left her? She was afraid and uncertain, full of doubt. And yet one thing shone clearly through the gloom—Nick had been a constant support to her, showing her how much he wanted her, gently coaxing her into loving him.

Just yesterday he had taken her to meet Natasha, and surely that was because he hoped they might somehow manage to heal the rift that had opened up between them. Would he have done all that if she meant nothing to him, if their relationship was just a spur-of-the-moment thing, a casual fling? She had to hope there was more. She couldn't go on this way.

For once, she had to take him at his word and trust in him. From now on she was going to meet life head on, which was why she walking along this stretch of sand, heading towards Nick's beach house.

Of course, she had rung Natasha. She had been desperate for news of her young niece, and at least her half-sister had recognised that she cared about the child and was worried about her.

'They're keeping her in overnight,' Natasha had said. 'It was late by the time the doctors worked out what they were going to do, but Nick was by my side all the while, explaining everything about the tests and so on. I don't know what I'd have done without him.' She pulled in a deep breath. 'Anyway, I'm going to stay here at the hospital so that I can be with Sarah. My husband—Greg—said he'd try to get here as soon as he can. He's been working away in the next county. We're both worried sick about her.'

'That's understandable,' Katie murmured. 'This must have come as quite a shock to you. I hope things turn out all right for you—will you let me know what happens?'

'Yes, I will.' Natasha hesitated. 'Thanks, Katie. I know you've been concerned for her all along and you were looking out for her. We've perhaps been hard on you, Tom and I. We both feel that we've misjudged you.'

'You've had a lot to deal with,' Katie said simply. 'You're my family. I just want to know that you're all doing well.'

It was a huge relief to know that they no longer bore her any ill-will, but the problems were still there. If she refused to sell the vineyard, they would go on struggling to keep their heads above water. What was Nick planning to do that would change all that? If things were to work out well for her half-brother and -sister, there could only be one loser.

She was overcome by doubts. If she was ever to make sense of any of this, she needed to see him, be with him…talk to him.

Katie pushed away a strand of chestnut hair that blew across her cheek in the faint breeze and walked closer to the water's edge. She paused to pick up a pebble and launch it into the ocean. It made a satisfying splash, and water droplets sprayed over her cotton dress. Waves lapped at her feet, cool, even after the heat of the day.

She halted for a moment, peering into the distance. From here she could just about make out Nick's house sheltered in the curve of the bay, and she set off once more towards it.

It was late afternoon, still warm, with the sun casting

its glow over all and sundry. Surely Nick would have finished his shift at the hospital by now?

It wasn't long before she reached the smooth stretch of sand that fronted his house, and straight away she saw that he was there. He was standing outside on the terrace, beneath the overhead deck, and he was facing her way. But he didn't see her because he wasn't alone and at this moment his companion was claiming all his attention.

A young woman was talking to him earnestly, her hand resting tenderly on his arm. Katie recognised her from her picture in the paper. This was Shannon, the woman he had once been engaged to, the girl he had supposedly abandoned.

Katie couldn't move. She stood and watched them, and after a second or two she saw Nick move closer to the girl and give her a hug.

The breath caught in Katie's lungs. She felt as though she had been winded, and she didn't know how to react. There was such a wealth of affection in that embrace, and it broke her heart. She stood transfixed, her pulse racing, a feeling of despair washing over her.

What was she doing, thinking that there might be a future for her with Nick? She was wishing on a moonbeam if she thought there was any chance he might have fallen for her. Hadn't Shannon always been there in the background? He'd made no secret of their relationship, had he? And in the end, hadn't he proved to be no different from her ex, professing to want Katie and at the same time making a play for someone else?

Slowly, her mind clouded by doubt and uncertainty, she started to turn away. She would talk to him later, when she had her head together a bit more. Seeing him with another woman was way more than she could bear right now. She loved him, and knowing that he was with someone else was just one more betrayal, perhaps the biggest betrayal of all because she had finally come to realise that he meant more to her than anyone in the whole world.

Her feet sank into the sand, slowing her down, but she made a huge effort to hurry away from there, even as she saw him glance in her direction and heard him call her name. She didn't look back but kept on going, putting as much distance as she could between her and the house.

'Katie…stop…let me talk to you.'

Still she kept on going. There was nothing to say, was there? She had made a mistake, and this was one from which she might never recover.

After a while he stopped calling after her, and even the silence was a rebuke. How could she have been so reckless as to fall for him? She meant nothing to him, did she? He had let her go without a fight. Perhaps he'd never wanted her in the first place, despite what he'd said.

She trudged on, oblivious to the call of the birds around her. She paid scant attention to the rare sight of brown pelicans nesting on the high bluffs or the black-headed terns that were searching for crustaceans among the rocks.

Minutes later, though, she stirred as she heard the drone of an engine in the distance. It was coming nearer, gaining steadily on her, the sound becoming louder and mingling with the crash of surf against the distant crags. She turned to see what was disturbing the peace and tranquillity of the bay.

'Nick!' Her eyes widened in astonishment as a dune buggy swung alongside her. 'What are you doing? Where did that come from?'

'It's mine. Hop in, I'll give you a ride along the beach.'

'No, thank you.' She shrank away from him. 'I don't think so. I really don't want to go anywhere with you.'

'Of course you do...you're just not thinking straight. Come on up here beside me.' The engine chugged to a slow, idling pace.

'I can't for the life of me think why I'd want to do that,' she muttered. 'I'd just as soon be on my own right now.' She frowned, looking the contraption over, studying the sturdy wheels and the open rails that allowed the warm air to move freely over its occupant. 'Anyway, I've never been in one of those things before. What's it for?'

He cut the engine. 'It's for catching up with headstrong young women who won't stop and take notice when they're called,' he said, reaching out a hand and grasping her by the wrist. 'Up you come. You'll like it... only hold onto the rail because the ride might get a bit bumpy around the rocks.'

She tried to resist, but his hold on her was firm and unyielding and after a while she realised that her struggles were fruitless and she may as well give in. There was no one around within shouting distance to come to her rescue, anyway.

Triumphant, he tugged her into the seat beside him. She glowered at him then settled herself more comfortably and brushed the sand off her feet before slipping on her sandals.

'Where are we going?' she asked as he started up the

engine once more. 'And what about Shannon—shouldn't you be with her? I saw you together. What happened? Have you just abandoned her? I'm sure she won't be very pleased to know that you're here with me.'

'Heaven forbid that I'd abandon her. No, she had to leave. She was only there on a quick visit—all she wanted was to let me know that she'd sorted out her problems.' He sent her a quick sideways glance. 'I thought we'd head along the beach to a nice, secluded spot…you never know when people are going to come along and disturb us on this section of the beach…and then you can tell me what's going on, why you came to see me and then turned away.'

'I decided what I had to say could wait until you were less busy,' she said in a pithy tone. 'It seemed to me that you had your hands full.'

'I thought that might be it.' The buggy gathered speed. 'You have a bee in your bonnet about Shannon, don't you?' he said, raising his voice to combat the sound of the engine. 'I keep telling you not to believe what you read in the papers. She's just a friend and she's been going through a bad time, but I guess you don't believe me, do you?'

Katie's mouth turned down at the corners. 'Perhaps it would help if you told me why she was at the hotel with you that night when the press caught up with you—and why, when I saw you with her just now, you had your arms around her?'

'Does that bother you?' He studied her thoughtfully for a moment and then turned his attention back to the beach ahead. 'Does it matter to you if I'm with someone else?'

'If it's another woman…yes, it matters.' She swallowed hard. There, it was out, she'd said it, something she'd hated to admit because it made her incredibly vulnerable.

'Good,' he said, in a satisfied tone, and she looked at him in shocked surprise. 'I hope that means you're jealous. I was beginning to think you'd never take me seriously.' He manoeuvred the buggy around an outcrop of rocks and steered it into a sheltered cove.

'I don't follow your reasoning,' she said awkwardly, looking at him wide-eyed. 'How can you care about me the way you say you do, if you're still seeing Shannon?'

His mouth flattened. 'Shannon is just a friend,' he said. 'I couldn't explain the situation before because she wanted to keep everything under wraps. The truth is, she's in love with someone her father doesn't approve of—he decided some time ago that he was a fortune hunter and did everything he could to break up the relationship. Of course, that was totally the wrong thing to do because it just encouraged them to have more clandestine meetings. Personally, I think the man she's chosen is okay. He cares about Shannon and wants the best for her.'

He parked the buggy by the foot of a cliff. 'Shannon was upset because her boyfriend was becoming wary of what her father might do—he'd threatened to cut her out of his life. So the boyfriend was thinking of going away because he didn't want her life to be ruined because of him. I was at the hotel that night when he'd tried to break it off with her, and she confided in me. We left the hotel separately, but the press had wind she was there and caught both of us on camera. They put two and two together and came up with five.'

'And now? After all, that was some time ago, wasn't it?' Katie looked at him doubtfully.

'Now she's trying to gain command of her life once more. She's made up her mind to go ahead and marry the man she fell in love with.' He gave a wry smile. 'To be honest, I don't think her father will cut her off. He loves her too much for that.'

'Oh, I see.' Katie's green eyes were troubled.

'I hope you do,' he said. 'But either way I'm glad you came to see me. Was there something special, or was it just because you couldn't stay away?' He grinned. 'I hope it was the last one.'

She pressed her lips together, still anxious. Even though he had put her mind at rest over Shannon, there was still a huge hurdle to face. She had to know what was on his mind when he spoke to Toby.

'I wanted to talk to you this morning,' she said, 'but I couldn't get through to your mobile.'

He nodded. 'I was swamped at work. We were inundated.'

'Yes, of course, I should have known.' She frowned. 'Is there any more news about Sarah?'

'They gave her a transfusion this morning and they're waiting to see if she perks up. From what the nurse said, she seems to be improving.' He paused for a moment. 'I think the doctors were worried about the cause of the anaemia initially, but now that the test results are back it appears it's as we thought. In time, she'll start to recover naturally. They say she just needs supportive care at the moment...rest, fresh air, a balanced diet.'

Katie let out a slow breath. 'That's good to know.'

'It is...and another snippet of good news is that I think Natasha and Greg will be getting back together.

They were always well suited—it was just that their money worries took over once Sarah came along. The fact that she's ill has brought them close to one another again.'

'I'm glad for them…and it's good to know that Sarah will have her father back with her.'

'Yes. It's always good when families are reunited. Which applies to the Delaneys, too, by the way. They moved Maria out of Intensive Care this afternoon. Apparently, her sister went to see her and they were able to talk for a while.'

'Oh, that's brilliant news.' Her face broke into a smile. 'That's been weighing on my mind for some time.'

'A lot of things seem to have been weighing you down lately.' He lifted a hand and gently stroked her face. 'Like this business of the vineyard. You're not happy about how it has affected Tom and Natasha, are you? I know things have been difficult between you.' His hand was warm against her cheek and she revelled in his comforting touch.

'It's worrying me,' she admitted. 'Though at least Tom and Natasha seem to have forgiven me. But I know they're going to have heavy burdens on their shoulders for some time to come, and I can't help feeling I might have done something to help them avoid that situation.'

'You still could.' He fingered the silky strands of her hair. 'If you let me help you.'

Her gaze meshed with his. 'Sell to you, you mean? I won't do that, Nick. I'm sorry. I made up my mind.'

'I know. I meant you could buy them out.'

She shook her head. 'How could I do that? I just don't have the means.'

'You could...' he paused to drop a kiss gently on her mouth, catching her off guard and setting off a flurry of warm sensation to fizz inside her '...if you'd allow me to lend you the money.'

She stared up at him, open-mouthed. 'But...but why would you want to do that?'

'Because I care about you.' He gazed down at the pink fullness of her lips. 'Because I want you to be happy. Because it's in my power to do it.'

Katie was shocked, thrown completely off balance by the enormity of his gesture. So this was his plan? To help her to keep the land that meant so much to his family? Words failed her, and her head was swimming with all kinds of thoughts, all of them leading to nowhere but utter confusion.

'I need to think about this,' she said huskily. 'I don't know why you're saying this to me. I never dreamed...'

She suddenly needed to escape the confines of the buggy. She slid down onto the sand and stared about her for a second or two, her mind in a daze. What he was suggesting was something she had never even contemplated...but why would he do such a thing?

He came to stand beside her, his arms folding her to him, his body close to hers, so close that it was all she could do not to cling to him and bask in the heady comfort of his warm embrace.

'What you're suggesting is incredibly generous,' she said huskily, her words muffled against the velvet column of his throat, 'but I don't see how I could accept. There's such a huge sum of money involved and I've no way of knowing if I could pay you back in the short or the long term. But thank you… I'm overwhelmed that you would even make the offer.'

The palm of his hand drifted lightly over the gentle curve of her spine, stroking her as though he would memorise every line, shifting to caress the rounded swell of her hip.

'You don't need to worry about any of that,' he murmured. 'It doesn't matter to me. All that matters is that you're happy and free from worry.' He gazed down at her. 'I don't know how it happened, Katie, but I've fallen for you big time. I'm completely out of my depth for the first time in my life and there's nothing I can do about it but accept it. I realised that some time ago. I love you… I need you… But most of all I want to make sure that you're safe and secure.'

The breath caught in her throat. 'I never imagined you would ever say that to me. I wanted it so much, but there was always this doubt at the back of my mind. I was scared. I'm still scared. I tried so hard not to love you because I was so sure I would be hurt…but it happened all the same, and now I'm…overwhelmed… elated…over the moon…' She closed her eyes briefly and absorbed the moment. 'I love you, Nick.'

He let out a ragged sigh and stooped to kiss her, exploring her lips with tender passion, sparking a trail of fire that flamed in every part of her being. 'Then nothing else matters,' he said softly, his voice rough edged as he came up for air. 'I'll always be here for you, Katie. You just have to learn to trust in me. I'll never hurt you, I promise you. You're part of me now. You've found your way into my heart, and we're bound together for all time.'

He darted kisses over her cheek, her throat, the bare

curve of her shoulder. 'Will you marry me, Katie? Please say that you'll be my wife.' His expression was intent, his eyes as dark as the ocean on a stormy day, and she realised that he was holding his breath, waiting for her answer.

'Yes… Oh, yes… I will,' she said in a soft whisper, gazing up at him, her heart filled with joy. She reached up to lightly stroke his face. She kissed him, running her hands along his arms, his back, wanting him, desperate to have him hold her closer, and he obliged, drawing her against him, moulding his thighs to hers and pressuring her into the safe haven of the cliff side.

'I want you so much,' he murmured, his voice husky with emotion. 'I can't get enough of you, Katie. You're everything I could ever want in a woman…so gentle, thoughtful, so considerate of everyone around you.' His mouth indented in a smile. 'When I saw you with young Sarah, holding her in such a worried fashion, I thought there was the woman I would want to be the mother of my children. You're the only one for me, Katie. I love you so much.'

She gave a sigh of contentment, her fingers roaming lightly over his chest. 'I'd like to have your children some day,' she murmured. Her gaze softened as she looked up at him. 'Of course, if we should be lucky that way, you know what it will mean, don't you?'

He shook his head and clasped her hand lightly, kissing her fingertips as though he would confirm his love for her with each tender kiss. 'That we'll face the future together as a family, come what may?'

'As a family,' she echoed. 'The Bellini family. And the name will go on through the generations, just as you wanted. Our vineyards would be linked under the same name as they were once before.'

'I hadn't thought of that,' he said. 'But, of course, it's true.' He smiled. 'It sounds like a perfect solution to me.' He wrapped his arms more firmly about her, and then he hugged her close and kissed her passionately, thoroughly, until her senses whirled and she was lost in a thrilling world of heady delight.

'I feel as though I've drunk too much wine,' she murmured contentedly. 'I feel as though my head is spinning and I'm so full up of happiness that I'm brimming over with it. Everything is turning out to be just perfect… you and me, and the solution to my brother and sister's worries. I never imagined things could turn out like this.'

'I'm glad you feel that way. I want to smooth out every glitch and make things perfect for you.' He laughed softly, running his hands over her as though to make sure she was really there, that he wasn't dreaming.

'I love you, Nick…only you. There's no other man I want in my life.'

He breathed a long sigh of relief. 'That's good. Because I really, really love you, Katie'

He bent his head and kissed her once more, and Katie clung to him and kissed him in return, loving him, loving the feel of him and wanting nothing more than to be with him for all time. For now she realised he was a man she could trust, a man who would be there for her always.It had taken her a long while to let down her guard, and finally she understood that he wasn't like other men. He would keep his promise to her, she could feel it in every part of her being, and she knew that she could look forward to a love that would last for ever.

She settled into his arms, kissing him tenderly, an ache of desire burning like a flame inside her. Why had she waited so long?

SUMMER SEASIDE WEDDING

BY
ABIGAIL GORDON

Abigail Gordon loves to write about the fascinating combination of medicine and romance from her home in a Cheshire village. She is active in local affairs, and is even called upon to write the script for the annual village pantomime! Her eldest son is a hospital manager, and helps with all her medical research. As part of a close-knit family, she treasures having two of her sons living close by, and the third one not too far away. This also gives her the added pleasure of being able to watch her delightful grandchildren growing up.

CHAPTER ONE

IT WAS June and the hot summer sun above made the confines of the car feel restricting as Leo Fenchurch drove along the road at the top of the cliffs in Bluebell Cove, a coastal village in the Devonshire countryside.

It had been a long morning. The first surgery of the day had been followed by home visits to the patients of the Tides Practice, where he was employed as one of the two doctors there, and now every time he glanced down at the sea, blue and dazzling as it danced onto the sandy beach, his collar felt tighter, his smart suit more a burden than an asset, and the yearning to pull into a deserted lay-by and change into the swimming trunks he always carried in the car was strong.

But needless to say he couldn't give in to the temptation. After a hasty lunch there would be the second surgery of the day to cope with and by the time that was over it would be half past six, so any sun-worshipping and bathing would have to wait until a summer evening unfolded.

The practice was on the road he was driving along, past the headland overlooking the sea, and situated in the centre of the village. As he drove onto the forecourt the red car belonging to Harry Balfour, the senior partner, pulled up alongside.

As the two men walked towards the main entrance to the surgery Harry said, 'There is something I need to discuss with you, Leo, before we grab a bite of lunch, so let's go to my room, shall we?'

'Yes, sure.' The fair-haired six-footer, who was top of the list of Bluebell Cove's most eligible men, had no problems with that.

The two of them worked well together, especially since Harry had recently married Phoebe and now seemed in a permanent state of bliss. He was a changed man from the brusque widower who'd returned from Australia to take over the practice. And the change in him was all due to meeting the love of his life after a marriage that had not been the most satisfying of relationships.

Phoebe Morgan had been the district nurse attached to the practice but was now no longer employed there because she was expecting their first baby, a brother or sister for Marcus, her son from her own disastrous previous marriage and a child that Harry loved as if he was his own.

A carefree playboy himself when he wasn't at the surgery, Leo had thought a few times when observing his partner's contentment that maybe he was missing out by never committing himself to any of the opposite sex who were ever ready to be in his company given the chance.

But the woman had yet to appear who could make

the most attractive man in Bluebell Cove want to settle down. Once long ago he'd thought he'd found her, but a force stronger than either of them had decreed that it was not to be.

'I had a phone call from Ethan while I was out on my rounds,' Harry explained once they were seated in his office.

Leo observed him questioningly. It had only been a few weeks since Ethan Lomax, who had been in charge of the practice before Harry had come and now lived in France, had brought his family over for the wedding of the man sitting opposite, so what was it now?

He was soon to find out. 'As you know, Ethan is working in a French hospital,' Harry explained, 'and has been approached by a junior doctor who is keen to get some experience of general practice, British style. Willing to assist if possible, he rang to ask if we could fit this person into the practice here for a few months. I told him I couldn't just say yes on the spur of the moment without discussing it with you, and would get back to him. So, what do you think?'

'An extra pair of hands would come in useful,' Leo said slowly, 'but how experienced is this guy?'

Harry was smiling. 'What makes you think it's a man?'

'So it's a woman?'

'Yes. Her name is Amelie Benoir. She's twenty-six years old and was top of her course at medical school, so I feel that an extra doctor in the practice for a while and one of such promise is too good an opportunity to miss, but first I want *your* opinion, Leo.'

'I feel the same as you,' Leo told him, 'and if this Benoir woman is what Ethan says with regard to ability *and* is as chic as his French wife, Francine, it will be a double bonus.'

'You never change, do you?' Harry commented with wry amusement, but Leo didn't rise to the bait. His mind was on the practicalities of the idea.

'So where would this French doctor stay?' he questioned, and then reverting back to form, went on, 'How about the apartment next to mine above the surgery? It worked for you and Phoebe when the two of you lived up there, didn't it?'

'I thought you weren't the marrying kind,' was Harry's reply to that.

'Who said anything about marrying? But I have to admit I envy you sometimes.'

'That is because I've found the right one,' he was told, 'and, having said that, going home to Phoebe and Marcus is the highlight of my day, so if this Amelie Benoir does come to join us here, I'd be obliged if you would go to the airport to meet her if she arrives in the evening. If it's during the day I'll do the honours, though evening would be better all round, I feel.

'Besides, with only the two of us as GPs, it's tough when one of us is missing, so I'll mention that to Ethan when I return his call and suggest she flies in after the surgeries, unless she's already found herself a niche over here by the time he speaks to her again. If she hasn't, and does come to join us for a while, I'm afraid she won't be living in the apartment across from yours.

Ethan has offered to let her rent his house in the village at a nominal sum for however long she stays.'

The following morning Harry announced that he and his predecessor had spoken the night before and arrangements were already in hand for the temporary addition to the practice to join them the following week.

She was to arrive next Friday evening, which would allow her time to get used to her new surroundings before presenting herself at the surgery on Monday morning.

Leo would meet her at the airport and give her the keys to Ethan's house, and Harry and Phoebe would make sure that a bed was made up and there was food in the fridge.

Having taken note of the arrangements, Leo put the new arrival out of his mind until such time as it had been arranged he should be at the airport to meet her. He carried on with his leisure pursuits as normal, which included swimming at every opportunity, tennis, and taking part in the village's social life in the form of dining out and attending local entertainment.

When Lucy, the elderly practice nurse who had worked at the surgery for as long as anyone could remember, asked him one morning if the trainee doctor was married or single, coming alone or accompanied, Leo had to tell her that he didn't know, hadn't thought to ask. Neither, it seemed, had Harry.

He appeared at that moment and when consulted merely said, 'Ethan's house is big enough to accommodate eight to ten people comfortably, so there won't be a problem regarding anyone she brings with her.'

'Especially if she's got lots of attractive sisters,' Leo joked, and Lucy smiled. She liked Leo Fenchurch, liked his easy manner, which some people misread. In reality he was a caring and experienced doctor who often concealed his feelings behind a casual bonhomie, which could be the reason why so many of the local female population sought his company.

Leo set off for the airport the moment the surgeries of the day were over on the Friday of the following week. It was a lengthy drive and he had no wish for the new arrival to be without someone to greet her when the aircraft touched down, which meant that he was still wearing the suit he wore for the practice, having had no time to change, and was hungry into the bargain, again because of the time factor.

Amelie Benoir's name was printed in large capitals on a piece of cardboard beside him on the passenger seat of the car and he was hoping that she would be one of the first off the plane so that he could take her for something to eat to appease his hunger.

The traffic wasn't good, but Friday nights never were, he thought as he watched the minutes ticking by. He strode into the arrivals lounge holding his piece of cardboard aloft with only seconds to spare as the first passengers from the French flight began to filter through.

His eyes widened. It looked as if his wishes were going to be granted. This had to be her, he thought as a tall, elegant woman with a sweep of shining blonde hair appeared amongst the first of the arrivals.

He reached out over the barrier as she drew level and held the card out for her to see, but there was no reaction, just a rather surprised smile and then she was gone, moving in the direction of the taxi rank. So much for that, he thought wryly. He'd been too quick off the mark there.

Passengers kept coming and no one stepped out of line and claimed to be Amelie Benoir. Eventually he was the only one there with his piece of card. As the last two, a rather nondescript couple, appeared, he was on the point of turning away when the woman called, 'Wait, please. I am she. I am Amelie Benoir.' As he observed her in dismayed surprise, the man that he'd thought she was with proceeded to the nearest exit.

He almost groaned out loud at the idea of mistaking the other woman for this untidy creature, but pulling himself together he said smoothly, 'Welcome to Devon, Dr Benoir. I am Leo Fenchurch, one of the doctors in the practice. If you will walk to the end of the barrier, I will take charge of your luggage, and then perhaps you would like some refreshment before we embark on what is quite a long drive to Bluebell Cove.'

It had been a shift like most of the shifts for junior doctors at the busy hospital where Amelie had first met the friendly Ethan Lomax. Who had set her imagination on fire when he'd spoken of the beautiful village on the coast of Devon where he'd lived before moving to France.

She had been allotted to Women's Surgical and had been nearing the end of what should have been a twelve-hour shift, but as sometimes happened it had been twice as long for various reasons, and for the last couple of hours Amelie had cast frequent glances at the clock because she hadn't wanted to miss her flight to the UK. If its relentless hands hadn't messed up her arrangements, there had always been the chance that exhaustion would.

But release had come at last and hurrying to her flat, which fortunately had been in the staff accommodation part of the hospital complex, she'd thrown off her hospital garb, showered, and replaced the clothes she'd taken off with the only jacket and trousers she possessed for travelling in.

Picking up her case, which fortunately she'd packed previously, she'd hailed a taxi from the rank outside the hospital gates and the last thing she remembered after settling into her seat on the plane had been wishing that it wasn't going to be such a short flight as the exhaustion that she'd had to fight to get there on time had taken over and even before take-off she'd been asleep.

It was why she was one of the last off the aircraft, drowsy and disorientated. She saw the card in the hand of a man who looked like the angel Gabriel in a suit and wished that she'd managed to find time to brush her hair properly instead of just rubbing it dry with the towel after she'd showered.

She was discovering that his likeness to an angel wasn't just in the golden fairness of him. He was offering her food and as it had been hours since she'd eaten, she would have kissed his feet if he'd asked her to. Yet there was nothing angelic about the hand that he'd extended to shake her ringless one. The contact was brief, but she felt a firmness and sense of purpose in its clasp.

'Yes, please,' she said in reply to his offer of food. 'I'm famished. I came straight off my shift with only a short time to spare before my flight was due to leave, and have slept all the way.'

He nodded. At that moment she looked like what she was, an overworked, underpaid junior doctor with the white mask of exhaustion that most of them wore.

The rest of her was made up of hair that was black as raven's wings in a short cut that would have looked stylish if she'd taken the trouble to run a comb through it, and there was a snub nose in the centre of a face with a wide mouth that looked as if it might smile a lot under other circumstances.

She was of average height, average weight, everything about her was average, except for her eyes. They made up for it, blue as the bluebells that the village got its name from, and as their glances met, his keen and perceptive and hers still verging on sleep, he thought that maybe she wouldn't be such a disappointment after all. If nothing else, she would be an extra pair of hands.

He took her to eat in a restaurant on the airport concourse and as she enjoyed the food he reflected it was only the smell and sight of it that was keeping her awake.

A visit to the powder room followed the meal and

Amelie sighed at the vision she presented in the mirror there. A quick flick of a comb through her hair improved it slightly, but the overall effect was far from how she would have wanted to appear on arriving in the UK for the first time to be met by a man who on closer inspection was more like a Greek god than an angel, but so what? She was off men, had been ever since she'd given Antoine his ring back.

The hurt and humiliation of what he'd done to her had made her feel unlovely and unloved when it had happened, but she felt she was over that now, had risen above those sort of feelings, and been grateful in a crazy sort of way for the long hours and other demands made of a junior doctor, which had left her with little time to brood. Yet it would be an eternity before she put her trust in or gave her heart to another of his sex.

Leo was waiting for her by the reception desk with her cases beside him when she reappeared, and didn't miss the fact that the black bob of her hair now hung smooth and shining around her face.

That's better, he thought, and almost laughed at the workings of his mind.

Amelie Benoir hadn't crossed the Channel to enter a beauty competition. She'd come to gain some experience in general practice and hopefully give assistance to Harry and himself at the same time.

'Thanks for the food,' she said gratefully. 'I feel much better now.'

'Good. I was a junior doctor myself once and remember the trials and tribulations just as much as the rewards. So if you want to nod off again feel free because it will be some time before we arrive in Bluebell Cove.'

'What is the house like where I shall be living?' she asked after they'd travelled the first few miles in silence, each not sure if the other wanted to talk.

'It was built for Ethan and his family a couple of years ago and is very spacious and attractive. It is opposite the surgery so you won't have to travel to get there. With regard to visiting our patients, Dr. Balfour is sorting out a hire car for you, though you will be with one of us until you know the district and have got the hang of the surgery routine.'

'And where do you live?' was her next question.

'Nowhere as sumptuous as where you will be living in Ethan's modern detached, or Harry Balfour's manor house,' he said laughingly. 'I live in an apartment above the surgery that supplies my needs.'

'So you do not have family?'

'My mother is alive. She lives in Spain with my sister and her husband. I'm not married myself, neither do I have any children. Families are the ties that bind, I feel. What about you? Have you left family behind in France?'

She shook her head and he thought there was something sad about the gesture. 'No. I have not left anyone behind. Both my parents are in the diplomatic service and spend most of their time abroad. I rarely see them.'

He nodded, 'I only asked because Ethan's house is big. If you'd wanted to bring anyone with you, he wouldn't have minded.'

'I might have done at one time,' she replied, 'but not now.' Silence fell between them once more.

It was gone midnight when Leo pulled up across the way from the surgery in front of the big detached house that was to be her home for the next six months.

Amelie had been half-asleep on the last leg of the journey but had woken up when he'd turned onto the coast road and been tuned in when he'd explained that the sea and the beach were below and that a house standing on a headland overlooking them called Four Winds because of its exposed position was occupied by a frail elderly woman who had once been in charge of the medical practice that they were heading for.

'I have lived in many places,' she told him, 'and the ones I have liked best were always beside the ocean. So this is a great adventure for me.'

'That's good, then,' he commented as he took her cases out of the boot and carried them to the front door of the house. While he was unlocking it he said, 'Ethan and his family were here just a few weeks ago for Harry and Phoebe's wedding, so all should be in order.' And with her close behind, he led the way inside.

Amelie looked around her, wide eyed at the spacious rooms and attractive, modern furniture, and Leo thought that this place made the apartment above the surgery look like a henhouse, yet did it matter? It was enough for his needs at the present time.

'If you would like to take a look upstairs, you should find that Phoebe has made up one of the beds for you, and there will be fresh food in the cupboards and the refrigerator,' he explained. 'If you need anything over the weekend, you know where to find me, above the surgery.'

'You will see a separate staircase leading to the apartment and there is a buzzer by the door. Now I shall leave you to settle in.' With a glance at her tired face, he added, 'Sleep well. Harry and Phoebe will be calling in to introduce themselves some time over the weekend and, as I've said, I won't be far away, so I'll say goodnight until eight-thirty on Monday morning.'

'Thank you for bringing me here, Dr Fenchurch,' she said, and he sensed the melancholy in her tone again.

Yet she was smiling as she went to the door to see him off and nodded obediently when he said, 'Be sure to lock and bolt the doors after I've gone.'

It was only when she was alone in the strange house that she'd escaped to that she allowed herself to think that with midnight already past, today should have been her wedding day.

Had Antoine even remembered, she wondered, or was he so engrossed in his new love that he'd shut the past out of his mind? Whatever the answer to that was, *she* was here in this beautiful English village and was going to make the most of the time by helping the sick and enjoying the change of surroundings, and along with that was hoping to find some kind of permanent healing for her own hurts.

She awoke the next morning to the sound of shrill cries in the distance and when she went to the window Amelie saw gulls circling around the headland.

There was a clear blue sky and already the sun was

out, warm and tempting overhead, even though it was only six o'clock. So tempting that instead of going back to bed and allowing herself the treat of a lie-in, the urge to explore her new surroundings was strong.

Within a very short time she'd breakfasted on some of the wholesome-looking food that had been left for her, had had a shower, and was striding along towards the beach in shorts and a cotton top to conceal a bikini, with a towel over her arm.

It wasn't just curiosity that was taking her there. It was a day that Amelie intended to fill with everything except thoughts of what might have been. Exploring Bluebell Cove was top of the list, and wallowing in hurtful memories at the bottom.

When she passed the house called Four Winds an elderly man was pottering around the garden and he gave a friendly wave when she appeared. The strip of golden sand below was deserted and as the sea pounded against the rocks and the gulls continued to screech above, she was out of the shorts and top and walking barefoot towards the water's edge in a matter of seconds, as if the wide expanse of ocean was a huge blue magnet pulling her towards it.

Leo had seen her go by from his vantage point above the surgery and had watched her walking towards the beach in amazement. Where was the exhausted young doctor of the previous night? he thought, never having dreamt that she would be up and about so early.

Getting her to Bluebell Cove and dropping her at Ethan's house had been enough to be going on with after a busy day in the surgery with journeys to and from the airport added on, so issuing warnings about dangerous currents and rip tides hadn't been in his mind at gone midnight the night before.

For one thing, he hadn't been expecting her to surface before midday and there she was, moving towards the delights of the cove with a spring in her step, which was more than he could say for himself.

He would have mentioned the tides if he'd had time to think the night before, but having not done so he couldn't let her go down there with no such thoughts in her mind. Within seconds he was following her, dressed in a similar manner in shorts and a T-shirt with swimwear underneath, and feeling less than chirpy at not having fulfilled his function as welcome party to Amelie Benoir.

She was in the water when he got there, swimming effortlessly quite a way out, and he groaned. He could murder a coffee and some toast, followed by a leisurely read of the morning paper, but first he was going to have to swim out to her, explain the dangers, and suggest that she swim nearer to the shore as Ronnie, the lifeguard, didn't appear on the beach until eight o'clock. The treacherous tides only surfaced rarely but strangers and locals alike needed to be aware of them.

When he bobbed up beside her in the water he gestured for her to swim back to the beach with him, and when they were on the sand she exclaimed, 'Dr Fenchurch! Do you also like to swim at this time of day?'

'Not unless I have to,' he told her dryly. 'I saw you walking past my place and came to warn you that there are dangerous tides on rare occasions that you need to be aware of. I should have mentioned it last night, but wasn't expecting you to be out and about so early after your exhaustion of yesterday.'

'Yes, I know,' she said apologetically, 'but my room was full of sunlight and I could hear the gulls. I just had to explore down here.'

She wasn't going to tell him that today she didn't want time to think, that she needed to be occupied every moment so that her thoughts wouldn't be of a wedding dress taken back to the shop, a bridal cake that had to be cancelled, and on a larger scale a honeymoon that hadn't materialised.

'So can I expect you to be watchful?' he asked, about to depart.

'Yes, of course. I will take note of everything that you say.'

'Good, and now I'm going back for some breakfast. Enjoy your weekend, Amelie.' And off he went with the thought going round in his mind that there was a solitariness about her that was worrying.

As he settled down to a belated breakfast and the morning paper, Leo was hoping the new addition to the practice would find her own niche socially and workwise, and that his part in the proceedings would now be completed.

He could understand her eagerness to go down to the beach and having seen her swim understood why.

She moved like a dream in the water, and now he supposed she would be exploring the rest of Bluebell Cove if she hadn't gone back to bed. He hoped that Harry and Phoebe would take up where he'd left off and make her feel welcome.

For his own day he'd arranged to spend time on the tennis courts later in the morning with Naomi, an aspiring fashion model. On Saturday afternoons he always drove into town, and tonight was joining Georgina, the attractive owner of the local boutique, and her friends for a meal. So *his* day was planned.

Amelie hadn't gone back to bed. She'd considered it, but knew that alone in the stillness of the bedroom the thoughts she was trying to keep in check would come sweeping over her and she would be lost.

Instead, she was going to explore the shops in the main street of the village, then walk as far as she could see on the road that ran along the top of the cliffs. And somewhere in the midst of her exploring she would eat.

The 'Angel Gabriel' hadn't seemed too cheerful when he'd found her already in the sea at just gone six o'clock in the morning, but she was afraid he would have to get used to that because she loved to swim; and if life at the village practice was as demanding as the job she'd just left, it might be her only chance at that early hour.

So far she hadn't met the senior partner but there was plenty of time for that. She'd met Leo, that was enough to be going on with, and for the rest of the weekend she wasn't going to butt into his life again.

The shops were to her liking. They reminded her of those in the French village where she'd lived as a child. Amongst them was a grocer's selling butter straight from the tub, a fishmonger's with the morning's fresh catch on display, and a combined village store and post office where people were good-humouredly passing the time of day without seeming to be in any hurry.

There was the feeling of life lived at a slower pace, she thought as she set off in the direction of the cliffs and the road that ran along the top of them. As she breathed in the fresh sea air and felt the sun on her face Amelie knew she'd done the right thing in accepting Ethan's suggestion that she come to Bluebell Cove *and she was here today of all days.*

She could see the sea in the distance as she walked along. The tide had gone out and there were more people down on the sand now than there had been earlier. She was in love with the place already, she thought wonderingly. What must it be like to live here all the time?

When she looked over her shoulder she was surprised to see how far she'd walked. The village was almost out of sight and having no wish to make her arrival in Bluebell Cove brought to the notice of others by getting lost, she began to retrace her steps.

Eventually she came to tennis courts that had been empty when she'd passed earlier but were now occupied by an attractive blonde with long legs. Partnering her, resplendent in tennis shorts and a short-sleeved white shirt, was the man she'd been hoping to avoid for the rest of the weekend.

Fortunately he was serving with his back to her and

with a few fast steps she was past before he'd had the chance to see her.

She was smiling as she neared the edge of the village. It made sense that a man like him would want someone as attractive as himself to have around him, she was thinking when suddenly the church bells began to ring out and as she drew nearer the reason was revealed.

A June bride, resplendent in a beautiful white dress and train, was being helped out of a wedding car that had stopped at the lychgate of the church, and Amelie felt as if a cloud had covered the sun.

So much for upbeat thinking and keeping occupied on this particular day. Who was she kidding? The hurt hadn't gone away. She'd learned to live with it, but it was still there.

Turning away blindly, she hurried past the shops until she came to a café and seated herself at a table farthest from the window.

CHAPTER TWO

THE tennis had been good, his companion pleasant to be with, and as the two of them walked along the main street of the village, seeking refreshment after the exercise, Leo was aware that the bells were ringing at the church and a wedding was taking place.

Not an unusual event on a Saturday in June, by any means, but it was attracting a lot of attention, as weddings always did, and when his tennis partner wanted to linger outside the church they separated, him to the café farther along the street and her to join those who were waiting for the bride and her groom to appear.

The place was almost empty when he got there, even cream teas were being overshadowed by what was happening at the church, but there was one customer sitting at a table at the back, staring into space, and he forced a smile.

Hot and sticky, he just wanted to relax but she was here again, the young French doctor looking so forlorn he just had to go across and say hello.

'So how's it going?' he asked easily, towering above her with racket in hand.

'Fine,' she said with a pale smile.

'You must be the only one not watching what is going on at the church. I thought that most women love a wedding.'

He was making conversation and knew it, out of his depth because she looked so glum, and he was dumbstruck when she said tonelessly, 'Not those who have been betrayed. Today should have been my wedding day too. I should have been a bride, but as you can see it has not happened.'

'Oh!' he exclaimed, and lowered himself onto the chair beside her. 'I am so sorry. I would never have brought up the subject of marriage if I'd known. It is not surprising that you aren't amongst the observers and well-wishers. Do you want to talk about it?'

She shook her head. 'No, I don't, Dr Fenchurch. I was managing to get through the day reasonably well until I saw the wedding and came in here to get away from it.' The pale smile was back. 'But I'm all right now.' Steering the conversation into less upsetting channels, she said, 'What has happened to your tennis partner?'

'Naomi? She's outside the church with everyone else, but we were about to separate in any case. We only meet once weekly for tennis. So why don't you let me take you back to the house before the bridal couple appear?'

'But you came in here for some refreshment,' she protested.

'I'll have a bite when I've seen you safely away from all of this,' he replied. 'If we take the long way round we'll miss the church. But, Amelie, I have to warn you there will be other weddings. June is the most popular month in the year so…'

'I'm not going to have a panic attack every time I see one,' she told him.

'It was because it was today of all days that it upset me so much, and I'm butting into your weekend again, aren't I? I am so sorry.'

'Don't be. You are alone in a strange place and I am happy to help in any way I can,' he assured her, and was surprised how much he meant it. 'So let's go, shall we?' And with a smile for the girl behind the counter as Amelie paid for what she'd had, he shepherded her outside and they set off in the opposite direction from the wedding.

Harry had rung him after breakfast, wanting to know if the previous night's arrangements had gone smoothly, and he'd been able to tell him that they had.

'So what's she like?' he'd wanted to know, and Leo had described her briefly.

'Something in your tone tells me that Amelie is not another chic Francine Lomax,' the senior partner had said laughingly.

Leo hadn't taken him up on that comment. Instead, he'd told him, 'She was down in the cove swimming at some godless hour this morning after seeming to be completely exhausted last night.'

'How do you know that?'

'I saw her go past with a towel over her arm and realised I hadn't told her about the rip tides, so went after her to be on the safe side.'

'And where is she now?'

'I don't know, but if her rapture on seeing Bluebell Cove is anything to go by, she'll be out seeing the sights.'

'We'll be calling round soon,' Harry had informed him, 'and if she isn't there we can stop by again later.'

It would seem that she hadn't been there because she was here with him, Leo was thinking when the surgery and the house opposite came into view. When she opened the door there was a note behind it.

He was observing her hesitantly as she bent to pick it up, undecided whether he should go and leave her to her private thoughts or offer to stay and keep her company for a while until he was sure she was all right to be left on her own.

Unaware of what was going through his mind, Amelie read the note and exclaimed, 'Oh, dear! Dr Balfour and his family have been while I was out.'

'Don't concern yourself,' he advised. 'I spoke to him this morning and he said he'll call again if he misses you, but for now, Amelie, would you like me to stay for a while or would you prefer me to leave?'

For the first time he saw the sparkle of tears in the blue eyes looking into his, but her voice was steady enough as she replied, 'I will be all right, thank you. You helped me through a bad moment and I am grateful, but I am sure that you have other things to do.'

As relief washed over him at being let off the hook he said, 'All right, if that is what you would prefer, but I'll leave you my mobile number just in case.'

'There is no need,' she protested. 'I will be fine once

this day is over,' and wished she hadn't been so quick to tell him the reason for her distress. She'd kept the hurt under wraps ever since the break-up with Antoine and would still have been doing so if she hadn't come across a village wedding.

Leo's relief at her insistence that she would be all right was short-lived. While he was out dining with Georgina from the boutique and other friends that evening he was on edge, knowing that he shouldn't have been so quick to latch onto Amelie's reassurances.

The day she'd been dreading wasn't over yet and the hurts that life was prone to hand out always seemed to multiply with the coming of the night.

It was as he'd said. She was alone in a foreign land and although he hardly knew her, he did have some degree of responsibility towards her because she was joining the practice on Monday morning and they would be meeting again. On a different level.

The folks he was with were aware of his wandering thoughts and Georgina asked, 'What's the matter, Leo? Aren't we entertaining enough for you tonight?'

He smiled and there wasn't a woman there who didn't wish he belonged to her, including Georgina, but she was aware that Leo was not the marrying kind, not where she was concerned anyway.

'I have got something on my mind,' he confessed. 'I'm sorry if I'm poor company.' He sent an apologetic glance in Georgina's direction. 'I need to pop out for a while. If I'm not back when you're ready to order, you know what I like to eat, Georgina.' And before anyone could comment he'd gone, striding out of the restaurant with a haste that didn't go unnoticed.

Ten minutes and once again he was outside the house where Amelie was staying, and when he saw that it was in darkness he was about to turn away when her voice came from behind him.

'Dr Fenchurch!' she exclaimed. 'I wasn't expecting to see you again today.'

'I just came to check that you're all right,' he said smoothly, as if he hadn't been fidgeting on her behalf for the last hour. 'I'm dining with friends in a restaurant not far from here so thought I'd call to make sure.'

'That is very kind of you and makes me even more sorry that I unloaded my troubles on to you,' she told him. 'But concern yourself no longer. I am fine. I beg you go back to your friends and remember you did give me your mobile number.' *Which I am not going to use, no matter what.*

'I shall have an early night to make up for my exhaustion of yesterday,' and as he made no move to take the hint, she said, 'Goodnight to you, Dr Fenchurch.'

He nodded. 'Goodnight to you too, Amelie.' At which she opened the door and disappeared from sight and he drove back to where Georgina and the others were waiting.

'So who was the woman?' someone asked jokingly.

He sighed and surprised them by saying, 'Her name is Amelie Benoir. She's the French doctor who is joining the practice for a few months. I only met her yesterday and I'm concerned that she is on her own in a strange place where she knows no one except me because Harry asked me to go to the airport to meet her last night. Does that satisfy your curiosity?' he questioned mildly.

'Yes,' the joker said laughingly, 'and we'll all be sure to ask for Dr Benoir when we're sick.'

As he listened to the friendly banter Amelie's face came to mind, framed by a glossy black bob, with a snub nose and wide mouth. So anyone who wanted glamour and the trappings that went with it would need to look in Georgina's direction.

It was hard to imagine anyone not being keen to marry the boutique owner *except himself,* and if anyone should ever ask him why, the answer would be that he couldn't see her as the mother of any children he might have.

In what seemed like another life he'd wanted Delphine, sweet and bubbly, to give him young ones when the time came, but it hadn't worked out that way.

They'd met at college, where so many romances began, and had known from the start they'd wanted to be together for always, but his love for her had been rent with an anguish that had ended in despair when she'd been rushed into hospital with a serious undetected heart problem and it had been too late to save her.

The pain he'd felt then had set the pattern for the years to come. It had been something that he never wanted to have to go through again. He was pursued all the time by women and laughed and joked with them, sometimes had the odd fling, but that was it. None of them could bring the kind of joy to his life that Delphine had.

When Amelie had told him that she was all right, it had been partly to reassure him and also because his kindness and concern on her behalf had helped to turn what could have been a ghastly day into a bearable one, and now she was determined that she wasn't going to lie sleepless and fretting about what might have been.

Antoine Lamont had been a junior doctor at the same hospital as herself. When he'd started paying attention to her she'd thought that the quiet, low-key guy, who had often been on the same shift as herself, had seen her as the right kind for him because she was as average as he was.

Gradually they'd drifted into an engagement with the promise of a white wedding on the very day she'd arrived in Devon with her heart set on a new life far away from the hurts of the previous one.

Her surmise that Antoine had chosen her because she had been the least demanding and overpowering of some of the women he'd known had been shattered when she'd called at his apartment unexpectedly one night in the hospital grounds and found him in bed with one of the nurses, a brassy, auburn-haired creature who was anything but average when it came to looks and curves.

It had been the end of her dream of contentment with a man she could love and trust and the beginning of pain and loneliness because of the deceit of it.

He'd tried to make amends, pleading that it had just been a one-off with the nurse, but she hadn't wanted to hear his pleas and subsequently Antoine and the girl he'd been in bed with had left the hospital together, leaving her to face the pitying looks of others as best she could.

Yet deep down Amelie thought she might have had a lucky escape and accepted that maybe she'd been more in love with the idea of getting married than with the man in question. But as she lay beneath the covers in the master bedroom of the big house that she was going to be rattling around in, she knew that the hurt of rejection had still been there when she'd seen the bride arriving at the church for her wedding that day, and it had been the same man who had met her at the airport who'd helped her to cope with it.

So far Leo had only seen her at her worst. On Monday morning she intended that he was going to see her at her best, with the ups and downs of her arrival in Bluebell cove blotted out.

If there was one thing that she never wanted to appear as, it was needy. With her parents always at the other side of the world, she'd had to fend for herself since her early teens and maybe that was why Antoine had seemed like a calm oasis in her often chaotic life, but he'd turned out to be just the opposite, and with that thought in mind she turned her head into the pillow and slept.

Sunday was uneventful except for a visit from the Balfours, Harry and Phoebe, with their toddler, Marcus.

The senior partner asked if she was happy with her living arrangements and said to let him know if she had any problems with regard to that or anything else.

'I'm aware that you've already met Leo,' he said, 'and the rest of the staff will be looking forward to meeting you on Monday morning, Amelie.'

'Yes, I've met Dr Fenchurch,' she replied. 'I feel I may have interrupted his weekend as I seemed to be everywhere he was.' She wondered if the man in question had told his partner at the practice about her unsuccessful attempt at matrimony.

She hoped not, though she hadn't asked him to keep it to himself, but if he had respected her privacy it would be a stick to measure him by and she was already intrigued by him.

The Balfours didn't stay long, but it was time enough for her to discover a couple of things about them: one, that they were deeply in love and both adored the child; and, two, that she liked them and hoped that Dr Balfour would be as pleasant to work for at the practice as he was outside it.

Monday morning saw Amelie poised and ready for action, dressed in a smart white blouse, short black skirt, and with her smooth ebony hair straight and shining around a face that was alight with anticipation.

She'd made up carefully, paying special attention to her eyes, which she felt were the best feature of a nondescript face, and when she stood in front of the mirror in the bedroom she felt that she'd done her best with what nature had given her because there was nothing wrong with her bone structure and the flesh on it, yet when she thought about a certain brassy red-headed nurse with breasts like balloons she did have her doubts.

Leo was emerging out of the private entrance to the apartments as she appeared on the practice forecourt and strode purposefully towards him, carrying a leather briefcase. She looked different again, dressed smartly as she was, from the dishevelled woman at the airport and the bikini-clad swimmer on the beach.

'Good morning, Dr Fenchurch,' she said as he fell into step beside her. 'It has come. The day I am to be part of your medical centre.'

'Yes, indeed,' he replied as he held open the main door of the surgery for her to go through. 'I hope you won't be disappointed in us.'

She smiled up at him. 'It is more that it should be me who does not disappoint you and Dr Balfour. When you met me at the airport it was what I saw in your expression…disappointment.'

Surely it hadn't been so obvious? he thought. It had been because he'd picked out the wrong woman to be her that the difference had seemed so great.

He didn't deny it. Instead, he said, 'It was very rude of me if that was how I appeared, and you are certainly proving me wrong so far. I hope that your first day is a good one, Amelie. Harry is already here and waiting to see you in his consulting room.'

'They came to see me yesterday. Dr Balfour and his family were most kind. I wondered if perhaps you had told them about my cancelled wedding.'

For the first time since she'd met him she saw Leo's pleasant manner chill as he told her, 'Certainly not! If Harry and Phoebe were kind, it's only because that is what they're like. I wouldn't dream of discussing what you told me on Saturday with anyone. Your private life is yours alone.' And with the coolness still there he pointed to the door nearest to them, said, 'That's Harry's room,' and disappeared down the corridor in front of them where all the activity seemed to be taking place.

She'd unintentionally insulted him, Amelie thought as she tapped on the door of the senior partner's room. Suddenly the morning wasn't so exciting and challenging. She was just a temp from across the Channel, a bride-to-be who'd ended up on the outside of things.

Somehow she managed to put on a good face for the head of the practice and smiled her pleasure when he told her that she was being provided with a hire car that would be available the next day.

'You'll be in the room next to Leo at the other end of the passage,' he told her, 'and for a time will do the home visits with him until you are familiar with the area.' He shook her hand. 'Welcome aboard, Dr Benoir. I hope you enjoy your time with us.' And that was that.

His phone was ringing so she left him to it and went to introduce herself to the receptionist at the desk opposite, who in turn took her to meet the rest of the staff, who were gathered in the kitchen for what she was to discover was a daily ritual—a mug of tea before surgery commenced.

The first thing she saw was that Leo wasn't there and wondered if he was still smarting from what she'd said earlier. On her part it had just been innocent curiosity, yet she could understand his annoyance at the inference that he might have repeated what she'd told him to others.

But there was no more time to dwell on that. There were hands to shake, names to remember, and by the time the introductions were over she was feeling more comfortable.

Amongst those present were the two practice nurses, Lucy the elderly one, and Maria, young, pretty and the daughter of the beach lifeguard.

The district nurse, Bethany, only recently appointed, was there too, as well as the cleaner, a pleasant woman who came early and finished early in time to get her children off to school.

As she drank the tea Amelie was still wondering where Leo was and when she moved nearer to the open kitchen door she could hear his voice coming from Dr Balfour's room and he didn't sound happy.

He'd gone outside to get something out of his car and on returning had found that the senior partner had left Amelie to introduce herself to the staff, instead of doing it himself, and his frown had deepened when Harry had said laughingly, 'She wandered off while I was on the phone. Don't fuss. I've told her she's getting the cherry on the cake.'

'And what might that be?' he'd gritted.

'Doing the house calls with you, of course.'

'Really. And how exciting is that not going to be… for her?'

She'd heard everything that was being said except

the last two words because Leo had lowered his voice. If she'd felt she'd upset him before, it was twice as bad now. He obviously had no desire to be lumbered with her on his house calls.

He joined them all in the kitchen seconds later and her glance raked his face for signs of how he was feeling now. She was surprised when he had a smile for her and asked, 'Are you all right, Amelie?'

'Yes. I'm fine,' she told him, relieved to see that he was back to his normal manner. 'I have met all the staff, except the manager of the practice, and someone said she will be along shortly.'

'That's Janet. She doesn't start until nine o'clock, but often works later than we do in the evenings. Bethany, the new district nurse, is her daughter.

'They're a good lot. Don't hesitate to ask any of them if you have any problems. Surgery will be starting in a few moments so let me show you where you will be providing health care for the folk in Bluebell Cove.'

'Are you still angry with me?' she asked in a low voice as he opened the door of the smallest consulting room in the practice.

'No, of course not. It was just you thinking I might have discussed your private life with Harry or anyone else that threw me off balance for a moment.'

He was beginning to wish they weren't having this conversation, didn't want to get any closer to this young French doctor who had butted into his weekend and now wanted to see into his thoughts. He'd actually fallen out with Harry over her and that was a first. They usually got on well.

A change of subject was called for and as the surgery was due to open its doors in a matter of minutes, what better way than to explain to her what was going to be required of her on her first morning?

'Harry and I have picked out a few appointments from today's list for you to deal with,' he explained. 'They are mostly women and children. Since Francine left to go back to her homeland we haven't had a woman doctor on the staff, so you can see the advantages of having you here for our female patients, young and old.

'If anything occurs that you haven't dealt with before, Harry and I are here for help and advice. So good luck on your first morning. And now, if you'll excuse me, I must prepare to meet my own patients. After surgery is finished we'll have a coffee and then it will be time for the home visits. You will be able to see a lot more of Bluebell Cove while we're out in the district as the area that the practice covers is both coast and country.'

With that he disappeared into the room next to hers and Amelie was left with the feeling that he was putting up with her on sufferance. What he'd said to Dr Balfour with regard to there being no pleasure in taking her with him on his rounds indicated that, and also there'd been the darkening of his brow when she'd asked him if he'd told the other man about her non-wedding.

He'd been all right about it afterwards, but there were signs that Leo was finding her heavy going, so a low profile was called for.

Her first patients were a harassed mother with a tearful four-year-old who was protesting loudly that she didn't want to see the doctor man. Both were surprised to see that the 'doctor man' was a smiling young member of their own sex who had a way with children, having worked in the paediatric wards of a French hospital.

Within seconds the child had stopped crying and the mother was calming down as she explained why they were there. 'Tiffany has an inflamed throat,' she said, 'and is very fretful. She won't eat and had a raised temperature during the night. It seems normal enough now, but I still felt she should see a doctor.'

'Yes, of course,' Amelie agreed. 'First I must look down the throat to check the degree of the inflammation.' Turning to the small patient, she said gently, 'Will you open your mouth for me, Tiffany, so that I can shine a light inside it?'

Not too keen on the idea, Tiffany clung to her mother and at her most persuasive Amelie said, 'Just one little peep, that is all. Can you do that for me?'

Reassured, the child nodded and opened her mouth and when, as promised, Amelie did a quick examination of her throat she saw there was infection around the tonsils.

'Has Tiffany had an inflamed throat before?' she asked.

Her mother shook her head. 'No, never.'

'Then let us see what a few days' rest and some paracetemol will do. They will help to relieve the soreness and then Tiffany will be more likely to want to eat. Ice cream is good for an inflamed throat too. If you should see pus on the tonsils, send for one of us immediately.

'Her temperature is normal at present,' she announced when she'd checked it, 'but may rise again in the night so be prepared.' She turned to the child. 'You have been a very brave little girl, Tiffany, and you can have some ice cream when you get home.'

'Thank you, Doctor,' her mother said as they were leaving. 'Are you new here? I haven't seen you before.'

Amelie's wide smile embraced them both. 'Yes, I am here from France for a while and am already in love with your village.'

'I have a woman's problem that I've wanted to discuss with someone of my own sex, so you might be seeing me again,' Tiffany's mother said.

'That will be fine whenever you are ready,' Amelie told her, 'and be sure to bring Tiffany back to the surgery if the inflammation persists.'

An expensively dressed elderly woman with an irregular heartbeat came next and was immediately dubious when she saw a fresh face behind the desk and a young one at that.

'I was expecting to see Dr Balfour,' she said haughtily. 'Are you fully qualified?'

'Yes, I am,' Amelie told her pleasantly. 'I have a degree and have been employed in a French hospital for the last two years. I am here to see how general practice works in the UK. So would you oblige me by unbuttoning your cardigan, Mrs…er…' a quick glance at her notes '…Arbuthnot, as any kind of change in the heartbeat needs immediate attention.'

'Yes, it is a little fast this morning,' she told the

patient when she'd listened to it intently. 'Has it happened before?'

'On and off, but not as severe as this,' was the reply.

'And you have seen Dr Balfour on those occasions? There is no mention of it in your records.'

'No. When it has happened before I've ignored it and it has gradually gone away.'

'But not today?'

'No. Not today.'

'Then an ECG is called for. If you will accompany me to the nurses' room it will be done, and whatever the feedback we will find out what, if anything, is wrong with your heart.'

As Esther Arbuthnot got slowly to her feet she said grudgingly, 'They say that a new broom sweeps clean, so maybe being passed to you for my consultation isn't such a bad idea after all. What is your name?'

'Amelie Benoir,' she said as she led the elderly woman towards the ECG facility, where Lucy would perform the test.

The speed with which the results came through had Esther Arbuthnot in a state of amazement that turned to alarm when she was told that there could be a problem with one of the valves of her heart and that there had been evidence of a minor heart attack some time in the past.

'We need to refer you to a cardiologist for further tests,' Amelie told her gently as she observed how the patient's bumptiousness was disappearing fast, yet not so fast that she wasn't already planning ahead.

'There is a top heart surgeon in Bluebell Cove,' Esther informed Amelie. 'His name is Lucas Devereux and he has a private clinic that he runs from his home.'

'He's the consultant I want to see. I can well afford it. He is married to Barbara Balfour's daughter Jenna, who was a practice nurse here until they had their first child. So if you would arrange for me to see him as quickly as possible, I would be obliged.'

'Yes, of course,' she assured her, 'and in the meantime no excessive exertion. Just take it quietly and rest whenever possible. I will be in touch as soon as I have an appointment for you.'

When she'd gone Amelie wondered how many Balfours there were in Bluebell Cove. They had to be related to Harry Balfour, the head of the practice, in some way. At the first opportunity that arose she would ask Leo who this Barbara Balfour was.

CHAPTER THREE

AMELIE's first morning at the surgery was over and as she waited for Leo's much longer list of patients to come and go before they set out on the home visits she was thinking how much she'd enjoyed her first taste of general practice.

She'd coped with the patients that had been passed to her by the other two doctors without having to consult either of them, and when Leo finally appeared and asked, 'So how was it?' she had a smile for him.

But there was uncertainty behind it and he thought she was unsure of him, still aware that he hadn't liked being questioned as to whether he'd passed on details of her private life to Harry. But she was not to know that though some saw him as lightweight, he cherished his integrity and admired that of others.

'I enjoyed it immensely,' she told him. 'I liked the one-to-oneness of it. In a hospital situation there are sometimes too many fingers in the pie.'

'So, are you ready for an interesting couple of hours visiting the sick and seeing the sights of Bluebell Cove when we've had a coffee?'

'Yes, of course,' she said obediently, and it was there again, a withdrawal of the unaffected easiness that she'd displayed when in his company previously.

Yet as he pulled out onto the coast road she was the first to speak, and it was to ask if Dr Balfour had relations living in Bluebell Cove. She went on to explain that a patient had mentioned someone called Barbara Balfour.

'Yes, he has indeed,' he replied. 'Harry was brought up in this place and when he got his degree came to work at the practice as a junior doctor like you. At that time his aunt, Barbara Balfour, was in charge of the practice and I'm told was a force to be reckoned with, but she had to retire due to ill health. She and her husband live in Four Winds, the large house on the headland.

'Barbara was instrumental in persuading Harry to come back to Bluebell Cove after losing his wife in an accident, and also helped Ethan Lomax with his problems at the same time. The lady in question is a household name here and revered by all who know her, but she is also something of a tartar, even though she isn't in charge any more.'

'And it is her daughter who is married to the heart surgeon?'

'Yes, she was Jenna Balfour before she married Lucas Devereux. So now you can place us all in our slots,' he said whimsically.

'All except you, Dr Fenchurch. You don't seem to have one. All the others appear to have roots in Bluebell Cove but not you. Where do you come from?'

'The north-west. I'm from Manchester.'

'So you are a long way from home.'

'Yes, but not as far from home as you are, though you seem contented enough.'

She shook her head. 'Not always, I'm afraid. Yet I know I'm going to be happy here, I can feel it inside. Bluebell Cove is so beautiful, how could I not be?'

He gave her a quick sideways glance and thought how different she was from other women he'd known. She had no airs and graces. She was just herself, an enthusiastic young doctor with, from the sound of it, parents who had put their careers before their daughter. Had they been around when in the not so distant past she had suffered heartbreak at the hands of some two-timing upstart?

But she was getting on with her life with an ingenious kind of acceptance that a lot of the women who sought him out wouldn't be able to boast.

'Our first call of the day is at the marine museum next to the harbour,' he said, bringing his thoughts back to the reason they were driving in that direction. 'The caretaker and his wife live in an apartment on the premises and they've asked for a home visit.'

'Why?' she asked, all eagerness on her first venture on house calls with him.

'I'm not sure. It was his wife who rang up and the message was rather garbled. If I understood it rightly, her husband is having some sort of severe gastric attack.'

'Oh, dear, that sort of thing can be most unpleasant,' she commented, and he tried not to smile. If they didn't come across something worse than that during the next couple of hours he would be surprised, but had to have a rethink when he saw the elderly caretaker.

He was deathly white and in a lot of pain, which his wife said had started in a milder way around and above the navel then had increased sharply and was now located at the lower right-hand side of the stomach. When he'd examined the patient Leo turned to Amelie, who had been watching intently.

'Would you like to examine our patient and give an opinion?' he asked, and turned to the man's wife. 'Dr Benoir is going to be working with us at the surgery for a while. She has come over from France to join us.'

Amelie was already doing as he'd requested and when she'd finished she straightened up, looked him in the eye and said, 'I suspect appendicitis.'

'I would agree,' Leo told her. 'The hospital will do a laparotomy and if that is what it shows, they will remove the appendix.'

He was quick to reassure the caretaker's wife. 'I'm sending for an ambulance and if it should turn out to be appendicitis your husband will be operated on without delay to avoid infection spreading.'

'You seem to be something of an expert in diagnosing appendicitis, Dr Benoir!' he commented, impressed by Amelie's confident diagnosis.

'I have seen it in a child. It was in the same place and very painful.'

'So you know that the most dangerous time with appendicitis is when the pain goes. It is the calm before the storm when the appendix bursts and peritonitis develops, so watch out for that.'

When the ambulance had come and gone, with the suffering caretaker and his wife on board, Leo drove them to the next house call, where they found a small boy with measles.

He had a high temperature, the usual rash, and was waiting for their visit in a darkened room as the illness made the small patient very sensitive to light.

'It was wise of you not to bring your boy to the surgery,' Leo told his mother. 'Measles is very infectious. Also I see that you are taking care of his eyes, which is good. Measles is a serious illness that was almost stamped out until the scare that the vaccine might be connected with autism. Am I to take it that your son hasn't had the three-in-one MMR?'

She nodded glumly. 'My husband and I did what we thought was best for him, but now I'm not so sure and am not going to leave his side for a moment until he's better.'

'Plenty of rest and lots to drink will help, and once the rash has gone you will see an improvement. He should stay in quarantine for at least four days so he doesn't infect anyone. Like all the familiar childhood illnesses measles will take its course and the young ones need plenty of care and love while it is doing so.'

As they were leaving the house Leo said wryly, 'Being a good parent is the job of a lifetime and not everyone gets it right or even wants to, but that child's mother was giving it a good try, even though she'd decided on the wrong course of action.'

The moment he'd made the comment about families

he wished he hadn't. Amelie's family life didn't sound fantastic, if it existed at all.

When he glanced across she was staring out of the car window, her face expressionless. He hoped he hadn't spoilt her first foray into the world of those not well enough to go to the surgery.

As they made their way back to the practice, once they'd completed all the home visits, Amelie's gaze was fixed on the sea below and suddenly she wound the window down and said urgently, 'The tide is coming in fast around the entrance to a cave down there and I can see children inside.'

He slammed the brakes on and flung wide the door and they ran side by side down the cliff path that led to the beach.

'Where is everyone?' he cried. 'There isn't anyone in sight.'

Waves were crashing against rocks and they could see two small girls crouching in the entrance to the cave, about to be swept out and battered against them any second.

There was no time for discussion between the two of them. Every moment was vital if they were to get to the children and bring them to safety, but this young doctor was in his charge, Leo thought frantically. If anything happened to her…

He was cold with horror at the thought as he clambered over the rocks and prepared to lower himself into the sea, with her close behind. Calling over his shoulder, he told her, 'I'll deal with this. Stay where you are, Amelie.'

It was too late. She'd run to a point farther along and was already striking out towards the cave and the children trapped there. A powerful swimmer himself, he saw once again that she was in a class of her own in the water.

As they reached the cave a huge wave swept into the opening and on receding brought the children with it. Amelie grabbed one of them, he took the second in his grip and they fought their way to the nearest rocks where they heaved them up to safety as two lots of frantic parents scrambled towards them.

'We only left them for a short time,' one of the mothers cried as she hugged her child to her. 'The men wanted a drink and persuaded us to go with them. The tide was way out then and the children *are* having swimming lessons.'

'The sea came in from the side and was in front of the cave where they were playing before they had a chance to escape,' he explained grimly, 'and it would have been too powerful for children as young as these to swim in a high tide such as this.'

'Yes, well, thanks,' one of the fathers said sheepishly. 'We'll know next time.' And with the children wrapped in towels, they moved towards the car park.

When they'd gone Amelie looked down at her soaking-wet blouse and skirt. Thankfully she'd kicked off her shoes in the car so at least they would be dry.

Beside her, Leo was stripping off his shirt and squeezing water out of his trousers, and when their glances met he said tightly, 'I suppose you didn't hear me when I called that I would handle it. I was having nightmares out there in case something happened to you while you were under my supervision.'

'Is that all you were concerned about?' she asked miserably, as the feeling that she was of no consequence to anyone surfaced once more. 'Concerned that I didn't embarrass you by drowning while I was in your charge? Had you forgotten that I can swim like the best of them?

'When I was young my parents had to take me with them on their postings abroad and often there was nothing else for me to do except go to whatever school was available and spend the rest of my time swimming. I even trained as a lifeguard one summer.'

It had been his turn to offend her, Leo was thinking, but it was no time for soul-searching. She was beginning to shiver in her wet clothes and he said, 'There is a long raincoat of mine on the back seat of the car. Take your wet things off and put it on before you catch a chill. I'll wait here until you've done that and then we'll be off. The village is only a short drive away and you'll be able to have a shower and a hot drink before the afternoon surgery starts.'

She nodded meekly and went to do as he'd suggested. Within minutes they were pulling up in front of the Lomax house and he was bidding her goodbye as he went to change his own clothes before returning to the practice.

Typically of village life, by the time they both arrived back at the surgery Harry and the rest of he staff had heard about their rescue in the cove and he'd opened a couple of bottles of wine for the staff to toast them, which Amelie felt was a more celebratory attitude than Leo's had been. Yet she supposed it was understandable. She might have felt the same in his position, so she could see his point of view.

That she could always see the other person's point of view was her Achilles' heel. She'd even seen Antoine's when he'd opted for someone more raunchy and lively than her. Had known she'd been wrong in thinking that because he was so ordinary and undemanding he would want her, who was the same, when all the time he'd had other ideas.

It hadn't made the hurt any less but she'd understood better and would be very careful in her next choice, if there was ever a next time.

At the end of the day Leo said, 'I'd like a word in private. Would it be all right if I popped across when I've finished here?'

'Er...yes,' she said, with bluebell eyes wide and questioning, 'but only if you aren't going to tell me off again.'

He sighed. 'I'm not going to do anything of the kind. I've got one more patient to see so should be about fifteen to twenty minutes. The guy has phoned to say that he's held up in traffic, so I'll come over when he's been, OK?'

'Yes. I'll be doing steak and salad. Shall I do it for two so that you don't have to cook when you get in, or are you dining out with friends?' she asked, and couldn't believe what she was saying.

He gave her a long level look and informed her, 'I

don't eat out all the time, you know. It's usually weekends when I do my socialising so, yes, thanks for the offer, Amelie. It will be a change from an endless round of ready meals.' *And a change from the kind of company I usually keep,* he thought, *which is long overdue.*

When he came he'd changed again for the second time and was dressed in a smart casual top and jeans, and Amelie thought how incredible he looked with his golden fairness and the trim six feet of him.

Without giving serious thought to how it might sound, she said, 'When you met me at the airport I was half-asleep and thought you were either the Angel Gabriel or some Greek god who had come back to haunt womankind.'

'Really?' he said dryly, with lips pursed and eyes rolling heavenwards. 'I lay no claim to my looks. I inherited them from my Nordic grandfather and in any case what we look like from the outside isn't always an indication of what goes on within.'

'What did *you* think when you saw me?' she wanted to know.

He was smiling and it took the sting out of what he was about to say.

'I thought you were odd, a bit scruffy and rather vacant.'

She laughed at the description. 'I can't deny any of that. I'd just worked twenty-four hours non-stop, had had the quickest shower of my life and flung myself into a taxi, praying all the time that I wouldn't miss my flight. They were calling it as I rushed into the airport and I made it with only seconds to spare, so must admit that my appearance was the last thing on my mind.'

He nodded. 'Yes. That was understandable.'

'And so are you going to tell me why you are here before I serve the meal? I won't be able to eat with curiosity gnawing at me.'

'I came to apologise for my tactless comments after we'd brought those youngsters to safety. You were incredible, so fast thinking and even faster in the water. Yet even though we were back on dry land with everyone safe and sound I was still imagining what it would have been like if I'd had to tell Harry that you'd drowned on your first day in the practice. I'm sure you can understand that.'

'Yes, I can,' she said soberly. 'I have this bad habit of always being able to see someone else's point of view. Though at that moment it wasn't working too well as you were making me feel that I didn't matter as a person, that I was just an encumbrance, the gauche, wet-behind-the-ears trainee that you'd been burdened with and wanted to take back to the practice intact for your own reputation.'

Stopping for breath, she wondered if she was suffering from some kind of verbal override. She'd hardly stopped talking since he'd appeared and supposed one reason might be that she was nervous in his company.

It was his turn to be amused. 'Thanks a bunch for that powerful description of your opinion of me. If I remember rightly, at the time you were wet in other parts of the anatomy besides the ears, and I'm not too sure about the gauche label. I'd give it five out of ten.'

'Now you're making fun of me.'

'Not at all. I have to say that whatever else you are… you're different. But getting back to why I came, do you accept my apology?'

'Yes, of course. And I thought what *you* did was pretty special too.' Before she said or did anything else that might be misconstrued, she added, 'If you will excuse me for a moment, I'm going to serve.' She indicated the dining room where the table was set. 'If you would like to take a seat.'

Watch it, he told himself when she'd gone into the kitchen. Don't let it get out of hand with this young doctor. She's sweet and caring but not in your league, Leo. She would soon tire of your sort of lifestyle. You aren't over the moon with it yourself these days, especially when you observe Harry and Phoebe. Yet there is something to be said for freedom.

They chatted about everything but themselves while they were eating—the practice, the village, the community and the social life of the place. Amelie listened intently as he described the events that were arranged during the various seasons.

When she discovered that in July there was to be what was known as the Big Summer Picnic, where everyone who went took food with them, either sweet or savoury, to be shared at long wooden tables covered with white cloths, she was already wondering what to wear.

'You haven't said where the picnic takes place,' she reminded him.

'On the field at the back of the village hall. That way

there is somewhere to scatter if it should rain, and in the evening there is a barn dance.'

'Do you go to these events?' she asked.

'Yes, usually. It depends on what is going on in my life at the time.' She wondered if that was significant or just a casual comment.

'That was lovely,' he said when they'd finished eating and she'd served coffee in the spacious sitting room. 'Maybe you'll let me do the same for you one evening in my sparse accommodation.

'I stayed at Mariner's Moorings, the guest house on the coast road, for a long time before I moved into the apartment and I've no thoughts of buying a property at the moment. I don't like to be tied down.'

Her expression was downcast as she told him, 'We have different ideas about that. My life has been like that of a Gypsy, lacking stability, especially when I was young, which I feel had something to do with my disastrous broken engagement and cancelled wedding. I thought marrying Antoine would give me security and was mistaken, so it will be a long time before I fall into that pit again.'

'You don't exactly sound as if you were head over heels in love,' Leo commented dryly. 'People *are* supposed to marry for love, you know.'

He was getting to his feet and glancing at the clock with the feeling that it was all getting a bit too intimate. They'd only known each other a few days. He'd been there for Amelie at the start. She should be able to cope from now on.

She was observing him questioningly and he said,

'Thanks for the meal and the hospitality, Amelie, Not having to do the cooking myself will give me more time to get up to date with a lot of medical info that's coming through and waiting to be absorbed. I'll pass it on to you when I've finished with it. Harry has already seen it.'

'That would be great, thank you,' she told him primly, and thought that he wasn't exactly lingering. Yet had she expected him to and, more importantly, had she wanted him to?

When he'd gone striding off across the few yards that separated the apartment and the large detached house, Amelie went to sit in the back garden beneath a sun still high in the sky, and began to go over in her mind what each of them had said. By the time she'd finished she couldn't believe that she'd been so up front about her life with a stranger.

But Leo didn't feel like a stranger. The things they wanted from life were poles apart, but it didn't prevent her from relaxing in his presence, and as she was only going to be working in Bluebell Cove for a few months, did any of it matter?

It was the end of her first week in the village and already Amelie had established a routine that began with a six-o'clock swim down in the cove each morning before the day got under way,

The beach was usually deserted at that time, apart from maybe a lone surfer. There was just the noise of the tide pounding in and the screeching of gulls overhead to break the silence.

On the third morning of that first week the lone surfer had turned out to be Leo, and when she'd appeared he'd come out of the waves carrying his board and watched her approach.

'Is this a regular thing for you?' he'd asked as they'd drawn level.

It was the first conversation they'd had that wasn't about work since Monday night, when he'd left rather abruptly. Even when there was just the two of them in the intimacy of the car while on house calls, they'd only talked about the two Ps—practice and patient—as if they were each wary of the other. So Amelie had been careful of what she'd said, even though the question he'd asked had been innocent enough.

'Yes, I've been coming down each morning at this time because it's so peaceful. It puts me right for the day. What about you? I suppose there is no novelty in having the sea so close for those who live here all the time.'

He had smiled. 'Of of course there is! I never cease to marvel at the view when I arrive at the headland. Harry was away from here for five years and Ethan has gone for good, but I don't want to leave Bluebell Cove ever.'

'Neither do I,' she'd said with unconscious wistfulness.

'Maybe we won't want you to when your time is up. Have you thought of that? You've only been with us a short time but Harry and I are already impressed with your medical knowledge and general aptitude.'

As he watched her face light up with pleasure he was

once again aware of the lack of guile of the young doctor from across the Channel who had even been ready with a good word for the guy who'd hurt and embarrassed her in the worst possible way.

Ignoring his vow to keep it cool between them, he said, 'How are you fixed for coming across to my place one evening? If you remember, I promised to return your hospitality.'

Her cheeks were stained with warm colour and her eyes wide as she told him, 'You don't have to do that. I'm sure you have better things to spend your time on than entertaining me.'

'Why not let me be judge of that?' he replied. 'So when would you like to come?'

'Whenever you say. All my evenings are free as I don't know anyone to socialise with.'

'Shall we say Friday night?' he suggested. 'We will drink a toast to the end of your first week in the practice.'

'That would be lovely.' She glowed. 'Thank you for inviting me…Leo. Is it all right if I call you by your first name when we're off duty?'

'Yes, I was beginning to wonder when you were going to drop the formalities.'

At that point she was throwing off the wrap she was wearing over her bikini and he felt his blood warming as he admired the smooth perfection of her body where everything was in such delightful proportion.

As if she'd sensed it, Amelie had kicked off her sandals and was running towards the sea. When she glanced over her shoulder she saw that Leo had thrown down the surfboard and was following her into the oncoming tide. As they swam together they were just two people enjoying themselves early on a spring morning.

Yet not for as long as they would have liked as not far away there was a waiting room that would soon be full of the people they had been trained to serve, and as they walked back to their respective dwelling places each was wishing they knew what the other was thinking.

But by the time Friday night arrived Amelie had forgotten their easy camaraderie on the beach. She was nervous.

She felt instinctively that she wasn't the kind of woman Leo would want to spend time with. He must have made the gesture out of politeness. How embarrassing *that* was going to be, especially if she had the verbal complaint again and gabbled all the time about something and nothing.

'Stop worrying,' she told her image in the mirror when she was ready to walk across to Leo's flat. Her ebony bob hadn't a hair out of place and the dress she was wearing always made her feel good because of its cut and colour. But she was still nervous at the thought of dining with the 'Angel Gabriel' again.

The windows of the apartment were wide open. She could hear music and laughter coming from above and hesitated. Leo hadn't said anything about anyone else being there.

When they'd made the arrangement on the beach she'd taken it for granted that it would be just the two of them, but it didn't sound like that. Had he invited some people round because she'd said she didn't know anyone to socialise with?

If that was the case, he should have warned her. There was no way she wanted to be an exhibit in front of a group of his friends. She turned quickly, went back to where she'd come from, and couldn't get the key in the lock fast enough.

It was an hour later when the doorbell rang and she got slowly to her feet, prepared to offer what now seemed like a weak excuse for not turning up for the meal that Leo had invited her to.

'So why didn't you come?' he asked unsmilingly. 'The food is spoiling.'

I'm sorry,' she said weakly. 'I was about to press the buzzer to your apartment when I heard what sounded like a party up above, and I couldn't face a lot of strangers at short notice. Why didn't you tell me you were having friends round so that I might have been prepared?'

He was frowning. 'I didn't tell you because I wasn't, that's why.'

'But I heard the voices and the music.'

'Yes, you probably did,' he commented dryly, 'but being new around here you won't know that there are two apartments. The other one, which Harry used to rent, is occupied by the new district nurse who has replaced Phoebe. She and her family are renting it until they find a house that suits them. They were the ones having the party.'

She listened to what he'd been saying in complete mortification. 'I am so sorry, but you should have told me. You are right about me not knowing about the other apartment. I remembered telling you I had no one to socialise with and thought you were doing something about it when I heard what was going on up above. But when it came to joining in the fun I could not face a room full of strangers.'

He sighed. 'The only person you would have found there is me, so do you want to come and risk my dried-up offerings, or put it down to experience?'

'I want to come,' she said immediately. 'If there is any excuse for the way I behaved it is that I haven't done any socialising since breaking up with the man who betrayed me. It took away a lot of my confidence in myself, but it is returning, and coming to Bluebell Cove is the best thing I've ever done, Leo.'

He was smiling again. 'So come on, then. The burnt offerings await us.'

CHAPTER FOUR

WHEN he'd invited Amelie to the apartment for a meal that morning on the beach and asked what night would be convenient, she'd said any night and indicated that her social life was non-existent, which was not surprising as she'd only been in Bluebell Cove for a week.

But it had caused him to wonder if it had been a hint. He was the only person she knew, both inside and outside the surgery, and he'd invited her to dine with him. It had been out of politeness and with the feeling of responsibility that had been there ever since he'd brought her to the village. He hoped she wasn't reading anything else into it.

To feel responsible for someone who had joined the practice from choice and who was already proving her worth was ridiculous, he'd thought afterwards. Amelie was no shrinking violet, yet neither was she streetwise and provocative, like some of the members of her sex who sought him out.

As he took her up the wooden staircase leading to the apartments that had been one of the focal points of Phoebe and Harry's romance, he was thinking that all his efforts in the kitchen were going to be well past their best because she'd panicked at the thought of meeting strangers. Yet wasn't that what she needed to do, and wasn't that what *he* was, in spite of them being forever in each other's company since she'd arrived…a stranger?

When he'd shown her into the apartment the first thing he did was check on the state of the hot dishes he'd prepared and left on a very low oven setting. They seemed to have survived and with his concerns about the role in which Amelie might be seeing him put to one side, he gave himself up to enjoying her company.

The evening that had started badly became an enjoyable occasion as Amelie relaxed into the situation.

She said how much she'd enjoyed the meal, having already decided that she would have eaten it even if it had been burnt to a crisp, but there'd been no need to do that. His cooking was better than hers, and the food hadn't been spoilt while she'd been dithering in the house across the way.

Over coffee they chatted about the hospital where she'd been based since getting her degree, and Leo told her so much about Manchester that she was keen to visit if the opportunity arose.

She was just as interested in anything connected with his life as he was in hers. Where she'd been nervous of spending time alone with him she was now relaxed and ready to talk. But remembering the last occasion when they'd dined together and she'd been verbal non-stop, she was wary of saying too much.

He thought the red linen dress she was wearing was a perfect foil for the raven's-wing colour of her hair, unaware that it was one of a scant selection in her wardrobe that was all the salary of a junior doctor allowed.

Having been with her the previous Saturday, when she'd come across a wedding in the village on the same day that it should have been hers, he wondered what sort of a dress she would have been wearing if it had come to pass, and felt a strange sort of protectiveness at the thought of her generosity in making allowances for her two-timing ex-fiancé's behaviour.

The door of the second bedroom was ajar while she was helping him to clear up after the meal, and the cot that Phoebe's little one had used while they had been living there was on view.

'That is from the time when Phoebe lived here,' he said laughingly. 'I'm not keeping it just in case. I like to be a free spirit and have no plans along those lines at present.'

She didn't join in the laughter. Instead she said, 'Neither have I. It will be a long time before I take any chances on love again. To feel unwanted is an awful experience.'

He didn't take her up on that or it would be there again, the compassion she aroused in him, which was crazy when he considered how long they'd known each other. But there was a simple dignity in the way she'd described her past and present life to him that pulled at his heartstrings.

When they went back into the sitting room Leo said whimsically, 'As you can see, my place is far less salubrious than yours. Phoebe managed to get around to painting the ceiling while she was resident here, but I feel that once she'd met Harry there were far more exciting things to do than decorating. So I'm going to remedy that the first chance I get, and when you come again you will see a big difference.'

So there was a chance she might be here again some time. Concealing her pleasure at the thought, Amelie went to the window and looked out into the night. The light was fading and a June moon shone like a great silver ball over the headland.

For the first time since she'd arrived at the apartment she let her mouth race ahead of her mind and said, 'Why don't we go for a swim in the moonlight, Leo?'

There was silence and she felt colour rise in her cheeks. He'd asked her round for a meal, not to go down to the beach.

He had come to stand beside her and into the silence that had followed the suggestion said, 'Yes, why not? I've done it before, and no doubt will do it again. It's a fantastic feeling. If you pop across and change into your swimming gear, I'll do the same and will meet you out at the front in ten minutes, OK?'

When they met up again he was carrying a beach bag containing a bottle of wine and two glasses, and with her thoughts still out of control she said, 'You are doing this because you're feeling sorry for me, aren't you?'

'Er, no,' he replied. 'I'm doing it because watching you in the water is something not to be missed, and it has given me an idea.'

'What do you mean?'

'Ronnie the lifeguard was saying the other day that he needed some help in the evenings, that the guy who shares the job with him is on long-term sick leave and the council is dragging its feet at finding a replacement. He said that just a couple of hours in the evenings would be much appreciated. At this time of year it's the busiest part of the day down there when folks have finished work and are ready to relax.

'Does the idea appeal to you? I'm sure there would be no problem with the authorities, as long as you were able to do a quick lifeguard refresher course. It would give them time to find someone permanent and it would help Ronnie, who is the father of Maria the young nurse at the surgery.'

Amelie didn't reply immediately. The idea appealed to her immensely, yet what she felt was behind it didn't. Leo had taken note of her comment about her evenings being empty, and to get himself off the hook had come up with an idea that could solve the problem. If she was down on the beach in the evenings as a lifeguard, she wouldn't be hoping that he would fill the gap.

But why should he? The man striding along beside her past the headland and down the steps that led to the cove where the last stragglers were beginning to wind their way upwards must have lots more interesting things to do with his kind of looks and personality.

'I wouldn't mind giving it a try if the authorities will allow it,' she said in a voice that told him she thought she'd read his mind. *So what if she did?*

Amelie had no idea how much she was getting to him

with her uncomplicated outlook on life and absence of coquettishness.

He felt sure the powers that be would agree to the idea, and he knew Ronnie would when he saw her perform. If he and they knew she'd been involved in rescuing the two young girls from the sea cave just a few days ago, he imagined they would jump at the chance of a temporary replacement. If Amelie was serious about what she'd said, he would start the ball rolling on Monday.

Not a lot moved in local government on Saturdays.

The tide was coming in less vigorously than it sometimes did and as they swam in its unaccustomed gentleness, with moonlight throwing shadows on the rocks and the sand that the sea hadn't yet reached, there was a tranquillity that they could both feel.

Amelie was so entranced by the magic of the evening that she fantasised about her role as temporary lifeguard leading to a permanent position if they didn't require her any more at the practice when her time was up. It would be one way of staying in Bluebell Cove, something she was increasingly keen to do, still saving lives but in a different way than at present.

They'd come out of the water, and were sitting on the rocks, idly watching the waves skipping over the sand towards them when Leo said, 'You being a doctor would fit in with the lifeguard role very nicely. Immediate medical assistance on the spot if needed, much better than simply having the required First Aid certificate.'

'Yes,' she said slowly, and almost told him he didn't have to sell her the idea. She was already sold on it. Sun, sea and sand were her life's blood. If at the same time as working at the practice she could put her abilities regarding those things to good use, why not?

The only problem was it being weekend tomorrow. It would be Monday before Leo could speak to anyone, and Saturday and Sunday loomed ahead as empty days.

'Why don't you come down here to have a word with Ronnie over the weekend?' Leo said, picking up on her thoughts. 'It would give you the chance to get to know him and find out what would be required of you in the evenings if the authorities are interested in employing you as a temporary lifeguard. He's a likeable guy.'

'Yes, I suppose I could do that,' she agreed.

It was almost as if he could read her mind. Though did he read it as far as realising that his eagerness to keep her occupied was beginning to show, was it another taste of the unwanted feeling that was bitter in her mouth?

If so, he ought to tell her. It was to be expected that Leo was living a full and happy life before she'd come on the scene, so it was to his credit that he was putting it on hold because he felt responsible for her.

But *she* didn't want it to be like that, just as much as she felt *he* didn't. She'd coped on her own for as long as she could remember, except for the short time that Antoine had been part of her life.

'Shall we go?' she asked flatly, as if the moon's light on sea and shore and the rugged cliffs behind them wasn't enough.

'Why the sudden drop in spirits?' Leo asked, as if

he didn't know. 'Shall we forget the idea of the beach patrol, Amelie? It was only a thought.'

'No, of course not!' she protested. 'It was kind of you to suggest it. I will come down here tomorrow and introduce myself to Ronnie.' Then it happened again, the words were out before she could stop them. 'What plans have *you* made for the weekend?'

Fortunately a cloud passed over the moon at that moment and he didn't observe her mortification at the intrusion into his life once again. Taken aback for a second by the directness of the question, he replied, 'Tennis tomorrow morning with my friend Naomi, a trip to town in the afternoon, and in the evening out for a meal with friends, maybe moving on to a nightclub later.

'On Sundays I do what chores have to be done, go to the pub for an hour late morning, and maybe drive into the countryside in the afternoon for a Devonshire clotted-cream tea.'

'What is that?' she asked curiously.

'Fresh scones, thick clotted cream that the county is renowned for and strawberry conserve or jam.'

'It sounds delightful.'

'It is,' he replied, and thought it would be so easy to suggest he call for her on Sunday and take her with him if she would like that, yet he wasn't going to. He had to ease off with the woman beside him, otherwise his well-planned bachelor life, stereotyped as it sometimes was, might fall apart if he veered off in a new direction, and *that* would cause some raised eyebrows amongst those he worked with at the practice.

He knew that Harry thought he was crazy, living the carefree life that he'd always led, but the senior partner was in love and had Phoebe and her child who loved him in return. Soon she would give birth to another little one that would be theirs entirely and his joy would know no bounds.

If he was in a situation like the other man's, he would approach life from a different angle, but he wasn't, and neither was he likely to be while mixing with the 'in crowd'.

The life he'd lived ever since losing Delphine was a defence against ever experiencing that sort of pain and heartbreak again. Even now, with the years having gone by, he still couldn't talk about it, so Harry could only judge him from outward appearances.

He got to his feet and said, 'I suppose we *had* better make tracks or Naomi will be calling for me in the morning and I won't be up.'

As they walked back to the village in the silent night Amelie risked another question about his private life, which she didn't think would offend. 'Does your tennis partner live locally?'

'Yes,' he said easily. 'She returned to Bluebell Cove, where she was brought up, some months ago after a distressing divorce, and we got to know each other at the tennis club.'

'Oh, I see,' she said, and thought what could be more appealing than an attractive blonde divorcee? Certainly not a nondescript junior doctor who couldn't even keep Antoine the unadventurous happy.

Their two residences were in sight and Amelie

knew she didn't want this time with Leo to end. Yet end it must, as the next thought that had come to mind was what it would feel like to be kissed by the Angel Gabriel.

When they stopped at her gate it was clear that the man by her side had no such thoughts. His mind was on more mundane things, such as a reminder to lock up securely before she went to bed and a wish for the best of luck with Ronnie down on the beach the next morning.

But she couldn't let him go with just that. Thanks were due because he had given up his evening for her and she said awkwardly, 'I've had a lovely time, Leo. Thank you for the meal and the rest of the evening.' Standing on tiptoe, she brushed her lips lightly against his cheek.

At the moment of contact he stepped back and Amelie felt her colour rise again. When would she ever learn? Antoine's treatment of her should have made it clear that she wasn't ever going to be any man's dream girl. Leo had backed off as if she was infectious, and that was after just a thank-you peck on the cheek. The pleasure of the time they'd spent together was disappearing like water down a drain.

He sensed her hurt. Could tell by her expression that he'd hit a nerve and wanted to kick himself for upsetting her, but Amelie wasn't to know that he was telling himself all the time to cool it with the young French doctor, and a peck on the cheek might soon transfer itself to the lips, and could go on from there.

'You don't have to thank me for *anything,* Amelie,' he

said abruptly, to bring an end to the awkward moment that had come out of nowhere. 'It is just a matter of being polite to a stranger who feels out of things because she knows no one here… And now I'm going to say goodnight.'

She nodded, and without speaking watched him move briskly towards the apartments without a backward glance.

'Ugh!' she breathed when she was inside with the door locked, as Leo had instructed. For someone known as the village Romeo he had taken a dim view of that butterfly kiss on the cheek, which was all it had been. What was the matter with the man?

Hadn't she made it clear that she wasn't in the market for love, or any of the trappings that went with it? And even if she had been, she was way out of his league, so why had he shied away from a simple expression of gratitude?

Up in the apartment Leo was also taking stock of those embarrassing moments outside the house across the way when Amelie had tried to thank him and been repulsed.

She wasn't to know how much she'd got through to him during the evening by just being there, and how much he'd known it would be a mistake to let those kinds of feelings take hold. The outcome of it was that it had to stop.

As from Monday morning it was going to be strictly business and nothing else between them. He'd played his part in making her welcome. Now she was on her own, socially and at the practice.

The hire car they'd arranged for her was there, waiting to be used, so he was going to suggest to Harry that she should do some of the house calls on her own, leaving him free of the close contact with her in his car, which couldn't be avoided.

He was as easy with women socially as he was with men, but it was all on the surface. With Amelie it wasn't like that and he knew why. It was as he kept telling himself, she was different, natural, easy to be with, and had a special kind of charm of her own.

With regard to what *she* thought of *him* he'd had a few laughs at the Angel Gabriel description and decided she was way out there. Angelic he was not! Caring and compassionate, yes, maybe, but never that!

The curtains were still drawn at the house across the way when he got up the next morning and he wondered if Amelie really was intending going down to the beach to introduce herself to Ronnie.

When he glanced across again, after having a shower and the leisurely breakfast that was part of the pleasure of Saturdays, the curtains had been opened and he caught a glimpse of Amelie as she passed the surgery in the direction of the beach.

She was dressed for swimming with her suit on under a sarong and was carrying a towel, so was obviously a woman of her word, he thought wryly, and wished he hadn't made the suggestion of her getting to know

Ronnie. He had to admit that he liked having her all to himself.

He was already dressed for tennis and had an hour to spare before Naomi was due to call for him. If he put on some speed he might catch Amelie before she got to the beach and persuade her to change her mind.

When he arrived at the headland he saw it was a vain hope. She was already down there, chatting to Ronnie, and there was no way he could intrude.

She looked upwards suddenly and he moved into the shadow of a nearby tree, hoping that she hadn't spotted him skulking up there. She was a pleasure to have around, he thought, but life was becoming more complicated by the minute.

Turning quickly, he headed back to the village and a morning on the tennis courts with Naomi that he wasn't going to enjoy as much as he usually did because each time the ball came over the net Amelie's face would be in the way.

She *had* seen him up on the headland. The white shirt and shorts he was wearing had made him stand out amongst the rocks and shrubs above and Amelie thought surely Leo wasn't so keen to get her off his back that he'd come to check that she was following through their discussion of the night before and having a word with Ronnie?

He was gone in a flash, most likely watching the time for his game of tennis, and she thought sombrely that he need have no further concerns on her behalf. The message had come over loud and clear the night before and no way was he going to see sight or sound of her out of surgery hours from now on.

In fact, she would go even further than that and ask Dr Balfour if she could start doing her share of house calls on her own as she felt confident enough to do so. If he agreed, the only time she and Leo would be in contact was during the morning and afternoon surgeries when for most of the time they would be closeted with their patients.

Her feelings were a mixture of rejection and annoyance with herself for letting her attraction to Leo blind her to the fact that he was just doing the polite thing by looking after her as he had been doing, but he need exert himself no further.

From now on she would be back to her own coping self, the self that he had yet to see, and after being told by the lifeguard that he would welcome her presence on the beach in the evenings and would speak to the authorities regarding her refresher course, he'd even suggested that she join him this very evening to get a feel for the role.

She'd agreed with the suggestion promptly. It meant that what would have been a lonely weekend wasn't going to be so bad because she would be spending most of the time with her other loves, sun, sand and the never-failing tides.

But what would it be like to be loved by the man she'd only known for such a short time, yet couldn't stop thinking about? The same man who'd made it quite clear the night before that she was just an encumbrance, so *he* wasn't going to look in her direction was he? She wasn't his type.

Still, her spirits were lifting as she walked around at the side of the lifeguard and listened to what Ronnie had to say about the organising of beach patrols and the dangers that were never far away.

There were lots of parents with children milling around and teenage lovelies out to attract young males by pouting in front of cameras, which prompted Ronnie to comment that he had a daughter their age.

'Yes, so I believe,' she told him. 'You are the father of Maria, the young nurse at the surgery, aren't you?'

He nodded. 'That I am. Maria has mentioned you often. So what do you think of Bluebell Cove? I hear Dr Fenchurch has been showing you around.'

'Yes, he has been most kind. As for Bluebell Cove, it's lovely. I would like to live here.'

'So what is there to stop you?'

Instead of answering directly, she replied, 'I don't know anyone here.'

'You soon will,' he assured her. 'Working in the surgery and helping out down here, you'll be known to everyone in no time.'

As they strolled around there was no cause for alarm. Everyone was behaving sensibly, and as Amelie listened to Ronnie describing the job and indicating the danger spots on the part of the coastline that he and his fellow lifeguard were in charge of the day dawdled along.

After his earlier furtive appearance on the headland Leo stayed away from the cove when the tennis was over and made his usual Saturday afternoon trip into the town, but by the time he arrived back in the village he was feeling that he couldn't avoid Amelie any longer.

He told himself it was to make sure she was all right after his rejection of her kiss on his cheek that she'd bestowed upon him, which was true in part, but the main reason was that he just wanted to see her, if only for a short time.

He felt that if only he would let her, she could bring a different dimension to his life, but the problem was he wasn't ready for it. The way he'd behaved when she'd kissed him had been proof of that.

On Amelie's part, her vulnerability was plain to see, and from the little she'd told him about her life till now it wasn't surprising.

Now she'd come to Bluebell Cove, where he'd found himself taking her under his wing, reluctantly sometimes and at others with great pleasure.

It had to stop. She'd had enough upsets in her life. He didn't want to be responsible for another. Added to that his own past had been far from easy, and the pain of it still clung to him, as did the dread of ever having to go through something like that again, and to avoid it he'd chosen the kind of life he'd been living ever since.

Until now he'd had no doubts about it, but along had come Amelie and everything was changing. He had to call a halt. She knew nothing of *his* past and the reason why he'd never turned to anyone else after losing Delphine.

He had never opened his heart to anyone and did not want to put his burden onto her.

She was the first person his glance rested on when he'd parked the car and was walking down the slipway. She was wearing a scarlet bathing costume that was the same colour as the dress of the night before, and once again the colour made a vivid contrast to her hair and the smooth olive skin of her face.

Ronnie was beside her as they chatted to a group of holidaymakers all in a happy mood. She looked carefree and relaxed amongst them, so much so that he turned on his heel and retraced his steps back to the car.

Leave well alone, he told himself as he reversed out of the car park.

Amelie didn't get a glimpse of him on that occasion. She was too engrossed with the people she was meeting down below, but Leo wasn't out of her mind, far from it. She'd been longing to see him all day. After him telling her what *he'd* had planned for the weekend, she'd been following him in his various pursuits in her mind, and not having seen him on the causeway she reckoned that he would be somewhere either in the town or on his way back.

Yet what did it matter where he was? He could at least have rung her first thing or called at the house for them to make peace. Though why should he? Leo had explained the night before in no uncertain terms the reason for his presence in her limited social life. So instead of fretting she should be grateful that someone like him had been prepared to take the trouble.

She left the beach in the early evening with a promise from Ronnie that he would be in touch as soon as he'd spoken to the powers that be, and windblown and sun-kissed she decided to have an early night.

That resolve was short-lived when Harry Balfour rang to invite her to supper. 'We usually have a few friends round on Saturday nights,' he said, 'and thought that maybe you would like to join us.'

'Our home, Glades Manor, is about a mile out of the village. If you don't want to walk, the car we've hired for you is on the practice forecourt in readiness for Monday morning and Leo has the keys.'

'I think I would prefer to walk,' she told him, 'and thank you for inviting me, Dr Balfour. I would love to come.'

Having already been told how Leo spent his Saturday evenings, she doubted he would be there, so there shouldn't be any awkwardness to cope with from that direction, and as she showered and dressed for the occasion in the red dress once again, it felt odd.

There hadn't been many days since coming to Bluebell Cove that Leo hadn't been a part of, she thought, and knew that the pleasant and interesting time she'd spent with the lifeguard on the beach, and the unexpected invitation to supper, were not going to make up for it.

CHAPTER FIVE

WALKING towards Phoebe and Harry's house in the warm summer evening was pleasant exercise and when Amelie eventually stood in front of the beautiful old building situated in a green glade that was surrounded by the fertile fields of Devon, it wasn't hard to guess from where the name of Glades Manor came.

As she stopped at the gates, taking in the scene, Phoebe came out to greet her, glowing in the later stages of pregnancy, and as the two women shook hands Amelie said, 'Your house is beautiful, Phoebe.'

'Yes, it is,' she agreed, with a smile for the young French doctor. 'The three of us are so happy here.' She patted her extended waistline. 'And soon there will be four.

'Come inside and meet the others,' she said, leading the way into the house.

Amelie obeyed cautiously, bracing herself for the introductions that must surely follow.

An elderly woman in a wheelchair turned out to be *the* Barbara Balfour, one-time head of the practice and Harry's aunt. The man standing beside her was her husband, Keith. An attractive blonde with a friendly smile was introduced as Jenna, daughter of the elderly couple, and her distinguished-looking husband was Lucas Devereux, the heart surgeon.

Elderly, grey bearded and the last to be introduced of the members of the small supper party was Desmond Somerby, the local Member of Parliament.

With the exception of Barbara Balfour, who was looking her over as if she was something under a microscope, they were all pleasant and friendly towards the newcomer in their midst. There was just one thing stopping her from enjoying herself: Leo wasn't there.

She knew why, of course. He would be somewhere in the town, hitting the night spots with his friends. When Harry had rung her she'd been relieved at the thought of not having the encumbrance label of the night before stuck on her once again, but it had been a long day without him and could be an even longer evening in spite of the good company she was with.

At one point in the evening the doctor who had made the Tides Practice her life's work wheeled herself across to where Amelie was sitting and said, 'They tell me at the surgery that you are doing well so far, Dr Benoir. How do you like our country and our National Health Service?'

Amelie's wide smile flashed out. 'I love everything about it, Dr Balfour, and feel privileged to have the opportunity of being employed in such a lovely place.'

The eyes that had looked her over speculatively when she'd arrived had lost their chill and the woman beside her was smiling as she said, 'That is what I wanted to hear. You have two excellent doctors to call on at the practice if need be, and our womenfolk will be happy to see someone of their own sex available to treat them. I hope that you enjoy your time with us.'

Amelie hadn't heard a car pull up outside because of the chatter inside, but a ring on the doorbell brought a moment's silence as Harry went to see who was there. The voice coming from the hallway was easily recognisable.

'I'm sorry to butt in,' she heard Leo say. 'I've only just seen the email you sent to say that Amelie might need the keys for the hire car to get here tonight. I went out at five o'clock and have only just got back, so I came to make sure that she found you all right and to see that she gets home safely.'

She had listened to what he was saying with a mixture of pleasure and surprise that had overtones of embarrassment as the rest of the guests observed her curiously.

When he appeared in the doorway of the sitting room, his glance went straight to her. Not caring that he had an audience, he said, 'I'm sorry about the car keys, Amelie. What did you do, walk or get a taxi?'

'It was such a beautiful evening I walked here,' she told him as the long day without his presence righted itself.

Phoebe appeared at that moment to call them in to supper, which was being served in the dining room, and with a smile for Leo said, 'You are just in time.'

'That is the best news I've heard today,' he said laughingly. 'I've had a joiner doing some work in the apartment for me. He was using a saw and it slipped and sliced into his hand, so I had to take him to hospital, and we were in A and E for ages, waiting for him to be seen. There'd been a pile-up on the motorway and quite a few casualties had been brought in just before we got there at five o'clock this evening He was seen to eventually, they put sutures in the cut and I've just taken him home.'

His gaze had been on Amelie all the time he'd been speaking, taking in the glow that a day on the beach had given her and admiring once again the red dress that suited her colouring so much.

He wanted to ask her what Ronnie had said about her helping out as a temporary lifeguard, and if she'd enjoyed her time down there with him. Ronnie was a staunch family man who loved his wife and children and would see that Amelie came to no harm.

Questions like those would have to be asked in the car on the way home, he decided, and made sure that he sat beside her at the supper table, telling himself that it was just in case she was feeling out of her depth amongst strangers.

It was gone midnight and he had her to himself at last, but before he could ask her about her day Amelie had a question for him.

'Why didn't you come down off the headland this morning?' she asked. 'Were you spying on me?'

'Spying? Of course not!' he protested indignantly. 'Checking up on you, yes. I wanted to make sure you were all right after last night, and from where I was standing it seemed that you were, so I went. Does that satisfy you?'

'Yes. I suppose so.'

'You don't sound so sure.'

'Well, last night you made me feel like an encumbrance, yet you are still involved in your unnecessary "duty" of keeping an eye on me, as on the headland this morning, and tonight.'

He sighed. 'What about tonight?'

'You came looking for me to make sure I would get home safely and...'

Her voice was thickening and when he gave her a quick sideways glance he saw the wetness of tears on her cheeks.

'You're crying, Amelie. What have I done now?'

'Nothing,' she sobbed. 'It's just that you are the first person to care a damn about me in ages. I know it's because you feel that you must under the circumstances, me being alone in your country and the rest of it, but you didn't have to, did you, Leo? You could have left me to my own devices.'

Pulling the car up at the side of the road, he took a tissue out of a box in the glove compartment and wiped her eyes gently. As she gazed at him tearfully he reached out and took her in his arms, and as she nestled against him he patted her shoulder and said, 'Shush, don't cry, Amelie. If you keep saying things like that, I'll be getting too big for my boots.'

She was smiling up at him through her tears. 'I don't think the Angel Gabriel ever had that problem.'

'Yes, well, we won't go into that,' he said dryly. 'I've

already explained that angelic I am not. Though I must admit that getting to know you is proving to be character building.'

'Now you're laughing at me,' she protested.

'No, I'm not,' he informed her gravely, 'but if I'm supposed to have your welfare at heart, I ought to be taking you home at the end of a long day, and while I'm doing that you can tell me what Ronnie had to say and if you are still keen on the beach patrol idea.'

He removed his arms from around her and switched on the engine, and as she settled back in her seat she told him, 'He is all for it and is going to speak to someone about getting me retrained and starting as soon as possible.'

'So you're happy about that?'

'Yes, I am, just as long as you'll come to see me down on the beach sometimes.'

'Of course. It goes without saying, if only to watch you swim.'

When they arrived at the house he saw her safely inside and when she would have asked him to stop for a coffee he forestalled her as he'd done before by saying, 'Make sure you lock up securely, Amelie.'

Pushing caution to one side, she asked, 'When will I see you again?' And he found himself ignoring the vows he'd made not to spend so much time with her.

'You know the Devonshire cream tea that I mentioned as part of my Sunday afternoon routine? How about I pick you up at three o'clock tomorrow and introduce you to yet another of the delights of this part of the world?'

'Yes. I'd love that,' she told him.

'It has to be on a promise, though.'

'What sort of promise?' she asked slowly, coming back down to earth.

'No more tears, Amelie.'

She smiled. 'I think I can promise that.'

The smile was still there as she went upstairs to the big empty bed in the master bedroom of the house. But Leo's expression was more sombre as he went to his own solitary bed. He hadn't wanted to leave her. Had gone against all his promises to himself to cool it with Amelie by arranging to spend time with her tomorrow. The last thing he wanted to do was cause her more heartbreak after her experience with the French guy. He should have had more sense.

But at least he wouldn't be as much in her orbit after tomorrow. On Monday Amelie would be on her own for home visits, and closeted away in her own small consulting room the rest of the time. If she went down to the beach in the evenings she would be fully occupied there, while he would be fretting on the sidelines, wanting her, yet not wanting her, because with commitment could come pain and hurt that knew no bounds. He accepted that what had happened to him and Delphine was likely to occur only in one in a thousand people's lives, but it had done nothing to ease the heartache and loss that had made him what he was now.

When Leo called for Amelie the next afternoon she was ready and waiting, bluebell eyes sparkling with the pleasure of being with him again. Dressed in white leggings and a turquoise casual top that showed off the tan that she was gradually acquiring, he could hardly believe that she was the same bedraggled woman that he'd gone to meet at the airport. It might be simpler if she was, he thought wryly, then he wouldn't be living from one moment of seeing her to the next.

Georgina had phoned earlier to ask why he'd been missing the night before. He'd told her about taking the joiner to hospital and she'd been mildly sympathetic, then changed the subject to a cruise she'd booked and asked if he wished he was going with her.

He'd made no comment but thought there wasn't anything he fancied less than that. Taking Amelie into the countryside was the uppermost thought in his mind and after they'd exchanged a few stilted sentences Georgina had rung off.

He took Amelie to a farm restaurant for afternoon tea, and as he watched her enjoying the food she said, 'I skipped lunch and saved my hunger pangs for this.'

'It would seem so,' he replied whimsically. Leaning forward, he wiped a blob of cream off the end of her nose with a paper napkin. As she smiled across at him it all seemed so right, the two of them together, light-hearted and in tune on a summer afternoon.

When they'd finished eating he said, 'Do you want to go for a stroll before we go back? There's an old and empty abbey not far from here. It's a tourist attraction now, a beautiful ancient building that brings a lot of visitors.'

She was observing him in surprise. 'I'd love to see it,

but are you sure, Leo? I wouldn't have thought it would be your type of thing.'

'Really? And so what *would* you expect it to be? A casino, a club, dining at the Ritz?' he said dryly, and it was clear that he wasn't joking. Before she could reply he went on, 'My looks are the bane of my life. They automatically say party person, and even my profession doesn't totally dispel the image. Sometimes I take the easy way out and just do what is expected of me.'

It might have been a good moment to explain why he lived the kind of life he did, which was a strange mix of dedicated doctor and playboy, but the day had yet to come when he was ready to confess that to anyone, so he told her, 'Yes, I am happy to visit the abbey. Shall we make a move in that direction? I'm not sure what time it closes on Sundays.'

She nodded and with the brightness of the afternoon dimming fell into step beside him. It was clear that her casual remark had hit a nerve where Leo was concerned. She'd better be more careful in future. Yet did she want to have to do that, watch what she said all the time?

When they arrived at the abbey and joined a party being shown around by a guide, he took her hand and said in a low voice, 'Sorry I was snappy. It was directed at life in general, not at you.'

'It's all right,' she told him, vowing to be more careful about what she said around him. Obviously she'd hit a sore spot, and she remembered when in fun she'd mentioned the angel Gabriel comparison, and he'd been quick to point out that the outside appearance of a person was just the shell. It was what was beneath it that mattered.

He was still holding her hand as they admired the stained-glass windows of another age and the empty cloisters that the monks had occupied. When they came out of the shadowed interior into the sunlight he said, 'Old buildings fascinate me. Take Harry's house, for example. It has a charm that modern architecture will never capture.'

She shrugged and there was indifference in the movement. 'My parents own a chateau.'

He was observing her in amazement. 'What? They live in a chateau?'

'Yes, though only rarely. They are away such a lot and are not in residence more than twice a year.'

'And what about you, Amelie? Don't *you* ever stay there?'

'Not if I can help it. The chateau is beautiful from the outside but dusty and damp inside.'

'You amaze me,' he said as they began the walk back to the restaurant to collect the car.

'Why is that?'

'It is difficult to describe. You seem frail, yet you are strong. Have no false pride, and can forgive those who hurt you.'

'Stop!' she cried. 'You are making me into what I am not.'

'So how do *you* see yourself?'

'As a very ordinary person in a beautiful foreign land.'

'I'll bear that in mind,' he said laughingly. 'You are a very ordinary person whose family own a chateau.'

'Yes, that is what I am, and would prefer a house with central heating.'

They were almost home and Leo was about to deliver a body blow. He was going to explain that he hadn't been able to resist spending the afternoon and early evening with her, but now it had to stop because he felt he wasn't being fair in monopolising her, as he had been from the day of her arrival in the village.

It wasn't the truth, of course. If the past wasn't still tugging at him, he would have no reason to back away from her and would 'monopolise' her to his heart's content.

But he'd never overcome the aching void inside him because after Delphine he didn't trust himself to be able to carry through the demands of complete commitment to another woman.

He wasn't sure how Amelie would react when he'd said what he had to say. She was not predictable, but he was soon going to find out. When they pulled up outside her temporary residence he said gravely, 'Can I come in for a moment?'

'Yes, of course,' she said brightly, with the pleasure of the time they'd just spent together coming through in her smile.

'Can I get you a drink?' she asked when they were facing each other in the sitting room.

He shook his head. 'No, thanks. I will say what I have to say and then I'll go.'

Her eyes widened and she said with a shaky laugh, 'That sounds ominous. What is it that I have done?'

You've changed my life, was the reply he would like to have had for her, but it would hardly fit in with what he'd been grimly rehearsing.

He watched the colour drain from her face as he began to speak in what he hoped was a voice of logical calmness. When he'd finished she said with quiet dignity, 'You have just made something that was light-hearted and casual seem as nothing. I have felt sometimes that you found me too much in your face. It was why you suggested I could occupy my evenings down on the beach, wasn't it? As to your comment about monopolising me, I don't hear you asking how I feel about that, if I liked it or not. It's more a matter of you offloading me, isn't it, Leo? I will bear in mind what you have said, and now will you please go.'

He took a step towards her and with her voice rising she said, 'Do not come near me, Leo. All my pleasure at being in your country is due to you and the practice, but mostly to you. Now it has gone and I have done nothing wrong that I am aware of.

'I will not repay Dr Lomax, far away in France, for his kindness by breaking my contract with the Tides surgery. But the moment it is complete I will be gone.'

He had listened in silence to what she had to say, the same as *she* had done while *he* had been saying *his* piece, and now he pointed himself towards the door and did as she'd asked, wanting to kick himself for not telling her about Delphine.

* * *

When he'd gone she walked slowly up the stairs and threw herself down on the bed. White-faced and tearless, she gazed up at the ceiling.

You are the unwanted one again, she told herself, and don't blame Leo. He has been merely doing the honours on behalf of the practice and now wants to end it so that he can get on with his own life again, so don't take offence.

Yet this time she didn't feel prepared to turn the other cheek. She'd done no wrong in being attracted to a man who had shown her nothing but kindness and was now wearying of the task he had set himself. The coming Monday morning at the practice was taking on the shape of an ordeal instead of the pleasurable time she'd been looking forward to.

In the apartment across the way Leo's thoughts were no happier.

He'd already suggested to Harry that Amelie should do the easiest of the home visits on her own as from Monday. So when she was informed of the arrangement she was going to see it as a follow-up to today's catastrophic clearing of the air, which would make everything worse between them.

What she'd said kept going through his mind. That he'd turned a relationship that had been light-hearted and casual into nothing. It had been a bit strong but he'd got the gist of it, and admitted he deserved top marks for the effort he'd put into spoiling it.

He'd even found her an evening job down on the beach to keep them apart, which she'd referred to coldly.

Yet he had known he wouldn't be able to keep away from her even then. She was the best thing that had happened to him in years, but because he couldn't forget the past he'd spoilt what they'd had.

She'd already been hurt by lover boy across the Channel, and been cursed with parents who were never there for her. He longed to make up for those things, but whether *he* would ever be the right one for Amelie was another matter.

He wasn't wrong about her reaction when Harry said first thing on Monday morning, 'You are on your own today with the home visits, Amelie. We're passing on to you the ones that should be the least traumatic. Although one can never be sure of that. Some of the calls we receive asking for a visit don't describe clearly enough the seriousness of the problem. Anyway, see how you get on. If you come across anything you can't handle, give one of us a ring.'

She managed a smile that was a cover-up for what she was really thinking, which was that Leo had to be behind her suddenly being seen as ready to work on her own.

As if Harry had read her mind he said, 'Having had you with him while he was doing house calls, Leo feels that you are ready to go solo.'

There had been no sign of him so far and she said casually, 'Where is Leo, Dr Balfour? I haven't seen him since I arrived.'

'Went out on an urgent call at eight o'clock and

isn't back yet,' he said briefly, and went to sort out his own day.

By the time Leo returned, Amelie was already dealing with her allocation of those in the waiting room, and as the morning progressed there was no time to dwell on anything but the problems of patients who had come for help and relief from the failings of the body.

Jonah Trelfa was one of those. A strapping sixty-year-old farmer with snow-white hair and a ruddy complexion, he'd come with chest pains and breathlessness, which had set alarm bells ringing.

Amelie had worked in a cardiac unit in the French hospital that she'd left in so much haste to catch her flight to the UK, and knew the signs of a heart problem.

'Is it just indigestion, Doctor?' he asked when she'd finished examining him, almost pleading for a reprieve.

'I don't think so, Mr Trelfa,' she told him gently. 'Your heart is not behaving itself at the present time and needs sorting. If you would like to come with me to the nurses' room they will do an ECG and we'll take it from there.'

The results indicated that atrial fibrillation was present and before she sent for an ambulance Amelie went to seek out one of the other doctors to confirm that she was doing the right thing.

Harry was with a patient but Leo had just returned from what had turned out to be a lengthy house call, and as their glances met she was relieved that their first meeting after the putdown of Sunday night should be about the needs of someone else rather than their own.

When she'd explained about Jonah's ECG she said, 'Could you spare a moment to examine him first before I summon an ambulance?'

'Yes, of course,' he replied, and when he'd done as she asked said, 'Send Mr Trelfa to the cardiac unit straight away. There are worse heart defects than atrial fibrillation, but no GP should hesitate to send a patient with that kind of problem to be checked out.'

As he turned to go he asked in a low voice, 'Everything all right?'

'Yes. Fine. Just doing my job *and* taking life as it comes,' she told him lightly, then closed the door behind him and gave her attention to Jonah, who needed her more than Leo did. But the feeling that life in Bluebell Cove had lost its sparkle was still very much in her mind.

She'd been totally content since arriving there with a place in the practice waiting for her, and with Leo, fantastic Leo, kind and supportive all the time. But now he wanted to opt out of their brief enchanted relationship for reasons that *he* understood...and *she* didn't.

By the time Jonah had departed in the ambulance to Hunter's Hill Hospital, exhibiting a stoic calm for someone with newly diagnosed heart disease, Leo was closeted with his own patients and the morning progressed in the Tides Practice until it was time for a quick bite and then off into coast and countryside to visit the sick and suffering. So far the only time they had spoken had been the brief exchange of words about a patient.

That was about to change. When Amelie went out onto the forecourt of the practice to acquaint herself with the car that had been provided for her, Leo was on the point of leaving but stopped when he saw her. Winding down the car window, he asked, 'So are you au fait with the arrangements for today, Amelie?'

'And what arrangements would they be?' she asked coolly.

'Doing the home visits on your own.'

'Yes. I'm "au fait" with most things', she told him. 'I'll phone if there is anything I am not sure of.'

'Of course,' was the reply, 'but we *are* talking about the practice.'

'Exactly,' she agreed, and settled herself behind the wheel of the hire car with a determination that had a message of its own.

Her first call was at the home of a smart middle-aged woman called Beverley McBride, who was much involved in village affairs, but not on this occasion.

A week ago she had been operated on for the removal of her gall bladder by keyhole surgery and of the three incisions made in her chest and stomach, two were healing well, but the third was not.

It had the redness of inflammation with a blueish tinge to it and Amelie prescribed antibiotics, along with a warning that if there was no improvement in a couple of days to contact the practice immediately.

'I'm surprised you didn't go back to the hospital as that is the place where you could have caught the infection,' she said when the patient was ready for off.

'Yes, I know,' Beverley agreed, 'but when I was

discharged they said if I had any problems I must see my GP.'

'Fair enough,' Amelie replied, unaware that she would be seeing Beverley McBride again very soon.

Her next call was a routine one at the moment. A daily visit to yet another middle-aged woman who had just had a bone from a bone bank fitted in her hip socket in place of her own, which had crumbled away, and was being given regular injections in the stomach to stop infection at such a delicate stage of her recovery.

It was all very exciting to be working on her own instead of being the onlooker that she'd been when out on the district with Leo, but it didn't take away the hurt she'd been carrying around with her ever since the previous night.

Having accomplished all the visits she'd been given to do, Amelie was driving back to the surgery when she was surprised to see Leo parked at the side of the road in the process of changing a flat tyre. When she would have driven past, he flagged her down.

When they'd separated outside the surgery and he'd driven off in the opposite direction from her, he'd thought so much for last night's diplomacy—a bull in a china shop would have been less clumsy.

He must have been insane to be prepared to cancel out their attraction to each other because of what had happened long ago, but its effect on him was still there in the form of always avoiding any kind of commitment with the opposite sex, and he'd felt that was where they were heading.

He'd never given much thought over the years to

what those he met saw him as, had been carefree and popular wherever he'd gone, but had always been on his guard.

Then along had come Amelie, younger than him and on her own due to the selfishness of others. He'd been jolted out of the life he'd led and was having to take a long, hard look at himself.

He supposed meeting her might not have led to so much soul-searching if he hadn't the example of Harry and Phoebe's love for each other always in front of him, along with the other man's comments about what he saw as Leo's empty life, a situation that would have lingered on if he hadn't met Amelie.

So what had he done? He'd called a halt to the wonderful thing that had been happening between them before it had had a chance to take hold because he was discovering that her happiness was very important to him.

For her to be hurt again by him would be unthinkable if he couldn't forget Delphine, so he'd been prepared to end it, hadn't slept a wink afterwards, and the result was she hadn't been prepared to stop on seeing him there by the roadside until he'd waved her down.

He wasn't to know that the desire to pull in beside him had been there but not the certainty that it was the right thing to do after what he'd said the night before, so she would have driven on if he hadn't signalled for her to stop.

When she went to stand beside him in a lay-by at the road edge, with a reluctance that didn't go unobserved, he was almost done and ready to be off, but looking down at his hands, which were decidedly oily, it seemed as if it was the right moment to say, 'I flagged you down to ask if you have any wipes with you to get my hands clean. I usually have some in the glove compartment but must have run out.'

He'd been so desperate to have a moment alone with her that he'd come up with a trite excuse to get her to stop, and as she fished a packed out of her bag and handed it to him he thought that it had been all he could think of at that moment, and hoped that in the near future Amelie would have no reason to look in the place he'd described as being empty of them.

As he wiped the grime off his hands the silence she was hiding behind continued, and wanting to end it he asked, 'So how has it gone, doing the rounds on your own?'

She spoke at last and her voice sounded stiff and formal. 'All right, thank you. Dr Balfour explained it was on your advice that I was doing some of the rounds on my own, and I felt quite sure that it was all part and parcel of last night's dumping.'

'That's an ugly word. I hate it.'

'But you don't hate what it stands for. You'd already put your plans into motion for getting rid of me with regard to our shared visits to the patients, and followed it up by preaching the gospel according to you. But as I'm used to the role of cast-off, it wasn't such a shock. Though there is one thing that puzzles me, Leo.'

'And what is that?' he asked bleakly.

'You've never made love to me or even kissed me. So why did you warn me off, unless you thought the nondescript French doctor at the surgery might fall in love with you and mess up your pleasure-loving private life?

'If that *was* the case, you need no longer concern yourself. You are just one of those who have found me surplus to requirements, so fret not.' And, wanting to make a statement, she strode across to her car with a graceful leisured step until, with her hand almost on the door handle, she was swung round and found her face only inches away from his.

'Did you listen to a word I said last night?' he demanded. 'Or were you so full of your hurt that it didn't register with you that I was trying to save you from more of the same kind of thing?

'No, I've never kissed you, or made love to you, and you think it's because I don't want to, do you? Well, how about this for an introduction?' Taking her face between his still oily hands, he kissed her, gently at first, then, as she became aroused, more demandingly, until she was limp in his arms.

It took another motorist pulling up noisily in the lay-by to bring them back to reality. With cheeks bright red and the rest of her weak with longing Amelie moved out of his arms and as they faced each other he said huskily, 'Now do you understand?'

'No!' she told him weakly. 'I don't. How can I?'

Opening the car door, she eased herself into the driver's seat and drove off into the summer afternoon, leaving him standing motionless, as if the last few moments had turned him into stone.

CHAPTER SIX

THE next morning, with all three doctors closeted with their patients in the first surgery of the day, Amelie considered that for anyone else those stolen moments in the lay-by would have been the beginning of a tender, breathtaking romance, but not when she was the woman involved.

Leo had asked her if she understood after setting her senses on fire but there was no way she could have said she did.

It was as if what had just taken place between them had been an ending rather than a beginning. She was bewildered by what was happening to them. Yet one thing had been made clear. Now she knew that given the chance she could love Leo with heart, mind and body, if he ever gave her the opportunity.

He was passionate, mind-blowingly attractive and kind. But there was no way she was going to let those things sweep her into a situation where she was going to be hurt again. Leo had got it right about that. A man with fewer scruples would have led her on, but not him.

It might work for someone else, a tougher woman, less vulnerable than she was, but not for her. If she was on her own for the rest of her life, it would be better than making a mistake now, so she was going to do as Leo had asked and stay away from him in every way except at the practice, where she would try to avoid him as much as possible.

Right now she had to focus on her patients, and she was surprised to see that her next one was Beverly McBride, her gall-bladder patient.

She had given her a supply of antibiotics to clear the infection and now she was back to say that the inflammation was disappearing, but during the night a clear water-like substance had started to come from the wound and it hadn't been just a dribble.

Needless to say, it was causing concern and when she'd examined the source of it and taken note of the much-improved state of the infected area, Amelie asked. 'Did it smell at all?'

The answer was no and she explained that it would be some sort of aftermath of the operation. That sometimes air and fluids are pumped into the area where that kind of surgery was to take place.

'It doesn't always happen,' Amelie told her, 'but I've seen it a few times. It is drainage, which is a good omen rather than a bad one. But on the other hand, if it occurs again I suggest that you ring the hospital just to be sure.'

'They told me not to get in touch with them if I had any problems,' Beverly reminded her.

'Yes, maybe they did, but one thing they *didn't* tell

you was that this might happen, so I feel you are entitled to put the ball in their court if they refuse to see you.'

When she'd gone, only partly reassured with instructions to ring the hospital, preferably, or otherwise the surgery if it happened again, Maria, the young practice nurse, came in with coffee. She paused for a second to say, 'My dad thinks you are a fantastic swimmer. He's looking forward to you giving him some help in the evenings down on the beach.'

Amelie smiled across at her from behind the desk and told her, 'I'm looking forward to it as well, Maria.' She added wistfully, 'From what he has told me, it sounds as if you are part of a very happy family.'

'Er, yes, I suppose I am,' she agreed, surprised at the comment but having no cause to disagree. 'Mum and Dad are fantastic. He's great with us kids *and* with those he meets on the beach.'

'Yes, I'm sure he is,' Amelie said with a vision of brief visits to a chilly chateau coming to mind and years of birthday and Christmas gifts sent by mail order.

Breaking into her sombre memories, Maria said, 'Have you seen Dr Fenchurch with the children who are brought to the surgery? He is fantastic too. Has lots of patience, makes them laugh, yet doesn't let a single thing escape him medically. Parents with a sick child nearly always ask to see *him*.'

Amelie swallowed hard. What Maria had said described him exactly. Leo was another man who would make a good father from the sound of it, but he seemed to have doubts about the rest of married life or he would have been spoken for long ago.

It was all becoming just too confusing and when Maria had gone back to the nurses' room she called in her next patient and so the day progressed.

At six-thirty Leo was still ensconced in his consulting room so she made a quick departure and went back to the house for a snack and a change of clothes before going down to the beach to renew her acquaintance with Ronnie the family man once more.

A short time later, with his day at the practice over now, Leo saw her leave from the window of his apartment and thought that Amelie must feel she had seen and felt enough of him for one day. His presence on the beach this evening would be about as welcome as a rip tide, and, going into his kitchen, he began to make himself a leisurely meal.

A couple of hours had passed and the sun was still high in the sky. He'd been watching for her return and so far it hadn't materialised. He hoped that Ronnie had sorted something out about getting her employed in the proper sense of the word as a temporary lifeguard and not as a voluntary performer. Giving in to the urge to go and find out, he set off for the headland.

When Amelie had arrived there earlier the beach had been packed with families and teenagers enjoying the sun and the sea as white-tipped breakers surged back to where they'd come from, but now the numbers were lessening as folks went to eat in the café at the top of the causeway, in a restaurant in the village or just went back home for whatever was on offer, and he saw her sitting on a rock, gazing out to sea as she ate an ice-cream cornet.

He smiled. Just seeing her again was making him feel better and he went striding down from the headland to join her, not sure of his welcome but chancing it nevertheless, and noting as he did so that there was no sign of Ronnie anywhere.

As if she sensed he was near, Amelie turned and her heartbeat quickened at the sight of the golden man who had captured her heart and was wishing he hadn't. Why was he there? she wondered. To carry on where they'd left off in the lay-by yesterday?

'Hi,' he said when he drew level. 'Where's Ronnie?'

'Gone back home for a well-earned meal.'

'So what sort of arrangement is this going to be?' he questioned. She was so amenable he wasn't going to allow anyone to take advantage of it, himself included.

'He's got permission from the authorities for me to help out in the evenings and at weekends if I so wish. I'm booked onto a refresher course this weekend, so can start immediately after that.'

'And are they going to be paying you for it?'

She was frowning. 'What is all this about, Leo? Yes, I will be paid at the rate for temporary employees, and I'm looking forward to being by the sea and being on hand to help anyone who might need me.

'It must be a wonderful feeling to be needed, though I wouldn't know. I'd begun to think that was all going to change, but I was wrong, wasn't I? Should have known better and taken note of what Lucy and Maria have told me—that you have only to give them a glance and half the women of the village would come running.'

That was one for him, he thought, cringing at the implication, but it was only partly true.

He'd spent a major part of the previous twelve months driving to and from Manchester to look after his mother while at the same time trying to hold on to the position in Bluebell Cove, which he'd only just settled into when she'd become ill. If his sister hadn't come over from abroad and offered to take their mother back with her, he would have had to leave the place that he'd fallen in love with on sight, the same as Amelie had.

Ethan had proved a good friend in those dark days by keeping the position open for him, even though he hadn't been there half the time, and he wasn't ever going to forget that.

Maybe he had gone off the rails a bit when his sister had stepped in. He'd been on a high after months of pressure, but it didn't mean he'd slept around or deliberately gone out of his way to attract the opposite sex. The reason for that had been because he'd never met anyone who could replace Delphine until now and here she was, sitting on a rock, licking a cornet and wanting him gone.

He hadn't come down to the beach to preach the gospel according to him, as she'd described it. It was a matter of needing to know that she was all right, and maybe get some feedback on that kiss. But after the conversation they'd just had he was beginning to wonder if it had actually happened. If he'd made her even more disgruntled with him, it would be just another mountain to climb.

'Is Ronnie coming back, or what?' he asked.

'No. He would have done, but I told him not to, that I would stay until the light went and that would be it. After all, there are enough notices around the place to warn the people who come here of the currents and the fast tides.'

He was looking around him. The beach was deserted except for a man walking his dog, and the light was going already, so he said, 'The light has almost gone and I know the guy with the dog. He's one of my patients who has lived here all his life and isn't likely to get himself into any trouble down here with the comings and goings of the tides. So I'll walk you back to the village.'

'Do I have a choice?' she asked coolly, concealing her pleasure at the thought.

'No, you don't,' was the reply. 'I am not leaving you down here on your own. It will be dark soon and in future don't be so generous with your offers to our friendly neighbourhood lifeguard.'

'Don't be so crabby!' she exclaimed, unaware that he wasn't sure if his suggestion that she help out on the beach had been a good idea.

'I'm not,' he told her, 'but I know what you're like.'

'No, you don't!' she declared. 'I can be strong and inflexible if I have to...so take care.' She was smiling but it didn't reach her eyes and he wondered whether she was referring to the past or the present.

On the walk back to their respective dwellings they chatted about local events, the surgery, the weather, everything but themselves, and when they reached her gate she was wishing him goodnight and whizzing up the drive with her door key in hand as if she was wary of him asking to come in.

There had been no likelihood of that, he thought. The wish to do so had been there, but after the hurt he'd caused the other night it wouldn't be the right thing to do.

In the days that followed they both still kept to his suggestion that they cool it. Their only lapses had been *the* kiss and their meeting on the beach when she'd been filling in for Ronnie.

The only time they were in each other's company now was at the practice, and both kept contact there down to the minimum. She was miserable and lonely, and he was causing much speculation amongst his socialising friends by never being available when it was party time.

Harry was the only person who guessed what was going on and he said nothing but thought a lot, along the lines that Leo was crazy if he was keeping the young French doctor at a distance. She was good at the job, a charming young woman, and he was a great guy.

But remembering all the ups and downs and misunderstandings that he and Phoebe had had before it had all come right, he could sympathise with Leo, whose attractions seemed to cause more misery than pleasure in his life. But something told him that Amelie would not be swayed by outward appearances, she would need more than that.

The stalemate between them was still in place the week of the Big Summer Picnic that was held on the field behind the village hall. It was free, the only thing asked of those who attended was that they bring their own food and drinks, otherwise it wouldn't be a picnic.

Amelie was looking forward to it as something to break into the routine she had fallen into of surgery and beach on weekdays, and the beach again for most of the weekend.

One of the most painful things about cooling it with Leo was them living so close to each other. When she looked across at his apartment it was as if it was a tree bearing forbidden fruit, beckoning her to come and taste. She sighed at the stupidity of the way they were behaving, but if ever they were to put an end to the painful pretence they were involved in, Leo would have to be the one to do it because it had come from him.

He looked on the closeness of their homes as a mixed blessing. It was comforting to know she was so near, but agonising not to be able to talk to her, hold her, and the blame for that was his alone for not facing up to the past.

Until now he'd never met anyone who'd made him feel uneasy about the memory time warp he was caught up in, but with the coming of Amelie a voice in his mind was telling him to look to the future and forget the past.

But he'd lived with the memory of Delphine for a long time, so would he be able to put it to one side and find happiness with Amelie?

Most of the surgery staff were going to the Big Summer picnic and, knowing how interested she was in any local event, he was pretty sure she would be amongst them. So if nothing else they would be around each other for a few hours if the warm lazy days of summer that had become a regular thing over the last few weeks didn't disappoint the picnickers.

He'd promised the vicar's wife he would be around all the time in case of accident or injury, and knew that Harry would also be there with Phoebe and little Marcus. And with Amelie also amongst those present, health and safety would be well represented should the need arise.

He had been right when he'd thought that Amelie wouldn't want to miss the picnic. The days were long without him in her life when she was away from the surgery. Even the time on the beach with Ronnie, which she really enjoyed, didn't make up for his absence. So *she* was hoping *he* would be at the picnic, if only for the chance to be near him in a less restricted way than when they were working.

She set off for the village hall with a picnic basket optimistically holding enough for two, and knew she could be asking for a disappointment, yet it was worth a try.

He was there before her, supervising the erection of

a carousel beside the large marquee that was always provided in case of rain. But today the skies were blue and the sun was beaming down graciously on to the scene below.

There was excitement in the air and soon the community feeling that such occasions brought forth would take over with a local band in place and the revellers ready to enjoy themselves.

Leo had seen her arrive and his spirits lifted. So far so good, he thought. The moment he was free he was going to go over and ask if he might join her, and if Amelie said yes he would take it from there, and if she said no, well…

She was chatting to Ronnie and his family, who had just arrived, and the last thing he wanted was for her to be drawn into their circle.

Jenna and Lucas hadn't arrived yet and surprisingly neither had Harry and Phoebe, but no doubt they were on their way. Then all the folks he enjoyed being with would be there, with his lovely French doctor top of the list.

The hierarchy of the Balfour family were expected, but would not be staying long as it might get too noisy for Barbara in her frail state. But she was insisting on attending, as anything that gave her the opportunity to be with those who were looking after her beloved practice in the same way that she had was a pleasure that didn't come often enough.

As they'd been about to leave the headland to take the road into the village, she'd asked Keith to turn the wheelchair round so that she could see the scene that was as familiar as her own face.

The sea bounding onto the golden sand with the same kind of power and purpose that she'd once had, and the cliffs rising towards them, worn by the sea and kissed by the sun with seabirds swirling above them, and in the distance the green and fertile fields of Devonshire.

'I love this place more than life itself, Keith,' she'd told her husband.

'Yes, I know you do,' had been his gentle reply, and he'd pointed the wheelchair towards the village once more.

'When we get there, put me in a sheltered spot under a tree, will you?' she asked. 'I'm going to have a nap before everyone begins to arrive.'

'Yes, anything you say,' he told her, and thought he must have said that a thousand times in their long life together.

When they reached the main street there were lots of folk about and they waved or called across to them, and Keith thought Bluebell Cove was Barbara's reason for living. It happened all the time when he took her out. The respect and affection that was always there went a long way to make up for her having to retire because of her lack of mobility, which had been followed by serious heart defects, but he knew more than anyone that inside she was the same old battling Barbara whose patients had been her life's blood.

There was only a scattering of folks there when they arrived at the field behind the village hall. Soon there would be lots of noise and excitement and then they would leave as it would be too much for his frail wife.

So he did as she'd asked, left her to rest in a secluded spot with the branches of an old oak tree protecting her from the rays of the sun, and went to have a word with Leo, who was helping members of the events committee erect the various kinds of amusements that would be there to entertain the picnickers.

There was no sign of Harry and Jenna, the other two Balfours, but both had young children to cope with and Keith and Leo were not unduly surprised. It would be unheard of for the members of that family not to be present on such an occasion.

As Amelie watched the two men chatting together, she had no idea that Keith had claimed Leo's attention just as he was about to approach her, so she was envisaging spending the time with Ronnie's family, who were lovely but not who she wanted to be with today.

Leaving her picnic basket on a nearby table, she began to stroll around the field, admiring the sideshows and carousel and taking note of the instruments, mainly guitars and drums, already in position on the stage.

As she came to the end of the field where there was less to see she gave a casual glance in the direction of the wheelchair and its occupant and paused. She'd only spoken to Barbara Balfour once, when she'd been invited to supper at Harry's, and had liked the elderly doctor's straightforward manner.

Feeling that she looked rather lonely there beneath the trees, Amelie went across to speak to her. As she approached it seemed that she was asleep with her head back and eyes closed, but when she reached her side she saw that it wasn't sleep that was holding her so still. She'd seen it so many times before in hospital.

By this time Keith had gone to talk to other friends and Leo, who had been observing Amelie's progress around the field, was about to join her. He could see her at the far end, bending over Barbara, and thought it was good that the two of them were getting to know each other.

When she looked around her to call for help he was coming towards her, and she cried, 'Leo! Come quickly!' then turned back to the woman in the wheelchair. He was by her side in seconds and saw to his dismay that she was trying to resuscitate Barbara who, at a glance, had already passed on to another life.

'It's no use. You are too late, Amelie,' he said sombrely. 'It could have happened some time before you found her and with no one around to see, she probably had a massive heart attack and was gone.'

So far they had been unobserved but now Keith was on his way back to check on his wife and something in the way they were bending over her made him quicken his step. When he stood looking down at the woman who had given her life to her patients and left only a little of it for her husband and child, he said soberly, 'I think she knew it wouldn't be long. As we were setting off to come here Barbara asked me to stop while she had what turned out to be a last look from the top of the headland at all the places she loved so much.'

'Jenna and Lucas have just arrived. Will one of you go and fetch her? It will be a great shock, though again maybe it won't. I feel that Lucas, as Barbara's cardiac consultant, will have prepared Jenna for this.'

'I'll go, Amelie, if you'll stay here with Keith,' Leo said, and she nodded gravely. Soon the field would be full of those out to enjoy the day. It was vital he get to Jenna quickly.

He found her chatting to friends with Lucas holding Lily in his arms, but his expression caused the chatter to dwindle into silence and into it he said gently, 'It's your mother, Jenna. Amelie found her a few moments ago down at the bottom of the field. She tried to resuscitate her but I'm afraid it was too late.'

Lucas passed the baby to one of their friends and with his arm around Jenna's shoulders they followed him to where Keith was seated by his wife's body on a chair that Amelie had found for him.

From that moment of extreme sadness the news began to filter around the field that battling Barbara Balfour had fought her last fight, that a failing heart had been the victor this time.

An announcement was made to say that Barbara had passed away and a minute's silence was called for before the local undertaker and his assistants arrived to take her to the chapel of rest.

There having been three doctors present, one of them her cardiac consultant who had seen her in the last few days, it meant there would be no necessity for an inquest, and everyone present stood with heads bowed as the sad little procession left the field.

When the vicar would have cancelled the event Keith had said not to, that, knowing Barbara's love of

Bluebell Cove and its inhabitants, she would want it to proceed, and with that thought in mind the band began to play again, the carousel began to turn, and children ran around excitedly, exactly how Barbara would have wanted it to be.

When the picnic was over Amelie and Leo walked back towards the surgery together. The events of the afternoon had made their differences seem minor. They'd managed the time together that they'd been yearning for, but under the worst possible circumstances, and still there was no sign of Harry.

'Where can they be?' Leo said as they sat in the garden of the house.

'It will hit Harry hard, losing Barbara. From what he's told me, the Balfours were good to him when his parents lost his little brother and were so wrapped up in their grief that he got pushed to one side. It was Barbara who persuaded him to come back to Bluebell Cove when he lost his wife, and it was here that he met Phoebe, who he adores.'

At that moment Leo's mobile rang and when he picked it up Harry's voice came over the line. 'I thought I might find you at Amelie's place,' he said. 'I take it that the picnic is over.' His voice had a lift to it that had to mean he didn't know that Barbara was no longer in the background of his life as she had been for so long.

'Er...yes,' Leo said uncomfortably, dreading what was coming next,

But Harry forestalled him by announcing jubilantly. 'We have a daughter, Leo! Phoebe and I have daughter and Marcus a little sister. Did you wonder where we were? She went into labour a couple of weeks early in the middle of the night, so we wrapped Marcus, who was sound asleep, in a blanket and drove to the maternity unit at Hunter's Hill. The baby arrived just before lunch.'

'That is wonderful news! Are they both all right?'

'They're fine and so is Marcus, who is trying to take it all in and wanting lots of love. I'm on top of the world, Leo, and must go as the obstetrician is due on his rounds any moment.'

'Before you go, there is something that you need to know,' Leo told him sombrely, wishing himself anywhere but at the other end of the line to the ecstatic new father. 'Your Aunt Barbara passed away at the picnic this afternoon. I am so sorry to be the bearer of such sad tidings in the midst of your joy, Harry.'

There was silence for a long moment then Harry said chokingly, 'What time did she die, Leo?'

'The church clock had just struck one when Amelie found her under the trees in the wheelchair. Why, what are you thinking?'

'That was the time our daughter came into the world. I had a feeling that it might be. As one life ended, another was beginning. Where are Keith and Jenna? I must speak to them.'

'They are all back at the house on the headland. Hopefully your wonderful news will help to lessen their heartache a little.'

Leo's expression was sombre as he put the phone down and Amelie thought that Antoine had done her a favour when he'd turned his attention to another woman.

If he hadn't, she would now be living a mundane life with a mundane husband. Would never have met the man sitting opposite her who had just done his best to soften the blow he'd inflicted on Harry in the midst of his rejoicing.

He was so special, she was so happy to be with him, and if they were going to continue as they had been without any possibility of a future together, at least she would have had the joy of knowing him.

Yet as he sat there dejectedly, having just turned Harry's euphoria into grief, she couldn't sit and watch and do nothing. Going across to him, she placed her arm around his shoulders and said softly, 'Don't feel bad, Leo. You had to tell him before he heard it on the village grapevine. Until now Keith and Jenna haven't known where he was to tell him about Barbara's passing. Better that it came from you.'

He nodded then, getting slowly to his feet, said, 'You were wonderful out there, but what a shame it had to be you who found her. Though I suppose it was a blessing in one way. Keith and Jenna were spared the sharp, agonising shock that is part of a sudden death by having you and I around.

'We work well together, don't we? And today I was hoping we might have played together at the picnic, but the fates had other ideas. Playful was the last thing I felt after what happened to Barbara.'

'So why don't we go for a walk where it is calm and peaceful and we can unwind? Then find a nice restaurant for dinner, my treat,' she suggested. 'There is nothing more we can do here.'

CHAPTER SEVEN

To avoid going anywhere near the headland and the Balfours' house, which was now in mourning, Amelie and Leo walked inland between hedgerows weighed down with flowers, and past Wheatlands, the biggest farm in the area, owned by the well-respected Enderby family.

While Amelie was observing its opulence, he said, 'Some spread, isn't it? Would you like to live in a place like that?'

She considered for a moment and then said, 'No. I don't think so. I'm not keen on large houses.'

'You mean like your family's chateau?'

She smiled across at him. 'You have it in one. My parents took it for granted that I wanted to be married in the chateau when I was engaged to Antoine. In fact, that's where the wedding was to be held.'

'But you didn't want to?'

'No. And now I will never be married in that place. If I ever got close to marriage again, which I seriously doubt I will, I would choose to have my wedding somewhere small and beautiful.'

'Like you,' he said in a low voice, and she turned away.

'Don't make fun of me,' she told him. 'You're the one with the looks.'

'And do you think I care about that?' he exclaimed. 'I'd rather be downright ugly than the village catch.'

She was laughing now and he thought how easy she was to be with. How uncomplicated her attitude to life was, or had been until he'd begun to cause confusion in her mind.

She was happy to be with him if he would let her, like now, but knew that could change if his conscience began to pull at the strings of his integrity again.

'So where are we going to eat?' he asked as a restaurant with a thatched roof appeared on the skyline. 'The place ahead is very popular. It is where Lucas proposed to Jenna over a clotted-cream tea on a cold day when the place was empty, or so she thought. Her family and friends were hiding in one of the other rooms ready to congratulate them when she'd said yes.'

'How lovely, but supposing she'd said no?'

'I take it you've seen Lucas Devereux?'

'Well, yes, of course.'

'There you have your answer, then, and in case you're thinking that it wasn't very romantic, being proposed to while eating a scone covered with jam and cream, surely we both agree that it is the people involved that matter rather than the location.'

'Quite,' she agreed demurely, 'as long as it isn't in the fish sheds down by the harbour, or on top of the refuse collection pile.'

If she'd been less confused about his feelings, she

might have rounded off the comment with *so do please bear that in mind*, but there was nothing in his manner to indicate that he'd changed his mind about what he'd said when he'd spelt out for her that they weren't going anywhere together on a permanent basis.

The restaurant wasn't as near as it had looked. When they were almost halfway there Leo said, 'I know a short cut. No use when in a car but much quicker when on foot. It is through remote woodland for part of the way but will certainly get us there more quickly. Do you want to try it?'

'Yes,' she agreed. 'I don't know about you but I'm hungry.' *And not just for food, she would have liked to have told him.*

The woods felt cool after being in the evening sun and everywhere was very still. After a while Leo said, 'Shall we rest for a few moments, if you can get your hunger pangs to subside?'

'Yes. I think I can,' she replied. 'Appetite will have to take second place to feet. We passed a stream only moments ago. I'm going to cool them off in it. Are you coming?'

'No, I'm fine here. Don't be too long or the place we're heading for will be full.'

She was already removing the sandals she was wearing and walking carefully towards the edge of a narrow rivulet running through the woods.

While she was gone he took a large clean handkerchief out of his pocket and when she came back and lay down on the grass beside him he began to dry her feet with gentle strokes.

She ached for him, Amelie thought as he bent to his task, but of his own free will Leo had taken desire out of their relationship because of something she still didn't fully understand, so maybe it was up to her to bring it back.

He looked up and found her bright blue gaze on him. 'What?' he questioned. 'What are you thinking?'

'I'm thinking that not so long ago I accused you of having never kissed me or made love to me, didn't I?'

His voice was flat. 'Yes, you did indeed.'

'So you dealt with one of the omissions that day in the lay-by, but so far haven't done anything about the other.'

'And you would like me to do so, is that it?'

'Only if you want to, but I must warn you I am no expert. It will be a first time.'

Was she serious? he thought raggedly. Amelie had no idea of the workings of his mind when it came to his personal life or she wouldn't have created this sort of situation.

It was another opportunity to tell her about Delphine, but to her it might come over as just another rejection, an escape route back to his life before she'd come on the scene.

The eyes looking up into his were wide and questioning. 'You don't want me, do you?' she cried, humiliated beyond reason. 'Why does my mouth always have to be ahead of my mind when I'm with you?'

He had no answer to that. Instead he said in the same flat tone, 'I think we should be on our way if you are as hungry as you said.'

'I've just lost my appetite,' she told him. 'Food would choke me.'

'You might change your mind when we get there,' he said placatingly. 'So up you get and off we go in search of it. Just one thing before we go, Amelie. You have just put yourself amongst almost every woman I meet. They all want me to bed them.'

'And do you?'

'You mean am I the local stud? I can't believe you're asking me that. I thought you were different, but it seems I was wrong.'

She was up and running, wanting to get as far away from him as possible so that he wouldn't realise just how much he'd humiliated her. But he was moving fast behind her and when he caught up said, 'Watch out for tree roots, Amelie,' as if they'd never had that dreadful conversation.

For the rest of the evening they were so polite to each other it was nauseating. But all the time the thought was rocketing around her mind that once again she had been the unwanted. And, she thought shamefully, she'd even mentioned her virginity like some sort of special offer.

She couldn't wait to get away from him so that her shame might be a more private thing. The moment they'd finished eating she went to pay for the meal, in keeping with her promise when she'd suggested they go for a walk and she could tell from his expression that he wasn't pleased about that either.

'I've asked them to order us a taxi,' he said when she

returned to the table. 'I didn't think you would want to walk back the way we came.'

'How right you are,' she said quietly. 'I never ever want to set foot in those woods again.'

'I meant no hurt by what I said,' he told her. 'You are young, vulnerable and enchanting. Can we just leave it at that and be friends?'

'If you say so,' she said bleakly, not to be comforted or given back her self-respect. At that moment they were told that their taxi was outside and she hurried towards the means of escape from her folly.

When it pulled up outside the house she didn't give Leo the chance to make any further comments, she had its door open and was running up the drive with door key at the ready once again. By the time he'd paid the driver she had disappeared from sight and he thought grimly the chances of her opening the door again if he rang the bell were slim.

So he made his way to his apartment and spent the next hour going over the awful events of the day that had started with discovering that Barbara Balfour was no longer with them, and ended with his refusal to do something he'd been aching to do for weeks—make love to Amelie.

The incident had been catastrophic in many ways. She'd taken him by surprise, for one thing, and another reason of a more irksome kind had been that it had been she who had done the asking.

It was clear that she hadn't been remembering his words of wisdom with regard to cooling their relationship at that moment. So where on earth did they go from here? Was he still so tied to the heartache of the past that he couldn't make love to Amelie when the opportunity was there?

He'd felt as if she was expecting him to jump at the chance when she'd made the request and had seen red. Of course he'd wanted to, but not under those circumstances.

When the phone rang he was praying that it might be her, but it was Jenna on the line with details of her mother's funeral and also with the news that Ethan was coming over from France for it on his own as both Ben and Kirstie were now at school there and after the upheaval of the move he and Francine didn't want to have to disrupt their education again.

'How is your father taking it?' he asked. and was surprised by her reply.

'Very well, considering. He has amazed us all by saying that now Mum has gone he's going to sell the house and travel the world, something he has always wanted to do but never got the chance. So what do you think of that?'

'Good luck to him. Do you think he will have any trouble selling Four Winds?'

'He might. The market is unpredictable at the moment.'

'If he goes ahead with his plans, I can find him a buyer.'

'Really! Who?'

'Me.'

'He would be happy about that, Leo. You and Amelie

were so kind to him when Mum died, and he has always liked you. If he does keep to what he is saying you will be the first to know, and now I must go as Lily is fretful tonight, almost as if she knows that her grandma isn't here any more.'

As he rang off he couldn't believe that he'd just said he would like to buy her parents' house if it came up for sale, and more unbelievable still that he'd had Amelie's love of Bluebell Cove in mind when he'd said it.

The apartment was good enough for him on his own, but it was not the sort of place he would want to bring his bride to if the church bells ever pealed out over the village for him. Acquiring the house might be easy enough, but as for the rest of it he was losing his sense of direction.

In the house across the way Amelie was weeping tears of humiliation and regret. She'd known it had been a big mistake to say what she had to Leo the moment the words had come out of her mouth.

While he'd been drying her feet, desire had risen in her in a hot tide. She'd craved his touch like a thirsty person for water, with disastrous results, and as if asking him to make love to her hadn't been awful enough, she'd told him about the icing on the cake!

The right thing to do would be to go back to France, she kept telling herself, but she was committed to working at the practice for six months and didn't want to break her contract. There was some time to go before it would be up, so all she could do was to continue avoiding Leo as much as possible.

It was the picnic and what had happened to Barbara Balfour that had thrown them so much into each other's company again, and those moments in the tranquil woodland setting had tempted her to say what was in her heart, but the vast waters of the sea would freeze over before she ever did that again.

She was halfway up the stairs on her way to bed when she caught sight of Leo through the landing window, striding across from the apartment, and quickly shrank back out of sight.

The day was almost over. It had been a ghastly one, and much as the sight of him always warmed her heart, enough was enough. She was too spent for any further conversation between them and what he could possibly want of her after the way they'd separated when the taxi had dropped them off she really didn't know.

Yet one thing she could be sure of—he wasn't coming across because he was having second thoughts about his refusal to do what she'd asked.

She was right on that count. Leo was coming to tell her about Jenna's phone call. To inform her that Barbara's funeral was to take place on the coming Friday and that if they could both be spared from the practice, he felt they owed it to Keith to be there, having been with him when he'd discovered that his wife had died.

But there was no answer when he rang the bell and when he looked up, the curtains had been drawn in the master bedroom. So the excuse he'd been going to use to see Amelie for just one more time before the day was done was not going to work. With measured steps he returned to his apartment.

She had heard him ring the bell from up above and was lying with her head beneath the pillows to shut out its noise. When it stopped she pulled the covers up around her and, too exhausted to even think any more, turned on her side and slept.

She awoke to a room full of sunlight and the sound of the church bells pealing not far away, and thought thankfully that it was Sunday. She had twenty-four hours to gather her wits before she and Leo came face to face again.

It was not to be the case. He came as she was finishing a mundane breakfast of cereal, toast and tea. This time she had to let him in. He'd seen her seated at the dining table as he'd walked up the drive and his first words when she opened the door to him were, 'Are you all right after yesterday?'

'Yes, I suppose so,' she told him, and before he had the chance to say anything else she added, 'Have you heard when the funeral is?'

'Yes, Jenna phoned late last night. I came across to tell you but there was no answer so I presumed you had gone to bed. It is on Friday at half past two for a private family service at the crematorium, followed by a public thanksgiving service in the church for Barbara's life and her dedication to those she served so well in a medical capacity. I spoke to Harry a few moments ago and he said the church service is to be relayed to anyone who can't get inside, indicating that a large attendance is expected.

'They're talking of changing the name of the surgery to the Balfour Medical Centre, which I feel would be very fitting, don't you? Especially as with Harry in charge there is still a Balfour involved.'

'Er, yes,' she agreed, taking in the image of him, drawn looking around the eyes but dressed in a smart top and jeans as if the events of the previous day had never taken place, while she was huddled at the table in an old T-shirt and shorts. But maybe that was because she cared and he didn't.

Yet she knew that wasn't true. He did care, but not in the way that she cared for him. She adored him. The more she saw of him the more she wanted to be near him, but yesterday had shown that they weren't going anywhere together.

He had a surprise for her and it brought her out of the doldrums into amazement. 'The family want you to read the lesson at the service in the church, if you will.'

'I don't know!' she gasped. 'I am a stranger here. What will those who have known Dr Balfour all their lives think of that? And though I speak English fluently, I do not always get it right.'

'You will,' he said confidently, 'and I won't be far away.'

As if, she thought. He might be near in body, but in mind and purpose he might as well be sitting on the moon instead of in a nearby pew. Yet she couldn't refuse, not about something like that, so she told him weakly. 'Tell them yes, I will do as they ask. But I hope that it will not offend.'

'It won't,' he assured her. 'Everyone knows that you found her and tried to save her, and now I must go. An acquaintance of mine, Georgina, who owns the boutique next to the post office, was taken ill with some kind of gastritis during the night and phoned to ask me to go round, and as she lives alone I stayed with her.'

'I see.'

'Yes, I'm sure you do,' he said dryly. 'The farmer who delivers the milk around here gave me a wink when he saw me coming out of there at six o'clock this morning. I'm going home to get some sleep now, Amelie, and am presuming that you are going to spend the day on the beach, helping Ronnie.'

'Yes, that is my intention when I have gathered my wits together,' she said stiffly, and with a sudden surge of jealousy said, 'Does your friend at the boutique not know that you are off duty at the weekend, that she should have called an emergency doctor?'

'I would expect she does,' he said, 'but what are friends for, Amelie?'

He was already moving towards the door and as if he hadn't made her miserable enough the day before, he departed with a wave of the hand and the casual observation that he would see her around, no doubt.

Of course he would *see her around*, she thought glumly when he'd gone. They both worked at the practice, didn't they? She would have that small comfort, if nothing else.

* * *

When she arrived there on the Monday morning it was as if a cloud of sadness was hanging over the place because the woman who had served it so well for many years until her own health had brought her to a halt had succumbed to a massive heart attack.

Lucy, who liked to chat before the day began, was white faced and silent. She had been Barbara Balfour's one and only close friend, had known her faults and her failings just as well as she'd known the woman's dedication to her calling.

They'd called her 'battling Barbara' but Lucy knew that her battles had never been for herself. They'd been with the authorities when she'd thought they had been failing a patient, or with the hospital if she'd thought they had been dragging their feet regarding appointments.

If Lucy had been close to her, so had Harry, especially during his young years. Phoebe had asked him if he would like their new baby daughter to be christened Barbara, but always one to call a spade a spade he'd said with a wry smile, 'It's a lovely thought, Phoebe, but I don't want our innocent little one to be called after my aunt, even though I had the greatest respect for her.

'She was a fantastic doctor, served her patients to the limit of her endurance, but when it came to her family, she fell far short. We both know loving families are what it's all about, and while we're on the subject I do not want to call our baby after Cassie either, as you once suggested.'

'My life with her wasn't a bed of roses by any means, so no to Cassie. The only name that warms my heart is yours, and if we can find one just as beautiful, that will be it.'

Amelie had been treating Leo with cool politeness since arriving at the surgery and every time anyone mentioned the funeral looming up on Friday she wished herself miles away because he had said he would be there for her and she didn't want him to feel it was something else she required of him on sufferance.

In the meantime, the waiting room was filling up with those who had problems of their own to contend with and would be expecting her to pull a cure out of the hat, or at the least some relief from the ills of body and mind.

Her first patient of the day was Martha Maguire, cook at the village school. She had itchy weals all over her skin, with yellowish white centres surrounded by inflammation.

When asked the usual questions regarding eating different foods not usually part of her diet, changing to a different kind of washing powder or the possibility of garden hazards, there didn't seem to be any answers to explain the rash.

'It looks like urticaria,' Amelie told her, 'or nettle rash, as it is sometimes known, and is rarely serious, except in cases when other illnesses are present, such as lupus erythematosus or vaculitis. It usually clears up without too much fuss by using calamine lotion for the raised areas on the skin and antihistamine tablets for inward treatment of the irritation. I'll give you supplies of both. Come back if there is no improvement during the next few days.'

Martha was smiling. 'Thanks, Doctor. Sounds like I made a fuss about nothing, but working in a school one is open to all the children's illnesses. Some of the parents send them when they should be at home, and even though what I've got isn't serious, I'm going to have to stay at home as they won't want me to handle food with a rash, and I don't blame them.'

'You didn't fuss over nothing, Mrs Maguire. It is always best to be sure when something strange happens to our bodies,' she told her.

Jonah Trelfa, who'd been a patient with a heart problem on her first day at the practice, followed the school cook. He'd come for a repeat prescription of the medication the hospital had put him on that day and was looking much fitter than he had done then.

As he lowered himself on to the seat opposite he said, 'I've just seen Dr Fenchurch going into the boutique. Is Georgina poorly?'

'I'm afraid I have no idea, Mr Trelfa,' she told him politely, acutely aware that Leo was giving his friend his full attention in whatever way she was demanding it. Yet she had to have a rethink when an ambulance came screeching along the road and stopped outside the shop. Seconds later paramedics came out with its owner on a stretcher and Leo by her side.

He watched as it disappeared from sight, then turned and went back into the shop. He was at the surgery when the staff stopped for lunch, and when about to go to the baker's across the way asked if he could bring her anything.

Her reply was 'No, thank you.' And before she could

ask about his friend, he nodded as if her refusal wasn't unexpected and went on his way.

By the time he came back there was no need to ask about the boutique owner. The news was filtering around the surgery that she had been taken into hospital with gastroenteritis.

She'd just said 'I see' when he'd told her he'd been in the boutique most of the night. But it must have been the way she'd said it that had prompted him to tell her about the milk delivering farmer's reaction when he'd seen him coming out of there.

She wanted to tell him she was sorry, yet what had she done wrong?

When he'd told her where he'd been during the night, she'd been too overwrought about the episode in the woods to take too much notice, and in any case did it matter?

He kept making it clear that he didn't want her, so why should he be blamed if he had a yearning for someone else, and in any case it hadn't been like that, he'd gone to answer a cry for help in his capacity as a doctor.

At the end of the day he caught her up as she was leaving and said casually, 'Is it the beach again tonight?'

'Er, yes,' she replied, and before he could say anything else went on, 'Have you heard how your friend is?'

'Yes. She's quite poorly. Last night it was severe stomach pains. I felt that she might have some degree of food poisoning that would clear itself, as it often does, but it was much worse this morning so I had her admitted to hospital.

'Georgina's mother is on her way from the Scilly Isles to be with her while she gets over this, so it should all end happily enough once she is clear of the infection, which is not always the case, is it, Amelie?'

She was her usual direct self as she asked, 'Are you referring to us?'

'I might be.'

'What happened on Saturday was my fault, Leo. It was stupid of me. Over the years I've learned never to take anything for granted. It helped a lot when Antoine dumped me for the red-haired nurse, but I didn't bring caution into play when I let my feelings get the better of me while you were drying my feet. So will you accept my apology?'

He groaned softly. 'You have nothing to be sorry about, Amelie. I also let my feelings get the better of me, so we're quits.'

'I thought we were on the same wavelength until yesterday,' she told him, 'even though you do have reservations, but it seems as if I was way out.'

They were at her gate. She was ready to do her quick skip up the drive, but he wasn't going to let her do it this time, at least not until he'd said his piece.

Gripping her arm, he swung her round to face him and said tightly, 'Do you want it on the drive, in the sitting room, the bath, or more traditionally on the bed?'

'What are you talking about?' she cried.

'Making love, of course. Surely I don't have to spell it out.'

The heat of anger was replacing the chill of the question she'd just asked. 'Oh, yes, you do! Thanks for offering to oblige me, but, *no, thanks*.'

She wrenched herself out of his grip and he made no move to stop her. Turning, he walked slowly towards the apartment, unlocked the door at the bottom of the wooden staircase and proceeded upwards, considering as he did so what he would have done if she'd taken him at his word.

When he'd gone Amelie shut the door behind her and stood in the hallway with cheeks flaming and eyes sparking fire as it registered that Leo had been telling her in a roundabout sort of way that he would do the asking if there was any to be done. Well, so much for that. He could ask until he was blue in the face from now on.

Barbara Balfour took her last ride through Bluebell Cove in a glass-sided coach on four wheels pulled by black horses that tossed the plumes on their heads proudly as they passed the silent crowds lining the pavements.

They were on the way to the private family service and Amelie, sitting next to Leo in one of the funeral cars, had a feeling that they were going to be paired off during both of the services that had been arranged.

Every woman's dream man and the nondescript French doctor as a twosome were bound to result in raised eyebrows in some quarters.

CHAPTER EIGHT

AMELIE'S surmise that she would be partnered with Leo had been correct and it had been a relief when the funeral was over and they had returned to the practice where a reduced staff had kept the place going during the absence of the three doctors and Lucy.

To Leo's amazement, Keith Balfour had taken him to one side after the service in the church and asked if he'd meant what he'd said to Jenna about buying his house.

He'd been the patient and loving husband of a difficult woman for many years and was now a changed character, already making plans for a world cruise with the intention of coming back from it to a newly built apartment on the coast road.

'Yes, I was serious,' Leo had told him. 'Four Winds is in a fantastic position. Whenever you feel ready, I will be only too pleased to discuss buying it. There is no rush,' he'd assured the older man with a dismal reminder of Amelie's closed countenance during the two services.

The only time it had lightened had been when she'd

stood in front of the mourners in the old Norman church and reverently done what had been asked of her by the Balfour family, reciting in her precise English the reading they had chosen.

He'd been near while she'd done it, as he'd promised he would be, but he might as well have been invisible for all the notice she'd taken of him, and if he hadn't been so keen to buy Four Winds House he might have been less enthusiastic when its owner had brought up the subject.

'I'm off on my world cruise in a few weeks,' Keith had told him in reply to him saying there was no rush, 'and would like it to be settled before I go, if that's all right with you.'

He'd assured him that it would be, even though his original interest had not been from the point of view of living there alone.

Autumn was on the brink, he'd thought as he'd returned to the surgery after the funeral. Days were shortening, harvests were being brought in, and even with a ready-made buyer for his property Keith Balfour wasn't going to have contracts signed before he went, but surely they could trust each other?

Amelie was back before him and already seeing a patient, but Harry had gone back to the hospital with Marcus to be with Phoebe and the baby, so there would be his patients to add to their lists today and some catching up to do as well.

When surgery was over at last, he put aside his longing to be with Amelie and drove to the hospital to bring Georgina and her mother home. The boutique owner was due to be discharged in the early evening and that would be one less worry on his mind.

She was just a friend who would have liked to have been more, but he'd made it clear that his feelings didn't match hers. His concern over her had been just that of an acquaintance, the kind of thing he would do for anyone in distress, and now that her mother had arrived he could step back and let her take over.

Amelie watched him drive off and felt the melancholy of the day increase.

Leo hadn't spoken to her since the funeral. Keith had buttonholed him and by the time he'd been free she'd been back at the surgery, trying to catch up from her absence earlier.

It would seem that he'd gone to visit Georgina, she thought miserably. She understood the other woman's need of his presence, yet he could have said something, if only goodbye, before he'd gone.

Maybe he felt he'd seen enough of her for one day, and on that thought she went back to the house, had a quick bite, and went down to the beach to keep the amiable Ronnie company.

Storm clouds were gathering when she got there and those present were hurriedly packing up their belongings and getting ready for the off before there was a deluge. Ronnie followed them soon after, not expecting to be needed after the general exodus, and Amelie was about to do the same when she was halted in her tracks by the appearance of an anxious mother who announced that they couldn't find their youngest child, a four-year-old boy called Freddie.

'I thought he was with his dad up in the front of the bus and he thought he was with me at the back with our twin girls,' she said frantically, 'and we can't find him. He is a little wanderer if he gets the chance.' She looked around her anxiously. 'The tide is going out, isn't it?'

She didn't get a reply. Amelie had gone round a bend on the rocky part of the shore to see if the child was playing in the next inlet, but the strip of sand was bare of anyone, especially a small child. Yet as she scanned the foam-tipped waves that were surging back to where they'd come from she saw a small blond head above them, rising and falling with each movement of the sea as it departed.

She called to the child's mother just once, then flung herself into the water and was immediately aware of the pull of the current beneath her. It was then that her swimming prowess came to her aid. Gathering up all her strength, she grabbed the little boy and began to fight her way back to shore, but with every stroke she slid further out and the child she was holding began to struggle and scream.

When a head of damp golden fairness bobbed up beside her she was overwhelmed with relief, and when the voice she'd been longing to hear bellowed above the crashing waves, 'Let him go, Amelie. I've got him,' together they fought their way back to the shore with Leo holding the protesting child.

'Where is Ronnie?' Leo spluttered angrily as he bent over the child, who was lying limply on the wet sand and whimpering softly. 'You could both have been drowned. The currents out there had a mind of their own tonight.

He needs to be checked over in A and E and neither of us have a phone handy. Where are his parents?'

'Here they are,' she said as Freddie's frantic parents came running across the sand. 'His mother came back down here after they'd left to avoid the rain that was threatening because they couldn't find him and had left his father searching for him at the top.'

She observed Freddie, who was now sitting up. 'Shall we give them back their precious little one?'

A crowd had been watching their endeavours from the cliffs and Freddie's parents, with arms outstretched and cries of relief and gratitude, were running towards them to claim their child.

'Have either of you got a mobile with you?' Leo asked as Freddie's mother wrapped him in a dry towel and hugged him to her, and his father turned anxiously to make sure their daughters were where he could see them.

'Yes, I have,' he said.

'Then may I?' Leo asked. 'I'm going to ring for an ambulance to take your child to A and E to be checked over. Fortunately his head was above the water most of the time so we can hope that he hasn't swallowed too much salty seawater, but he hasn't spoken since we rescued him so there could be some extent of trauma, and bruising where we had to hold him so tightly.'

'What brought you to the beach?' Amelie asked when there was just the two of them left beneath a golden harvest moon that had replaced the storm clouds.

'You, of course, I've just brought Georgina and her

mother home from the hospital and wanted to tell you how beautifully you read the lesson this afternoon.'

'Why didn't you tell me then?' she enquired perversely.

'With the temperature at zero, I think not.'

She was shivering now in her wet bathing suit and he said quickly, 'Why don't we go back to either your place or mine and have a shower, followed by a glass of wine to celebrate bringing young Freddie safely on to dry land?'

There was no immediate reply to the suggestion. Amelie was imagining what she looked like and deciding it would take more than a shower and a glass of wine to rectify her appearance after her recent battle against the currents, yet what did it matter? There'd already been one demise in Bluebell Cove in recent days. Thank goodness they'd prevented another and a child's at that.

'Yes, all right,' she agreed, and went on to say, 'Better if we go to the house. There is a shower in the main bathroom and another in the master bedroom.'

'Fine,' he said easily, 'and how about when we've cleaned ourselves up I go for fish and chips?'

'Mmm, that would be nice,' she agreed weakly.

When she'd showered and shampooed the salt out of her hair Amelie put on a cotton robe with a tie belt and after fastening it at the waist got a man's equivalent out of the wardrobe, which Ethan had left behind. Knocking on the bathroom door, she called to Leo that she would leave it outside on the landing for him.

'It's all right, I'm decent. You can bring it in,' he

replied, and she pushed the door back slowly to reveal him standing barefoot wrapped in a towel. He was a sight to see, six feet, trimly built, with broad shoulders rising above the towel and a scattering of golden hair across his chest.

They stood facing each other without speaking for what seemed an eternity then he took a step forward and loosened the ties around her waist, and with the release of them the smooth, perfect, lines of her nakedness were revealed. His glance went over them and he let the towel that was covering him fall to the floor.

The heat of the attraction they had for each other was like a bright flame engulfing them, willing them to let it consume them. He felt ready to put down the burden of grief that he had carried for so long, and be the person he'd once been. He had the beautiful woman in his arms to thank for that and as he bent his head to kiss the cleft between her breasts she stroked his hair gently. She was melting with the desire he was arousing in her and when he lifted his head and their glances held, he said softly, 'Maybe this will make up for what didn't happen in the woods.'

He felt her stiffen and knew he'd said the wrong thing, brought back the memory of her humiliation, and even before she spoke he knew what she was going to say.

'Nothing could make up for that, Leo, unless you can tell me why you pick me up then put me down all the time. It does nothing for my self-confidence.'

She was retying the belt on her robe to let him see that the moment was over, but he didn't need telling. For the first time he'd felt he could make love to her without Delphine's face before him and go on from there, but Amelie, unaware of his past heartache, had brought up the subject of some of her own.

He'd got the message and it was hurting like a knife thrust that he of all people, who was generally thought to be every woman's dream man, should be spurned by the only one he'd ever wanted.

Where had it all gone wrong? he thought bleakly as he told her, 'I'm going back to my place in the robe you've found for me and will take my wet clothes with me. I'll return it in the morning.'

He went swiftly down the stairs and out into the night. Seconds later she saw the door close behind him as he disappeared into his apartment, and she thought that the day had ended as it had begun: miserable, sad… and hurtful.

Slumped in a chair by the window, Leo gazed out into the darkness and wondered where the delight of them getting to know each other had disappeared to. It was ironic that Amelie, who he ached for so much, should turn away from him when so many others would have jumped at the chance.

He'd felt their relationship was back on course as they'd walked home from the beach but had been wrong. He was attracted to her because she was different from any woman he'd ever met. When he'd let the towel fall he'd known she wanted him as much as he wanted her, but the barrier he'd put up that night in the woods was still there.

Amelie hadn't made love with the Antoine guy or she wouldn't still be a virgin, and as the memory came back of her telling him that she wasn't very experienced in the art of love-making, tenderness washed over him at the thought of how she'd wanted him to be the first.

So what had he done? Torn a strip off her for being so honest and without guile, and ever since they'd seemed to be on a downward path.

On Monday morning the surgery was fully staffed and back to normal after Friday's funeral. Harry announced on his arrival that they had chosen the lovely name of Freya for their baby daughter and that her christening was to take place on the following Sunday.

When he and Leo were briefly closeted together before the day commenced he said, 'Jenna is going to be one of her godmothers and we would like you to be her godfather, if you will, Leo.'

He had noticed that his friend and partner in the practice was not his usual brisk and capable self, and that the young French doctor on loan to them wasn't exactly chirpy either, so it didn't need a lot of brain power to work out that the oddly matched pair were not as happy as of late. But Leo's pleasure at being asked to be a godparent at the christening brought a smile and a ready acceptance.

'All the staff will be at the christening,' Harry told him meaningfully, and this time Leo's smile was wry.

'Is that so?' was the reply.

There was a knock on the door and when Harry called out for whoever it was to come in, Amelie appeared, seeking their advice with regard to a patient with an illness she hadn't come across before.

Leaving her in the company of the head of the practice, Leo left the room with a brief 'good morning' to the woman of his dreams, who was observing him warily.

As he proceeded to his own consulting room he was thinking that it was going to be his turn to be taking part in something special on the coming Sunday. He had been there for Amelie when she'd read the lesson at the funeral service to celebrate the ending of a life, and now it was his turn to take part in a joyful ceremony to acknowledge the beginning of a life.

It would be a cause for rejoicing rather than grief, the christening of little Freya. Would Amelie be there for him, as he'd been there for her? He doubted it. Togetherness was beginning to seem like a thing of the past.

As his first patient of the day ambled in, Leo put his own affairs on hold and had a smile of welcome for the local barber, Ambrose Whittaker, who was a genial old tease, always wanting to know why Leo wouldn't let him give him a short back and sides.

But not today. His face was pale and puckered with pain as he lowered himself down onto the nearest chair. 'I was out in the *Molly Maid* yesterday and slipped on the deck,' he said as Leo observed him questioningly. 'I've hurt my back something awful and I can't feel my legs properly.

Ambrose's life revolved around two things—his barber's shop on the harbour front and his boat, *Molly*

Maid. But today the only woman in his life was out of favour because he'd hurt himself on her timbers.

'Can you ease your shirt off and show me where the pain is?' Leo said.

'It's at the bottom of my back and down my legs,' he was told.

He examined the hardy old fellow carefully and pronounced, 'It could be pressure on a nerve root from the fall that is causing so much pain, but only the hospital can sort that out for you, Ambrose. If there is a prolapsed disc or pressure on a nerve, CT scanning or an MRI should reveal the cause.'

'I'm going to send for an ambulance to take you straight from here to A and E. Is there anyone I can get in touch with to go with you?'

He shook his grizzled head. 'Not unless the guy at the fishing-tackle shop next door could come with me, but he's only just finished looking after that young nephew of his who was hurt when his father crashed the car, and he has a business to run, don't forget. No. I'll be fine on my own just as long as they can sort out the pain.'

'I will prescribe you some painkillers,' Leo told him, 'and will ask someone from the chemist across the way to pop over with them while we're waiting for the ambulance. You should find movement easier once the pain is under control, but finding the source of it is vital to avoid permanent damage to your back.

'Take a seat in the waiting room, Ambrose, and once the ambulance arrives, the paramedics will help you carefully on board.' Knowing how much the boat meant to him, he asked, 'Where is the *Molly Maid*? Safe in the harbour, I hope.'

'Aye, that she is. No back pain on earth would stop me from seeing her safely anchored.'

It was lunchtime, and during the short break there was reference amongst the staff to the coming christening, but not from Amelie's direction. She didn't join in the conversation and Leo decided it meant she wasn't intending to go. If that was the case, it showed even more clearly that togetherness was not the order of the day… or the night!

For the moment he was prepared to let it ride. It was only Monday. There was the rest of the week to come before Sunday was upon them. His main concern at the moment was that she might decide to pack her bags and go back to where she'd come from, which was unthinkable.

Amelie was delighted for Leo's sake that he was to be one of the godparents for Harry and Phoebe's baby. She knew he would fulfil the pledges he made at the christening to their fullest degree, and wondered why she could be so sure of his feelings about something like that yet be totally confused about the way he felt about her.

The other night it would have been wonderful to have given in to the longing that he aroused in her and she in him, but what he'd said had brought those awful moments in the woods back and taken all the magic from the moment.

Unaware that he'd been ready to put his memories of what had happened to Delphine behind him, Amelie was constantly wondering if she would be faced with his changing moods all the time if she gave herself up to him. She'd told him once how much she needed security and there would be no secure feeling to be got from that.

But one thing *was* clear. She wanted to be at the christening for him, as he'd been at the funeral for her, and tried to imagine what it would be like if it was their child being christened, a beautiful girl or boy with their father's golden fairness.

But that sort of thing was disappearing into the realms of fantasy. At present they were further away from that kind of magic than they'd ever been. So it was a matter of going to the christening as just a friend and keeping a low profile.

In the middle of a week made up of endless days and miserable nights there was a surprise in store for Amelie in the form of a phone call from her parents to say they were on two months' leave and were staying in a rented apartment in London until it was up.

'So when are you coming to see us?' her mother wanted to know.

'I'm not sure,' she told her as the shock of hearing her voice was beginning to subside. 'I'm working in general practice in a beautiful village in Devon, so it will have to be when I have some free time. I don't want to cause the two doctors I'm working with any inconvenience.'

'Fair enough,' was the reply, without any overtones of

disappointment, and that had been it, but Lisette Benoir had sighed deeply as she'd replaced the phone. It was her husband's fault that she saw so little of her daughter and she was caught in the middle.

Their appearance in her life again had made Amelie feel threatened, though she didn't know why, and on one of the rare occasions when she and Leo spoke at the surgery he observed her keenly and asked, 'What's wrong?'

The temptation to tell him that he knew very well what was wrong was there, but she knew he was referring to her uneasy expression of that moment and told him stiffly, 'My parents are on vacation in London for the next two months. I've had a phone call out of the blue.'

'Really!' he exclaimed. 'And how do you feel about that?'

'That it was a duty call. I presume they got my number here from Ethan. The French hospital where I was based knew I had come to England at Ethan's suggestion.

'He didn't say anything about them trying to get in touch with me when he came over for the funeral, so it must have been only in the last couple of days they've tried to find me.'

'So what next? Are you going to go to see them?'

'Yes, when I can. I've told them my responsibilities are here in Bluebell Cove first and foremost.'

'I'll bet that went down like a lead balloon. How long is it since they last saw you?'

'A year. I will go one weekend, maybe on a Saturday for the day.'

'I'll take you there, if you like.'

Amelie could feel her colour rising. What was that supposed to mean? Was it a peace offering? The kind of thing he would do for anyone? Or a casual sort of reprimand aimed at her reluctance to make the effort? Or was Leo curious about the two high flyers who put lifestyle before caring?

He hadn't mentioned his family much, but he'd said once how it had been stressful when he'd first joined the practice, travelling backwards and forwards to Manchester to look after his mother who had suddenly become quite ill with a chest and breathing problem.

So there had been no reluctance to put family first on his part, and if the practice had been in the charge of anyone other than Ethan at that time, he might have had to quit living and working in one of England's most beautiful counties.

'Thanks for the offer,' she told him. 'I'll bear it in mind.'

'Yes, I'm sure you will,' he said as anger sparked off inside him, 'then you'll forget about it. For goodness' sake, Amelie! You will have to get a local train at some ungodly hour to take you to the mainline station for a longish journey to the capital, followed by shoving and pushing on the tube or taking a taxi.

'It would be the same on your return journey, going through all that palaver again, unless your parents wanted to bring you back to Bluebell Cove in the family limo.'

She was smiling. 'You obviously know the stresses of getting to London and back off by heart. Of my parents you know nothing at all, or you wouldn't have made that last comment. I am not allowed to interfere in their lives, so if your offer is still there when the time comes, I will accept it gratefully.'

He would take her to the ends of the earth if need be, as long as they could be together. As for her parents, time would tell what he thought of them when he met them.

His mother now lived abroad with his sister. He loved them both dearly and they felt the same about him. There was nothing he wanted more than to show Amelie what proper family life was like, but their relationship was a fiasco at the present time.

It was a mellow Sunday in August when those involved in the christening of Freya Katherine Balfour arrived at the village church.

The name of Katherine had been chosen in respect of Phoebe's much-loved sister Katie, who had always been there for her in difficult times and shared her moments of rejoicing. Along with Jenna, she was to be the other of the baby's godmothers, with Leo taking on the responsibilities of her godfather.

As the christening party walked to the front of the church, watched by the silent congregation, Phoebe's little boy, Marcus, was holding tightly onto Harry's hand and he was gazing down at him lovingly, while beside them Phoebe was carrying the baby that she would soon be passing to the godparents in turn during the ceremony.

For Amelie, sitting as close as she could to the font, there was a surprised smile from Leo that warmed her heart as he walked slowly past.

When he'd seen her and their glances had held, he'd thought tenderly how could he have ever thought she wouldn't be there? She was a part of this community now, with or without him, though he hoped that he was a part of the reason she had come to feel so at home there. When they arrived at the manor house afterwards, where there was a buffet laid on, he would take her to one side and…

They were taking up their positions in front of the font and the vicar was ready to start the service. His special time with Amelie would come later, he thought as he prepared to repeat the age-old words that would bind him to this child for ever.

Glades Manor was filled with well-wishers who had gone to share in the christening meal and the community spirit that was always there, be the gathering large or small.

The christening party had left before the rest of the congregation so as to be there to greet them when they arrived, and now Leo was searching for Amelie amongst the throng and telling himself with every passing second that she wasn't there.

Unbelievably, there was no sign of her and he thought grimly she must have seen her presence at the christening to be as much as she was prepared to be involved in on his behalf. So nothing had changed after all.

He was choking on the bitter taste of disappointment. Had Harry and Phoebe noticed her absence? he wondered. Probably not surrounded as they were by friends and well-wishers, and the rest of the surgery staff were enjoying themselves too much to notice that the young French doctor was giving the party a miss.

The urge to go and find out why she wasn't there was overwhelming but Phoebe had just put the baby in his arms and was about to take his photograph, and when that was done Harry and little Marcus were at his elbow, wanting to show him a new garden room that had just been added to the house.

So it was almost the middle of the afternoon before he could get away without offending anyone, and he drove to the village with the determination to find out if it was because of him she'd skipped the party.

He had part of the answer as soon as the house that Ethan had loaned her came into view. The car in the drive wasn't a limousine but it had the same luxurious kind of history and he didn't need to think twice about who it belonged to. It would seem that Amelie's wealthy parents had arrived.

They had to be the reason for Amelie's absence at the gathering at Glades Manor. He was ashamed that he had been so quick to judge. While turning the car round to go back to where he'd come from, she came to the door and waved for him to stop, then she was coming down the path towards him.

'I had a call on my mobile as I was coming out of

church,' she explained, 'to say that my parents had arrived and were here outside the house. I couldn't get to you to explain and hurried back here to greet them.'

'Where are they now?' he asked in a low voice,

'Inside. I'm about to make a meal but it will be a scrappy affair as I wasn't expecting them.'

'Are you going to introduce me?' he wanted to know, with the thought that it was an ideal moment to get to know the strange Benoirs. Strange because they seemed to have had little time for their daughter, had put their jobs first, which was unthinkable to anyone who loved children.

She was observing him doubtfully. 'Do you want me to?'

'Does the sun rise and set? Of course I do. I'm interested in anything connected with you, and with regard to you making a meal at such short notice, why don't we take them to the christening party instead, to save you the trouble of cooking and to introduce your family to Harry and Phoebe and your other friends?'

'Do you think we should?' she queried doubtfully.

'Yes, I do. There's loads of food and it will give your parents a chance to see something of English country life with all its attractions.'

'All right, I'll suggest it to them, but first, if that is what you want, I'll take you to be introduced.'

He was laughing. 'So you're going to chance it. Take the risk?'

'It won't be a risk. They'll be dumbfounded to discover that I know someone like you.'

'So lead on and we'll take it from there,' he said with

returning seriousness, while straightening his cuffs and wondering how the suit and tie would go down with her parents. Any other day than today he would have been in shorts and a cotton top, but the christening had called for more than that and so here he was dressed to kill, being introduced to two people that so far he had no cause to like.

He sensed that Amelie was on edge and as they entered the house he took her hand in his and gave it a squeeze that was meant to say, 'Don't worry. I'm going to marry you in any case,' but only ended up being what it was—a squeeze.

CHAPTER NINE

LISETTE and Charles Benoir were more or less what he'd expected them to be. Early fifties, smartly dressed, and very much in control of the situation, which was more than could be said of their daughter. Amelie's cheeks were flushed because where to some families there would be nothing strange in them turning up unexpectedly, clearly it was not the case with hers.

They were cordial enough when she introduced him to them and only by the flicker of an eyelid did either of them show surprise at the vision he presented.

It seemed that as Amelie hadn't been able to say exactly when she would be able to visit them in London, they had driven to Devon to seek her out and do some sightseeing at the same time.

She was clearly amazed that they'd made the effort and even more so when they'd graciously agreed to his suggestion that the four of them should join those still partying at Glades Manor—as long as their friends would have no objection, Charles Benoir stipulated.

'You have obviously shown some sense for once in coming to this place,' he said, addressing his daughter stiffly, with as good a command of the English language as hers.

Leo saw her mother flinch, watched the colour drain from Amelie's face, and in that moment all the loving protective tenderness he felt for her overwhelmed him. He'd felt the same way about Delphine. It had been there alongside the sexual chemistry, and now the kind fates were giving him a second chance to experience the wonder of that kind of love.

Maybe when Amelie understood the source of his caution she would forgive his behaviour. He hoped so. And as for the grumpy old guy who had just embarrassed her, he would take her away from that kind of thing if she would let him.

'What is *your* function in the community?' was Charles's next question.

'I am a partner in the village medical practice where your daughter is on loan to us at the moment,' he replied, and added, with a special smile in her direction, 'We will not be wanting her to leave us when the six months are up as Amelie is a very able member of the medical profession.'

'Ah! I see,' was the comment that greeted that information, and Leo wondered exactly what it was that Charles saw. But he was more interested in what Amelie had to say, and for the present she was saying nothing. The shock of finding her parents in Bluebell Cove and her father's sour manner were rendering her speechless.

It was always she who'd had to travel to them, so what had changed? She could tell they approved of Leo, his looks, his easy manner and the clothes he'd worn for the christening.

They must be wondering what part he played in her life, if any, and she thought wryly that she didn't know the answer to that herself. The only thing she was sure of was that she loved him and didn't know how to handle it.

The newcomers were made most welcome by Phoebe and Harry and when Amelie heard them ask her parents how long they were intending to stay, she was relieved to hear that it would be for just a couple of days before they headed off to Cornwall.

It was good to see them after a long absence, but she didn't want them butting into this precious thing she had with Leo. One-sided it might be, but it was still very important.

When Leo was about to leave them in the early evening she went out to the car with him and he said in a low voice, 'What do you think has brought this on, coming all the way from London to see you?'

'I don't know,' was the answer, 'but there will be a reason and it won't be because they were desperate to see me.'

'Don't say that,' he chided. 'None of us can choose our parents. Their manner may come from the kind of job they do. I felt sorry for your mother. She would seem not to have the same steel in her heart as your father. I take it that he rules the roost.'

'Yes, he does.' With pleading in her glance she went on, 'I wish you didn't have to go.'

'I can't intrude any longer into your reunion with them in spite of how flat it might be. Did you ask Harry if you could have the next two days off while they are here? I don't mind and I'm sure he won't.'

'No,' she said firmly. 'My parents have always put their job first, so I intend to do the same. I will be with them in the evenings, and during the day they intend to explore the coast and countryside.'

He was frowning. 'You can be quite inflexible when you want to be, Amelie.'

'Is that a reminder of when we were both fresh from the shower on the night we pulled Freddie from the sea?'

'It might be.'

'You don't understand, do you?' she said wearily. 'For as long as I can remember, I've felt unwanted, first by my parents and later by Antoine. Then I met you and everything was wonderful, until that night in the woods when I wanted us to make love and you rejected me. So is it surprising that I am not going to want to make that mistake again? If that seems inflexible, fine!'

She'd glanced over her shoulder a couple of times to make sure that Lisette and Charles hadn't been within earshot while she'd been opening her heart to him, but before he could reply to what she'd just said, she told him hurriedly, 'My parents must be thinking this is a long goodbye. I must go.'

'Yes, of course,' he agreed, reluctant to leave her after she'd explained her feelings so achingly and with such honesty. He said, 'It's been another day of mixed emotions, and it isn't over yet. So I'll leave you to catch up with what has been happening in your parents' lives, Amelie.' He smiled quizzically. 'Something tells me that you won't be in a hurry to tell them what has been happening in yours.' And with one last lingering look at the face that was still flushed and apprehensive, he pointed his car towards the apartments.

She wanted to run after him, throw herself into his arms, and, whether he wanted to hear it or not, tell him how he had changed her life, that she could endure anything her father had to say as long as he, Leo, was by her side, but that wasn't going to happen because they were waiting for her, seated in the back garden, watching a glorious sunset.

When she brought out a tray of drinks and joined them she had the strangest feeling of disquiet. Her father cleared his throat and said, 'We have sought you out because there is something that you have to be told.'

She thought, Here it comes, the reason they are here.

'Your mother and I are getting divorced,' he said without preamble, and she felt her jaw go slack.

'Why?' she gasped, and he actually managed a smile.

'Maybe we have seen too much of each other, working together as we have for so long,' he said, with a glance at her mother. 'We have both met other people and when the divorce comes through will be spending the rest of our lives with them.'

'You will be welcome to visit, of course,' her mother said hurriedly.

Amelie thought, Leo, where are you? Come and

tell me I'm dreaming this. I'm on the outside of things again, the afterthought again.

Yet did she want him to come and see her like this, taken aback, distressed to be told that her parents' marriage was over? She'd seen little enough of them before, so what would it be like now?

She'd asked if they required separate bedrooms and when they'd said no, they would be fine, she couldn't believe it was happening, her parents about to divorce sleeping in the second-largest bedroom of the house where Ethan had told her she must feel free to have someone stay with her if she needed company. That her first house guests would be them had been the last thing she could have imagined.

When they'd gone up to bed she decided she had to get out of the house for a while to calm down. Letting herself out quietly, she began to walk to the place she loved best.

It wasn't yet midnight, there were still a few folks around, but when she reached the headland it was deserted and the Balfours' house was in darkness, which left her a solitary figure staring out to sea.

Leo had seen her come out of the house. He hadn't been able to settle after returning to the apartment and had stood gazing out of the window for a long time, wishing he hadn't left her so soon on this strange day of highs and lows.

When he saw that she was on the move he set off to follow her. There was no way he was going to let her go out into the night alone, especially in the direction of the headland and the beach, which were her favourite places, as they were his, but not at this time of night.

The purchase of Four Winds House was going through. In the last week he'd had it surveyed and paid a holding deposit, and though Keith wasn't going to get his wish before he went on his cruise, the sale would be well along the way by the time he came back.

When she heard a step behind her Amelie turned quickly. There had been no one around when she'd arrived and when she saw Leo standing there she couldn't believe it.

'What are you doing out here?' he asked gently. 'Is something wrong, Amelie?'

'Yes,' she sobbed. 'Didn't I tell you there would be a reason for my parents' visit? They're getting divorced and it's all so cold-blooded. Both of them are going to marry someone else. Knowing what they're like, I'm surprised they even bothered to tell me.'

'Whew!' he exclaimed. 'Was it on the cards?'

'Not that I knew of,' she told him between sobs, and when he tried to take her in his arms to comfort her she moved away and said chokingly, 'How do we know it would work out for us if you ever wanted me enough to marry me? I don't want to be hurt again.'

'You wouldn't be,' he assured her gently, with his new resolve firmly in place, but it was not the time or place to tell her about Delphine.

He held out his arms again but she wouldn't let him hold her close and, still sobbing, she said, 'How can I be sure? Half the time you don't want me near you, and the rest of the time you are everything I've ever dreamt of, so how do I cope with that sort of situation? Please, go away, Leo. I want to be alone.'

'All right,' he agreed grimly, 'but I'm not moving until you start making tracks for home. I shall be following you at a distance until I've seen you safely inside.'

'Please yourself,' she said wearily. 'Do whatever you think best, but leave me alone.'

He did as she'd asked once he'd seen her back where she belonged.

Back in the apartment, he was remembering that night at the airport when he'd gone to meet her and how he'd been disappointed and amazed that the odd-looking creature drifting sleepily towards him in the arrivals lounge was the young French doctor they were taking on at the surgery for six months.

They'd come a long way since then, but not as far as he wanted them to. Patience was still the name of the game, and after what Amelie had said about them back there on the headland, he might need plenty of it. In the meantime, he was going to do what she'd asked him to do, leave her alone for a while, and then when he felt she was ready he would tell her about Delphine, how at last he was ready to let her memory be a sweet and distant thing instead of a constant reminder of pain and grief.

After a sleepless night Amelie was up and about before her parents came down for the breakfast she'd prepared, and leaving them to clear away afterwards she was at the surgery in good time for Monday morning's overflow from the weekend.

When she and Leo met up again he was coming out of the staff kitchen with a mug of tea in his hand, and when she would have stopped to apologise for the way she'd told him to go the night before he didn't give her the chance. As the words trembled on her lips he wished her a brief good morning and disappeared into his consulting room, shutting the door behind him.

So much for that, he thought as he drank the tea. But how long was he going to be able to keep it up?

When a young guy who looked like a student presented himself in front of him in the late morning he looked far from well and was anxious to explain why he was there.

'I've been to a few late-night parties with my college friends over the last week,' he said, 'and I think I might have picked up some sort of virus. My throat is raw, I keep feeling faint, and I've got a rash.'

'Any aversion to bright lights?' was Leo's first question. The young man shook his head. 'Show me the rash, then.' And in keeping with the patient having no problem with a bright light, he concluded that it was not the dreaded red rash of meningitis.

'Does it itch?' was the next thing he wanted to know.

'Yes, a lot,' was the answer to that, and as Leo examined it more closely he saw that there were red raised areas on the skin and where the patient had scratched them they'd turned to blisters.

'What have you been taking at these parties?' he questioned.

'If you mean drugs…nothing,' was the reply. 'My parents would go ballistic if I ever did that.'

'I was not referring to anything in particular,' he told him. 'Just trying to get a picture of what has caused this. Have you been on, or near a farm at all?'

'Er, yes. The parents of one of my mates have a farm. I was at a party there last week.'

'Did you handle any live stock on the farm?'

'I was around some cows that didn't look too lively.'

'Did you touch any of them?'

'I might have done, but why are you asking me all this?'

'It is possible that you might have contracted anthrax from the cattle. I'm going to take some blood samples and send them to the laboratory for a fast result.

'In the meantime, I'll give you something for your throat, which is very inflamed. Then go home, tell your parents what I've said, and that you have to rest until the results come through.

'There are two kinds of anthrax infection—cutaneous anthrax that affects the skin and is reasonably easy to cure, and pulmonary anthrax that affects the lungs and is much more serious. In your case, I would think from my experience of the illness that it is the less serious of the two.

'We will soon know if I'm right, and if I am the authorities will need the name of the farmer and the address of the farm as it will have to be inspected to see if the infection came from the animals themselves or from the land on which they were grazing, where it could have lain dormant for many years.

'I'll be in touch as soon as I have any news from the path lab. If it is what I suspect, we'll take it from there.'

By that time the youth was looking decidedly nervous, having got the picture of how rare anthrax infection was in humans and how serious it could be, and he went to do what he'd been told to do…rest, which was the only good thing about it. It gave him a very good reason for lying on top of his bed for hours on end, watching television.

For Amelie it was a morning of the usual things—a young pregnant woman with unpleasant morning sickness, a patient recently diagnosed with diabetes and suffering from the side-effects of the medication he'd been prescribed, which called for a change of plan, and an elderly woman who'd forgotten to take her blood-pressure medication with her on holiday and was desperate for reassurance that it wasn't out of control.

All of which she had given her full attention, but when one of the receptionists came round with elevenses and she had a few moments to herself, the flaws in her family life came flooding back and with them the memory of how she'd let Leo see how unsure she was of the future. She needed security like she needed to breathe.

She was deeply in love with him but wasn't sure of

his reactions sometimes. And her parents, enjoying the delights of Devon, with Cornwall to come, would appear to have not given a second's thought to how she would react to their news.

Why she felt so upset about that she didn't know as she rarely saw them in any case, but the truth of the matter was that they'd spoilt it, taken away the wonderful feeling of security that had been hers ever since she'd come to Bluebell Cove and met Leo.

The vicar's wife had been in earlier, selling tickets for a hoe down on the coming Saturday night, and on impulse Amelie had bought one, without knowing what she was going to do with it as she wasn't in the mood for socialising.

Yet she could feel her batteries beginning to recharge after the upset of the night before. She was coming out of the slough of despondency. Her parents' insensitivity was not going to spoil her life any more, she told herself.

They were due back in the village from their stay in Cornwall early on Saturday evening and after a brief stop were driving back to London. So once they'd gone she was going to go to the hoe down.

It would be on her own as Leo had already demonstrated that he'd taken her demand to leave her alone seriously. So it would not be a night of nights or anything of that kind, but it would be better than staying in and moping.

In the days leading up to Saturday the young student

with the rash had it diagnosed as the anthrax bacterium of the cutaneous type, which was treatable with penicillin. So he was still at home, resting and taking the medication, with Leo keeping a firm watch on his progress.

The hay-fever sufferers were paying the penalty of heavy pollen counts and the added problem of harvest reaping, which meant that theirs was a continuous presence in the waiting room. But for the rest of the population of Bluebell Cove there was a general air of well-being.

As the weekend drew near and still in a more positive frame of mind, Amelie was debating whether to buy tight jeans and a check shirt to wear for the hoe down. Having seen something along those lines in the window of the boutique, she decided to brave the cold stare of Leo's friend Georgina and go to try them on in her lunch hour.

The owner wasn't there, she was relieved to see. A young, brown-haired girl was serving and as she moved along the rails of fashionable clothes her enthusiasm was waning because it would normally have been Leo that she was out to please. But in the present state of affairs she didn't even know if he would be there.

Yet she already had the high leather boots to go with the clothes, and the jeans and shirt fitted perfectly when she tried them on, so those things and the fact that she felt she needed cheering up all combined to persuade her to buy, and moments later she left the shop with a spring in her step.

On Saturday night she was ready in good time. The clothes she'd bought looked good on her. She hadn't a hair out of place beneath a cowboy hat that she'd found in one of the cupboards in the house, and she thought wistfully that all she lacked was Leo. Without him, nothing was the same.

But he was still giving her some space, keeping as far away from her as possible out of working hours and during them acknowledging her presence only briefly.

She was waiting for her parents to arrive. She wasn't planning on going to the hoe down until they'd been and gone.

A flask of coffee and sandwiches for the journey were waiting for them. She knew her father wouldn't want to linger after he'd been for petrol to get them home and typical of the man their car pulled up outside the house at exactly the time he'd said it would, and as soon as he'd dropped her mother off he went to the garage.

The moment he had gone Lisette asked urgently, 'Do you love Leo Fenchurch, Amelie?'

'Yes,' she told her, surprised at the question. 'I love him more than life itself.'

Her mother nodded, as if that was what she wanted to hear, and went on to say, 'Then if he asks you to marry him, tell him yes. Turn your dreams into reality. That kind of love comes only once in a lifetime. Don't let it pass you by.'

Amelie was listening to what she was saying in complete bewilderment.

'Why are you telling me all this?' she asked.

'Because I know what that kind of love feels like,' Lisette replied, 'but mine was lost to me and I ended up marrying Charles.'

'And is that the reason why you're divorcing?'

'Yes, that's the reason. Charles doesn't think people should have feelings. Given the chance, he would exchange me for a robot without batting an eyelid.'

'So *my* feelings of rejection come from that tarnished point of view, do they?' Amelie said. 'Yet you've always gone along with it.'

'I had no choice because you are not his child,' was the incredible reply. 'He had always wanted me. Charles was head of my department, as he is now, and he said he would marry me and that I could keep you, as long as he came first in everything and you were always kept out of sight in the background. Does that explain what has happened over the years?'

Groping her way to the nearest chair, Amelie sank down on it. 'So who is my father?' she croaked.

'He was an Englishman called Robert Templeton. Robbie was killed in a skiing accident when I was four months pregnant. We were planning to be married before you were born. He was the only man I've ever loved, so you see why I say if Leo loves you as much as you love him and he asks you to marry him, don't hesitate.'

'I've got to be asked first,' she said flatly. 'And why are you telling me all this now after allowing me to feel so unwanted all my life?'

'Charles would never let me. He is a proud man and said he would throw both of us out if I told you, and it is he who is the wealthy one. I own nothing. But now I see you with this man and know it is the time to speak because I can tell he will love and protect you.'

They could hear the man she had known as her father all her life coming up the drive and Lisette said, 'He thinks I have found someone else but it isn't so. It's just an excuse to get away from him.

'There is just one thing before we leave,' she said pleadingly. 'If you marry your doctor, please let me come to the wedding.' Then, reverting back to her usual manner, she kissed her lightly on the cheek and went out to join her father, leaving Amelie to follow her to where their car was parked at the roadside as if nothing unusual had happened.

She went back inside on leaden feet and when the door closed behind her she knew she wanted Leo there to hold her, talk through with her what she'd just been told, but there'd been no sign of him at the apartment all day and the hoe down would have started by now. She could hear country and western music filtering through from the village hall.

As she stood irresolutely, fighting back tears, she saw him coming up the drive, and when she opened the door to him he looked at the clothes she was wearing and said, 'So you *are* intending going to the hoe down, Amelie. I was beginning to think you were giving it a miss.'

When she didn't answer he told her, 'I've stayed away from you for as long as I could but not any more. I saw your parents driving off as I was coming up the road. Was everything all right with them?'

Ironically, now he was there she found she couldn't speak; she was still in shock, so she just nodded and desperate to bring the moment back to normality picked up her handbag and her ticket for the hoe down and with a grimace of a smile pointed to the door.

CHAPTER TEN

AS THEY walked the short distance to the village hall Leo glanced at her a few times and wondered what was wrong, but something told him not to press her to tell him.

It was significant that her parents had stopped off on their way back to London and had left Amelie in this state. Slow anger was kindling inside him at the thought of them bringing any more insecurity into her life.

On the other hand, the state she was in with her ashen face and the lack of response speechwise could be for some other reason than the Benoirs, yet he doubted it. He'd had plans for tonight, big ones, but with Amelie clearly emotional all he could do was register concern.

The hoe down was in full swing when they got there, and a barn dance was in progress, so he took her out onto the village green and in the scented autumn night asked gently, 'Are you going to tell me what's wrong, Amelie? I've never seen you like this before. It's as if you're in shock.'

'Charles isn't my father,' she croaked, and he observed her incredulously.

'Who told you that?'

'My mother, the one person who is sure to know.'

'So that is what it's all about,' he said slowly. 'Why he's so crabby. Not all men have Harry Balfour's generosity of spirit. How do you feel about that?'

'I don't know,' she said raggedly. 'It was so unexpected I'm still in shock.'

'What made your mother tell you after all this time?'

'She didn't want me to make the mistakes she made.'

'And what were those?'

'Not marrying the man she loved and losing him in an accident, I suppose, then marrying a man she *didn't* love. It was all so sad, Leo.'

He reached out for her and held her close, and there were no requests to leave her alone this time. As he looked down on the shining crown of her dark head he said, 'The past creeps up on us when we least expect it, Amelie. I've made *my* peace with my past. Would you like to hear about it?'

'I suppose so,' she said listlessly, and he led her by the hand away from the noise to a bench outside the church and when they were settled he said, 'You are the only person I have ever spoken to about this.'

Her eyes widened, he had her full attention now. 'When I was twenty-five and in my last year at medical school I fell madly in love with one of my fellow students. Her name was Delphine and we were both of the same mind, that we wanted to spend the rest of our lives together, but it was not to be.

'Delphine had an undetected heart defect and in the middle of our wedding arrangements she was rushed into hospital with a cardiac arrest that proved fatal. The heartbreak and pain that followed her death were indescribable, feelings I've never forgotten. So much so that I've spent the last ten years on the social merry-go-round instead of putting down roots and having a family, because I didn't want to risk ever having to go through that again.

'But then you came along and changed my life for ever. Being with you, falling in love with you, didn't feel like a risk, it felt like it was heaven sent, yet still I was haunted by the past. But not any more, Amelie. Finally I'm free of the guilt and of the fear, free to tell you how much I love and adore you.'

There were tears in her eyes. 'Couldn't you have told me about Delphine before?' she asked gently. 'I would have understood you so much better. Poor Delphine. Poor you.'

'Yes,' he agreed. 'I won't ever forget her but it will be without the nightmare that I've carried around with me all this time. I am ready to move on if you'll only say you love me.'

The bluebell eyes looking into his would have been enough answer but she asked tenderly, 'How many times would you like me to say it? Ten, twenty, a thousand times, or more?'

'More,' he murmured with his lips against her hair. And then he was kissing her, and kissing her, until she said breathlessly, 'I can't believe that only an hour ago I was feeling so miserable, yet now I have a father who would have loved me had he lived, and a better understanding with my mother, but you are my true joy-bringer, Leo, with your love and tenderness and the desire you arouse in me. The Angel Gabriel would find you a hard act to follow.'

He was smiling at the comparison and, taking her hand, he brought her to her feet and asked, 'Can you smell food, Amelie? They will be serving supper at the hoe down about now, and it is always a feast of delight, so shall we join them? And then, afterwards, would you like to go for a drive?'

'Absolutely,' she replied dreamily. 'Whatever you say.'

For the first time in her life she was totally content and it was all due to the man beside her. He hadn't asked her to marry him yet, but she felt sure he would when he was ready.

The meal was, as Leo had said it would be, a feast, with cheeses galore and fresh vegetables from village gardens served as salads and soups, along with ham from the pig farms and fruit from the trees, and fresh loaves from the bakery, crispy and warm.

They sat with Harry and Phoebe and their two little ones, and while the two women chatted the head of the practice said to Leo, 'So have you been to fix it with the bellringers yet, and suggested to Ethan that he gets a season ticket for crossing the Channel? Since he went to live in France he's been over here more than he's been over there.'

'Is it so obvious?' he replied laughingly. 'We have to fix a date first, but it won't be long, I hope.'

It became clear that Leo hadn't meant a lazy cruise around the neighbourhood when he'd suggested they go for a drive as the road signs indicated that he was heading for the airport.

Minutes later they were parking there and as she stood gazing around her on the tarmac he said, 'This way, Amelie.' She followed him to the arrivals lounge. The walkway from the aircraft was deserted, as he had hoped it would be, and as she observed him questioningly he went down on one knee and said, 'This is the place where my life began again. Will you marry me, Amelie?'

She was laughing, joyful peals of delight. 'Yes, please,' she cried, and if she'd had any ideas that the request might have been impulsive rather than planned, he opened his clenched palm and revealed a solitaire diamond ring.

'I bought it weeks ago,' he told her. 'Yet the chance to ask you never seemed to materialise, but now all our problems are sorted, so how soon can I put a band of gold on your finger next to the diamond, Amelie?'

'Soon.' She glowed. 'I would like to be married while it's still harvest-time if possible. How long does it take to get a licence?'

'And a memorial plaque.'

'What for?'

'For *this* spot, to commemorate *this* event, if the airport authorities will allow it,' he teased. 'And now come here, my lovely French doctor, and let me show you how much I love you.' As he kissed his wife-to-be a cheer went up from the curious and the romantics who had been gathering to watch.

As they approached the village on their way home, Leo pulled up across the way from the headland and said, 'I have something to tell you, Amelie. Would you like to get out of the car for a moment?'

Taking her hand, he took her to the same spot where they'd met unexpectedly on the night that her father had told her about the divorce. Turning her towards the solitary house that once again was in darkness as Keith was still on his cruise, he said, 'This will be my wedding present to you.'

Her eyes were round pools of amazement. 'You mean that we...'

'Yes, I mean that we are going to live here. I bought this house for us. I know how much you love the water and this house has the best sea views of anywhere in Bluebell Cove. The sale is going through and as I'm a first-time buyer it shouldn't take long. Would you like to wait until it is ours before we marry, or just set a date now and hope it might have gone through when the day arrives?'

'I'd rather wait,' she said joyfully, 'so that we can start our life together in this wonderful house.'

'Me too,' he said, holding her close. 'And now I'm going to take you home to bed in your posh lodgings, then it will be bed for me too in the apartment, and soon I won't ever have to do that again.'

EPILOGUE

SEPTEMBER was almost gone, October was waiting at the gate, and the house was finally theirs. The sale had gone through smoothly and they'd been sure enough of its completion to fix a date and arrange their wedding.

The church was full and if there were some present who wondered how the young French doctor had managed to capture Leo Fenchurch, they needed only to observe his expression as Amelie appeared on the arm of Charles Benoir, dressed in a white wedding gown that set off her dark tresses and clung to her slender curves.

There were no bridesmaids, but Phoebe Balfour, with whom Amelie had become firm friends, was her matron of honour and Harry was Leo's best man.

His mother and sister were there from abroad, and on being introduced to her new mother-in-law who, though frail, had the same looks and personality as her son, Amelie had felt that here was a kindred spirit.

Her own mother was seated in one of the front pews, elegant and withdrawn on the outside but inside rejoicing that it was all coming right for her daughter.

She and Charles had brought a very special wedding present with them for Amelie and her new husband. It was the news that the divorce was off. They'd both only been fantasising about having someone else and had decided to stay together because they'd been partners too long to change their ways, and if they'd never thought her to be particularly striking before, today their daughter, Amelie, looked radiant and would continue to be so because she and Leo had reached out and taken hold of the kind of love that lasted for ever.

The evening reception, the final part of the wedding festivities, was over. Their special day was coming to an end, but not yet. They'd arrived at the house and after he'd unlocked the door Leo bent and, picking Amelie up in his arms, carried her over the threshold and up into a large bedroom with a breathtaking view of the sea.

Laying her gently on the bed, he looked down on her and said softly, 'It's been a long journey for us both, Amelie. But at last we are together, and if I have my way we'll stay here in Bluebell Cove for ever.'

Amelie smiled up at her handsome new husband. 'This place has healed us both. I could never consider being anywhere else. I came here because I was running away, but instead I have finally come home, and that is all because of you, Leo. I do love you so much.'

'And I love you, my beautiful French wife.' And with his eyes darkening with tenderness and desire, 'Now

I'm going to show you just how much, Amelie, because we're in the right place and it's the right time.'

And after that it felt as if there was only the sea, the sand and the two of them in the whole wide world.

WEDDING IN DARLING DOWNS

BY
LEAH MARTYN

Leah Martyn loves to create warm, believable characters for the Mills & Boon® Medical Romance™ series. She is grounded firmly in rural Australia, and the special qualities of the bush are reflected in her stories. For plots and possibilities she bounces ideas off her husband on their early-morning walks. Browsing in bookshops and buying an armful of new releases is high on her list of enjoyable things to do.

CHAPTER ONE

IT WAS winter. Early morning. And cold.

Emma burrowed her chin more deeply into the roll-collar of her fleece as she jogged the last of the way home across the park.

The cawing of a crow disturbed the peace. Emma slowed her step and looked about her. She loved this time before sun-up. The moist atmosphere never failed to lift her spirits. And heaven knew she could do with a bit of that. Mist was everywhere, as translucent and filmy as a bridal veil. It seemed to have a life of its own, breathing up from the earth, softening the stark winter outlines of the trees.

Emma clicked back into the present, regaining her momentum. She hadn't time to be indulging in fanciful thoughts. Another long day at the surgery loomed. But time for Kingsholme to keep functioning as a viable medical practice was running out. Her father's sudden death almost three months ago had left Emma in disarray. Both personally and professionally. If she didn't line up another partner quickly, the medical practice that had been founded by her grandfather would have to close. One lone doctor, namely *her*, couldn't hope to generate enough income to keep the place functioning.

The end result would be for the practice and the beautiful old home that encompassed it to go under the auctioneer's hammer.

The new owner, perhaps someone with an eye to the tourist potential of the district, would probably turn it into a bed and breakfast. And their little town would be left without a resident medical officer.

Emma's spirits plummeted to a new low. The nerves in her stomach began knotting up again.

I *should* be able to get a doctor interested enough to work here, she berated herself. Even a decent locum who could fill the gap until a suitable partner came along. Perhaps her interviewing technique was all wrong. The few people who had actually showed, had taken one look at the set-up and promptly, if a bit awkwardly, fled.

Lifting the latch on the back gate, she made her way along the path and ran quickly up the steps to the verandah. She had time for a shower and marginally less time for breakfast. And then she'd better open the surgery and start seeing patients.

In her consulting room later, Emma threw her pen aside and lifted her arms in a long stretch. It had been another crazy morning. She couldn't go on like this. She just couldn't…

A soft tap sounded on her door before it opened. 'Moira—' Emma managed a passable smile for the practice manager '—come to tell me it's lunch time already?'

Moira Connelly, who'd been with the practice for at least twenty years, came into the room and closed the door. She looked pointedly at Emma's untouched cup of tea and the half-eaten muffin and clucked a motherly concern. 'You don't eat enough, Emma.'

Emma lifted a shoulder in a resigned shrug. 'I'll be out in a tick. Perhaps we could open a can of soup for lunch.'

'I'll manage something.' Moira flapped a hand in dismissal. 'Actually, I came to tell you there's a Dr Declan O'Malley here to see you.'

A sudden light leapt into Emma's green eyes. 'Has he come about the job?'

Moira shook her head. 'Apparently, he knew your dad.'

'Oh—' Emma bit her lips together, the grief she felt still raw and unchannelled.

Moira paused, pulling the edges of her cardigan more closely together, as if warding off a sudden chill. 'I expect he wants to offer his condolences.'

'I guess so…' Emma's short ray of hope faded into a heavy sigh. 'Give me a minute, please, Moira and then ask Dr O'Malley to come through.'

Emma watched the door close behind Moira and then swung off her chair and went to stand at the picture window, looking out. She imagined this Dr O'Malley was a contemporary of her father's from Melbourne. In earlier times Andrew Armitage had forged a rather distinguished medical career before the call of *home* had brought him back here to the town of Bendemere on the picturesque Darling Downs in Queensland.

Emma had spent holidays here, been happy here. So it had seemed only natural to come flying home when her world had fallen apart. Her return had coincided with the resignation of her father's practice partner. Emma had stepped in, proud to work alongside her father. In the past year she'd begun to pull the shattered bits of her life together until it was almost making a whole picture again.

Then her father had suffered a massive heart attack, leaving her to cope alone.

Declan O'Malley prowled the reception area. In a few seconds he'd know whether Emma Armitage would welcome his visit or tell him to go to hell. God, he hoped she'd be reasonable. The situation demanded she be reasonable.

'Oh, Dr O'Malley—' Moira fluttered back into reception. 'Sorry to keep you waiting. Emma was just finishing up.' She waved towards an inner corridor. 'Second door on your left.'

'Thanks.' Declan acknowledged the information with a slight lifting of his hand. He paused outside what was obviously Emma's consulting room, took a deep breath, gave a courtesy knock to warn of his imminent entry, and then moved in with every intention of being at his diplomatic best.

Emma turned from the window. Her throat dried. Every molecule in her body felt as though it had been swiftly rearranged. She'd been expecting a man in her father's age group, a man in his sixties. But Declan O'Malley in no way fitted that description. He looked in the prime of his life, all six feet of him. Mentally roping off the very mixed emotions she felt, she went forward and offered her hand. 'Dr O'Malley.'

'Emma.' Declan ditched formality, enfolding her hand easily within his own. 'Your father told me such a lot about you.'

Well, it's more than he told me about *you*, Emma thought, blinking several times in quick succession, long lashes swooping against her pale cheeks.

'I can imagine what a difficult time this must be for you.' Declan's words filled an uncomfortable gap. 'I would have been in touch before this but I've been out of the country. I've just caught up with things in general.'

She nodded. His voice was deep and resonant. Smooth like red wine. Emma could feel its impact like a thump to her chest, momentarily disarming her. 'Please… have a seat.' She indicated a conversation area in front of the big bay window.

As they settled, Emma took several quick, all-encompassing peeks at him, recording short finger-combed dark hair, a lean face, strong features, olive complexion. And blue eyes reflecting a vivid intensity that could see things she didn't want seen…

Declan looked at the woman he had to deal with here. Emma Armitage was strikingly lovely. She had amazing facial bones and her hair looked cornsilk-soft, blonde and straight, just brushing her shoulders. But it was her eyes that drew him. They were green like the deepest part of the forest, framed within thick tawny lashes. And they were accessing him warily. He had to step carefully here. He didn't want to embarrass her, hurt her. But he'd come on a mission and, somehow, he had to accomplish it.

But how to begin?

'So, how come you knew my father?' In a lightning strike, Emma took the initiative.

Declan refused to be put on the back foot; instead he cut to the chase. 'When I was an intern at St John Bosco's in Melbourne, your father was my boss. I'm where I am today in medicine because of Andrew. In the early days of my training, I was ready to chuck it. Oh, boy was I ready! But your dad talked me out of it. He was an amazing man.'

A new loneliness stabbed through Emma's heart. 'Yes, he was…'

A pause. Awkward. Until Declan resumed gently, 'Over the years I kept in touch with your dad. Any career-change I considered, I ran it past him first. He was my mentor and I considered him my *friend*. And I don't use the word lightly.'

Emma nodded, swallowing past the lump in her throat. 'I appreciate your taking the time to come here.' Her mouth compressed as if shutting off the flow of emotion. 'You must be very busy in your own practice.'

'I'm between jobs, actually. That's another reason why I'm here.'

Emma straightened in her chair, the oddest feeling of unease slithering up her backbone. 'I don't understand.'

Declan's perceptions whipped into high awareness. Something in her eyes and the defensive little tilt of her chin held him back from explaining further. The last thing he needed was for her to start resenting him before they could speak properly. So, softly-softly. 'Uh...this could take a while.' He glanced briefly at his watch. 'Could we perhaps have a spot of lunch somewhere and talk?'

Emma held back a harsh laugh. He just had no idea. 'I don't have time to go out to lunch, Dr O'Malley. Patients will be arriving soon for the afternoon surgery.'

'You're the sole practitioner?'

'Yes,' she said, thinking that was another story in itself.

He'd assumed she'd have engaged a locum, but obviously not. Declan thought quickly. Emma Armitage had a brittleness about her—she was obviously worked to death. He cursed his lack of foresight and sought to remedy it swiftly. 'Understood.' He gave a brief shrug. 'I'm here and available. Put *me* to work.'

So, what was he saying? That he'd share her patient list? Emma's eyes widened. She didn't want to be blunt but she had only this man's word he was a competent doctor. First and foremost, she had a duty of care to her patients… She turned her head slightly, raising a hand to sweep her loose fair hair away from her neck. 'Is that a good idea, do you think?'

Declan sat riveted. Her little restive movement had briefly exposed her nape, with skin as tender and sweet as a baby's. He tried without success to dismiss the unexpected zip of awareness through his gut. What was the question again? Idiot. Got it. 'Sorry.' He gave an apologetic twist of his hand. 'You'll need some ID.' Reaching back, he took out his wallet and spun it open in front of her. 'Driver's licence.'

Emma nodded, registering that the photo on the licence matched the face of the man sitting opposite her. So he was who he claimed he was.

'My card as well.' He held out the buff-coloured business card towards her.

Frowning a bit, Emma took it, almost dazzled by the impressive array of letters after his name. 'You completed your orthopaedic speciality in Edinburgh, Scotland?'

His hesitation was palpable. Then he said, 'Yes. It was always the discipline I felt drawn to.'

She handed the licence back with the ghost of a smile but retained his card. 'Should I be addressing you as Professor O'Malley, then?'

'I wouldn't think so.' In a second his eyes were filled with unfathomable depth and shadows. 'Declan will do just fine. So—' he slid his wallet back into his pocket '—going to let me loose on your patients, then?'

'Why wouldn't I?' Emma felt a curious lightening of her spirits. To be able to share her workload, even for a few hours, would be wonderful. 'I'll give you the ones who like a good chat.'

'I guess I asked for that.' Declan's look was rueful and he uncurled to his feet. 'I'll grab a burger somewhere and my bag and be back in—' he checked his watch '—twenty minutes?'

Swept along by his enthusiasm, Emma stood hastily. 'Take whatever time you need.' She began to usher him out. 'You can use Dad's consulting room.'

Declan stopped, looked down at her, his expression closed. 'If you're sure?'

Emma nodded, leading him down the corridor to the room next to her own. She opened the door and went in.

Declan followed hesitantly. Soft early afternoon light streamed in through the windows, leaving a dappled pattern across the large desk and the big leather chair behind it. A big chair for a big man, Declan thought. A man with a big heart that had in the end let him down far earlier than it should have.

'It's been cleaned but basically everything is as Dad left it.' Emma moved across to touch the tips of her fingers to the rosewood patina of the desktop.

Declan felt emotion drench him. Yet he knew what he felt at the man's loss was only a fraction of what his daughter must be feeling. He spun to face her, questioning softly, 'Are you sure about this, Emma?'

'Quite sure. It will be good to see the place being used again.' The words were husky, as though she was pushing them through a very tight throat.

Declan wanted to reach out to her. Hold her close. Feel the press of her body against his. Take her grief into himself... Oh, for crying out loud! He cleared his throat. 'I'll see you back here, then, in a half-hour or so.'

'Feel free to come straight through and get yourself set up,' Emma said as they left the consulting room and she pulled the door closed. 'I'll just need to make a call and verify your registration before you take surgery.'

Declan inclined his head, acknowledging her eyes were clearly weighing the effect of her statement on him. He gave a mental shrug. As far as his accreditation went, he had nothing to hide. 'Good,' he agreed. 'You should do that.'

'And I'll brief Moira,' Emma added. 'She'll make sure the patients find you.'

'Moira.' Declan lifted a dark brow. 'The lady I spoke to in reception, right?'

Emma nodded. 'She's been with us for years. I sometimes think she could treat most of the patients herself.' Her eyes lit impishly, her full mouth hooking into a half smile.

The impact of that curve of her lips hit him like a sandbag to the solar-plexus. He flicked back the edges of his jacket, jamming his hands low on his hips. 'Let's try to push through early, then.' He paused, his blue gaze roaming over her in an almost physical caress. 'We do need to talk, Emma.'

For a second Emma felt as though she could hardly breathe, his proximity sending a warm rush of want to every part of her body. Feminine places she'd almost forgotten existed. She pulled back, regaining her space. 'We'll arrange something…'

Even though the circumstances weren't ideal, it was good to be back in a consulting room with his feet under a desk again, Declan thought. At least he was doing something useful and if it lasted no more than the rest of the day, he'd give it his best shot.

He was amazed how the time flew. He saw a steady stream of patients, each without exception with a comment about his presence in the practice. He'd answered as honestly as he could, 'I'm helping out Dr Armitage for the moment.' And whether that situation became permanent still depended on so many things. So many.

He called in his final patient for the day, Carolyn Jones. She looked anxiously at Declan. 'I was expecting to see Emma—Dr Armitage.'

'Emma's passed some of her patients over to me today, Mrs

Jones,' Declan offloaded with a cheerful smile. 'I'll do my best to help.'

Carolyn gripped her handbag more tightly. 'I...really just wanted a chat…'

'That's fine,' Declan encouraged, leaning back in his chair, his look expectant. 'I'm here to listen.'

'I want to go back on my sleeping pills. I've tried to do without them for a couple of months now but I just can't manage—' Carolyn stopped and swallowed heavily.

For a second Declan considered a quick consult with Emma. But she had enough on her plate. He could handle this. He leaned forward, speed-reading the patient notes.

The lady was sixty-one but there was nothing leaping out at him to warrant extra caution. He raised his gaze, asking, 'Is there a reason why you can't sleep, Carolyn?'

'I've a difficult family life. Emma knows about it—'

'I see. Suppose you tell me about it as well and see how we go?'

Carolyn lifted her shoulders in a long sigh. 'My husband, Nev, and I are bringing up our three grandchildren. Their ages range from seven to ten.'

'Hard going, then,' Declan surmised gently. 'What circumstances caused this to come about?'

Carolyn gave a weary shrug. 'The whole town knows about it. Our son was a soldier serving overseas. He was killed by a roadside mine. Our daughter-in-law, Tracey, took off and then got in with the wrong crowd. Started seeing someone else. She was always a bit *flighty*.'

Declan raised his eyebrows at the old-fashioned word.

'She's with this new boyfriend now. We've heard they're into drugs. I don't understand how she could just dump her children…'

Declan's caring instincts went out to his patient. But, on the other hand, there were strategies she could try that might induce natural sleep—

'The children are still unsettled, especially at night,' Carolyn said, interrupting his train of thought. 'I just can't get off to sleep and then I'm useless the next day.' She paused and blinked. 'I've really had enough....'

So, crisis time then. Declan thought quickly. As a general rule, sleeping pills were prescribed in small doses and only for a limited time-span. But his patient sounded desperate—desperate enough to... He got to his feet. 'Carolyn, excuse me a moment. I've been out of the country for a while. I'll just need to recheck on dosage and so on.'

Declan came out of his office the same time as Emma emerged from hers. Her brows flicked in question. 'Finished for the day?'

'Not quite.' He accompanied her along to reception. 'Actually, I wanted a word about a patient, Carolyn Jones.'

'The family have ongoing problems,' Emma said quietly.

'I gathered that.' Declan backed himself against the counter and folded his arms. 'Carolyn wants to go back on her sleeping pills. I wondered about her stability.'

'You're asking me whether she's liable to overdose on them?'

'Just double-checking.'

'She cares too much about those children to do anything silly,' Emma said.

'Quite. But still—'

'The sleepers Carolyn takes are quite mild,' Emma cut in. 'They don't produce a hangover effect next day.'

A beat of silence until Declan broke it. 'You realize more than two weeks on those things and she's hooked?'

Oh, for heaven's sake! Emma almost ground her teeth. Declan O'Malley needed to stand outside the rarefied air of his theatre suite and realize family practice was about people not protocol. 'If you're so concerned, make it a stopgap solution. In the meantime, I'll try to figure out some other way to help her. But if Carolyn can't get sleep, she'll go dotty. Then where will the family be?' she pointed out.

'OK...' Declan raised a two-fingered salute in a peace sign. This obviously wasn't the time to start a heated discussion with the lady doctor. 'I'll go ahead and write her script.'

He took a couple of steps forward and then wheeled back. 'Are you around for a while?'

Emma felt the nerves in her stomach tighten. What was on his mind now? 'My last patient just left so I'll be here.'

'Good.' Declan's eyes glinted briefly. 'I'm sorry to push it, but we do need to talk.'

Emma twitched her shoulders into a barely perceptible shrug and watched him go back to his consulting room. Then she went into the work space behind reception and began slotting files back into place.

Moira joined her. With the information Emma had discreetly passed on to her about the new doctor, Moira's eyes were rife with speculation. 'Do you think he'll stay?'

At the thought, Emma managed a dry smile. 'I haven't offered him a job yet. And, even if I did, I expect Dr O'Malley has far more exciting challenges than working in a run-down practice in a country town.'

'You never know.' Moira's voice held a bracing optimism.

No, you never did. Thinking of her father's untimely death, Emma could only silently agree. 'Moira, it's way past your home time. I'll lock up.'

'If you're sure?' Moira looked uncertain.

'I'll be fine. Go.' Emma flapped a hand. 'And have a nice evening.'

There was still no sign of Declan some ten minutes later. Carolyn was obviously still with him. Perhaps it would help her to talk to a different practitioner, Emma thought philosophically. Heaven knew, she herself had no extra time to allot to her needy patients. Well, even if Declan helped only *one* of her patients in the short time he was here, it was a plus. Deciding there was no use hanging round in reception, she went through to the staffroom.

Declan found her there. He gave a rat-a-tat on the door with the back of his hand to alert her.

Emma's head came up, her eyes blinking against his sudden appearance. 'Hi…'

'Hi, yourself.' One side of his mouth inched upward and a crease formed in his cheek as he smiled. 'I smelled coffee.'

Emma averted her gaze to blot out the all-male physical imprint.

In a couple of long strides, he'd crossed the room to her.

Emma lifted the percolator, her fingers as unsteady as her heartbeat. 'Milk and sugar's there on the tray.'

'Thanks.' He took the coffee, added a dollop of milk and lifted the cup to his mouth. 'Could we sit for a minute?'

Emma indicated the old kitchen table that been in the staff room for as long as she could remember. 'You were a long time with Carolyn. Everything OK?' she asked as they took their places on opposite sides of the table.

'I hope so.' Declan's long fingers spanned his coffee mug and he said thoughtfully, 'We talked a bit and I suggested a few things. Some tai chi, a good solid walk in the early evening could help her relax enough to induce a natural sleep. Even a leisurely swim would be beneficial.'

'The school has a pool but it's not open to the public.'

'Pity. She's obviously quite tense.'

'And it's a situation that's happening more and more,' Emma agreed. 'Grandparents taking on the caring role for their grandchildren. Even here in this small community, there are families in similar circumstances as the Joneses.'

Declan took a long mouthful of his coffee. 'Does Bendemere have anything like a support group for them? Somewhere they can air their fears and worries in a safe environment?'

Emma resisted the urge to shriek. 'This isn't the city, Dr O'Malley. We're a bit short of facilitators and psychologists who could lead a group.'

'But a doctor could.'

Was he serious? 'Don't you think I would if I could?' she flashed. 'I'm so stretched now, I—'

'No, Emma, you're misunderstanding me.' His look was guarded and cool. 'I meant *me*—I could help.'

'You?' Emma huffed her disbelief. She wasn't understanding any of this. 'Are you saying you want to stay on here?'

'You need a practice partner, don't you?'

'But you know nothing about the place!' Emma's thoughts were spinning. 'Nothing about the viability of the practice. Nothing about *me*.'

He stared at her for a long moment. 'I know you're Andrew's daughter.'

'And you'd make a life-changing decision on the basis of that?' Emma's voice had a husky edge of disquiet.

Oh, hell. He was doing this all wrong. No wonder she was confused. He'd meant to lead up to things gently and objectively, explain himself, choose his words carefully. But just getting his head around Emma's crippling workload, the plight of Carolyn Jones and others like her had spurred him on to get matters sorted and quickly.

'Emma—' He paused significantly. 'I didn't just come here to offer my condolences. There's another reason why I'm here in Bendemere.'

Emma tried to grasp the significance of his words. 'Perhaps you'd better explain.'

Declan watched as she drew herself up stiffly, almost as if she were gathering invisible armour around her. He knew what he was about to tell her would come as a shock, maybe even wound her deeply. But he had to do it. 'Your father contacted me shortly before his death. He offered to sell me his share of the practice. I'm here to arrange payment and finalise the details of our partnership.'

Emma's mouth fell open and then snapped shut. She clutched the edge of the table for support, becoming aware of her heart thrashing to a sickening rhythm inside her chest. 'I don't believe Dad would have done something like that.'

'I have a letter of confirmation from your father and the legal documents.'

'Dad wouldn't have just *thrust* someone on me. Someone I didn't even know!' She felt the pitch of her anger and emotion rising and didn't care. 'And I don't have to accept your money, Dr O'Malley, nor do I *have* to take you on as my practice partner.'

Declan's gaze narrowed on her flushed face, the angry tilt of her small chin. Damn! He hadn't reckoned on any of this. 'It was what your father wanted, Emma.'

Emma gave a hard little laugh. 'Emotional blackmail will get you absolutely nowhere, Dr O'Malley.'

'Please!' With a reflex action Declan's head shot up, his vivid blue gaze striking an arc across the space between them. 'Give me a little credit. I realize this has come as a shock to you. And I'm sorry. I'd hoped Andrew might have given you some idea of what he wanted, paved the way a bit, but obviously time ran out on him. But we can't leave things here, Emma. We really can't.' His mouth compressed briefly. 'I suggest we take a break and let things settle a bit. I'm staying at the Heritage Hotel. We could link up there later this evening and talk further. Dinner around seven. Does that suit you?'

'Fine,' Emma responded bluntly. It seemed she had no choice in the matter.

'Let's meet at the bar, then.' Declan grabbed at the grudging acceptance.

CHAPTER TWO

EMMA hitched up her little shoulder bag and determinedly pushed open the heavy plate glass door of the restaurant. She loved this place. As it was winter, the lovely old fireplace was lit, sending out warmth and flickering patterns to the wood-panelled walls. The atmosphere was charming and tonight was the first time she'd come here since… Her teeth caught on her lower lip. She and Dad had come here often. The Sunday lunch at the Heritage was legendary.

But this evening her dinner companion was someone far different than her father.

Heart thrumming, Emma made her way along the parquet flooring towards the bar. Declan was there already. She saw him at once, his distinctive dark head turning automatically, almost as if he'd sensed her approach. A shower of tingles began at the base of her backbone, spiralling upwards and engulfing her. She swallowed. He was wearing dark jeans and an oatmeal-coloured sweater that looked soft and cuddly. Oh, get real, Emma! Cuddles and Declan O'Malley were about as compatible as oil and water.

'Hello again.' Declan nodded almost formally. And blinked. Wow! Gone was the harassed-looking medico. Emma Armitage could have sauntered in from the catwalk. She was wearing black leggings and a long-sleeved, long-line silver-grey T-shirt, a huge silky scarf in a swirl of multicolour around her throat. And knee-high boots. 'You look amazing.'

'Thanks.' Her shrug was so slight he hardly saw it. 'I love your outfit too.'

So, the lady did have a sense of humour after all. A quirky one at that. Declan's grin unfolded lazily, his eyes crinkling at the corners. 'We seem to have that sorted, so let's try to enjoy our evening, shall we? Would you like something to drink?'

In a leggy, graceful movement, Emma hitched herself up on to one of the high bar stools. 'A glass of the house red would be nice, thanks.'

For a while they talked generalities and then Declan glanced at his watch. 'I reserved us a table. Shall we go through?'

'It's rather crowded for a week night,' Emma said stiltedly as they took their places in the restaurant adjoining the bar.

'I've been quite taken with the town,' Declan rejoined. 'Tell me a bit about its history.'

Emma did her best to comply and it wasn't until they'd come to the end of their meal and were sitting over coffee she said pointedly, 'It's been a long day, could we wind things up so we can both get on about our business?'

'OK, then.' Declan's moody blue eyes were fixed unflinchingly on hers. 'I'll get straight to the point. About six months ago I received a letter from your father telling me about his deterioration in health.'

For a few seconds Emma stared at him in numb disbelief. 'Dad told *you* and he didn't tell me? Why? I was his daughter, for heaven's sake.'

Declan could hardly bear to watch her grief. 'I know it sounds an old chestnut, Emma,' he said gently, 'but perhaps he didn't want to upset you any further than you had been. You had other things going on in your life, didn't you?'

Emma's face was tightly controlled. 'What did Dad tell you about that?'

'Almost nothing—just that you'd had a few personal problems.'

Like mopping up the emotional fallout after her rat of a fiancé had dumped her for her best friend…

'And that you'd come back to work in the practice,' Declan finished diplomatically.

Emma curled her hands into a tight knot on her lap. 'What did he tell you about his health? That he had only a short time to live?'

Declan's frown deepened. 'Nothing like that. But, from what he told me, I drew my own conclusions. If it hadn't been for the fact that I, myself, was in somewhat of a personal crisis at the time, I'd have come back to Australia to see Andrew immediately. Instead, I called him. He was concerned for you, for the future of the practice if the worst happened. We talked at length. It was then he offered to sell me his half of the practice.'

'I see.' Emma swallowed through a suddenly dry throat. But she understood now why her father hadn't told her anything about his plans. He would have had to reveal the uncertain state of his health. So instead he'd trusted Declan O'Malley to set things right. But did that mean she had to accept him as her partner? She didn't think so. 'I'm sure Dad wouldn't have wanted you interfering in my life.'

'That's not what Andrew had in mind, Emma.'

'So, you're here as some kind of…white knight?' she grated bitterly.

'I'm here because I want to be here,' Declan said simply. 'Because it seems like a worthwhile thing to do. You need a partner. I need a job. Isn't that the truth of it?'

She looked at him warily. 'Why do you need a job? You obviously have medical qualifications beyond the norm. Career-wise, the world should be your playground. Why aren't you working in your chosen discipline somewhere?'

'It's a long story.'

'There's plenty of coffee in the pot,' Emma countered. 'And we're quite private here.'

Declan felt the familiar grind in his guts at the thought of rehashing everything.

At his continued silence, something like resentment stirred in Emma and she couldn't let go of it. 'Dr O'Malley, if you've ideas of entering into partnership with me, then I need to know what I'm getting. That's only fair, isn't it?'

He took a long breath and let it go. 'My surgical career is, to all intents and purposes, finished. I can't operate any longer.'

Faint shock widened Emma's eyes. How awful. She knew only too well what it was like to have your world collapse with no redress possible. 'I'm sorry.'

'Thank you.' The words escaped mechanically from his lips.

And that was it? Emma took in the sudden tight set of his neck and shoulders. He had to know she needed more information. Much more than the bald statement he'd offered. She felt about for the right words to help him. But in the end it was a simple, softly spoken, 'What happened?'

Declan rubbed a hand across his forehead. 'After I'd completed my general surgery training, I decided to go ahead and specialize in orthopaedics.' His blue eyes shone for a moment. 'On a good day when everything in the OR goes right and you know it's your skill that's enabling a patient to regain their mobility, their normal life, and in some instances their whole livelihood…it's empowering and humbling all rolled into one.'

'Yes, I imagine it is,' Emma said, but she had the feeling he had hardly heard.

'I was fortunate enough to be accepted at St Mary's in Edinburgh.'

Emma's eyes widened. 'Their training programme is legendary. I believe they take only the brightest and best.'

'I was lucky,' he said modestly.

Hardly. Obviously, he was seriously gifted. Which fact made Declan O'Malley's reasons for opting to come in as her partner in a country practice odd indeed, she thought, noticing he'd hadn't touched his coffee. Instead, he'd spanned his fingers around the cup, holding on to it like some kind of lifeline.

'After a long stint in Scotland, I'd decided to head back home. I was still finalizing dates when I had a call from an Aussie mate. He was coming over for a holiday in the UK, beginning in Scotland. I postponed my plans and Jack and I bought a couple of motorbikes.'

'Fuel-wise cheaper than cars, I guess,' was Emma's only comment.

'Jack and I found a couple of high-powered beauties for sale locally. Those bikes took us everywhere. Life was sweet—until we had the accident.'

Emma winced and she automatically put her hand to her heart. 'How?'

He gave a grim smile. 'A foggy afternoon, an unfamiliar road. A bit too much speed. And a truck that came out of nowhere. Jack received a broken leg. I was somewhat more compromised. I ended up with lumbar injuries.' He expanded on the statement with technical language, ending with, 'The outcome was partial paralysis in my left leg.' He grimaced as if the memory was still fresh.

Emma gripped her hands tightly. He must have been sick with worry and conjecture. And fear. Her antagonism faded and her heart went out to him. 'What was the result? I mean, you don't appear to have any deficit in your movement.'

His eyes took on a dull bleakness. 'I've regained most of it but my muscles are unpredictable, my toes still get numb from time to time. Added to that, I can't stand for excessively long periods. And that's what orthopaedic surgeons have to do. You need to have muscle strength, be in control. I can't risk a patient's life by breaking down in the middle of a long operation. So, career-wise, I'm stuffed.'

'But you could do other kinds of surgery,' Emma said hopefully.

'I don't even want to think about that. I want to do what I was trained to do—what I do—*did* best.'

But sometimes you had to compromise. Emma knew that better than most. 'You could lecture, Declan.'

He made a disgusted sound. 'Take up a *chair* in a hallowed hall somewhere? That's not me. I'm a doer. I'd rather change direction entirely.'

'In other words, come in as my partner—' She broke off. 'You might hate it.'

'I don't think so.' Blue eyes challenged her although his mouth moved in the ghost of a wry smile. When she remained silent, he went on, 'Emma, don't you think it's just possible Andrew considered he was acting in the best interests of *both* of us? He knew the extent of my injuries, the uncertain state of my career in medicine and he knew, without him, you were going to need a partner—someone you could trust. And you *can* trust me, Emma,' he assured her sincerely.

Emma felt almost sick with vulnerability. Heaven knew there was no one else beating the door down to come and work with her. But this man? On the other hand, what choice did she have? He had all the power on his side and, she suspected, the determination that her father's wishes would be carried out. There was really no get-out clause here. None at all. 'How do we go about setting things in motion, then?' Her voice was small and formal.

Declan breathed the greatest sigh of relief. They'd got to the trickiest hurdle and jumped it. 'You're overworked and under-capitalised. If we tackle the problems together, Kingsholme could be brought up to its potential again. Why don't we give it six months? If we find we can't work together, I'll get out.'

'And where will that leave me?'

'Hopefully, with a fully functioning practice. You'd have no difficulty attracting a new partner and I'd recoup my investment. It would be a win-win situation for both of us.'

Emma knew the decision had already been made for her. She wanted to—*needed* to—keep Kingsholme. Declan O'Malley had been Dad's choice of a suitable practice partner for her. She had to trust his judgement and go along with that.

Otherwise, she was back to the mind-numbing uncertainty of the past weeks. 'Have you come prepared to stay, then?'

'I've brought enough gear to keep me going for a while.' Declan kept his tone deliberately brisk. 'If it suits you, I'll continue at the surgery until Friday and then, on the weekend, we can go over what practical changes need to be made. I'd imagine you'd have a few ideas of your own about that?'

'It depends on how much money you want to spend,' Emma shot back with the faintest hint of cynicism.

He answered levelly, 'There'll be enough.'

On Friday afternoon, they held a quick consult after surgery. 'What time do you want to begin tomorrow?' Emma asked.

Declan lifted his medical case up on the counter. 'I'm flexible. What suits you?'

'I need to do an early hospital round. We could meet after that.'

'Why can't I come to the hospital with you?'

Emma looked uncertain. 'It's all pretty basic medicine we do here.'

'And nothing I'd be interested in?' Declan's gaze clouded. 'Emma, if we're partners, we share duties. Right?'

She coloured slightly. 'I was just pointing out there'll be none of the drama associated with Theatres.'

'So, it'll be a change of pace. I can handle that.'

Could he, though? Emma wished she felt more certain. On the other hand, why not think positively? She'd already capitulated over him becoming her partner. It was time to just get on with things. 'Hospital at eight o'clock, then? I'll give you the tour.'

'That's what I want to hear,' he drawled with his slow smile.

For a split second Emma registered a zinging awareness between them. Raw and immediate. Like the white-heat of an electric current. She repressed a gasp. Declan O'Malley exuded sex appeal in spades. He was about to step in as her practice partner. And they were going to be working very closely together for at least the next six months…

Emma had enjoyed her Saturday morning run. Leaning forward, hands on the verandah railings, she breathed deeply and began to warm down.

'Great morning for it,' a male voice rumbled behind her and she jumped and spun round, her heart skittering.

Emma straightened, one hand clenched on the railings, her senses on high alert, as Declan O'Malley came up the steps. His sudden appearance had made her flustered and unsure. 'I run most mornings.' She felt his eyes track over her and, before she could move or comprehend, he'd lifted a hand and knuckled her cheek ever so gently. Emma felt her breath jam.

'It's good to see those shadows gone,' he said, his voice throaty and low and further tugging on her senses. His eyes beckoned hers until she lifted her gaze. 'I gather you slept well?'

She nodded, breath rushing into the vacuum of her lungs. She'd slept well for the first time in weeks. She wasn't about to analyse the reason. But she had a fair idea it was all to do with the fact that at least for the next little while, her future was settled. Her teeth caught on her lower lip. 'I thought we were to meet at the hospital.'

Hands rammed in his back pockets, Declan shifted his stance slightly as if to relieve tense muscles. 'I was awake early. Thought I might come over and persuade you to have breakfast with me.'

'Or you could stay here and have breakfast with *me*,' Emma rushed out. 'I'm sure I could cobble something together.'

'I didn't mean to gatecrash—'

'You're not.' She took a thin breath. 'Give me a minute to have a shower and change.'

He followed her inside to the kitchen. 'I could knock us up some breakfast—that's if you don't mind someone else rattling around in your kitchen?'

'Not remotely.' In a reflex action, Emma jerked the zipper

closed on her track top right up to her chin. 'Uh...I did a shop last night. There's plenty of stuff in the fridge.' She almost ran from the room.

Sheesh! Declan spun away, thumping the heel of his hand to his forehead. Why on earth had he done that? *Touched* her. He hadn't meant it to happen but at that moment his hand had seemed to have a life of its own. Oh, good grief. Surely, the idea had been to reassure her he was trustworthy. Well, that premise was shot. Instead, he'd gone to the other extreme and created a damn great elephant in the room. He hissed out a breath of frustration and tried to take stock of the kitchen. He'd promised her breakfast. He'd better start delivering.

Emma showered in record time, towelled dry and dressed quickly in comfortable cargos and a ruby-red sweater. She wasn't about to drive herself crazy thinking about earlier. It was hardly a professional thing for Declan to have done. What she couldn't work out was her instinctive response to his touch… Oh, Lord. Suddenly, her body was stiff with tension. Almost jerkily, she lifted her hands, bunching her hair from her shoulders and letting it spiral away. At least he'd got on with the breakfast. There was a gorgeous smell of grilling bacon coming from the kitchen.

'How's it going?' Emma asked, buzzing back into the kitchen, determined not to start walking on eggshells around him. They were about to become partners in practice. Nothing else. 'Find everything?'

Declan looked up from the stove. 'No worries. It's a great kitchen.'

'Tottering with age but very user-friendly,' Emma agreed. Opening the door of the fridge, she peered in and located the orange juice. She poured two glasses and handed one across to Declan.

'Thanks. I'm doing bacon and scrambled eggs.'

'Lovely.'

Declan lifted his glass and drained it slowly as he watched the eggs begin to thicken and fluff. He could get used to this.

The warmth and the clutter of the old-fashioned kitchen. The comforting aroma of food cooking. The feeling of solidness, of family. The place just breathed it. He could get some idea now of how desperate Emma had been to hang on to her home. 'Your idea?' He pointed to the sun-catcher crystal that dangled from the window in front of the sink.

Her tiny smile blossomed to a grin. 'My *alternative* period. You about done here?'

'I hope it's up to scratch,' he said, catching the drift of her flowery shampoo as her head topped his shoulder.

'Mmm, smells good.' Emma gave him a quick nod of approval. 'I'll get the plates.'

'I used to run a bit,' Declan said as they settled over breakfast.

'You can't now?'

His mouth pulled down. 'I seem to be stuck with a set of prescribed exercises these days.'

Emma looked up sharply with a frown. Did that mean he didn't trust his legs on a simple run? 'I understood you to say it was standing for long periods you had trouble with. Short bursts of running would seem OK, surely? And drawing all that fresh air into your bloodstream works magic.'

Well, he knew that. 'Maybe it'll happen. In time.'

So, end of discussion. Emma pursed her mouth into a thoughtful moue, realizing suddenly that her own emotional baggage didn't seem nearly as weighty as her soon-to-be-partner's. Determinedly, she pulled out her social skills and managed to create enough general conversation to get them through the rest of the meal. She glanced at her watch, surprised to see the time had gone so quickly. She swung up from the table. 'If you'll start clearing away, I'll just feed the cat.'

Declan gave a rusty chuckle, looking sideways to where the big tabby sprawled indolently on the old-fashioned cane settee. 'Looks like he wants room service.'

Emma snorted. 'Lazy creature. I think the mice run rings around him. He belonged to Mum.'

Declan hesitated with a response, a query in his eyes.

'She moved back to Melbourne about a year ago,' Emma enlightened him thinly. 'Dad bought her an art gallery in St Kilda. It had an apartment attached so the whole set-up suited her perfectly and Dad went there as often as he could before he died. She never really felt at home here in rural Queensland. Missed the buzz of the city, her friends.'

Declan was thoughtful as he stood to his feet, processing the information. At least now he knew where the bulk of Andrew's estate had gone and why the practice was all but running on goodwill. And why Emma's stress levels must have been immense as a result.

Between them, they put the kitchen to rights in a few minutes. Hanging the tea towel up to dry, Emma felt an odd lightness in her spirits.

'Emma, I wonder if you could spare a few minutes now? There are a couple of business decisions I'd like to run past you.'

His voice had a firm edge to it and Emma came back to earth with a thud. 'Let's go through to Dad's–*your* surgery,' she substituted shortly. 'I'll give the hospital a call and let them know we'll be along a bit later than planned.'

They took their places at the big rosewood desk. 'Fire away,' Emma invited, locking her arms around her middle as if to protect herself.

Declan moved his position, sitting sideways in his chair, his legs outstretched and crossed at the ankles. 'First up, I'll need to see some figures from your accountant. Could you arrange that, please?'

'I do have some current figures,' she replied. 'I organized that when I needed to see what state the practice was in after Dad—' She stopped. 'I'll get them for you directly. Perhaps you'd like to study them over the weekend.'

'Thanks.' He nodded almost formally. 'That will help a lot. Now, your office system—'

'Yes?'

'It seems a bit outdated. You obviously have computers installed but no one seems to be using them.'

She'd wondered when they'd get to that. 'I encouraged Dad to get them soon after I moved back and we had the appropriate software installed. Moira did an evening course at the local high school, but at the end of it she said it was all beyond her. Dad said he felt more comfortable with his own way of doing things.'

'I see.'

'I tried to get things operational myself, but then, with Dad gone, it all came to a screeching halt. Any time I had to spare has had to go on face-to-face consults.'

'The system must be got up and running,' he insisted. 'If it's too onerous for Moira, then she'd be better—'

'I won't let you sack her, Declan,' Emma swiftly interjected.

He raised his head and looked at her coolly. 'Emma, don't go second-guessing me, please. I was about to add, Moira would be better staying with what she does best. She's obviously invaluable to the practice. She knows the patients well and that helps facilitate appointments. But what we do need is someone with expertise who can come in on a permanent basis and get our patient lists up to date and their medical history on to the computers. Can you think of anyone suitable?'

'Not offhand,' she said stiffly. It all made sense though and, belatedly, she realized the shortcomings he'd pointed out had probably been one of the reasons the doctors she'd interviewed had vetoed working here. 'I'll have a chat to Moira. Better still, I'll call her now.' She felt almost goaded into action, reaching for the phone on his desk. She hit Moira's logged-in home number and, after a brief conversation, replaced the receiver in its cradle. Raising her gaze, she looked directly at Declan. 'Moira's coming in now. She says she may have a few ideas. I hope that's in order?'

Declan spread his hands in compliance. He wished Emma didn't see him as the bad guy here. But he'd promised Andrew he'd do what he could to save the practice and if along the way he had to tread on a few toes—gently, of course–then he'd do it. He hauled his legs up and swivelled them under the desk. 'I noticed we don't seem to have the services of a practice nurse. What's the situation there?'

'We used to have one, Libby Macklin. She took maternity leave, intending to come back, but found it was just too much with the demands of the baby. We didn't get round to replacing her.'

Declan placed his hands palms down on the desk. 'Would she like to come back, do you think?'

Emma nodded. 'I see her quite often. The baby's older now, of course, and Libby's managing much better. I know she'd appreciate some work but I just haven't been in a position to offer her any…'

'Sound her out then,' Declan said, refusing to acknowledge Emma's wistful expression.

'I'll go and see her after we've been to the hospital. Now, about patient lists.'

'I'm listening.'

'I'm not sure how you'd like to work it, but perhaps we could do a clean swap? You'd take over Dad's patients,' she suggested.

'That sounds fair. And I'm thinking we could schedule a weekly practice meeting, air anything problematic then. Suit you?'

Heck, did she even have a choice in the matter? A resigned kind of smile dusted Emma's lips. 'Fine.'

Declan frowned and glanced at his watch. 'How long will Moira be?'

'Not long. She lives only a few minutes away.'

'Yoo-hoo, it's me!' As if on cue, Moira's quick tap along the corridor accompanied her greeting.

Declan uncurled to his feet and dragged up another chair. 'Thanks for doing this, Moira.'

'No worries.' She flapped a hand and leant forward confidentially. 'I'll get straight to the point. My granddaughter is looking for work.'

'Jodi?' Emma's gaze widened in query. 'I thought she was full-time at McGinty's stables.'

Moira's mouth turned down. 'James, the youngest son, has returned home so he's taken over much of the track work. Jodi's there only one day a week now.'

Declan exchanged a quick guarded look with Emma. Moira was obviously a doting grandmother but they couldn't afford to be giving jobs away on her say-so. 'Moira, we'd need to have a chat to Jodi about what the job here entails,' he stressed diplomatically.

'Of course you would.' Moira smiled. 'That's why I've brought her in with me. She's outside in reception.'

'Ask her to come in then,' Declan said briefly, turning to Emma as Moira left the room. 'What do you think?' he asked quietly. 'You obviously know this young woman. Are we doing the right thing here?'

'Jodi is very bright. Providing her technical skills are up to speed, then I think she'll do a good job. Oh—here she is now.'

Declan got to his feet again as Jodi bounded in, all youthful spirits and sparkling eyes. 'Hi.' She linked the two doctors with a wide white smile.

'Jodi.' Declan stuck out his hand in greeting. 'Declan O'Malley. Emma you know, of course.'

'Hello, Jodi.' Emma beckoned the teenager to a seat. 'Moira says you're looking for some work.'

'Yes, I am.' Jodi slid her huge leather satchel from her shoulder and on to the floor beside her chair. 'Nan's told me a bit about what you need here. I could easily manage to give you three days a week, if that suits. I work track at McGinty's on Fridays and I've just got a day's work at the supermarket on Thursdays. So I could give you from Monday to Wednesday.'

Declan leaned back in his chair and folded his arms. 'How old are you, Jodi?'

'Eighteen. At present I'm taking a gap year before I start Uni.'

'What are you studying?' Declan asked.

'Applied science. Eventually, I want to be associated with the equine industry, combine research and field work. Horses and their welfare are my great passion. I'll need to do my doctorate, of course.'

'That's really worthwhile, Jodi,' Emma said warmly. 'Best of luck with your studies.'

Declan made a restive movement in his chair, his dark brows flexed in query. 'How are your computer skills, Jodi? We'd need you to be able to collate information, get the patients' histories logged in and kept up to date.'

'I'm thoroughly computer literate.' Jodi twitched a long hank of dark hair over her shoulder. 'I work quickly and thoroughly and I'm quite aware of the confidential nature of the job here. I'll sign a clause to that effect if you need me to.'

Emma bit hard on the inside of her cheek to stop the grin that threatened. This kid was something else. 'We'll probably get round to that, Jodi. But, if Dr O'Malley agrees, I think we can offer you the job. Declan?'

'Uh—' Declan's eyes looked slightly glazed. He rocked forward in his chair. 'Let's agree on a trial period, Jodi, if that suits—say a month? And we'll see how things are going then?'

'Absolutely.' Jodi shrugged slender shoulders. Bending down, she flipped open her satchel. 'I'll leave you my CV. And there are several character references as well.' She placed the file on the desk. 'If there's anything else you need to know, I'll be available on my mobile.' She smiled confidently and whirled to her feet. 'So, I'll see you both on Monday, then.'

'Good grief,' Declan said faintly after Jodi had swished out of the door. 'Do you get the feeling *we're* the ones who have just been interviewed?'

Emma chuckled. 'It's the Gen Y thing. They're inclined to set out terms and conditions to prospective employers. But isn't she marvellous?'

'Made me feel about a hundred and six,' Declan growled. 'Hell, was I ever that young and enthusiastic about life?'

Emma stood and pushed her chair back in. 'Probably we both were.'

'Mmm.' Declan's tone was non-committal. 'Well, we seem to have made a dint in what needs to be done here so, if you're ready, I'd like to see over your hospital.'

CHAPTER THREE

BENDEMERE'S hospital was old but beautifully kept. Declan looked around with growing interest. 'This place has a long history, obviously,' he remarked.

'My grandfather actually funded the building of it,' Emma said proudly. 'These days, much of the accommodation is given over to nursing home beds for our seniors. Anything acute is sent straight on to Toowoomba by road ambulance. Or, in the case of serious trauma, we stabilise as best we can and chopper the patient out to Brisbane.'

'Do you have a theatre?' Declan began striding ahead, his interest clearly raised.

'A small one—just here.' She turned into an annexe and indicated the big oval window that looked into the pristine operating space. 'Dad did basic surgical procedures. And Rachel Wallace, our nurse manager, has extensive theatre experience. She insists the maintenance is kept up. Shame it's not used any more…'

'It's all here though, isn't it?' Declan's gaze roamed almost hungrily, left and right and back again, as if to better acquaint himself with the layout. 'Who did the gas when your dad operated?'

'Oliver Shackelton. He's retired in the district. And, even though he won't see seventy again, I know Dad trusted his skills to the nth degree.'

'Interesting.' Declan pressed his lips together and took a

deep breath. This was his natural environment. But he didn't belong here any longer. Suddenly, it all came at him in a rush, a heartbeat, the past coming forward to link with the present. He felt the sudden tightening of his throat muscles. It was over. He was finished as a surgeon. He couldn't operate any more. At least not in any way that was meaningful—from his standpoint, at least…

'Declan…are you OK?'

Declan's head came up, looking at her without seeing. 'Sorry?'

'We should get on,' she cajoled gently.

'Yes, we should.' He turned abruptly, as if to shut out the scene he'd walked into so unguardedly. He felt weird, in no way prepared for the hollow feeling in his gut as he snapped off the light and closed the double doors on the annexe.

Emma's gaze moved over him. 'Sure you're OK?'

He saw the compassion in her eyes, the softening, felt her empathy. But he wasn't a kid who needed to cry on her shoulder. 'I'm fine,' he said, his tone gruff as if brushing her concern aside. 'Fill me in about hospital staff.'

Emma gave a mental shrug. He hadn't fooled her for a minute. Well, if that was how he wanted to handle it, that was his business, his life. 'I've sent out an email to the nurses to advise them you were joining the practice.' She didn't add they'd probably done their own research on the Internet in the meantime. 'Rachel is our nurse manager,' she reiterated as they made their way along to the station. 'We have three other permanent RNs who alternate shifts and Dot Chalmers is permanent nights. Ancillary staff are rostered as necessary.'

'Leave and sick days?' Declan fell into step beside her.

'Covered by a small pool of nurses who mainly live in the district.'

'That seems like a reasonable set-up,' Declan said. 'I imagine the staff value their jobs quite highly.'

'And the folk hereabouts value *them*,' Emma said, leaving him in no doubt that any changes there would be unacceptable. Just in case he was thinking along those lines.

'Hospital maintenance is covered by a local firm, as is security. And Betty Miller is our indispensable hospital cook.'

Declan nodded, taking everything on board. He began to quicken his pace.

'Patients now?'

Emma rolled her eyes. He'd have to learn to slow down if he was going to relate to the locals. 'Is there a fire somewhere?' she enquired innocently.

'Forgot.' He sent her a twisted grin. 'I'm keen to get cracking, that's all.'

'Hello, people.' Rachel, tall and slender, came towards them, her nimbus of auburn hair stark against the white walls of the hospital corridor. 'And you are Dr O'Malley, I presume?' Beaming, the nurse manager stuck her hand out towards Declan.

'I am.' Declan shook her hand warmly. 'And it's Declan. I've just been getting the lay of the land from Emma. It looks like a great little hospital.'

'We're proud of it.' Rachel spun her gaze between the two medical officers. 'Um—I was just on my way for a cuppa.'

'Don't let us hold you up,' Emma insisted. Despite it being a small hospital, she knew the nurses worked hard and deserved their breaks.

'OK, then. I won't be long.' Rachel began to move away and then turned back. 'I knew you'd be along so I've pulled the charts on our current patients.'

'Take your time.' Emma smiled. 'And thanks, Rach. We'll be fine.'

'I guess you know this place like the back of your hand,' Declan surmised as they made their way along to the nurses' station.

Emma sent him a quick look. It still seemed surreal that this once highly ambitious, powerful man was now to all intents and purposes her practice partner. Her hand closed around the small medallion at her throat. No doubt, for the moment, the newness of what he'd taken on was enough to keep him motivated. But what would happen when the grind of family practice began to wear thin? Where would his motivation be then?

In a dry little twist of quirky humour, Emma transposed the scenario into equine terms. Surely what Declan was proposing was like expecting a thoroughbred racer to feel fulfilled pulling a plough…

'Something amusing you, Emma?' Declan lifted a dark brow.

'Not really,' she said, going behind the counter and collecting the charts Rachel had left out.

'OK, who's the first cab off the rank?' Declan asked, settling on one of the high stools next to her.

'Russell Kernow, age seventy-five, lives alone,' Emma said. 'I saw him at the surgery a week ago. He was presenting with an incessant cough, raised temperature. I prescribed roxithromycin. His condition didn't improve and I admitted him two days ago. He was seriously dehydrated, complained his chest felt tight. I've placed him on an inhaler twice daily and the cough seems to have diminished slightly. I've sent bloods off as well.'

'So, you're testing for what—serology, pertussis, mycoplasma?'

'Plus legionella,' Emma said.

Declan raised a dark brow. 'Is that a possibility?'

'A remote one, but Russell's house is fully air-conditioned. He spends much of his time indoors. And we've since found out the filters on his air-con unit haven't been changed for two years.'

'Still…legionella is drawing a fairly long bow,' Declan considered.

Emma bristled. If he was going to start telling her her job, they were going to fall out before the ink was dry on their partnership papers.

Their eyes met. He could see the spark of hostility in her gaze. Hell, he didn't want to blow things with her before they even got off the ground. 'Just thinking aloud,' he said hastily. 'It's your call. When do you expect the results?'

'Soonish,' Emma said, faintly mollified. 'I've requested the path lab to fax them to us here.' She turned, stroking a stray lock of hair behind her ear. 'Next patient is Sylvia Gartrell, age sixty-five. Recently had surgery—hysterectomy and bladder repair. Post-op seven days. The air ambulance delivered her to us yesterday.'

Declan ran his index finger between his brows. 'What's the problem?'

'Her bladder function hasn't yet returned to normal. She's having to self-catheterise and she's finding the procedure difficult to manage. Currently, the nurses are giving her some guidance. It seemed the safest option to have her here until she feels competent to go it alone. At the moment she's convinced she'll be stuck with this problem for ever so she needs emotional support as well.'

'Why was she released from hospital in the first place?'

Emma sighed. 'Same old story. They needed the bed.'

'Oh, for crying out loud! We'll need to keep a close eye on her, be mindful of the possibility of infection.'

'We're all aware of that, Declan.'

He sighed. 'OK, then, who's next on our patient list?'

'Only one more. Ashleigh Maine, aged eleven. Poor little kid had a bad asthma attack yesterday. Scared the life out of her.'

'So what's her prognosis?'

'She's getting some relief from a nebuliser and of course she's on a drip. Her home situation is not as good as it could be, though. Dad still smokes.'

Declan swore under his breath. 'I realize tobacco is the drug some folk cling to when they're under stress but surely, if his child is suffering, the man has to take stock of his actions?'

'Normally, Ashleigh's condition is fairly well managed but it only needs a change in routine and she's struggling again.'

'Are you aware of the study on asthmatics that's been

carried by the Jarvis Institute in Sydney?' Declan asked pointedly.

Emma's gaze was suddenly uncertain. 'It's a breathing technique, isn't it? I think there's a new physio in Toowoomba who's a graduate from the Institute. We got some leaflets. I was going to investigate it further just before Dad…died. Do you want to take the child on to your list?'

'Fine with me,' he replied calmly. 'I'll chase up the physio and get the parents in for a round-table chat. I've a few ideas that might help as well.'

Emma defended her corner quietly. 'I did try to put the parents in touch with the Asthma Foundation. They run camps and things that Ashleigh could attend with other youngsters with the same health problem. They declined.'

Declan's response was swift. 'Leave it with me, Emma. I'm new to the place. They'll take notice, believe me.'

Emma opened her mouth and closed it. She hoped he wouldn't jump all over the family. It wasn't the way things worked in rural medicine. If the Maines took offence, that would be the end of the doctors getting access to Ashleigh. Oh, help. Which way should she jump? Forward, if she had any sense. 'You will tread gently, won't you, Declan?'

His jaw hardened. 'I'll do what I need to do, Emma.'

'Not with my patients, you won't,' she flared. 'Bendemere is a close-knit community. You can't go around upsetting people.'

Hell, this was a minefield. She was guarding her territory, whereas he was used to giving orders and having them carried out immediately. OK, then. Back off, he told himself. 'If we want this partnership to work, Emma, we have to trust each other's medical skills. You haven't had any complaints about my patient contact, have you?'

'No…' She lifted her hands in appeasement. 'It's just—we're not used to working with each other yet.'

His mouth pulled tight. Was this what he was about to sign on for—bickering over someone who couldn't grasp that his inability to quit smoking was stuffing up his child's health?

He lifted his gaze to glance meaningfully at her. 'Just let's try to keep it professional, then.'

Emma gritted her teeth. That was a low blow. She'd done everything she could under very difficult circumstances to keep their relationship professional. He'd been the one to overstep this morning when he'd touched her cheek! She tried to steady her thoughts. She'd have to swallow her angst with him if she didn't want everything turned into ashes. New jobs had been promised and already there was an air of expectation about the town. She breathed a sigh of relief when she saw Rachel heading towards them, a tea tray in her hands. 'I thought you might need this,' she said. 'And Betty's made us some of her special ginger biscuits,' she added brightly, sensing an air of tension between the two.

'Lovely,' Emma said faintly.

'I'll take a rain check, thanks, Rachel.' Declan spun off his stool. 'I'll get on and make myself known to our patients.'

'Then I'll accompany you,' Rachel said.

'There's no need.' He gave an impatient twitch of his shoulder. 'I'm sure I can manage.'

Rachel's raised brows spoke volumes, before she swept up the patient charts. 'My hospital, my call, Dr O'Malley. Besides, I need to strut my stuff occasionally,' she said cheekily. 'It's ages since I walked the wards with a posh doc.'

Emma watched them walk away together, saw Declan turn his head, heard his rumble of laughter as he interacted with Rachel. She made a little sniff of disapproval. Shaking off a disquiet she didn't understand, she took up one of Betty's ginger biscuits and dunked it in her tea.

By Sunday afternoon Emma was going stir-crazy. It wasn't that she didn't have a million things she could be doing. She just couldn't settle to anything. Declan had offered to be on call for the weekend so that had left her with more free time than she'd had in months. She'd done a tour of the garden and picked a bunch of winter roses to bring some warmth and friendliness to reception. At least Moira would appreciate her gesture. She doubted Declan would even notice.

She was back to *him* again. She still had the feeling of things being not quite right between them. He'd erupted into the practice and into her life and she'd hardly had time to take stock. He hadn't exactly steamrollered over her but he hadn't wasted any time in putting his plans into action. But then she'd given him tacit permission, hadn't she? Because the alternative had been too bleak to contemplate.

Oh, help. Emma turned her restless gaze towards the kitchen window. It would be dark soon. Suddenly she was beset with a strange unease. She couldn't begin the first week of their new partnership with so many of her questions unresolved.

They needed to talk.

Now she'd decided, she wouldn't hold back, although her heart was slamming at the thought of what she was about to take on. They'd already exchanged mobile phone numbers. She'd find him about the place somewhere.

He answered on the fourth ring. 'O'Malley.'

'Hi—it's me—Emma.'

'Problem?'

She took a shallow breath. He wasn't making this easy. 'Are you busy?'

'Er—no. I've just been for a jog.'

Emma blinked uncertainly. 'How did it go?'

'Pretty good,' he said, sounding pleased with himself. 'What's up?'

'Nothing, really. I wondered whether we could get together this evening—just sort out a few things before work tomorrow…'

'OK…' He seemed to be thinking. 'Want to grab a bite to eat somewhere, then? Or, better still, come to me. I've moved into the log cabin at Foley's farm. Know where it is?'

'Yes.' Emma's fingers tightened on the phone. The Foleys lived about a kilometre out of town. 'I thought it was only a holiday let.'

'I struck a deal with the Foleys. It's mine for as long as I need it.'

'I see...well, that's good. About dinner—I've made soup. I could bring some over.'

He curled a low laugh. 'You're obviously intent on feeding me. But soup sounds good. I did a shop this morning. I'm sure we'll find something to go with it.'

Declan felt a new spring in his step as he threw himself under the shower. How odd that Emma must have been thinking about him just at the same moment he'd been thinking about her...

Emma was glad he'd found somewhere to live, and the log cabin was a comfortable option for the time being, she thought, guiding the car carefully over the cattle grid that marked the entrance to the farm. The cabin was barely five minutes drive further on and in seconds she saw the lighted windows come into view. As she pulled to a stop in front of the cabin, her heart began its pattering again, the nerves in her stomach lurching and flailing like a drunken butterfly.

Out of the car, she took a moment to look up at the sky. It was the same night sky she'd been seeing since she was a child, the same stars. But tonight she noticed them in a way she never had before. The Milky Way was its usual wash of grey-white light, peppered with twinkling stars. But tonight, as she watched, one lone star shot across the heavens, leaving a glittering trail of light before it disappeared.

'Stargazing?' Declan's deep voice was husky behind her.

'Oh—' Emma spun round, giving a jagged half-laugh. He was standing on the sheltered front porch. 'I didn't know you were there.'

'Saw your headlights. Coming in?'

'Mmm.' Suddenly, for no reason at all, anticipation was a sweet ache in her chest, a flutter in her breathing. She held her vacuum jug of soup tightly and followed him inside.

The cabin was open-plan and modern with the lounge area and kitchen melded into one living space. 'Oh, good,' Emma said lightly. 'You've got the fire going.'

'Glass of wine?' Declan offered as they moved across the timber floor to the kitchen. 'I have a nice local red.'

'OK, thanks.' Emma placed her soup on the counter top. 'You should be comfortable here.'

Declan didn't comment. Instead, he took up the wine he'd left breathing and poured two glasses. He handed one to Emma, unable to stop himself gazing at her with an intensity that made his heart stall for a second and then pick up speed. She was wearing jeans that clung to her legs and outlined a pert little backside. Her top was a frilly button-up shirt, the neckline open just enough to expose a hint of cleavage. Her hair had a just-washed, just-brushed shine about it and when their gazes met and she smiled at him he felt a jolt to every one of his senses. Hell. How was he going to get through the evening without wanting to…?

'What?' Emma raised a quick brow.

He shrugged, breaking eye contact quickly. 'I guess we should drink to the future of our *partnership*.'

Emma's mind went blank. They seemed to have travelled half a lifetime in a few days. Even this morning, she'd woken with a start, wondering whether she'd dreamed it all—that she actually had a partner for the practice, someone to rely on, to confer with—to trust. 'I guess we should.' She gave a tinny laugh to disguise the sudden attack of nerves. Lifting her glass to his, she echoed, 'To our partnership.'

'What kind of soup did you bring?' Declan cringed at the banality of his conversation. But his brain felt like shredded cheese.

'Minestrone.'

'A meal in itself.' He sent her a crooked grin. 'I put some herb bread in the oven to warm when I knew you were bringing soup.'

Emma savoured another mouthful of the full-bodied wine. 'You know about food, then?'

He lifted a shoulder modestly. 'I went along to the farmers' market this morning. I thought I might have seen you there.'

Emma blinked rapidly. 'I used to go when I had time to cook.'

'The produce is amazing,' Declan said, indicating they should take their wine through to the lounge area. 'I couldn't stop buying stuff.'

Emma chuckled. 'And I'll bet the stall-holders couldn't wait to sell you *stuff*. The whole town will know who you are by now.'

'They will?' He looked startled.

'And that you're living here and fending for yourself.'

He groaned. 'It won't be daily casseroles at the surgery, will it?'

'Not just casseroles.' Emma sent him an innocent wide-eyed look and curled herself into the big squishy armchair. 'There'll possibly be apple pies as well. Bendemere will want you to feel at home here.'

'I think I'm beginning to already.' He'd taken his place on the sofa opposite her. 'By the way, I released young Ashleigh this afternoon.'

'Any problems?'

He was about to ask if she'd expected any. Except he'd seen the flash of worry in her eyes. 'None at all,' he elaborated. 'And I have Aaron and Renee coming in for a chat tomorrow.'

Emma felt a flood of relief. If he'd already got on first name terms with the Maines, then he must have at least listened to her concerns and trod softly. 'They're not bad parents. They're just—'

'Young?' Declan gave a rueful smile. 'I'll be gentle with them, Emma, but I promise I'll get through to them, whatever it takes.'

Well, she guessed she couldn't ask for more than that. She took another mouthful of wine and then leaned forward to place her glass on the coffee table between them. In a second her thoughts began racing like an out of control juggernaut. She'd come to ask Declan something. She tried to think of the best way to say what she'd come to say but, in the end, there was really no lead-in for the questions she needed answers to.

'Declan—' she paused and wet her lips, tasting the sweetness of the wine '—I need to run something past you.'

'About the practice?'

'No.' Emma swallowed hard. 'I want to know the extent of your involvement with my father.'

'I thought I'd told you.'

Not nearly enough. 'You mentioned Dad was your boss when you were at John Bosco's and that he took a special interest in you. Was there a reason for that? I mean, there must have been a large group of interns. Why did he single you out?'

So here it was, sooner than he would have liked. Deep down, he'd known someone as astute as Emma would not have been content with the glib kind of scenario he'd painted about knowing her father. Very deliberately, he took a mouthful of his wine and placed his glass next to hers on the coffee table. His jaw tightened. 'I was about ten, I suppose, when your dad started visiting our home.'

Emma stared at him uncertainly. 'Was someone ill?'

He shook his head. 'My mother was a nurse. She and Andrew worked together in Casualty at the Prince Alfred in Melbourne.'

Oh. She hadn't expected that. She quickly put dates and ages together in her head. Dad would have been married to Mum by then… 'What were the circumstances? How did—*why* did Dad become involved with your family?'

He looked at her steadily. 'Are you sure you want to hear this, Emma?'

Emma had no idea where their conversation was leading and her stomach was churning. But she knew she needed answers. 'Yes.'

He rocked his hand as if say, *so be it*. 'My parents, me and my two younger sisters were just a regular little family living in the suburbs of Melbourne when my dad was killed in an industrial accident. Suddenly our lives were turned upside down. Overnight, Mum was a sole supporting parent with three kids to feed and educate. She had no choice than to switch from part-time to full-time work.'

Emma shook her head. She'd been indulged as a child and had wanted for nothing in a material sense. 'It must have been very hard on you all.'

'No, not hard, exactly.' His mouth lifted in a token smile. 'Just different. I know I had to grow up pretty fast. Erinn and Katie were only little girls.'

'You had to be the man of the house.'

He shrugged. 'Mum worked an early shift. We went to a neighbour's until it was time for school and Mum was always home for us in the afternoon. We missed Dad, of course, were bewildered for a time. But, after a while, kids being kids, we accepted our lives as they were, changes and all. But I guess Mum had worries she never told us about. Well, how could she?' The muscle in his jaw kicked for a second. 'It was about that time Andrew began calling round. Mum merely said he was a friend from the hospital. Sometimes he brought groceries, had a kick of the football with me. He seemed to enjoy being around us kids. Told us he had a little girl called Emma.'

Emma licked lips that seemed bone-dry. 'H-how long did he keep coming to see you? Weeks, months…?'

'Couple of months, I guess. I was a kid, Emma. Time didn't mean much. I just remember when he stopped coming. I asked Mum about it. She said he'd left the PA and gone to another hospital. He wouldn't be able to see us any more.'

Emma lifted eyes that were wide and anguished. 'Do you think they were…*involved*?'

'I don't know,' he said evenly.

She swallowed hard, as if unable to voice the questions crowding her head. Had Dad fallen in love with—? 'What was your mother's name?' she asked.

'Anne,' Declan said quietly. 'She was called Anne. She died a couple of years ago.'

Anne O'Malley. The name sat frozen inside Emma, along with a block of emotions. She'd never heard her father refer to anyone by that name. Never. But obviously Dad's involvement with Declan hadn't ended there. 'Was it pure chance you and Dad met up again when you were an intern?'

'It seemed like chance. Perhaps he'd simply seen my name on the intake list. I do know he was extremely interested in my welfare. But he was discreet. I never felt I was treated differently than the others. But I knew I could go to him with any problems.'

Emma smiled sadly. 'That sounds like Dad. But you mentioned wanting to chuck in medicine. Why was that?'

'My mother had a stroke…' Declan's words were drawn out softly, seeming to echo in the close confines of the cabin. 'She was only forty-eight. Both Erinn and Katie were at Uni. Money was tight. I figured I could get a *real* job, start bringing in the big bucks.' He rubbed at his jaw. 'God only knows what I thought I was capable of doing. When I told Andrew, he was shocked. He told me I had the potential to make a fine doctor.' Declan gave a rough laugh. 'At the time I remember wondering how *potential* was going to pay the bills. Mum's rehab was dragging on and I knew it would be a long time before she could work again—if ever. Then, suddenly out of the blue, she was whisked off to a private clinic with the latest methods. I gathered Andrew had arranged it. I have the feeling he paid for it as well.'

Emma just nodded. If she'd had any doubts before, then she had none now. Dad had fallen in love with Anne but he'd stayed with his wife. *For my sake?* she wondered now. Or maybe Anne had sent him away so as not to break up his family. They'd never know. Emma was not about to ask her own mother. Ever. Sometimes, it was better not to revisit old wounds, old memories.

Somehow, they got through the rest of the evening. They ate their soup and the warmed herb bread and made desultory conversation.

'What made you decide to go for a jog?' Emma asked later, washing the platter they'd used for the local cheeses and crisp slices of apple they'd eaten instead of dessert.

'I went out on to the porch, took one look at the paddock and all that space and thought, why not?'

'And it was good?'

'It was fine,' he hedged. He didn't tell her he'd begun to ache all over. He felt almost relieved when Emma glanced surreptitiously at her watch. The evening had strained them both. 'Cup of tea before you go?'

'No, I won't, thanks,' she said almost hurriedly. 'I'll just grab my Thermos jug.'

Declan managed a quick smile. 'I'll walk you out.'

'Thanks.' Emma's return smile was edged with vulnerability.

On the lighted porch, Declan paused and looked down at her. 'Are you OK?'

'You've given me a bit to think about.'

His mouth drew in. She'd sounded shaky and the eyes that lifted briefly to his were guarded and shadowed. Almost in slow motion, he took the Thermos from her unprotesting hands and set it on the outdoor table. 'Come here…'

Emma fought a losing battle as he gathered her close. Every caressing detail of his hands was conveyed to her through the thin stuff of her shirt, lapping at the edge of her resistance. Confusion and need struggled for supremacy.

'Half-truths wouldn't have done,' he said quietly.

'I know,' she said huskily, not trusting her voice too far.

Declan frowned down at her. A tiny chill wind had come in a flurry behind her, separating tendrils of her hair from around her face and fluffing them out. For an instant, she'd looked so young. And so alone.

'It's just—I don't quite know where I fit any more,' she said quietly, an admission that was heightened by her evident uncertainty about *what* to think.

'You were the sunshine of your father's life, Emma. Hell, you must know he'd have moved mountains for you?'

Her mouth trembled. 'Perhaps he was just overcompensating. Perhaps he felt guilty that he'd rather have been with Anne and all of you.'

Declan swore under his breath. 'That's rubbish. Did you ever feel second-best?'

She shook her head. 'It's been a bit of a revelation all the same. About Dad.'

'With hindsight, would you have rather stayed in ignorance?'

Letting her breath go on a heavy sigh, she stepped away from the weight of his hands. 'I honestly don't know.'

CHAPTER FOUR

DECLAN immersed himself in his Monday morning surgery. It was better he did, he thought, grabbing a quick coffee between patients. Anything to keep his mind from flipping back to last night and Emma's reaction to what he'd told her. Now he wondered whether he'd done the right thing in telling her anything.

He could have pleaded ignorance. But secrets had a way of surfacing when you least expected. And, in reality, did any of it matter now? Emma seemed to think so. He sighed and reached for his phone when it rang softly. 'Yes, Moira?'

'Your eleven o'clock's cancelled, Declan, and the Maines are here already.'

'OK, I'll come out. And don't forget I'm going to need extra time for this consult, Moira.'

'All taken care of.'

'Thanks.' He replaced the handpiece and got to his feet. Moments later, he was ushering Aaron and Renee Maine through to his office. When they were settled, he said, 'Just for the record, you're not on trial here. But obviously I need your input if we're to sort something out for Ashleigh. Do you have any idea what may have triggered her asthma this time?'

'She had a cold.' Renee kept her gaze averted. 'Sometimes, no matter what we do, she can't seem to throw it off.'

'I know my smoking doesn't help…' Aaron came in. He paused and chewed his bottom lip. 'Renee and me have talked a bit—' He stretched out his hands, his knuckles white as he clasped them across his jeans-clad thighs. 'I reckon I have to quit. And no mucking about this time.'

'Well, that's very good news.' Declan leaned forward earnestly. 'There's a great deal of help I can give you for that.'

Aaron shook his head. 'I'm gonna chuck out my cigarettes—go cold turkey.'

'That's pretty drastic, Aaron.' Declan was cautious. 'And I'd like to give you a physical before you start, if that's OK?'

'Yeah, whatever. I just want the poison outta me system.'

'Dr O'Malley—' Renee paused, nervously winding a strand of dark hair around her finger '—could you explain just what happens when Ashleigh gets an attack? This time, it scared us spitless. We had to call the ambulance.'

'Sure.' Declan swung round to the bank of filing cabinets behind him. 'I actually put together some reading matter for you.' He pulled out a file and opened it. 'There's a chart here that will give you an idea of the body's reaction during an asthma attack.' So saying, he flipped out the chart and placed it in front of the young parents. 'As you know, asthma affects the lungs,' he explained. 'When someone experiences an attack the tubes begin narrowing, making breathing difficult.'

'Oh—that's the wheezing sound Ashleigh makes?' Renee looked at Declan fearfully, fisting her hands and crossing them over her chest.

Almost an hour later, during which Declan had drawn diagrams for the parents and explained in depth the crippling effects of an asthma attack on their daughter, Renee said, 'I feel like we're really getting somewhere at last. And we'll need to go to the physio's appointment with Ashleigh, then?'

'It's essential.' Declan was unequivocal. 'One of you should be there and learn the breathing technique with your daughter.'

'We can do that.' Renee's mouth trembled into a shaky smile. 'We're ever so grateful to you for explaining everything. Thank you, Dr O'Malley.'

'Yeah. Thanks, Doc,' Aaron said awkwardly. 'Thanks a lot.'

'Ashleigh's a great kid,' Declan complimented them. 'Take care of her.'

'Oh, we will.' Renee linked hands with her husband and they stood together.

'Er—when do you want me for this medical, Doc?' Aaron's chin came up and his shoulders straightened as if he'd at last taken charge of his life and his family.

'The sooner, the better.' Declan opened the door of his consulting room for them. 'Sort out something with Moira as you leave.'

Emma was in some kind of shock. She knew the signs and she also knew it would pass. But finding out about Dad... Clicking off her computer, she got to her feet. Possibly, it had had the same impact as finding out as an adult that you were adopted.

But she and Declan had got through the first week as practice partners without any major dramas. She should be glad about that. Not that they'd seen much of one another. Well, not for long enough to have talked about anything other than the patients. Now it was Friday and they were about to begin their first staff meeting. Moira had been invited to attend.

'Let's keep this as brief and to the point as we can,' Declan suggested as they sat at the table in the staffroom.

'I don't have any complaints,' Moira said in her forthright style.

'How's Jodi shaping up?' Declan flipped his pen back and forth between his fingers.

'Very well,' Emma came in. 'She's caught on exactly to what we need.'

'Good.' Declan turned to face Emma. 'Libby still OK to start with us on Monday?'

'She can do a four-day week,' Emma said. 'If we're happy to work around that?'

'Fine with me,' Declan said economically.

'Libby's coming in for some orientation tomorrow,' Emma

relayed. 'She and I will go over things so she's up to speed and then she'll start officially on Monday—if that's all right with you, Declan?'

'Sounds very proactive. And make sure we pay Libby for the Saturday hours, please, Moira.' He lifted his head and raised an eyebrow between the two women. 'If that's all the staff business, then?'

'I've nothing else,' Moira said.

'Nor me.' Emma shook her head.

'Right.' Declan scooted his chair back from the table and stretched out his legs. 'Moira, feel free to take off, then. And thanks for making my first week such a smooth ride.'

'Oh—how nice of you to say so, Declan,' Moira responded coyly. 'I think we're going to make a great team.' She stood to her feet, sending the two doctors a broad smile. 'See you both on Monday.'

'Have a nice weekend,' they chorused.

Moira was barely out of the door when Declan rounded on Emma. 'Any patients you want to consult about?'

'A couple.' She gave an inward shrug. Did he always conduct his meetings at this pace? 'The lab confirmed Russell Kernow has whooping cough.'

'Poor old boy! Probably jabs for that weren't around when he was a kid. Not much we can do, though. It will just have to run its course. And the good thing is he's not infectious any longer. So, you'll release him then?'

Emma nodded. 'From a funding point of view, we can't justify keeping him indefinitely. Someone from the Rotary has been round to his home and replaced the filters in his air-con units and the meals on wheels will start calling again.'

Declan ran a finger across his chin thoughtfully. 'We should probably keep up a regular home visit, though.'

'I'll tee up with Libby to pop in on him each day. Anything untoward, she can report to us,' Emma said.

'Great.' Declan smiled and raised his arms and locked them at the back of his neck. 'How about your gynae patient, Sylvia?'

Emma was surprised he'd remembered such a small detail as a patient's first name. 'She's gone home. Her bladder function is still incomplete but she's managing much better. Her husband is at home for support and I aim to see her regularly until everything is back to normal. How was your consult with the Maines?' Emma pressed back a strand of hair behind her ear, shifting the angle of her gaze to look fully at him.

'Er—productive, I think.' Declan caught the concentration of her gaze, noting how the forest-green of her eyes was unusually dark, her expression almost wistful. His heart thumped, the memory of her feminine softness under his hands making his body tighten uncomfortably. Hell…he was almost tempted to cancel his plans for the weekend. And do what? the practical part of his brain demanded.

'And?' Her mouth was smiling. Just. More a tiny upward flick at the corners. 'Wakey, wakey, Doctor.'

'Huh!' Declan gave a crack of laughter. 'Slipped out of focus there for a minute. What were we talking about?'

'The Maine family.'

'Right.' He spun a finger up in comprehension. 'Aaron is chucking the smokes and Ashleigh is booked to see the physio next week. All on the file.' He cranked a dark eyebrow at her. 'You all set to cover for the weekend?'

She nodded.

'Good. Looks like we can wrap it up, then.' He clicked his pen closed and pushed it back in his shirt pocket. 'I'll just grab my bag and be off.' In one fluid movement, he'd stood to his feet and pushed his chair in.

Somewhat more slowly, Emma followed suit. She caught up with him again as he came out of his office, pulling the door closed and locking it. 'You seem in an almighty hurry to get out of the place.' Emma tried to dismiss the odd stab of disappointment she felt, almost running to keep up with him as he strode back out to reception.

'I'm driving to Brisbane.' Declan hoisted his medical case on to the counter top and wheeled to face her. 'Erinn is flying in for a conference. It's been ages since we've been able to catch up.'

'No wonder you're excited, then.' Emma managed a quick smile. 'So, what kind of conference is it?'

'Erinn is an OT,' he said, as if that would explain everything.

Emma blinked. An occupational therapist. 'And Katie? What does she do?' Emma knew she was holding him up but suddenly, for reasons she didn't want to analyse, she needed to put him together with his family. See them as a unit. Something *she* didn't have any longer.

'Katie teaches high school. Year eights. The *littlies,* as she calls them. Loves it.'

He laughed and then drawled sing-song, 'And they're both married to good guys and both have two kids each.'

Emma wrinkled her nose at him. 'So why aren't *you* married?' she asked lightly.

'Dunno. Never happened.' Raising an arm, he flipped his case off the counter top. 'Er...if there's a crisis of any kind—call me,' he instructed. 'I'll come galloping back.'

Her laugh cracked in the middle. 'On your white charger?'

'You bet. Isn't that what knights do?'

'Very cute.' Head thrown back, Emma caught his gaze. Her smile widened. Declan smiled back and, for just a moment, a blink of time, there was a connection of shared awareness. Sharp. Intense. Then, suddenly, their smiles retracted as quickly as turning off a light switch.

They both looked awkwardly away at precisely the same moment. And Declan was gone in the time it took for him to stride down the ramp to the parking area at the front of the surgery and cross to his car.

Against her better judgement, Emma watched from the window. In seconds he'd taken off, the bonnet of his silver-grey Audi a flash in the setting sun as he passed the border of flowering plumbago and was lost to sight. Emma stifled a sigh and drew back. He was on his way.

Suddenly all the places in her heart felt empty.

A peculiar kind of separateness engulfed her. She had nowhere to go.

And she realized she'd wanted to go with Declan. Be close with him. Meet his sister. Gather the warmth of family about her. *Oh, dear God.* Lifting a hand, she pressed it against her mouth. Where did she think she was going with any of this?

She needed to get a serious grip.

Keep busy. That was the best option. The only option. She locked up and set the alarm and then looked at her watch. It was still relatively early. She had time to pop in on Sylvia.

'How is everything going?' Emma asked as they sat side by side in the Gartrells' comfortable lounge room.

The older woman smiled. 'Tom's treating me like a queen. Doing the washing and everything. And we do the cooking together.'

'You know not to lift heavy pots and things,' Emma warned.

Sylvia flicked her hand dismissively. 'I just give the orders and Tom takes direction. We're quite a team.'

Emma chuckled. 'I'm sure you are. Now, how about the rest of you?'

Sylvia leaned forward confidentially. 'I think I may have had a breakthrough with the water. It's coming much better.'

'That's brilliant, Sylvia. You're still measuring the output?'

'Like you told me.'

'And how much are you still retaining?'

Sylvia thought for a second. 'About fifty mils. And I used the catheter to get that away. But I must say it's getting a bit tiresome.'

'Well, I think you can stop, now.'

'I can? Really?'

'Yes. Most of us retain that amount of urine naturally. I'd say nature's taken over and your body is well on the way to a complete recovery.'

'Oh, my!' Sylvia's hand went to her chest. 'You know I thought it would never happen. Even turning on the water at the basin like the nurses said didn't help. I was beginning to think I was some kind of oddity.'

'Oh, Sylvia, of course you're not! It's been a struggle but you'll reap the rewards of having the surgery done now.'

'Yes. And now I can power on again, get into my garden and help with the grandkids much more.'

'But not for a while yet,' Emma cautioned. 'You've had major surgery, Sylvia. Now, barring emergencies, could you come and see me in two weeks and we'll check everything is where it should be?'

'I can do that, dear.'

'About medication…' Emma flipped open the file she'd brought with her. 'I'd like you to stay on the hormone cream the specialist prescribed. Do you have enough for the next two weeks? If not, I'll write you a new script.'

'I have one repeat left,' Sylvia said. 'That nice new partner you have wrote me a script when he popped in on me at the hospital.'

'Oh—' Emma frowned. That would have been on that Saturday morning when they'd only just firmed up their partnership. But there was nothing on file… She lowered her gaze and rechecked the information. Oh, yes—there it was, in Declan's precise handwriting. So, why hadn't she seen it? She bit her lip thoughtfully. Probably because she hadn't been looking for it. Hadn't expected Declan to have become involved so quickly in a hands-on kind of way with their patients. She blinked a bit, not quite able to admit that she was missing the solidarity of his presence already.

Emma got to her feet. 'I'll see myself out, Sylvia. Don't get up.'

'Tom should be back any minute,' Sylvia said. 'He's just gone to get our usual Friday fish and chips for tea. Why don't you stay, dear? He always buys extra.' A grin tweaked a dimple in her cheek. 'Still can't get used to the fact there's only the two of us now. Stay,' she invited again.

Emma was tempted. Lord, how she was tempted. The need to be with family, surrogate as it was, was almost unbearable.

But, in reality, it would solve nothing. 'It's a lovely thought, Sylvia. And thanks. But...er...I've another patient I need to catch up with,' she invented hurriedly.

Sylvia nodded. 'Another time, then. And Emma?' Reaching up from her sitting position, the older woman squeezed the tips of Emma's fingers. 'Be kind to yourself, dear. Your dad would have wanted that for you.'

CHAPTER FIVE

HE WAS back.

Declan blew out a calming breath and switched off the ignition. He'd made good time from Brisbane and driven straight to Kingsholme, telling himself if Emma was out it was no big deal.

He stretched, felt a crack or two in his spine and shoulder joints, shrugged inwardly and swung out of the car. He'd go round to the back of the house. If the kitchen door was open, he'd know Emma was home.

Oh, hell. He worked his legs as he walked along the path at the side of the house. His joints felt as stiff and rusty as the Tin Man from *The Wizard of Oz*. Mounting the shallow steps to the verandah, he stood, quietly absorbing his surroundings.

It was a typical back verandah found in countless rural settings in Australia. A mish-mash of everyday items, from the outdoor shoes left to dry to the weathered wooden ladder that was being used as a plant stand. Two lovely old wicker chairs painted a silvery-blue were parked against the wall and in between sat a matching round wicker table covered with a patchwork cloth. On the table sat a little tea tray, a cup and saucer and a glass jar of…what? Shortbread? Something like that…

Declan took a hard breath and tunnelled a hand back through his hair. There was an odd feeling about the setting. A loneliness. Emma? His heart twisted. He hated that conclusion.

Moving purposefully across the verandah, he called a greeting from the open kitchen doorway. And waited, his heart banging like a drumbeat in his chest. There was no reply. Yet he knew she was here. He could *feel* it.

Warily, he took a couple of steps into the kitchen and looked around, his eyes widening, his face working at the sweetness of what he saw.

Emma was lying curled on the cane settee. It was obvious she was asleep, her pose unconsciously sexy yet vulnerable. Desire and need slammed into him with the intensity of a punch to the solar plexus, dizzying, like sudden gravity after weightlessness.

He felt a hard wedge in the region of his stomach and his jaw clenched. Oh, sweet heaven. This felt almost like voyeurism. Swallowing the dryness in his throat, he moved closer. 'Emma…'

His voice seemed to fall on Emma's skin like a caress, easing her out of sleep into wakefulness. 'Declan?' Her eyes shot open, her voice foggy with confusion. She jack-knifed to a sitting position. 'How long have you been there?'

'Just arrived. I didn't mean to intrude. Your kitchen door was open—'

'It's OK.' She lifted her hands, sweeping her hair back behind her ears. She gave a husky laugh. 'I started reading—must have fallen asleep.'

He frowned. 'Do you do that often—leave your door open? I could have been a burglar.'

She sent him a weighted look. 'What were you intending to steal—the kitchen chairs? The cat? This is a country town, Declan. No one locks their back doors.'

His mouth grew taut. 'I was concerned for you, that's all.'

Soft colour licked along Emma's cheekbones and she protested gruffly, 'Well, as you can see, I'm fine.' She stood to her feet. 'I thought you'd be back much later than this.'

Declan gave a twitch of his shoulder. 'Erinn's conference broke up at lunchtime. We both took off soon after. How was *your* weekend?'

Lonely without you, she was tempted to reply. But quickly thought better of it. 'Couple of call-outs,' she said. 'Nothing serious. So you had a good time with your sister?'

'Yes,' he said economically. 'Erinn and I had a few laughs, caught up on the family news.'

'As you do. Something to drink?' she asked, moving to the fridge, opening the door and peering into the contents, trying in vain to stem the smile that just wouldn't go away. He was back and somehow, in some odd way, her world felt right again. Which was crazy, she decided, leaning in to extract pear juice, a ginger cordial and soda water. She spun round and moved back to the bench. 'You'll like this,' she said, expertly mixing the three ingredients and then pouring the finished product into two tall glasses. She topped each glass with a sprig of mint and passed one across to Declan. 'It's delicious,' she promised when he hesitated over a taste test.

He held the glass to his lips and tasted once and then again, licking the residue from his lips. 'It's good,' he agreed and drank thirstily.

'Let's catch the last of the rays,' Emma invited, putting her own half-finished drink aside and leading the way out on to the verandah.

Ignoring the outdoor chairs, Declan moved to stand with his back against the railings. 'I'm a bit stiff after the drive,' he explained.

'So, was the trip back all right, then?' she asked, her hip almost touching his as she stood beside him.

'Mmm.' Why on earth were they talking such generalities? Stuff it. He couldn't hold back any longer. He turned to face her. 'I thought about you a lot over the weekend…'

Emma swallowed. Her heart tripped. He was bending towards her, his blue eyes capturing hers with an almost magnetic pull. 'I…'

'Thought about me too?' he murmured hopefully.

She had. She couldn't deny it. But would it help either of them if she told him that? Did she need the complication an admission would undoubtedly bring? She felt her heart bang out of rhythm, her gaze moving restlessly, almost fearfully, as though to find a way out of the dilemma.

The late afternoon sun felt intoxicatingly warm against her back. There was no urgency in the air. Just a languid kind of sweetness.

Declan leaned closer to her, slowly.

In a second, Emma felt her body trembling from the inside out. Was this what it felt like before a first kiss? Her mind went blank. After Marcus had defected, she'd thought she'd never again trust a man enough to experience another *first kiss*.

But she wanted it. How she wanted it.

Declan was so close to her now she could see the faint shadow across his jaw line, the slight smudges under his eyes. His face reflected a toughness, a strength.

'Emma…' he said, his voice low, this last second before his kiss.

Her mouth trembled. She could feel his breath on her face. It smelled minty, a faint residue from his drink. She lifted her gaze and stared at him, mesmerized by the yearning she saw in his eyes. The desire to be kissed by him was irresistible and, before she could second-guess the wisdom of it all, she was leaning into him.

Declan took her face in his hands, his need materialising in the softest sigh, before his mouth found hers. The kiss rolled through his blood and raw need slammed into him like nothing he had ever known before. Her lips parted and her own longing seemed to match his, overwhelming him like the heady aroma of some dark heated wine.

Applying a barely-there pressure through his hands, he whispered the tips of his fingers down the sides of her throat, then in a sweep across her breastbone to her shoulders, gathering her in.

Emma clung to him. And the kiss deepened, turned wrenching and wild. She felt a need inside her, an overwhelming need to be touched like this, held like this.

And *stroked* to the point of ecstasy by this man.

But it wasn't going to go that far. At least not today. She felt Declan pulling back, breaking the kiss, slowly, gently, his lips leaving a shivering sweetness like trails of insubstantial gossamer.

A long beat of silence while they collected themselves.

'Have we broken every rule in the official partnership handbook?' Declan asked in a deep voice, wrapping her closer.

She licked her lips. 'Possibly…probably.'

He bent to her, pressing his forehead to hers. 'It's all been a bit…'

'Unexpected?' Emma was dizzy with the newness of it all.

'Huge understatement,' he declared. 'Bone-rattling would be more apt. Ah, Emma…' His fingers lifted her chin, his mouth only a breath away as he said her name and then his lips were on hers. Again. And it felt so right the second time around. To taste slowly and blissfully instead of devouring as if there were no tomorrow.

Emma felt intoxicated, as though she were swimming through warm treacle toffee, loving the vital male taste of him, the warmth of his arms around her, the long, slow getting-to-know-you kind of kiss that she guessed neither of them wanted to end. Because then there would be questions, post-mortems.

And no answers.

But of course the kiss had to end. Good things, unexpected pleasurable things, always did. This time at Emma's instigation. Slowly, she pulled back, untwining his arms from where he'd looped them around her shoulders and took a decisive step away from him.

Declan's shoulders lifted in a huge sigh. 'I guess I should go,' he murmured and hesitated. Then, as if still compelled to touch her, he reached for her, running his hands down her arms, lacing his fingers with hers. 'Before we get into any more trouble,' he added wryly, placing the softest kiss at the side of her mouth. 'See you tomorrow.' He let her go abruptly, turning away and making a swift exit across the verandah and down the steps to the path.

He didn't look back.

At work on Monday morning, Emma was still dazed by what had happened, her whole body still sensitized by Declan's kisses, her thoughts far from clear. She'd been woefully unprepared for the avalanche of emotions she'd felt—and never experienced before. Not even with Marcus, whom she'd almost married.

She went along to her consulting room, lifting a hand to touch the corner of her mouth where Declan had imprinted that last lingering kiss. He'd be arriving at the surgery very soon. Suddenly she felt fluttery, the expectation of seeing him intense, sizzling and her former safe world was spinning out of control.

Declan left the log cabin hardly noticing the chilly winter morning, still trying to untangle the strands of emotions inside him. He'd *kissed* Emma. God, how had he let that happen? He should have been concentrating on cementing their professional partnership, not reacting to his hormones like a randy adolescent.

But they'd only kissed, for crying out loud. People did that all the time. It didn't mean they were about to move in together! Emma would see it for what it was. Opportunity, time and place, the uniqueness of their circumstances and no doubt capped off by a build-up of emotional overload. He heaved in a controlling breath and concentrated on the road.

But, by the time he reached the surgery, the rationalisation he'd concocted was rapidly being drowned out by the clang of warning bells. He was kidding himself. It was nothing to do with hormones. It was about feelings. It was about Emma Armitage.

OK, play it by ear, Declan self-counselled as he made his way along the corridor to his consulting room. He stowed his medical case and straightened his shoulders. Moira had informed him Emma was already in. Closing the door to his surgery, he moved along to her room. Her door was slightly open. Nevertheless, he rapped before he went in. 'Morning.'

'Good morning.' Emma lifted her gaze from her computer, snapping a smile into place. 'You're in early.'

Declan held out the cake tin he'd brought in. 'Thought we could share this for morning tea for the next hundred years or so,' he said deadpan.

Emma frowned a bit. 'What is it?'

'Fruit cake—old family recipe. Katie sent it via Erinn.'

'That was nice of her.' Emma looked at the rather battered cake tin with its old-fashioned English hunting scene on the lid. 'My Nanna had one of these,' she said with a laugh and got to her feet. 'May I look?'

'Help yourself.'

'Mmm…I love that smell,' Emma inhaled the classic lusciousness of rich dried fruit laced with brandy. 'Pity, though.'

He raised a dark brow.

'I think it'll be long gone before a hundred years are up. I'll leave it in Moira's safekeeping,' she added, replacing the lid carefully. 'Thank Katie when next you speak to her, won't you?'

He nodded absently. There was a beat of silence. Then, softly, as if the words were being pushed up through his diaphragm, 'Are you OK about yesterday, Emma?'

Emma didn't try to misunderstand him. Looking up, she saw the uncertainty clouding his gaze. Lord, she didn't want to have this conversation. She gave a little twist of her shoulder and asked a question of her own, 'How *OK* are you about it?'

Declan felt his heart walk a few flights of stairs. His mouth worked a bit before he answered, 'I'm not.'

'Did you enjoy kissing me, Declan?'

He looked startled at her frankness. Then, throatily, 'I'd have to be dead from the feet up not to have enjoyed kissing you, Emma. You're lovely…'

'Oh!' Suddenly, there was an ache in her stomach that was

half pleasure, half pain. And a new awareness was beating its wings all around them.

'We shouldn't let it happen again, though.' Declan sounded as though he was trying to convince himself. His hand reached out towards her cheek, then drew back sharply before it could connect with her skin. 'We're supposed to be operating a professional partnership here, aren't we?'

Her mouth dried. Was he saying they couldn't have both? Yet she ached for him. For the physical closeness they'd found yesterday. For more and more of his long, slow kisses. She was still searching for an acceptable reply when the harsh jangle of the phone in reception split the air.

'Monday morning,' Emma said resignedly.

Within seconds Moira's head popped around the door. 'We have an emergency at the primary school, folks. Neal Drummond needs a doctor there.'

Declan looked a question at Emma. 'Neal's the head teacher,' she said. 'What's happened, Moira?'

'Adam Jones has fallen out of a tree and impaled himself on the fence. It's his upper arm. The child is Carolyn Jones's grandson,' she added for Declan's benefit. 'He's only seven.'

'Then I think we should both go,' Declan said firmly. 'It all sounds a bit iffy.'

'Tsk…' Moira shook her head at the unfairness of it all. 'As if that family needs more trouble.'

'Let's not get bogged down in sentiment, Moira,' Declan growled. 'We can sort all that out later. Let's move it!' He flung the words at Emma from the doorway. 'I'll gather up some gear. Meet you in reception.'

'That's a bit unfeeling.' Moira's feathers were clearly ruffled. 'This could well be the last straw for Carolyn.'

'Declan's still finding his way in rural medicine to some extent,' Emma said diplomatically. 'I imagine the school will have contacted Carolyn but the last thing we need is for her to go into orbit at the accident scene. Whatever else, Adam will have to be kept calm.'

'I'll get her on her mobile then.' Moira as always was one

step ahead. 'I'll tell her to go to the school office and wait there. She'll listen to me.'

'Thanks, Moira.' Emma nodded gratefully. 'And prepare her for the fact that Adam will probably have to be sent on to Toowoomba Base. Carolyn will want to go with him.'

'So she'd better pack a bag then.'

'Yes.' Emma picked up her medical case and hurried through to reception.

Declan was already there, taking delivery of the emergency supplies Libby had hastily assembled.

'Paeds drug box, IV kit and emergency oxygen—is that all you need?'

'That's brilliant, Libby, thanks.' Declan slung the emergency pack over his shoulder. He sent a quick grin at the nurse. 'In at the deep end on your first day.'

Libby returned a pert look. 'That's what I'm here for.'

'Not sure how long we'll be,' Emma warned.

'Go!' The RN shooed them towards the outer door. 'Moira and I will juggle the lists around somehow.'

'We'll take my wheels,' Declan said as they sped across the car park. In seconds they were seated and belted up. 'What kind of fence are we talking about here?' He ignited the motor and shot the car towards the street.

'Probably the ten-foot wrought iron fence at the rear of the school grounds,' Emma said. 'There are several huge Moreton Bay figs close to the fence line. I'd guess Adam's scrambled up one of those and fallen.'

'For crying out loud!' Declan muttered, anger and dread in equal portions catching him by surprise. 'Those old spiked fences have no place anywhere near a school!'

'It's precisely because they are *old*,' Emma pointed out patiently. 'They're heritage-listed.'

It was barely half a kilometre to the school but time enough for Emma's uncertainty to intensify at the thought of the possible scenario they were facing.

Neal Drummond was waiting for them. 'Thanks, both of you, for coming,' he said after Emma had made swift introductions.

'What action have you taken so far?' Declan asked quickly.

'Our year one teacher has gone up to Adam. She's physically supporting him as best she can. We've also positioned a couple of ladders so that you'll have access of sorts to the injured child.' Neal escorted them swiftly along to the accident scene.

'So, do you have any idea why Adam went climbing?' Emma asked carefully.

'Don't know yet.' Neal's mouth tightened. 'His grandmother's on her way in. We'll perhaps get a clearer picture then.'

Emma explained what initiative she'd taken to keep Carolyn at arm's length from the accident scene.

'Thanks for that, Emma.' Neal nodded his relief.

'Ambulance, fire and rescue services been alerted?' Declan queried.

'Both ambulances are out on other calls. The base will get one to us asap. Fire and rescue will be here when they can muster a team.' The head teacher ran a hand distractedly over his crew cut. 'We do have a staff member who does regular climbing. He could be of some help in the interim. He's just nipped off home to get his ropes. Right, here we are.'

'Hell's bells!' Declan's face was grim. One look at the accident scene told both doctors it was going to need a painstaking and skilled team effort to achieve a successful outcome for Adam.

Just then, the boy's plaintive little cry, high-pitched and heart-rending, brought the doctors into swift consultation.

'He'll be bordering on shock with the pain.' Emma shaded her eyes, frowning up to where the dense foliage of the tree overhung the fence where the child was impaled. 'That set-up with the ladders isn't going to be effective, Declan. There's no way we can work on Adam like that.'

'Well, not for long,' Declan agreed. 'But if you could manage to get up there and begin the drugs regime...'

'What will you do?' Emma looked worried.

'Wait until the abseiling ropes arrive. Hopefully, I'll be able to secure myself to one of those big branches.' Declan raised his gaze to where the giant fig spread upwards towards the heavens. 'From there I can lower myself almost to the exact spot where Adam is impaled and support him on my lap. That'll allow me the freedom to use both hands to work on him.'

They'd need to intubate. Emma asked hesitantly, 'Sure you're OK with that?' She'd noticed the sudden tautness in Declan's stance. The thinly veiled tension. He was wound tight. Oh, sweet heaven. The uncertainties of his physical fitness must be eating him up. She dived in feet first. 'Do you want to swap roles here?' she asked in a swift aside. 'It's no big deal, if you'd rather…'

'I'm not a cripple, Emma,' Declan shot back with dark impatience. 'Yet!'

'I know—I didn't mean—' Emma swallowed the constriction in her throat, steeling herself as Adam's agonized sobbing almost jettisoned her composure entirely. 'Do what you have to do, then. Just, for heaven's sake, let's get this child some pain relief. Oh—' She turned, catching sight of the male figure sprinting across the quadrangle. 'Here's the bearer of the promised ropes, by the look of it.'

'Mike Foreman,' the young teacher introduced himself. 'What do you want me to do, Doc?'

'We'll need to set up a pulley system.' Declan's response was clipped. The two men went into a huddle.

Emma left them to get on with it. Quashing her fears, she slung the emergency pack over her shoulder and began moving purposefully up the ladder. Her stomach swirled. She breathed deeply and then collected herself. 'Hi.' She looked up shakily to where the young teacher was perched. 'I'm Emma.'

'Chrissy. Are you the doctor?'

'Yes. And you're doing wonderfully, Chrissy.'

'It's been awful, just trying to hold him like this. Poor little boy…'

'I know. Just keep on doing what you're doing. That'll be a great help.' Emma was aware of curtailing her movements, doing everything in slow motion. Adam's broken little sobs spurred her on.

'Hush now, baby,' Emma soothed gently, popping the oxygen mask over the little boy's face. She began assessing her small patient. His skin was cold and clammy, indicating shock. But his pulse and BP were better than she'd feared, raised but stable. Good. She could safely administer the painkiller and anti-nausea drugs. She'd follow up with midazolam. Its light anaesthetic properties would help to combat post-traumatic shock and ease the youngster through the ordeal ahead.

She selected the wide-bore cannula. She was taking no chances with this little one. If Adam began bleeding or, heaven forbid, going into sudden shock, they'd need to run through high-volume fluids to resuscitate him.

But, as long as the foreign object stayed where it was in Adam's arm, until it could be surgically removed, then the child was reasonably safe from haemorrhaging.

Although they still had a way to go.

With the drugs safely administered, Emma leaned more of her weight into the ladder, using both hands to secure a light absorbent pad around the child's injured arm, and then carefully and gently tucking the youngster into a space blanket. She sent the ghost of a smile to her counterpart.

Chrissy looked on in awe. 'I wouldn't have your job for anything. But, whatever you've given Adam, it's starting to work. I can feel him relaxing.'

'The drugs are doing their job, then. And that sounds like our backup arriving.'

Leaves swirled above them and then Declan's command rang out, 'One more hitch should do it, Mike. Right, I'm here—thanks.' Sitting suspended in his harness, he eased the weight of the child across on to his lap. 'Well done, team.'

Emma felt her heart lift. 'And you,' she rejoined quietly.

'Hmm.' He looked at her narrowly for a moment. 'How's our patient doing?'

'Drifting off.'

'Enough for me to get an airway in?'

'I should think so.'

Declan nodded. 'OK, I'll have a go.'

'I think this is where I leave you, guys.' Chrissy began backing down the ladder.

'The fire and rescue crew are ten minutes away,' Neal Drummond relayed from the foot of the tree.

'Have you got the airway in?' Emma's concern was more immediate.

'Almost there… Right, it's done. With a bit of luck—and heaven knows we've earned it—Adam will be in la-la land by the time the rescue guys get here.'

At last Adam was cut free. At the fireman's signal that the mission had been successful, a subdued cheer went up and, from his anchor in the tree, Mike paid out the guide rope, lowering Declan and his precious cargo to the ground.

'Nice work, folks.' The paramedics had arrived to witness the rescue. 'We'll take over now.' Gently, Adam was stretchered to the waiting vehicle, one officer supporting the little injured arm with the foreign object still *in situ*. 'Heading to Toowoomba Base, right, Emma?'

'Yes, please.' Emma bent over Adam for a final check of the IV line that was running in fluids.

'Just hang on a tick, guys.' Quickly, Declan scribbled some notes to go with their young patient.

'Declan?' Emma said in an urgent undertone. 'I can manage the patient lists if you'd like to go with Adam to the hospital.'

'And what possible use would I be there?' he growled, adding his signature and handing the notes across to the waiting ambulance officer. 'Thanks, mate. We'll be in touch with the surgeon later.'

'No worries, Doc.'

'Adam's grandmother is going with you,' a subdued Emma reminded them.

Jim Yardley, the chief paramedic, raised a hand in acknowledgement. 'All covered, Emma. Thanks.'

There was a strange lull for a few moments after the ambulance had pulled away. A kind of eerie hiatus. Emma heard the soft rustle of leaves above them and looked up. 'I hate this feeling,' she said.

Declan eyed her sharply. 'Adam will be all right, Emma. His arm will be a bit iffy for a while but kids spring back remarkably quickly.'

A furrow etched between her eyes. He just didn't get it. 'I know all that. I just meant the feeling of uncertainty. Wondering why this child did what he did this morning. Was there an upset at home? Should we be taking better care of Carolyn and her needs—the whole family?'

'For crying out loud!' Declan began gathering up their paraphernalia, impatience in every beat of his movements.

Emma felt her spine stiffen. What kind of response was that? Declan O'Malley had a lot to learn about family medicine, that was for sure. Her teeth bit into the full softness of her lower lip. She didn't need this aggravation. And she didn't need a practice partner who was on a completely different wavelength. After checking they'd left nothing behind, she followed him across to his car.

'Look—' Declan stood awkwardly beside the open lid of the car boot after loading everything inside '—just give me a bit of space here, all right?'

Emma felt a needle of guilt prick her conscience. He sounded on edge and the eyes that lifted to hers were guarded and shadowed. She swallowed. 'Are you OK?'

The corners of his mouth tightened. 'I'm fine.'

Of course he wasn't fine. Her heart bounced sickeningly. She should have realized. He'd spent most of the morning on an emotional roller coaster, no doubt agonizing whether he was going to be able to cut it in a rural practice where physical stamina counted just as much as his medical skills. But he'd done so well. So well. Her gaze faltered. 'Declan—I realize this morning has been difficult so if you feel we need a debrief, you only have to say.'

His blue eyes bored into hers. 'I'll bear it in mind.'

In other words, butt out. *Great.* Emma felt completely put in her place. At this rate they'd be lucky if the contract they'd signed lasted as long as six weeks—let alone six months!

By the time they'd got back to the surgery, Emma knew what she had to do and, by the end of the day, she'd accomplished most of it. She hesitated about telling Declan what she'd done. Would he even care…? Her train of thought was interrupted by the rap on her door and the man himself poked his head in.

'Moira said you'd finished for the day,' he said by way of explanation.

Emma beckoned him in, drawing back in her chair as if to reclaim her space. She took a deep breath, ultra-conscious of him as he walked forward and planted his hands on the desk in front of her. 'What's up?'

'I've an update on Adam. They've operated. Bit of a mess but the foreign object came out cleanly. They'll hit him with antibiotics for the next little while. Should be a straightforward recovery.'

Emma nodded, feeling the awkwardness between them cloy and magnify. She made a quick decision and swung off her chair. 'Let's go through and get a cup of tea. I'm parched—unless you need to be somewhere else?'

Several expressions chased through his eyes before he said with a rough sigh, 'No… A cuppa sounds good.' He tacked on a forced smile. 'Perhaps we can make some inroads into that fruit cake as well.'

'We'll give it a good shot,' Emma said, relieved that he'd at least agreed to have some down time, if only for a little while.

Switching on the electric jug, she got mugs down from the cupboard, all the time conscious of Declan's restive movements about her kitchen. She cut slabs of the fruit cake and set them on a plate and then, when the water boiled, she made a pot of tea. She didn't care how many cups it took, she was going to make Declan O'Malley talk to her about this morning.

'Delicious cake,' she said a bit later, swiping a crumb from the corner of her mouth. 'Family recipe, you said?'

'Mmm.' Declan was on his second cup of tea. Taking up his mug, he looked at her narrowly over its rim. 'Spit it out, Emma.'

Her eyes widened innocently. 'The cake?'

'No, not the cake.' His voice rumbled with dry humour. 'You want me to spill my guts about my reactions this morning, don't you?'

Her shoulders twitched. 'I wouldn't have put it quite so bluntly. But if it would help you to talk…'

His blue eyes traced her features one by one, then flicked back to lock with hers, their expression uncertain. 'I—realize I lost it a bit. I jumped all over you. It's the last thing I wanted to do.'

Emma drew in her breath sharply, and suddenly it was there in the air between them. The raw, overwhelming need, the awareness. The fear if it all went wrong. But, for now, they had to stay on track, keep it all professional. She moistened her lips. 'It's OK.'

'It's not OK,' he contradicted. 'I'd like to think it was a one-off but, realistically, I guess I'm going to have to face more of those knife-edge moments in the future—'

'But you'll also learn to cope, Declan,' she responded earnestly.

He snorted. 'Well, let's hope so. Otherwise, I'm not going to be much use to you as a rural doctor, am I?'

'Was it just the fact you doubted your physical capability in the situation?'

'That and the frustration I felt.' He sat back, linking his hands around his mug and staring broodingly into its contents. 'The fact is I *should* have been able to whip Adam into surgery here. Think how much easier it would have been for the family. How much more comfortable for Adam not to have had the road trip to Toowoomba.'

'But it would have been quite the wrong decision for *you*!' Emma's voice was ripe with emotion.

'I know that too,' he agreed, a small rueful twist to his mouth. 'It doesn't make the frustration any less, though.'

'Frustration you can live with,' Emma declared quietly. 'It would be a far worse outcome if you were to rush in when you're not ready.'

'Just to prove a point,' he tacked on dryly.

'Exactly.'

She was wise as well as beautiful. Declan ached to hold her again, feel the silkiness of her hair glide through his fingers. He closed his eyes briefly. He'd better face the fact. Emma Armitage had got to him as no other woman had. Ever. He wanted—*needed* her to think well of him. It mattered. A hell of a lot. He certainly didn't want her to think of him as some kind of lame dog she had to carry in the practice. He blinked and focused as Emma began speaking again.

'Don't keep beating up on yourself over this, Declan. In an ideal situation, the firemen would have been on hand to do the tree climbing today. We should have had only to carry out our role as doctors. But, like it or not, that's run-of-the-mill rural medicine,' she ended, spreading her hands in a philosophical shrug.

Declan frowned and changed the subject. 'I had a long conversation with Neal Drummond this afternoon.'

'About what?'

'Opening the swimming pool for use by our senior citizens.'

Emma's widened gaze registered her surprise at his proactiveness. 'What was his response?'

'He's willing but he'll have to confer with the school's P&C committee before he can give us an answer. I figured if we could get some water aerobics going for the seniors, it would be of immense benefit health-wise, lessen their stress levels, be a social outlet as well.'

'It would certainly benefit patients like Carolyn Jones. Well done, you.'

Declan's mouth kicked up in a crooked smile. 'Well…I'm slowly getting the hang of this kind of community medicine. Perhaps, by the end of our six months' trial, I'll be taking it in my stride.'

Emma's heart skipped a beat. But if he wasn't—what then? 'Um—I've done a bit of organizing of my own. While Carolyn's away in Toowoomba, I'm having Adam's two older siblings to stay with me.'

He huffed dryly, 'Why am I not surprised?'

'I'm a hands-on kind of girl,' she defended.

'I'd have to agree with that.' The look he sent her was blue-metal hot.

Emma's insides heaved crazily. She felt heat rising, warming her throat, flowering over her cheeks. Suddenly, her train of thought was gone, her thoughts all over the place. 'It just seemed the logical thing to do.' The words pumped up jerkily from her chest. 'Lauren and Joel know me. Before their lives went pear-shaped, Carolyn did some housekeeping for Dad and me. The kids used to come with her sometimes. They had the run of the house. Moira's round there now, helping them pack a few clothes. The school bus can pick them up from here in the mornings and drop them back. It'll be good.'

Declan's gaze softened. 'You're so like your father, Emma. He believed in actions speaking louder than words too.'

Emma dipped her head, sudden tears blurring her eyes. He couldn't have given her a nicer compliment.

CHAPTER SIX

CHILDREN made the house a home, Emma thought indulgently, watching as Lauren and Joel scooped up their breakfast cereal with obvious enjoyment. 'Now, I'll get on and make your school lunches,' she said, placing some buttered toast on the table between them. 'What would you like on your sandwiches, guys?'

'Anything will do,' ten-year-old Lauren said shyly.

Blue-eyed Joel sent an innocent look at Emma. 'It's tuck shop today.'

'We're not allowed tuck shop.' Lauren gave her younger brother an old-fashioned look.

Probably because their grandparents couldn't afford to hand out money they didn't have. Emma's soft heart was touched. Poor babes. 'Why don't we have a treat today, then? Let's do tuck shop.'

The children stopped eating and looked at Emma. 'Could we?' Lauren fisted a small hand across her chest.

'You bet,' Emma said.

'Yay!' Joel yelped with delight. 'Can I have a burger?'

'Please,' Emma directed, hiding a smile.

'Please…' Joel parroted with a grin.

'What about you, Lauren?' Emma sent the little girl a warm smile. 'Like a burger as well?'

Lauren nodded her wheat-blonde head. 'Yes, please, Emma.'

'Good. Now, what do we have to do—write out an order or something?' Emma racked her brains thinking back to her own primary school days.

'We write what we want on a piece of paper and put it in our lunch box with the money.' Joel was only too happy to provide the answers.

'And the tuck shop ladies make up the lunch orders,' Lauren filled in quietly.

'Right.' Emma looked from one to the other. 'That sounds easy-peasy.'

Lauren giggled.

'And you can get other stuff too,' Joel said around a mouthful of toast.

Emma reached for her scribble pad and a pen. 'Let's get started, then.' While the two pairs of young eyes watched intently, she wrote the orders for the burgers and then asked, 'Now, what else would you like, Lauren?'

The little girl thought for a minute. 'Could I have a strawberry yoghurt, please?'

'Of course, you may.' Emma wrote diligently. 'Joel, honey?'

'Packet of chips—please?'

Emma raised a brow. It wasn't the most nutritious of choices, but hey, today's lunches were meant to be a treat. 'OK, done.' Emma stuffed the notes into the waiting lunch boxes and enclosed the appropriate money. 'Now, if you've finished breakfast, hop off and brush your teeth.'

Joel took off along the hallway, making *vroom* noises as he flapped his arms like an aeroplane coming in to land, almost colliding with Declan, who was making his way in. 'What's that all about?' Declan cranked a dark brow in query.

Emma chuckled. 'Joel's on a high because I said they could have tuck shop today.

'He's not the only one on a high.' Declan's eyes and voice teased.

'It's lovely having them here.' Emma's blood sang. 'This house was made for children.'

And perhaps she'd fill it with her own one day. The wild idea of him being the father of those imaginary children stopped Declan in his tracks, sending rivers of want and doubt and sheer amazement cascading through his bloodstream. The thought was crazy… 'Er...I came in early. Thought you might want a bit of a hand. But I see I needn't have worried.'

'No—' She saw his gaze settle on her mouth and linger. And suddenly she could feel his presence, his masculinity like the ticking of a time bomb… 'They're great kids. Ah—here they are again. All set?' She snuggled them into their anoraks, gave Lauren a hug and laughed as Joel squirmed away. Handing them their backpacks, she ushered them outside to wait for the school bus.

'It's cold out there—' Emma was rubbing her arms as she came back into the warmth of the kitchen. 'Would you like a cup of tea?'

'I've put the kettle on for a fresh pot.'

'Oh—good. That's good.' Emma's voice trailed away and she glanced at her watch. 'You *are* in early.

'I couldn't stay away. It's more fun here.'

There was a moment of awkward silence while they smiled at each other in a goofy kind of way. Then the water boiled and Declan turned away to make the tea. Tea made, he turned back with the pot cradled in his hands. 'Am I making myself too much at home here? Just yell if I am.'

'No—it's nice…' The words spilled out on their own and she squirmed at her transparent honesty. 'I'll get the mugs.'

'So—did you happen to find out the reasons for Adam's misadventure?' Declan asked her.

'Mmm, I did, actually. I had a little chat to Lauren last night when she was getting ready for bed. I didn't press her,' she added, seeing Declan's sharp look of concern. 'Lauren volunteered the information. She said her gran lost her temper and smacked Adam on the legs.'

Declan's mouth drew in. 'Hard?'

'With a rolled-up newspaper.'

So, not too hard, then. They didn't need a case of child

abuse to add to the already difficult situation. 'What was the problem?'

'Adam wet the bed—again.'

'He's obviously disturbed. Poor little kid.' Declan shook his head. 'So, as doctors, what do we do—start looking for definitive solutions for this family?'

'If there are any.' Emma sighed. 'Carolyn will be beside herself.'

'Wallowing in guilt is not going to solve anything.'

'That's a bit hard.'

'So is what's happening to these kids. Be realistic, Emma. Do we know where the mother is?'

'Tracey?' Emma pulled her thoughts together. 'Toowoomba somewhere, I think. Carolyn has an address.'

'So, will she let Tracey know what's happened?'

'I don't think they speak much.'

Declan blew out a frustrated breath through his teeth. 'So, Tracey is living in a twilight zone with her junkie boyfriend while the grandparents slave their guts out to raise *her* kids. That's not good enough. Those kids need their mother.'

'They need a functioning mother,' Emma countered. 'And stability—which they have now with their grandparents.'

'They could still have that but Tracey should be there as well, sharing the load. Carolyn and Nev are nearing an age when they should be thinking of enjoying their retirement. They shouldn't have this extra burden of having to rear their grandchildren because their daughter-in-law chooses to opt out of her responsibilities.'

Emma rolled her eyes. 'So, what are you going to do—drag Tracey back by the hair and make her be a proper mother to her kids?'

'No, Dr Armitage.' Surprisingly, Declan grinned. 'I'll go and see her, talk to her and try to get her into some decent rehab programme.'

'You're quite serious about this, aren't you?'

'Yes, I am.' Declan's look turned pensive. 'I'm remembering my own childhood, when our lives suddenly turned upside-down.'

'I don't see the connection,' Emma said. '*Your* mother appears to have made a wonderful job of raising you and your sisters.'

He shrugged. 'Given a different set of genes, who knows how she might have coped? It's both as simple and as complicated as that. Anyway, I'd like to try to see Tracey. Ascertain what I can do to help.'

Emma was about to offer to accompany him but she held back. She guessed this was something he needed to do off his own bat. He was on a steep learning curve but he seemed to be getting the hang of family medicine with all its uncertainties and pitfalls. She should be grateful. 'When will you go?' she asked instead.

'This afternoon, if I can get away reasonably early. I'll make a few phone calls first, see what's out there in the way of help for Tracey. When I get to Toowoomba, I'll swing by the hospital and see Adam, have a word with Carolyn and hope she can give me Tracey's address.'

'Just—don't expect too much, Declan, from yourself or—' Emma's flow of words was interrupted by a loud banging on the front door of the surgery. She jumped to her feet.

'Wait!' Declan cautioned. 'Let me get the door.'

Emma stopped mid-stride. 'But surely it's an emergency!'

'We don't know that for sure. And people are aware you live alone, Emma.'

'Oh—' Beating back a shadowy unease, Emma fell in behind Declan as he went to the front door. Switching off the alarm, he unlocked the door and slid it open. 'Yes?'

A man dressed in workman's clothes rocked agitatedly from one foot to the other. At Declan's appearance, he pulled back uncertainly. 'You a doctor, mate?'

'Yes, I am.' Declan's response was clipped. 'What's happened?'

The man jerked a thumb over his shoulder. 'I'm the foreman from the building site across the road, there. One of the guys slipped off the scaffolding—tore his hand on a bloody wall spike. Bleeding's pretty bad.'

'You go!' Emma practically pushed Declan out of the door. 'I'll follow with my bag.'

As quickly as she could, Emma followed the men across the road to the site. 'Who and what do we have here?' She hunkered down beside Declan.

'Brett Cartrell, de-gloved hand.' Declan's dark head was bent over his patient. 'Did you bring morphine?'

Emma delved into her case and handed him the drug plus an anti-nausea medication. Ah…not good. She clamped her teeth on her bottom lip, seeing where the skin had been forcibly pulled back from the workman's hand. The injury would surely need microsurgery.

'Crikey, Doc…' Brett was pale and sweating. 'This is killin' me—'

'I know, mate.' Declan slipped the oxygen mask into place. 'Breathe away, now. That's good. IV now, please, Emma.' He shot the painkiller home. 'Normal saline.'

Emma knew it was their best option to stave off shock. Prompting a vein to the surface, she slid the cannula into place.

'What's the ETA on the ambulance?' Declan brought his gaze up, addressing the shocked faces of the men around him.

'They'll be a while, the base reckoned,' Cam Creedy, the foreman, said.

'God, I love that euphemistic term,' Declan growled, running a stethoscope over Brett's chest. 'Breathing's OK,' he relayed in an aside to Emma. 'Could you get a pressure bandage over the injury, please?'

Quickly and gently, Emma secured the bandage. 'Sling now?'

Declan nodded. 'I'll hold his hand steady while you do that.' He addressed the site foreman. 'I take it you'll be doing a report for the Workplace Health and Safety people?'

'Goes without saying.' Cam Creedy pushed back his hard hat and scratched his head. 'I don't know how it could have happened. I always get the guys to check and double-check before they climb anywhere.'

'Accidents happen,' Declan said darkly. 'I can vouch for that.'

Emma sent him a sharp look. He seemed in control and there was none of the edginess of yesterday. She daren't ask him if he was OK. He'd probably shoot her down in flames and she didn't want that. Not when they seemed to be forging a more positive kind of relationship.

'Here's the ambulance,' someone said.

After the handover, they walked back across the road to the surgery. 'So, when can we expect the third?' Declan asked.

'Sorry?'

'Accidents usually happen in threes, don't they?'

'Who said that?' Emma looked at him with scepticism.

'No one of note, but haven't you noticed when, for instance, your car packs up, then something else breaks down and then you wait with trepidation for the third thing to go wrong?'

'That's rubbish!'

'That's what the guy said when he accidentally threw out an antique vase worth thousands.'

'You're making it up.'

'We'll see,' he grinned, standing aside for her to precede him through the front door of the surgery. 'Morning all.'

Jodi avidly sought details of what had occurred. And then shrieked, 'Yeuch! Declan—look at your shirt! It's all bloody.'

'That's the third one,' Declan deadpanned, holding the offending garment away from his chest. He turned to Emma. 'My shirt's ruined. See, told you so.'

'You fool.' Emma's chuckle was rich and warm. 'Come through and I'll find you a spare one.'

Later that afternoon, Declan made his way to the address Carolyn had given him—reluctantly. 'Tracey won't come back,' the grandmother had said as they'd sat over a cup of coffee in the annexe off the children's ward.

'Have you told her about Adam's accident?' Declan had asked gently.

'She wouldn't be interested. Nev and I will have to rear these children as best we can.' Her shoulders lifted in a weary sigh and the corners of her mouth wilted unhappily. 'Ryan wouldn't have wanted this for us.'

'I don't imagine he'd have wanted this for Tracey either,' Declan pointed out with quiet diplomacy. 'Was he your only son?'

'Our only child. We couldn't have any more.' She paused. 'And I suppose I could have tried harder with Tracey…' Carolyn's mouth trembled. 'She's only a little thing. The babies took it out of her…her own mother was useless, no help there.'

Now, Declan hesitated before gingerly ascending the shallow steps. What a falling-down dump. The verandah was crumbling and sagging on rotten footings and saplings and long-stemmed weeds were shoving up through the cracks in the floorboards. He stood on the edge of the verandah and looked out, feeling a surge of anger swell in his chest. This just wasn't on…

'Whaddya want?'

Declan turned, his jaw tightening.

A young man was standing at the front door. He looked malnourished and unkempt, his hair dreadlocked and grubby, his skin pasty. 'You a cop?'

'No,' Declan said clearly. 'I'm a doctor.'

'We didn't send for no doctor. You're narc squad, ain't yer? Leave us alone…'

'Sorry, can't manage that.' Declan took a step forward. 'I need to see Tracey.'

'You can't—just—just leave us alone…' the young man whined, trying to block Declan's entry, but his slight build was no match for Declan's powerful bulk. 'Hey—you hurt me!' he yelped accusingly, trying to regain his balance. 'I'll get ya for this—'

'Whatever works,' Declan said through clenched teeth. A few strides took him to the end of the short hallway leading to an enclosed back verandah-cum-kitchen. There was a sight that had his worst fears realized. Tracey Jones looked a washed-out, defeated figure.

She was standing against a set of louvred windows, the light from the solitary naked bulb elongating her shadow. She was barefoot and wearing a threadbare dressing gown. Her stance spoke of defiance mixed with a fear so tangible Declan felt he could almost reach out and touch it. 'Hello, Tracey,' he said gently. 'I'm Declan O'Malley, your children's doctor from the Kingsholme practice. I've come to tell you Adam's had an accident. He's in hospital.'

Tracey gave an audible gasp and her hand flew to her mouth. 'It's not my fault—' She shrank back as if she'd been threatened with violence.

'No one is saying it is, Tracey. But you're Adam's mother and we need to talk about that.'

There was a long silence. Then Tracey slowly moved forward as if sleep-walking and sank down on one of the old wooden chairs set against the rickety kitchen table. She bowed her head and clasped her hands between her knees. 'My kids must hate me…'

Declan let the statement go unanswered. Instead, he cast a quick all-encompassing look around him. It was a scene of abject poverty. He'd expected no less but he'd also expected chaos and there he'd been wrong. Every surface was scrubbed clean; even the mismatched crockery was washed and stacked neatly on the shabby dresser. Declan's jaw worked for a second. It was a pathetic sight, yet he sensed hope that something could be salvaged here.

He pulled out a chair and sat down with Tracey at the table, his hands placed squarely in front of him. 'Would you like to see your children again, Tracey?'

'They wouldn't want to see me,' the young woman whispered brokenly. 'I—left them.'

'Mind telling me why you did that?' Declan's voice carried a gentle reassurance.

There was a long silence while Tracey rubbed at a spot on the edge of the table.

'I guess you were gutted when Ryan was killed,' Declan surmised. 'Maybe you flipped out, lost the plot for a while. Am I right?'

Tracey's gaze sprang to his. 'Yes…' she said on a ragged breath. 'H-how did you know?'

'I've been there.' Declan's voice flattened. 'Life gets complicated. Sometimes it's hard to ask for help, even when we know we should. I can give you that help now, Tracey, if you want it badly enough.'

Tracey made a sound somewhere between a sob and a moan. She looked at Declan, the pain of loss and uncertainty in her eyes.

'Your kids miss you…' Declan's smile warmed the bleak little kitchen. 'They need you. And I think you need them. If I didn't think that, I wouldn't be here.'

'Where are they now?' Tracey's gaze widened in query, her question a whispered plea. 'And what happened to my baby?'

Quietly and non-judgementally, Declan filled her in.

'I don't suppose Carolyn will ever forgive me,' Tracey said bitterly. 'She never wanted Ryan to marry me but I was pregnant with Lauren and we loved each other, despite what she said. But I had the kids so quickly and Ryan was away a lot. It was hard…'

'I know. Carolyn knows that too now. I think she and Nev would be over the moon if you came back.'

Tracey pressed a lock of hair to her cheek, her eyes wide with fear and doubt. 'I couldn't just rock back as if—as if nothing has happened. I'd need someone to help me.' She sent Declan a beseeching look. 'Could you… Dr O'Malley?'

Declan nodded, as if her response was what he'd hoped for. 'I can do that, Tracey.' He paused and then, 'When was your last fix?'

Tracey drew back sharply, her expression shocked. 'I never injected! I only took a few pills and that—not enough to get hooked on anything. It was just something to…make the pain go away. And Robbie kept getting them for me.' Her teeth came down on her bottom lip. 'He's garbage. I never want to see him again.'

'I don't think you need worry about *him*. I'd say he's done a runner. Now—' Declan pushed his chair back and stood to his feet '—let's get you sorted, Tracey Jones. What do you say?'

Tracey scrambled awkwardly to her feet. 'I'd like a shower but there's no hot water.'

'Do you have clothes?'

'Some—the ones I brought with me. And they're clean,' she added with an edge of defiance.

'Go and get dressed, then,' Declan said kindly. 'And pack up what you want to take with you.'

'Everything?' It was a frightened whisper.

Declan's look was implacable. 'You won't be coming back, Tracey.'

Her throat jerked as she swallowed. 'Then what?'

'You'll come with me to the women's shelter. You can have a shower and a hot meal and they'll give you a bed. I'll leave you a mild sleeper so you'll get some decent rest.'

'How...long can I stay there?'

'As long as you need. No one is about to judge you, Tracey, please believe that. The people at the shelter will arrange a medical check-up for you and, later on, some counselling, if that's what you'd like.'

'OK…' Tracey nodded. 'I s'pose I could talk to someone.'

'Good.' Declan smiled again. 'I'll check in with the shelter each day and, as soon as you're feeling up to it, I'll take you to see Adam.'

About a kilometre out of Bendemere, Declan pressed Emma's logged-in number on his hands-free phone. She answered on the third ring. 'Where are you?'

'Nearly home.'

'How did it go with Tracey?'

'OK, I think. Long story. Could I swing by?'

'Of course. Have you eaten?'

'No. Have you?'

'Not yet.'

'I'll pick up some takeaway, then.'

'No need.' There was a hint of laughter in her voice as she added, 'I've made a curry.'

'It must be your destiny to feed me,' he responded, matching her jokey tone.

'Mmm. Must be.'

'Are the kids OK?'

'They're fine. I've just tucked them in. Lauren's reading *The Wind in the Willows*.'

'Ah—I loved those guys—especially old Badger. Who's Lauren's favourite?'

'Moley, I think. She says he's cuddly.'

'Nice.' Declan laughed lightly. Oh, boy. He began to feel almost punch-drunk. The tone of the conversation was doing strange things to his insides. It could have been *their* kids they were talking about. An unfulfilled yearning as sudden as a lightning strike filled his veins.

Emma.

Who else in the whole of his adult life had ever made him feel this way? As though his feet were hardly touching the ground, his head in the stars.

But at the same time scared him to blazes…

What was happening here? Emma began to set the table, a mixture of a kind of thrilling uncertainty and just plain happiness flooding her. *Declan.* Her practice partner. Her friend. Yes, he was both of those. But he had become more than that. Unless she was reading it all wrong.

But she didn't think so. Lately, he'd been watching her in that way he had. Kind of thoughtful and expectant all mixed up together. And a little bemused, as though he didn't quite know what universe he'd stumbled into. Let alone why he had.

And there was more. Emma pressed her fingers to her mouth, reliving his kisses all over again. Parting her lips, she imagined tasting him again, just the action flooding her body with sensation and desire…

'Emma?'

'Ooh!' she squealed and spun round from her X-rated reverie to see him hovering at the kitchen door. Her hand flew to her throat. 'I didn't hear you arrive,' she said, all flustered.

'I was quiet,' he said, moving inside. 'Didn't want to wake the kids.'

'I've just checked on them. They're well away.' She went towards him and they met in the middle of the kitchen. 'What do you have there?' Emma indicated the carrier bag he was toting.

'Some wine and a chocolate dessert.'

'Lovely. But you didn't need to—' Emma felt she could hardly breathe.

'I can't keep letting you feed me.'

Oh, you can, you can.

Emma savoured the last of her dessert as it rolled off her tongue. 'Oh, that was gorgeous,' she said with a sigh.

'Not bad,' Declan said. 'I think the packaging might have been a bit deceptive all the same.' In fact the dessert had turned out to be nothing more exotic than a rich vanilla ice cream with a swirl of chocolate and a sprinkling of hazelnuts. 'No doubt the kids will finish it off.'

'Mmm, they'll love it. Coffee?'

'No, thanks.' Declan rolled his shoulders and stretched. 'Do you have a green tea, by any chance?'

'I have a whole selection of organic teas,' Emma said grandly, getting lightly to her feet. 'I'll have a peppermint, I think.' She made the tea quickly, passed a mug to Declan and then resumed her chair. 'Are you going to fill me in about your visit to Tracey now?'

Declan did, quickly and concisely.

Emma looked thoughtful. 'You don't think she'll do a runner from the shelter, do you?'

Declan took a mouthful of his tea. 'No…' he said eventually. 'Her self-esteem has taken a battering. But, unless I'm a very poor judge of character, I think she'll be back with her kids quite soon. She's had a huge wake-up call. And Carolyn's anxious to mend fences as well. I'm tipping they'll forge a workable relationship when things settle down.'

'Should we say anything to Lauren and Joel yet?'

'Not yet. I have faith in Tracey but I'd hate to raise the kids' hopes and see them dashed. Let's tread carefully for the next little while.'

'You're right.' She gave a short nod. And then the emotions from a very crowded couple of days kicked in and she said without thinking, 'You've no idea how wonderful it is to have someone to talk to about this stuff. And not even on a professional level—just to talk to.'

'Oh, but I do, Emma,' he said softly. 'I couldn't wait to get back and talk to *you*.'

She blinked. He was watching her in *that* way again. 'I guess it's good, then—that we can communicate so well. For the success of the practice,' she concluded, the words so far from where her thoughts had travelled, they made no sense at all.

'Why are you spinning this, Emma?' Declan kept his voice low. 'What's happening here is about us—you and me. We could have met anywhere in the world but we just happened to meet here. The practice has nothing to do with it.'

'I'm afraid…' she heard herself say.

'Of me?' His voice rose. 'Or of what we could mean to each other?'

'You were all for cooling things between us very recently,' she accused bluntly.

'Yeah—well, I was nuts to think emotions could be put in little boxes and only opened when it seemed the right time. There's no *right time*. Is there?'

Emma's green eyes flew wide with indecision.

'Don't you trust me?' His tone was still patient.

She licked her lips. 'I once trusted a man with my whole life…'

'I know about that.' Declan's gaze didn't waver.

'Dad told you?' Emma fisted a hand against her breast. 'He *told* you?'

'Normally, he wouldn't have broken your confidence. You must know that. But he was worn down, worried about the future—your future. And, whoever he was, the man who let you go was an idiot.'

'So you're implying I fell in love with an idiot?'

'He might have been a charming idiot,' Declan compromised. 'They exist.'

'He was sleeping with my best friend.' With the benefit of time blurring the pain, Emma found she could talk about it objectively. 'It was going on right under my nose and I didn't twig. And when Marcus finally had the decency to tell me he wanted to break our engagement, *she* had the gall to suggest there was no reason why we couldn't still be friends!'

'I hope you got mad.'

'Mad enough.' Emma smiled unwillingly. 'When I finally steeled myself to go round to our apartment to collect the rest of my things, Marcus was there.'

'And?' Declan's mouth twitched.

'He was embarrassed as hell. Said he was just nipping out to the shops. In other words, he hoped I'd be gone by the time he got back.'

'Bad move.' Declan's eyes glinted wickedly. 'And you *were* gone, of course.'

'Of course.' Emma sliced him a grin. 'But not before I'd interrupted the wash cycle he'd left going and chucked in a pair of my red knickers with all his obscenely expensive white business shirts.'

'Wow!' Declan looked impressed. 'I see I'll have to watch my back around you, Dr Armitage.'

She made a face at him and then, 'I was in a well of self-pity for a long time. That's probably why I didn't notice Dad's deteriorating health.'

'But you're over this guy, Marcus, now?'

'The man was indeed an idiot,' she said with asperity.

'So, we agree on something at last. Come on.' Declan reached for her hand across the table. 'Walk me out. It's time I went home.' There was regret in his voice and his eyes had gone dark.

'You could stay here tonight.'

There was a beat of silence.

A thousand questions wanted to leap off Declan's tongue. But he held back. Obviously, she hadn't meant stay as in *stay*. And, even if she had, it was too soon.

For both of them.

'There are a zillion bedrooms in this place,' Emma explained jerkily—just in case he'd imagined…

'There would be. It's a big house.'

'Um—thank you for today and everything. I have a feeling it will all turn out—'

'Stop.' He pressed his finger against her lips. 'This is about us, Emma.'

'Is it?' Her hands went to his waist. 'Shame we don't seem to have come up with any solutions *about us*.'

'On the contrary.' His voice dropped to a husky undertone. 'I think we've lit a bit of a lamp tonight, don't you?'

A lamp to find their way? Could it be as simple as that? Emma closed her eyes, giving herself up to the pure sensation of his hands running over her back, whispering against the soft cotton of her shirt.

'Come on the journey with me…' Declan bent to kiss her, tenderly at first, as if to soothe away her doubts and fears, then with an eagerness and urgency, as if to imprint his faith on what they had together.

Was this the time to let her feelings run free and just *trust* him? Emma agonized as she opened her mouth under his and kissed him back.

CHAPTER SEVEN

IT WAS two days later and Lauren was icing cup cakes with Emma at the kitchen table after school. 'Is Mum ever coming home?'

Oh, please heaven, *yes*, Emma thought, her eyes clouding, but what to tell this sweet child? 'Lauren,' she said carefully, leaning over and gently curving her hand around Lauren's slender little wrist. 'Your Mum's been sick.'

'Like vomiting and stuff?' Lauren asked.

'Well, not quite like that. But a lot of worries have made her sad and just not able to be with you all.'

Lauren set two huge dark eyes on Emma. 'How do you mean?'

Emma's mind scrabbled for a truth that might be acceptable. And then in a flash she remembered the explanation one of her trainers in paeds had given to a child whose circumstances had not been dissimilar to Lauren's.

'You've seen a balloon burst, haven't you, Lauren?'

The little girl's eyes widened and then she nodded.

'Well, your mum's problems just kept piling up and up and each problem was like another puff into the balloon. And then it was just one problem too many and the balloon exploded.'

'And she ran away…'

'Yes.' Emma met the child's gaze steadily.

Lauren looked suddenly lost. 'Was she mad at us?'

'Oh, honey, no...' Emma scooped the little girl close to her. 'Your mum was just mixed up.' Emma smoothed a hand over Lauren's fair hair. 'But she's been staying with some people who are helping her and she's feeling so much better, we think she'll be home with you again before too long.' Emma mentally crossed her fingers about that. But, from what Declan had said only that morning, it seemed Tracey had made a remarkable turn-around and had begun a tentative re-connection with Carolyn. Tomorrow, Declan was taking her to see Adam at the hospital.

'She might be back in time for our sports day,' Lauren said, her little hand still trustingly in Emma's.

'Yes, she just might.' Oh, Tracey, please don't screw up, Emma pleaded silently to the absent mum. Please come home where you belong.

The next morning, Emma welcomed a new patient, Rina Kennedy, into her consulting room. 'You're new to our community?'

'We've just bought the garden centre,' Rina answered in her soft Irish brogue.

'That's interesting,' Emma said. 'It looked like closing there for a while.'

Rina made a face. 'I don't think the former owners had a clue what they were doing. But we aim to fix all that. It'll be grand when we've done a makeover.'

'Very good luck with it, then.' Emma smiled. 'Now, Mrs Kennedy, what can I do for you today?'

'Call me Rina for starters. And I hope you don't think I've gone soft in the head for coming to see you, Doctor, but I wanted to ask you about the best way to avoid getting sun damage to our skin. We've been hearing such terrible things about skin cancer since we've moved to Australia and our two little girls have the fairest complexions.'

'You're right to be concerned,' Emma said. 'Our summers here are hotter and the sun's rays far more intense than you'd be used to in the Northern hemisphere.'

'That's what I thought…'

'But mostly,' Emma went on, 'folk who suffer sun damage to their skin can only blame themselves, because they don't take a blind bit of notice of what health professionals have been telling them for years. And that is to stay out of the sun in the hottest part of the day, to cover up with light protective clothing and, most importantly, to use sunscreen with the highest protection factor. A thirty-plus rating is the best.'

'Could you write all that down for me, please, Doctor?'

Emma smiled. 'I'll give you some fact sheets and you can read up on it. But if you're sensible and keep a healthy respect for what excessive exposure to the sun can do, you shouldn't have any problems.'

Rina jerked a hand at the window. 'It's a lovely garden you have out there,' she said with an impish grin. 'But there's always room for another shrub or two,' she added, unashamedly drumming up business. 'You must come along to our official opening when we've done our revamp. We'll have some grand bargains.'

Emma's head went back as she laughed. 'Let's know the date and I'll make sure all our folk from the practice are there with bells on and nice fat wallets,' she promised. What a nice cheery person, she thought. Spirits lighter, Emma began to make her way through the day's patient list and, at the end of it, she popped in on Declan.

'Hi.' He looked up from his computer, his eyes crinkling into a smile.

'Is our Friday staff meeting still on?"

'Hell, yeah. This is where we function properly as a practice. Thrash out all the hairy bits.'

Watching his strong mouth, so sexy in repose, curve upwards in a smile, Emma felt her heart pick up speed. 'See you shortly, then.'

'I can't believe how the time seems to be flying these days.' Moira looked around the team with a happy smile. 'Mind you, they say it does when you're having fun.'

'It's certainly been interesting,' Declan said. 'OK, folks, any problems?'

'Cedric Dutton,' Libby said with feeling. 'One of our patients on the list for a home visit.'

Declan reclined in his chair and stretched out his legs. 'What's up with Mr Dutton?'

'For starters, he lives alone. He had a stroke some while ago. He was treated in Toowoomba Base. But he's not reclaiming his independence at all.'

'Do we know why not?' Declan cut to the chase.

Libby shook her head. 'The Rotary arranged the necessary safety modifications to his house, and the meals on wheels folk call but he appears to be just sitting in front of the television. It's not like he doesn't know better—he's an educated man. He used to work as a surveyor with the council.'

Declan's eyes lit with sympathy. 'The stroke will have come as a great shock to him.'

'If Mr Dutton's not moving about, we have to be concerned about pressure sores.' Emma looked keenly at Libby.

'We do,' Libby agreed. 'And he's so very thin. But he wouldn't let me touch him, let alone explain anything. There are a dozen things he could be doing to gain a much better quality of life.'

Declan's mouth drew in. 'Possibly there's a residue of post-trauma. Sounds like he's scared to try himself out. Does he have family?'

'He's a bachelor,' Libby said. 'Extended family in Brisbane.'

'Has anyone talked to him about the stroke itself?' Declan queried. 'The repercussions to his body?'

'I imagine the nurses tried but he's such an old chauvinist,' Libby emphasized with a roll of her eyes. 'He called me *girlie*!'

Declan cracked a laugh. 'Want me to have a word, then, Libs?'

'Please, Declan, if you have time. He lives in one of the

cottages along by the old railway line, number fourteen. Seems very much a loner, from what I could gather.'

'Possibly another candidate for our water walking if we can get it up and running,' Declan considered. 'Which reminds me, I've been invited to a meeting of the school's P&C committee on Monday night. It's on the agenda to be discussed.'

'Hey, that's great,' Libby enthused. 'I've a list a mile long of folk who'd benefit. We'd possibly need to arrange transport, though.'

'The council could be pressed into doing that,' Moira contributed.

'Hang on, people.' Declan lifted a staying hand. 'We've only got to first base yet.'

'But it's a positive first step and all down to you,' Emma said, enthusiastic and proud on his behalf.

Declan acknowledged Emma's praise with a twist of his hand. Rocking forward, he doodled something on his pad and thought life played weird tricks sometimes. *Very weird.* A year ago, he'd never in his wildest dreams have imagined he'd be here in rural Queensland practicing family medicine. Rather, he'd expected to be planning a quick rise to the top in his chosen field in one of Australia's big teaching hospitals...

Emma was now so tuned in to his body language she could read Declan like a book. He was doing his best to settle in, even enjoying the challenge to some extent. But was he also acknowledging that community medicine could never match the heart-pumping discipline of being a top-flight surgeon? And, if he was, could he let his dreams go so easily? Suddenly, the six months he'd promised for their trial period seemed so little time to work out whether they had a future together.

Or apart.

'Oh, Emma, while I think of it—' Moira cast a quick enquiring look across the table '—Jodi wondered whether Lauren and Joel would like to spend some time out at the stables tomorrow. Apparently, there are a couple of quiet ponies they could ride and Jodi would be there to supervise them. She thought—well, we both thought—it might be a nice treat for them and, being Saturday, it could help fill in the time a little?'

Emma was touched by Moira and Jodi's kindness. In truth, she'd been wondering how she could keep the kids occupied over a whole weekend. There wasn't a lot to do in Bendemere. She jumped at the offer. 'I'm sure they'd love it, Moira. But is Jodi sure it's OK with the McGintys?'

Moira shrugged. 'My granddaughter could sweet-talk a crow into singing like a canary if she had a mind to. I'll tell her it's all right then, shall I?'

Emma nodded. 'Did she mention a time?'

'Morning's good. And, speaking of the children—' Moira looked at her watch. 'Do you need to see to them?'

'No, they're spending the night back home with their grandfather.' Emma smiled. 'He was picking them up from school. Promised them pizza for tea, I believe.'

'Good old Nev,' Moira nodded in approval. 'How's Tracey doing?' she asked gently. The whole practice in one way or another was now involved in the Jones's ongoing saga and were all rooting for the family to be healed and reunited.

Declan rubbed a hand across his chin. 'I'm visiting Tracey tomorrow. She thinks she's ready to see Adam. I'm picking up Nev and taking him along with me. He, at least, seems very optimistic things will work out.'

'He's the calming influence on Carolyn,' Moira said wisely. 'And he's always had a soft spot for Tracey.'

'There's still a fair bit of sorting out to do yet.' Declan was cautious. 'Now, anything else on the agenda, guys?'

There wasn't a lot, so the meeting wrapped up quickly and Libby and Moira left.

'How optimistic are you, really, about Tracey getting things together?' Emma looked earnestly at Declan, her chin resting in her upturned hand.

'Reasonably.' He flexed a hand. 'I've spoken to her on the phone each night and she's surprised me with her turnaround. But then, the folk at the shelter have been working with her and her self-esteem has received a huge boost. Apparently, she's been absorbing the counselling sessions like a sponge.'

'Lauren has been quietly eating her little heart out about things, worrying whether her mum left because she was mad at them. I tried to reassure her and I hope I haven't jumped the gun but I indicated Tracey might be back home soon.'

'It's best to keep positive around the kids,' Declan said slowly. 'I mean, what's the alternative?'

Emma bit her lip. 'Awful,' she agreed.

'Hey, don't let's drop the ball.' In an abrupt gesture of reassurance, Declan pressed her hand and then got to his feet. 'Are you busy tonight?'

'Er...no.'

'Like to go out somewhere to eat later?'

'Um...' Emma flannelled. He'd taken her by surprise. 'Where would we go?'

'You choose. Better phone and book, though. It's Friday night.'

'OK… Are you heading home now?' she asked as they walked slowly along the hallway and through to the main part of the house and eventually to the kitchen.

'I thought I'd call in on Libby's old chap first. See what I can sort out for him. I'll pick you up about seven?'

'Or we could meet at the restaurant.'

'Let's be old-fashioned.' His mouth tipped at the corner. 'I'll call for you.'

Emma pulled back, her nerve ends pinching alarmingly. So, were they going on a date? The thought thrilled her and panicked her in equal measure. 'Fine. Seven's good.'

As Declan opened the back door, a gale-force wind nearly knocked him back inside. 'Hell's bells, when did the weather turn foul like this?'

'Ages ago, probably without our knowing. We've been cloistered indoors. And it's freezing, Declan.'

'Rats!' Declan turned up the collar on his windcheater. 'After Scotland, this is nothing.'

Emma began to rub her upper arms vigorously. 'You won't say that when the power lines come down.'

'Is that likely?'

'It's happened a few times since I've been here.'

'Snap decision then.' His eyes narrowed on her face and suddenly the intensity of his regard hardened, as though he'd made up his mind about something. 'Change of plan. I'll drop by Cedric's, then head home for a shower and, on my way back to you, I'll grab some stuff for dinner. Not a takeaway,' he promised. 'I'll cook.'

How could she refuse? It would be such a relief not to have to venture out on such a wild night. 'If you're sure? But I've stuff in the freezer—'

'Please. Let it be my treat, Emma.'

Emma gave an uneasy huff of laughter. 'And you *can* cook?'

'I promise it'll be edible. Just trust me on this, all right?'

Well, she had to, didn't she? Emma thought as she closed the door after him and turned back inside. About dinner and about a lot of other things too.

Declan felt the wind tear at his clothes as he made a dash to his car. But, far from being intimidated by its force, he felt exhilarated, wild, powerful. As if he could do anything he really set his mind to.

If only that were an option.

Following Emma's directions, he soon found his way to the row of neatly kept cottages and drove slowly along until he found Cedric Dutton's. Hefting his case off the passenger seat, he swung out of his car. Making his way to the front door, Declan lifted his hand and banged loudly. When there was no response, he called, 'Mr Dutton? I'm a doctor from the Kingsholme surgery. I'd like a word. Could you let me in, please?'

Declan waited and listened and, finally, there was a shuffling inside and the door was opened just a crack. Two faded blue eyes under bushy brows looked suspiciously out. 'Who're you?'

'I'm a doctor from the Kingsholme surgery,' Declan repeated. 'May I come in?'

A beat of silence while the elderly man digested the information. 'No law against it, I suppose,' he said, unlocking the chain and holding the door open.

Once inside, Declan extended his hand. 'Declan O'Malley, Mr Dutton.'

'New around here, are you?' Cedric looked over the imposing male figure while he held Declan's hand in a fragile grip.

'Yes. I'm in partnership with Dr Armitage.' Unobtrusively, Declan watched his patient's general mobility as Cedric led the way back inside to the lounge room.

It took a little time for the elderly man to settle himself into his armchair. 'So—why did you want to see me?' he asked, seeming to sense the importance of Declan's visit. 'That girl's being talking to you, I'll bet?'

'Libby Macklin is a Registered Nurse, Mr Dutton. It's part of her job to check on our senior patients. We depend on her to tell us how your health is. She was concerned for you and she's a skilled professional, otherwise, she wouldn't be employed at our practice. You should have let her check you over.'

'Maybe.' Cedric shrugged a skinny shoulder.

'How's your general health, Cedric?' Declan's voice was gentle. He didn't want to antagonize his new patient from the outset.

'Days get a bit long. I'm not as fit as I used to be.'

'I understand that. What about your exercises?' Declan asked. 'Are you doing them? You know they're essential to help your muscles recover from the stroke.'

The elderly man hesitated. 'Sometimes I do them. But it's hard when everything's crook…'

'I know.'

Cedric looked sceptical. 'What would you know about it—young fella like you?'

Declan snorted a hard laugh. 'Oh, believe me, Cedric, I know.' Briefly, Declan explained something of his own circumstances.

'I get a bit *down*,' Cedric admitted. 'Like you said—'

'Depression is all part of the syndrome.' Declan leaned forward, his hands linked between his knees. 'When your body won't do what you want it to, you feel robbed of self-respect. And it's hard when you lose everything you could once be sure of.'

'My word, that's it!' Cedric looked impressed. 'For a while there I couldn't even get my pants on.' His mouth compressed in a reluctant grin. 'Or do up any buttons. And shoelaces were a lost cause.'

Declan nodded sympathetically. 'Was it explained to you just what a stroke is?'

'Something about a blood clot, isn't it?'

'Exactly. A stroke happens when a clot blocks a blood vessel or artery in the brain. It interrupts the blood flow and suddenly the body is out of whack.'

'Like damming a river,' Cedric acknowledged thoughtfully. 'I never cottoned on. But I do now you've explained it.'

'So you can see why those exercises are so important, can't you?'

'Reckon I can.' Cedric thought long and hard. 'So, this Libby, the nurse, she could help me with that, could she?'

'Yes.' Declan nodded. 'But I want you to come into the hospital one day a week for the next while and see our regular physiotherapist, Michelle Crother. I'll arrange transport for you.'

Cedric sighed resignedly. 'I suppose that'd be the thing to do.'

While he had Cedric's tacit acceptance of the changes he wanted to implement, Declan thought he'd push gently ahead with another suggestion. 'What about getting back into a bit of social life? Do you play cards?'

'I don't mind a game or two.'

'Then you might enjoy coming along to the seniors' club.' Since his involvement with Carolyn Jones, Declan had done his homework and clued himself in on what was available to the older residents of the town. 'They meet regularly on a

Wednesday at the farmers' hall and the CWA provide lunch. From what I hear, it's a friendly group. They'd make you welcome.' Declan grinned disarmingly. 'You'd possibly know most of them anyway, an old-timer like you.'

'Probably would.' Cedric looked down at his hands. 'I lost touch a bit when I had the stroke…'

'So, how's your appetite?' Declan infused enthusiasm into his voice, sensing Cedric was apt to drift off into introspection. 'Are you managing with the meals on wheels?'

'Food's OK.' Cedric shrugged. 'Sometimes I don't feel like eating much.'

'Once we can get you out and about a bit more, all that will improve. Get yourself out into the sun as well. That will keep up your vitamin D requirement. Very important, whatever our age.'

Cedric nodded, taking it all on board. Then he lifted his eyebrows in a query. 'What did you say your name was, Doctor?'

'O'Malley. Call me Declan. I'll be your medical officer from now on, if you're agreeable?'

'You seem all right,' Cedric said grudgingly. 'Not bossy like some.'

Like the women, Declan interpreted wryly. But at least he'd made headway with this old man. Stirred him up enough to take an interest in his own welfare. And that felt surprisingly good. 'Now—' Declan flipped open his medical case '—how would you feel about me checking you over while I'm here?'

'Fair enough, I suppose.' Cedric looked around him with agitation. 'Where do you want me?'

'Just there's fine.' Declan slung his stethoscope around his neck and grinned. 'And I promise I'll keep the prodding to a minimum.'

Emma's heartbeat was thrumming. Surely he'd be here soon. It seemed ages since he'd left to visit his patient. An age in which she'd had a leisurely bath and dressed in comfortable trousers and a fine woollen black top. She'd brushed her hair and left it loose and kept her make-up to a minimum.

Why was she fussing so? They were simply sharing a meal. He'd probably prefer to eat in the kitchen. But then, perhaps she should make the evening special and set the small table in the dining room. Would that look a bit contrived? He'd hate that. Although, just in case, she'd go ahead and light the fire in the dining room…

Finally, a knock sounded at her front door.

'Hi.' Hands occupied with his shopping bags, Declan leaned forward and planted a lingering kiss on her mouth when Emma opened the door. 'Sorry, I'm a bit late. It's a wild night out there. I nearly got blown to bits.'

'Hello…' Emma said when she could breathe again. The touch of his mouth had sent up sparks. She wanted to stop him right there, wrap her arms around his body and just *hold* him. She wanted him. So much. But he was already at the worktop unloading his shopping. 'What are we having?' she asked, peering over his shoulder.

He tipped his head on one side and grinned down at her. 'Char-grilled spiced lamb cutlets with ratatouille.'

Emma gurgled a soft laugh. In other words, grilled chops and vegetables. 'I'm impressed.'

'You're not.' He sent her an indulgent half-amused look. 'But give me my moment of fame here.'

'What can I do to help?'

'Ah—' he indicated the array of vegetables he'd bought—red and yellow peppers, zucchini and vine tomatoes. 'These have to be cut into bite-sized pieces.'

'Even though we're starving hungry?'

'Even though.' Declan gently elbowed her out of the way to select a knife from the kitchen block. 'Just do what the main man tells you, please? It'll be worth the wait.'

Emma was still chuckling to herself as she set about her task. Since he was going to so much trouble to feed her, she definitely *would* set the table in the dining room.

* * *

They took a long time over dinner, as though neither of them wanted it to end. 'How did I do, then?' Declan asked finally.

Emma smiled. He'd given her a look so warm, she'd felt its impact skidding and sliding across her nerves and along her backbone before settling in a swirling mass in her belly. 'You did so well, I just might have to keep you. This was such a good idea,' she rushed on. 'To have dinner at home.'

'Yes, it was.' Declan's gaze shimmered over her face and then roamed to register the gleam of lamplight that threw her tawny lashes into sharp relief against her flushed cheeks. He moved a bit uncomfortably as his body zinged to a new awareness. He took a careful mouthful of his wine, his eyes caressing her over the rim of his glass. He ached to touch her intimately, to breathe in the sweet scent of her silky hair, stroke the softness of her naked body as she lay next to him…

'Coffee?' Emma felt a quicksilver flip in her stomach. She'd been aware of his overt scrutiny.

'Not for me, thanks.'

She swung to her feet. 'I'll clear the table and stack the dishwasher, then.' She sent him a quick smile. 'Go through to the lounge. We'll be more comfortable in there.'

Declan extinguished the candles they'd used on the dinner table and then crossed the hallway to the lounge room. He went to stand at the window, drawing back the curtains slightly in order to check the state of the weather himself. In the glow from the street lights he could see the trees bending, their foliage swirling into a mad dance in the wake of the wind's rushing passage.

He turned when Emma came in. 'How long do you think the storm will take to get here?' He opened his arms in invitation and she slid into his embrace.

'I'm no expert.' Emma rested her head against his shoulder. 'But I'd rather be here than out driving somewhere—wouldn't you?'

'That's a no-brainer,' he said. 'Of course I'd rather be here.' He looked down at her. 'That's if it's all right if I hang about?'

'I'd have turfed you out ages ago if it wasn't.'

Declan gave one of his lazy smiles. 'Would I have gone, though?'

'Of course you would.' Emma stroked the tips of her fingers across the small of his back, her hands already addicted to the sensation. 'You're an old-fashioned kind of guy.'

Declan looked pained. 'Are you saying my clothes need an update?'

Emma's mouth widened in a grin. They were shadow dancing again—fooling around, as if it was obvious to both of them that if their conversation became too serious, too personal, then anything could happen…'Stop fishing for compliments,' she said. 'You know you dress very well.'

'I undress very well, too,' he rejoined daringly.

Emma's heart twanged out of rhythm. 'Do you?'

'Mmm.' Declan registered the tiny swallow in her throat. 'So,' he said softly, moving so that his hands rested on the tops of her arms and feeling the tremble that went through her, 'what do you want to do with the rest of the evening?'

Emma opened her mouth and closed it again, knowing deep in her heart that this was a moment of no return. Was she ready? Were *they* ready? They'd never know unless they put their trust in one another, reached out and gathered life in. 'You could stay—if you like…?'

His eyes locked with hers, dark in shadow, tender in their caress. 'My whole body aches with wanting you, Emma. As long as you're sure?'

'Yes.' He should have come into her life sooner, but he was here now. And that was all that mattered. 'Yes.' She looked at him and smiled, feeling the weight of indecision drop from her like an unwanted heavy garment. 'I've never been more sure of anything.'

Declan made a deep sound in his throat that could have been a sigh. Then he drew her close, lowering his mouth to claim her lips.

That was all it took. Like a spark on straw, the fire of their passion took hold and in a breath it was raging.

Declan whispered harshly against her mouth. 'I meant to take it slow…'

She arched back with a little cry. 'No—not slow.' Her hands threaded through his hair and she trapped his face, holding him. 'I need you, Declan—'

He turned his head and gently nipped the soft flesh below her thumb, his eyes pinpoints of desire when she gasped an indrawn breath. 'Which bedroom?'

'Mine.'

Clothes flew off in a flurry, Declan swearing over a leg of his jeans that refused to leave his foot. Finally, he stepped back and stared at her. At the tendrils of corn-silk hair draping gently on to her creamy naked shoulders. At the swanlike gracefulness of her neck. At the small line of muscle delineating the length of her upper arm. The sweet roundness of her breasts. The shallow dip of her tummy…'Emma—' He felt his voice catch on a painful swallow. 'You're—' He shook his head. 'You're beautiful.'

'And you…' She hardly realized what she was doing, reaching out to slide her fingers down over his diaphragm, over his belly and dip into the shallow nook of his navel.

Suddenly, Declan made a gravelly sound of protest, jamming his hand over hers to stop its movement. 'Wait…' He looked around blankly and then hooked up his jeans, slipping a tiny packet from the back pocket. 'I never know whether there's a right time to do this,' he growled.

Emma felt herself blushing, crossing her arms tightly across her ribcage. He'd turned his back and she could see the shallow hollow just above the base of his spine. A tiny jagged laugh left her mouth. 'No need for diagrams, Declan—just do it…'

Oh, God…it was like stumbling into paradise. He touched her teasingly, his hands light and seductive in their rhythm. Instinctively, he knew what would please her, excite her, bring her to the brink but not quite tip over.

Emma was wild for him, a wildness she'd never known,

drawing him closer, feeling him hover at the core of her femininity before plunging in. She gasped, dragging him in more deeply, her head arching back as she called his name, feeling the sweet ripeness of her release gathering and then splintering her into a thousand pieces. Her name exploded on Declan's tongue as his climax followed hers a millisecond later, their hearts thumping a wild tattoo as they fell back to earth.

After a long time, they pulled back from each other, two sets of bruised lips, two pairs of eyes hazed with a new kind of wonderment.

'So…' he said.

'So,' she echoed huskily.

Lifting a hand, he knuckled her cheek gently. 'Why did we wait so long?'

CHAPTER EIGHT

EMMA had no time to answer.

'I don't believe this!' Declan's expletive hit the air as his mobile rang. 'Can't we get two minutes to call our own?'

'Where's your phone?' Emma was out of bed and reaching for her gown.

'Pocket of my jeans.'

'Here.' She hooked them off the floor and tossed them to him. It had to be an emergency somewhere. She knew that instinctively.

They had trouble, the police sergeant, Gary Bryson, informed Declan. Part of the roof at the farmers' hall had blown off. The hall had been packed with the usual Friday bingo players. There was confusion, to say the least. No one was sure about injuries but could the doctors come? Declan closed off his phone and in clipped terms relayed the message to Emma.

'Right.' She snatched up her own mobile off the bedside table. 'I'll get on to the hospital and alert them we might be sending patients in. They'll automatically recall any staff who are available.'

'Let's just be grateful the power lines haven't gone down,' Declan said as they dressed hurriedly.

'Don't count your chickens quite yet,' Emma warned. 'But at least the hospital has a backup power supply. It'll kick in if the worst happens.'

Declan grunted a non-reply, looking broodingly at Emma as she twisted her hair quickly into a ponytail. A frown touched his eyes. He felt as though he'd been catapulted from a delicious dream with no time to wallow in its aftermath. But he could still smell Emma's perfume, still feel the softness of her skin beneath his hands.

His mouth tightened. He wanted more and he couldn't have it. They'd taken a huge step into the unknown tonight. They'd needed time and closeness to talk about it, wind down, make love again, this time slowly, softly, sexily—

'Your top's inside out,' Emma said, breaking his thought pattern.

Impatiently, Declan dragged the T-shirt over his head and rectified it. 'The timing's all wrong for this, Emma.'

Well, she knew that. Emma's head was bent as she pulled on a pair of sturdy boots. But they were rural doctors. They had to attend. Emergencies didn't choose their time to happen. Heaven knew what they'd find when they got to the hall. And she didn't want to be doing this any more than Declan. The timing *was* all wrong. She'd wanted a blissful few hours with him. Their newness as lovers surely demanded that. She'd wanted to hold him and have him hold her and just *talk*. About nothing. About everything. But it seemed as though an unkind fate had stepped in and now her emotions were all over the place. Declan's too, if she was a betting woman. She popped upright from the edge of the bed. 'Ready?'

They went in Declan's car. Halfway to the hall the street lights flickered and faded and the night around them was plunged into darkness.

'I've a couple of lantern torches in the boot' was Declan's only comment.

The rain had started in earnest by the time they got to the hall. 'Let's proceed with caution,' Declan warned, handing Emma one of the torches and taking the other himself.

'We should go through the front entrance,' she said. 'It seems the least affected.' To her relief, the State Emergency Services people were already on the scene, their bright orange overalls lending a sense of security. Emergency lighting was rapidly being put in place. 'That's John Cabot, the team leader for the SES,' she told Declan. 'We'll speak to him first.'

Introductions were made swiftly and Declan asked the question on both their minds, 'What's the damage, John? Do we know yet?'

'Less than we feared, Doc. Most of the folk had already left. Just a few stragglers having a last cuppa, from what we know. The roof over the rear of the hall has pretty much gone but the rest seems intact. I've a couple of guys up there presently checking and getting tarpaulins into place to keep out the rain. Let us know if you need more lighting.'

'Thanks, John.' Declan nodded, taking it all in. 'We'll let you get on with it, then.'

'Oh, look—' Emma made a dash forward. 'There's Moira! What on earth is she doing here?'

'I'm on the driving roster for our seniors' group at the church,' Moira explained agitatedly. 'And I'd just come to collect them when the roof went. This is Agnes—' She indicated the elderly lady slumped in a chair beside them. 'I think she's hurt quite badly,' Moira added in a frightened whisper.

Declan had already sized up the situation. His seeking gaze went quickly around the hall. 'Moira, is there a first aid room or somewhere we could make Agnes more comfortable?'

'Er—yes—yes…' Moira visibly pulled herself together, pointing to a room at the side of the hall. 'And, mercifully, it's still intact.'

'Over here!' Declan hailed the two ambulances officers who had just arrived and explained what he needed.

'Take it easy,' he instructed as they settled the elderly woman on the narrow bunk bed. Agnes looked glassily pale against the deep purple of her cardigan. 'Can you tell us what happened, Agnes?' he asked gently as he began his examination.

'Sitting at the table…' Agnes moistened her lips slowly. 'Something hit me—fell forward—hard, terrible hard…'

'That must have hurt, Agnes.' Emma held her hand to the injured woman's wrist. 'Thready,' she reported softly.

Declan replaced his stethoscope. 'Let's step outside for a minute.'

'What's the matter with me?' Agnes asked fretfully.

'It'll be all right, dear.' Moira took the older woman's hand and held it. 'The doctors will look after you.'

Emma followed Declan out of the room. 'What do you think?' she asked quietly.

'Hard to tell, but she could have a splenic haematoma. She'll need a CT scan asap.'

'We'll send her on, then?'

'Obviously.' Declan gave a dismissive grunt. 'We don't have the equipment to do it here, Emma.'

It was hardly her fault if their little hospital didn't have the advanced facilities of a city radiology department! 'I'll escort Agnes across to the hospital, then,' she said shortly. 'Stabilize her before the road trip to Toowoomba.'

'Do that.' Declan's voice was clipped. 'And call through to Toowoomba, please. Tell them we want a CT scan immediately on arrival. And to make sure they have a supply of O-neg blood ready in case she needs to go to surgery.'

For heaven's sake! Emma's fine chin darted a centimetre upwards. She knew what protocol to follow. Did he ever stop to consider how they'd managed before he'd come? Well, amazingly enough, they had! Then she softened. Giving orders came as naturally to him as breathing. 'Are you worried about a bleed?'

'Without a scanner we can only second-guess.' And it was frustrating him like hell. 'If you'll do the necessary for Agnes, I'll see if there are any more casualties here. So far it looks pretty quiet.'

They went back to the first aid room and Emma explained what they needed to do.

'I'll follow across to the hospital directly, Agnes.' Moira squeezed the older woman's hand. 'Don't worry about a thing.'

'Right, let's get you on board, sweetheart.' The paramedics moved in to make the transfer.

With Moira disappearing out into the night, Declan took a quick look around. Thankfully, the damage was only in one part of the hall. He was still considering the injury to Agnes when he heard his name called. He turned sharply. John Cabot was heading towards him.

'One of my lads has hurt himself, Doc. Breaking all the rules and trying to lift debris on his own.'

'I'll take a look at him.' Declan hitched up his bag and followed the SES leader. 'Who do we have, John?'

'Jason Toohey. One of our local football stars.'

Declan found the young man sitting hunched over, hands crossed, supporting his elbows. 'Where are you hurt, Jason?' Declan hunkered down beside his patient.

'Shoulder.' Jason pulled in a harsh breath. 'Put it out again, I reckon.'

'What do you mean *again*? Does this happen often?'

'I play league, Doc. It's contact sport.'

'I'm well aware of what rugby league is,' Declan muttered. 'I want you over at the hospital so I can look at you properly.'

John Cabot looked on worriedly. 'What do you think, Doc?'

'Shoulder dislocation,' Declan said briefly. He looked about him. 'Is the other ambulance here?'

Gary Bryson joined in the conversation. 'Just heard they've gone to collect a pregnant woman. Roads to Toowoomba are flooded. Looks like she'll have to have the baby here.'

Bendemere didn't take midwifery patients. At least not on a regular basis. But Declan guessed there would be protocol in place for just such an eventuality. And he guessed too that Emma, as usual, would have things well in hand. 'We need to get Jason over to the hospital.'

Rachel Wallace arrived just as Jason was being settled into the treatment room. 'Sorry, guys.' She looked from Declan to the young nursing assistant, Talitha, and made a grimace. 'I'd have been here earlier but when I went to reverse out of the garage, I found a damn great tree had fallen across the driveway. Took me a while to move it.'

Declan's eyes widened ever so slightly. 'You moved a fallen tree on your own?'

'With the help of a chainsaw.' Rachel coughed out a self-deprecating laugh. 'And it was more of a sapling really. But there was no way I could have reversed the car over it. Hi, JT.' She made a sympathetic face at the young man on the treatment couch. 'Is it the shoulder again?'

'Yep.' Jason managed a weak smile, raising his hand in acknowledgment, then wincing as he lowered it quickly.

'Let's get Jason on some oxygen, please,' Declan directed.

'We've all become accustomed to popping Jason's shoulder back in,' Rachel said, adjusting the oxygen. 'Relax now and breathe away, JT. Big tug coming up.'

Not if he could help it, Declan thought. 'I'll just try a manoeuvre here, Rachel,' he informed the nurse manager quietly.

She went to the head of the bed and waited. She watched intently as Declan gently and smoothly reduced Jason's dislocation until his shoulder was safely back in its socket. 'Wow…' Rachel puffed a little breath of admiration. 'You're good.'

Declan's mouth compressed for moment. It was what he'd trained for, for heaven's sake. But nevertheless Rachel's compliment had warmed him like a favourite woolly jumper on a winter's morning. 'Let's get a sling on that arm now, please.'

'Thanks, Doc,' Jason said, perking up. 'Looks like I'll be back in time for the semi-finals weekend after next.'

'No, you won't, old son.' Declan flipped out the patient chart from its rack and took the pen Rachel handed to him. 'You're out for the rest of the season. That shoulder needs resting.'

'Stuff that!' Jason struggled upright, dangling his legs over the side of the treatment couch. 'The team needs me. I play second-row forward.'

'And correct me if I'm wrong.' Declan's tone was professionally detached and even. 'But isn't that the position where you regularly shoulder-charge your opposite number?'

'So?' Jason looked sulky.

'So,' Declan elaborated, 'if you continue playing, you'll be lucky if your shoulder's not hanging by a thread by the end of the season. And you'll be very unlikely to have a future in league at all. How old are you, Jason?'

'Nineteen.'

'So, you've plenty of time to get your footy career up and running again.'

Jason gave a howl of dissention.

'Hey, JT, listen to Dr O'Malley, hmm?' Rachel came in with an overbright smile. 'This is his special field of medicine. He knows what he's talking about.'

Jason's lip curled briefly. 'So—what do I have to do, then?' he asked ungraciously.

'I'd like you to have a CAT scan on that shoulder,' Declan said. 'We need to know why it keeps dislocating. In the meantime, chum, it's rest. Want me to have a word with your coach?'

Jason shook his head. 'I'll tell him at training.'

Declan replaced the chart, backing against the treatment couch and folding his arms. 'It won't be the end of the world, Jason.' His tone was gentle. 'We'll make a plan of action when we see the results of your scan. Maybe the problem can be resolved with some appropriate physio. In all probability, you'll be back on the field next season. Call the imaging centre first thing on Monday. They'll give you an appointment. And I'd rather you didn't try to drive, so can you get a lift across to Toowoomba?'

Jason nodded and stood gingerly to his feet. 'Uh—thanks,' he added grudgingly.

'You're welcome, Jason.' Declan's mouth tightened fractionally. 'If you could hang around for a bit, I'll organise a request form for your X-ray.'

'We can fix you up at the nurses' station for that,' Rachel said helpfully. 'And JT, I'm sure you could do with a cup of tea. Or an energy drink, if you'd prefer. Talitha will show you where to go.'

'Follow me.' The young nursing assistant grinned impishly. 'Unless you'd like a wheelchair?'

'No way!' Jason looked horrified. He paused for a second and then, as if he could see he had no other choice, shuffled out after Talitha.

Declan worked his shoulder muscles and lifted his arms in a half-mast stretch.

'Long day?' Rachel commiserated. 'Got time for a hot drink?'

'Perhaps later.' Declan smiled. 'I'll look in on Emma first. See if she needs any backup.'

'Oh—OK, then. I'll be around for a while, if you change your mind.' She sent him a quick grin. 'We'll raid the kitchen.'

'Oh— Hi.' Emma had stepped out of the room that had been quickly rearranged as a delivery suite, to find Declan hovering. She blinked a bit. 'Is something wrong?'

'I came to see if you needed any backup.'

She shook her head. 'We're fine. Dot's a midwife and the baby's well on its way. Shouldn't be any problems.' She looked closely at him and put her hand on his arm. 'You look tired. Why don't you take off? You've a big day tomorrow with Tracey.'

Declan's gaze narrowed. Was she patronizing him? It sure felt like it. His eyes swept over her pale blue hospital gown. 'I'll wait.'

'You don't have to, Declan. I can get a lift home with someone.'

By the time Declan had formulated a reply, she'd turned away and re-entered the delivery room. He had a frown in his eyes as he made his way back to the nurses' station. Damn it! he raged silently. What an awful way for their evening to have turned out.

With the baby boy safely delivered and his mum tidied up, Emma felt a surge of relief. In the little annexe, she stripped off her gown and tossed it into the linen tidy. It had been a very long day. Day and a bit, she realized after a glance at the wall clock. Oh, Lord, she needed her bed. She stretched, feeling the protest of internal muscles, and felt heat rising from her toes upwards until she flushed almost guiltily. She couldn't believe she'd been so wild with Declan, almost frenzied. She stifled a groan. She hoped he'd gone home. She needed time to gather herself. They'd taken a giant step into the unknown. It had seemed the right one at the time but now, in the fuzzy light of the early hours… The smell of coffee, fragrant and rich, drew her towards the hospital kitchen.

And that was where she found her new lover and the nurse manager. All her insecurities from her past relationship, coupled with the most awful kind of disappointment, washed through her like a power-shower of pain. She pulled back, freezing at what she saw—Declan and Rachel were sitting very closely together, their foreheads almost touching, utterly engrossed in quiet conversation. At least Rachel was the one doing the talking, while Declan seemed enthralled, drawn towards her, listening. Emma felt the drum-heavy beat in her chest, the sudden recoil in her stomach. Surely she hadn't misplaced her trust again? Surely…

It was the longest minute of Emma's life. She stood undecided, wanting to run, yet with all her heart wanting to stay. The decision was taken out of her hands when Rachel looked up. 'Emma…hey… Everything OK?'

'Fine.' Emma took a deep breath. 'I smelled coffee.'

'Help yourself.' The nurse manager pressed a strand of auburn hair behind her ear and got to her feet. 'I'm off to crash for a while. I'm on an early.'

Two sets of eyes followed Rachel as she left and then Declan pushed up out of his chair. 'I'll get you a coffee.'

'Don't bother. I've changed my mind.' The words were said tonelessly, like a recorded message.

'Let's get you home, then.' Declan moving with speed, was already ushering her out of the door.

* * *

'You seemed very cosy with Rachel back there,' Emma said as they drove. Suddenly she felt she was fighting for her very existence, her emotions unravelling like a ball of string.

'Just killing time,' Declan answered evenly. 'Waiting for you.'

A beat of silence and then, 'I—guess you'd have a lot in common with Rachel. She's worked all over the world in the OR. She's smart and savvy. *And available*.'

'Don't do this, Emma.'

Emma felt her throat thicken. 'She was practically in your lap.'

Declan pulled air into his lungs and let it go. 'Emma, if you're waiting for a reaction, I'm not biting. We just have to accept the evening turned out light years from what we'd hoped for.' He paused. 'What about coming home with me?'

'To the cabin?' He must be out of his mind.

'That's where I call home at the moment.'

'Declan—' Emma made a weary little gesture with her hand '—I'd rather be on my own, if you don't mind.'

'So you can do what?' Declan felt nettled. 'Talk yourself into believing that making love with me was a huge mistake? Or, better still,' he revised with heavy sarcasm, 'that you can't trust me now?'

Emma felt her stomach churn. He was too near the truth for comfort.

Declan gave a fractured sigh and then he spoke quietly. 'I realize you feel vulnerable—hell, don't you think I do as well? But don't blow this up into something it's not, Emma. Come home with me. I'll sleep on the couch. There's hardly anything left of the night, anyway. But at least we'll be together. I hate the thought of you rattling around in that great house on your own.'

'I was doing it long before you came on the scene, Declan. I'm used to it,' she dismissed. 'Besides, the power's back on. I'll be fine.'

With a weary shake of his head, Declan aimed the car towards Kingsholme.

When they turned into the driveway at the surgery, he cut the engine.

Emma's head spun round in query.

'I'll come in with you,' he said. 'Make sure it's all safe—that no water's come in, or worse.'

'Thanks—but there's never been any problem before.'

In other words, I can get along without you very well; you don't need to come in at all. Declan's hands tightened on the steering wheel. 'It won't take a minute.'

Once inside, Emma stood stiffly in the kitchen, listening as Declan went from room to room, checking things were in order. It seemed only seconds until he was back and poking his head in the door.

'Seems fine, very snug. I'll say goodnight, then.'

'Yes— OK—thanks.' Emma voice sounded thick and vaguely husky.

'I'll be here about eight in the morning,' Declan said. 'To drop the kids off as arranged.'

She nodded. Words, all of them mixed up, tried to force their way from her lips. Words like, *Perhaps I was wrong. Perhaps we need to talk. Can things ever be right between us again?* Instead, she stood there awkwardly. 'Take care on the road back to the cabin.'

Declan's lips twisted in self-mockery. Obviously, she couldn't wait to be shot of his company. He lifted a hand in a stiff kind of farewell but no words came readily to mind. He turned and left quietly.

The next morning, Emma made a concerted effort to corral her private thoughts and concentrate on the children's chatter as they drove to the stables. But it was difficult. Declan had had very little to say when he'd dropped them off—well, nothing personal anyway. But she'd hoped, unrealistically perhaps—? 'There's Jodi waiting for us!' Lauren was beside herself with excitement.

'Now, I want both of you to do exactly what Jodi tells you,' Emma instructed. 'Horses can be a bit tricky.'

Jodi spent some time showing them the basic skills in looking after the horses. 'Now, I'll have to take each of you separately for a ride,' Jodi explained to the children. 'Lauren, you can go first. Joel, you'll have to wait a bit, OK?'

'I don't wanna ride.' Joel tugged his cap further down on his forehead. 'I'd rather help feed the horses.'

'Right, you're easily pleased.' Jodi grinned. 'Come with me, then, dude.'

Jodi was back in a few minutes and began saddling a chestnut pony. 'This is Lady Marmalade,' she told an entranced Lauren. She showed the little girl how to mount and then positioned her feet in the stirrups. 'Lady has a soft mouth,' Jodi explained as Lauren took up the reins. 'That means she'll go exactly where you want her to with just a touch on the bridle.'

Watching on, Emma said, 'Thanks for doing all this, Jodi.'

'No worries.' Jodi gave a dimple-bright grin. 'It's good for kids to learn to be safe around animals and have fun while they're doing it. All set?' She looked up at her young charge. 'I'll lead Lady for a while until you get used to sitting on her back and then I might let you have a ride by yourself.'

Lauren's little face was alight with happiness.

Jodi pointed to the paddock adjoining the track. 'Now, for starters, we'll be taking Lady over there.'

Lauren small hands clutched the reins, her thin little shoulders almost stiff with anticipation of her first riding lesson.

Jodi looked a question at Emma. 'Coming along?'

'I thought perhaps I should keep an eye on Joel.'

'He'll be fine.' Jodi flapped a hand. 'He's with the guys. And there's a new puppy over at the barn. He'll have fun with him. Isn't it a gorgeous morning after the storm?' Jodi chatted light-heartedly as they made their way towards the big paddock.

Emma began to feel her spirits lighten. It was indeed a lovely morning. The sun had risen, dispersing the mist, and a brilliant burst of gold-tipped fingers spanned the horizon.

* * *

Lauren was going beautifully, Emma decided and, even though she didn't know terribly much about riding in general, she could see the little girl was a natural. Already her seat was easy, her little back straight, her body moving in tune with the pony's rhythmic gait. She watched as Jodi gave a thumbs-up sign and then stepped away, leaving Lauren in charge of her mount. With a tap of her heels, Lauren urged Lady forward and the pony responded, picking up her pace into a bouncy brisk walk.

Emma thought the smile on the child's face would have dimmed even the Christmas lights. Oh, sweetheart, Emma's heart swelled. I wish your mum could see you now. She'd be back home in a flash.

And then it happened.

A black streak in the form of a wilful, naughty puppy tore across the paddock in front of Lady. Without warning, the pony took fright, breaking into a jerky canter and racing through the grass. Lauren cried out…and so did Emma.

Jodi began sprinting to try to contain the pony but Lady was having none of it.

'Oh, no!' Emma's hand went to her heart as Lauren lost her seat and tumbled to the ground. Emma ran as if she was possessed. Lauren was in a little heap on the ground, hunched over and looking into the distance at the pony that had careened away to the far side of the paddock. 'Is she hurt?' Emma skidded to a stop and dropped to the ground beside the child.

'She landed like a pro.' Jodi had her arm around Lauren. 'She's one smart little girl.'

'Ooh…' Emma felt a sob of relief in her chest.

'I fell off,' Lauren said as though the fact amazed her.

'Yes, you did.' Jodi squeezed her shoulders. 'I did too when I first began to ride.'

'Did you?' Lauren looked a wide-eyed question at her mentor.

'Broke my wrist.' Jodi held up a strong, straight arm. 'But you'd never know now, would you?'

Lauren shook her head. 'I don't think I broke anything.'

'Just let me take a little look at you, Lauren.' Emma bent to the child. She did a quick neuro check and asked Lauren to turn her head and lift her arms. 'Now, can you squeeze my fingers really hard? Good girl. Now, stand up for me, Lauren. And walk a straight line, please, sweetheart. Good. That's lovely.' Emma's heart fell back into its rightful place.

'I'll go and catch Lady.' Jodi scrambled upright. 'And we'll get her back to the stables.'

'Can I ride her back?' a now recovered Lauren asked eagerly.

Emma looked doubtful but Jodi said, 'If you feel up to it, Lauren—of course you can. But I'll lead her, just to make sure she doesn't get up to any more tricks.'

The ride ended with no more mishaps. 'I'll collect Joel now,' Emma said. 'And we'll get out of your hair.'

'Don't be silly,' Jodi dismissed. 'Mrs McGinty's invited us up to the house for morning tea. She loves kids—and company.'

'We can stay, can't we, Emma?' Lauren pleaded.

How could she refuse the child? 'Well, I guess it would be rather rude if we didn't,' Emma gave in gracefully.

'Good.' Jodi looked well pleased. 'Let's round up young Joel.'

Lauren skipped ahead.

'You will let them come again, won't you, Emma?' Jodi asked as the two young women made their way slowly across to the barn. 'Lauren's little mishap was just that. I would never have put her on a pony that was unsafe.'

Emma managed a little smile. 'I'm not sure just how long the children will be staying with me but, while they are, I guess if you can manage the strain then I can too.'

CHAPTER NINE

EMMA was glad she'd had the distraction of the children's company throughout the day. But now it was almost nine o'clock and the long night stretched ahead of her.

She felt too restless to watch television, her thoughts too fragmented to read. And sleep was out of the question.

She wandered aimlessly about the kitchen. She could probably do some meal preparation for next week. Perhaps freeze some simple meals for the kids. When the firm rap sounded on her back door, her heart slammed into her ribcage with such force she had to gulp down her next breath.

It had to be Declan. No one else was likely to be banging on her kitchen door at this time of night. Like water draining out of a bath, the tension trickled out of her shoulders and the knots in her stomach began to loosen. Thank heaven he'd come. Now, she could apologise for her crazy reaction last night and they could get back on an even keel again. So simple when you thought about it.

Declan waited for Emma to answer the door. Physically, he was wiped. His eyes felt as if they'd been back-filled with fine sand sprinkled with wood ash and hisguts knitted into a tight uneasy series of knots. He lifted his shoulders in a huge controlling breath. Hell, would she even let him in?

In an agitated gesture, Emma wiped her hands down the sides of her jeans and went to open the door. She raised her gaze, looking out on to the lighted verandah. 'Declan…' Her voice shook and suddenly her limbs felt as though they were being held together by string. He looked dark and achingly familiar in his black sweater. His hair was mussed as though his fingers had run through it over and over and light stubble sprinkled his jaw and chin.

'This couldn't wait until surgery on Monday,' he said. 'May I come in?'

Emma held the door wide open.

Declan walked into the kitchen and then spun to face her. 'I thought, as you're temporary guardian of Tracey's children, you'd need to know how things went today.'

Emma felt the impact of his words right down in her gut. It wasn't what she'd expected to hear at all. And he was being so formal—as if they were medical partners and nothing more. Was that what he wanted? Had she ruined everything? She said the first thing that came into her head. 'Have you eaten?'

Declan rubbed his forehead with a long finger. 'Nev and I stopped for a bite on the way home. A coffee would be good, though–if you wouldn't mind,' he added, as if unsure of her response.

'Of course I don't mind. Sit down.'

'Kids in bed?' Declan dropped on to a chair at the head of the scrubbed pine table.

'Ages ago.' With her back towards him, Emma drew in a few calming breaths and set water to boil. She got down mugs and instant coffee and stood them on the bench. 'We had a very full day,' she said, shaking the contents of a packet of chocolate biscuits on to a plate.

'Oh, yes. How did the riding go?'

'A bit mixed.' She laughed jaggedly and filled him in. Then the jug boiled and she made the coffee, added milk and took it across to the table.

'Lauren's OK, though?' Declan took up his coffee mug and looked at her over its rim.

'Took it entirely in her stride. She wants to go back again and Jodi's happy to give her some riding lessons.'

'Good.' Declan drank his coffee slowly, looking into space, almost as if he'd run out of words.

A silence, awkward.

'How was Tracey, then?'

Declan brought his gaze up sharply. 'Things are still a bit iffy between her and Carolyn.'

'Well, they were never going to fall into each other's arms.'

'How naïve of me.' He gave a grunt of mirthless laughter. 'I was actually hoping they might have. I guess I'll never understand women.'

Emma recognized his response as a not too subtle dig at her own recent behaviour and swallowed any comeback she might have made. Instead, she'd stay entirely professional. 'How was Adam when he saw his mum?'

'A bit quiet. Tracey had some one-to-one time with him later in the day and they seemed much more in tune with each other by the end of it.'

'He's been a lost little boy,' Emma said quietly. 'So—has the family come up with any plan for the future—or even if there's to be one?'

'I'm not about to let Tracey slip through the cracks,' Declan said emphatically.

'You can't be all things to all people,' Emma reminded him.

After a long, assessing kind of look at her, Declan lifted his mug and drained the last of his coffee. 'I've arranged some joint counselling for the family. And Nev's come up with a kind of plan. He's going to try to persuade Carolyn to take a holiday with her sister at the Gold Coast.'

'So, Tracey could come back home without Carolyn peering over her shoulder?' Emma caught on quickly.

'It could work,' he justified.

'Small steps, then?'

'Better than none at all,' Declan said and got to his feet.

Emma swung upright after him. 'You'll keep me in the loop about Lauren and Joel, won't you?'

Declan scrubbed his hands across his face in a weary gesture. 'That goes without saying.' He moved towards the door. 'I'll get going, then.'

Emma's heart beat fast. If she didn't speak now, she had a terrible feeling the opportunity she sought would be lost for ever. 'I'm sorry about last night.'

Declan went very still. 'What part of it are you sorry about, Emma?'

Oh, dear God—what on earth was he thinking—that she regretted making love with him? Goosebumps ran up her backbone. 'Could we talk—properly?' Emma didn't miss his cautious look, nor the way he seemed to gather himself in.

'I guess an opportunity might present itself next week.'

'Next week?' Emma echoed stupidly. Then she thought—perhaps this is his way of breaking things off? Well, this time she intended fighting for what she believed in. And she believed in *them*. 'I—thought perhaps tomorrow?'

Declan felt the strength drain out of his legs. He'd been convinced it was never going to work between them. That Emma, for her own reasons, didn't want it to work. He swallowed deeply. 'You have the children.'

'I'll ask Moira to come over and stay with them. She won't mind...'

'OK.' Declan spread his hands in a shrug. 'Would you like to meet somewhere or—'

'No,' Emma cut in. 'I'll come to you. I should make it by afternoon.'

'Fine.' he nodded. 'Just one thing, Emma.'

'Yes?'

What could have passed for the flicker of a smile crossed his mouth. 'Don't bring food.'

Declan couldn't keep still. When would she get here? She hadn't specified a time. He'd been for a run, had a shower and a badly needed shave. 'For crying out loud, just get here...' he intoned softly. Already Emma Armitage had stirred such powerful feelings in him; she was so sweet and funny. Sexy.

But did she want a future with him? The thought that she might not made nerves tighten low in his belly. He stopped his train of thought.

It would be dusk soon. He slid a look at his watch and took a deep breath. He was on a knife-edge, his emotions seesawing from high to low and back. In the quiet still of late afternoon, he heard her car long before he saw it. His heart gave an extra thud as he hurried outside to wait for her.

Emma had steeled herself for a great deal of awkwardness when she and Declan faced each other. Little speeches, none of them right, ran through her head. And she had to face the fact that he hadn't seemed in any hurry for this conversation they had to have.

She drove slowly towards the cabin. She was going to her lover—wild for just the sight of him, the touch of him. Oh, Lord—her heart was hammering as she brought the car to a stop. Did he still want *her*?

Well, she'd never find out by sitting here. Throwing open the door of her car, she swung out.

Declan was standing there. Waiting.

'Hi,' she croaked.

'I thought you'd never get here.' His gaze snapped over her.

'Moira got held up.'

'Not literally?'

'No.' A ghost of a smile crossed her lips. 'Just a domestic drama.' She wanted to reach up and touch his newly shaven jaw, place her hands on his chest, but felt too held back by the air of tension running between them. She swallowed nervously. 'Are you OK?'

He gave a tight little smile. 'Dunno yet.'

'Oh—'

Declan saw the pitch and roll of emotion in her eyes. The uncertainty. Oh, hell. He didn't want to put her through the wringer like this. He spoke quietly into the stillness. 'Would you like a hug in the meantime?'

She nodded. 'Please…'

He closed the space between them in one swift move and gathered her in.

Emma felt herself melt into his arms, the familiar ache, the quivering in her stomach. She could have happily stayed there for ever.

'What are we going to do about this, Emma?' Declan asked, his voice a little rough around the edges. 'We seem to be going in circles.'

Emma's heart gave a sickening lurch. She pulled back, her hands creeping up to rest on his shoulders. 'The whole weekend's been manic. I've been wanting to talk but we haven't seemed able to connect.'

'No.'

'I never meant to hurt you, Declan.'

'In my heart of hearts, I knew that.' He lifted a hand, his knuckles brushing softly over her cheek.

'Thank you.' His kiss came seconds later, a long exquisite shiver of a kiss that twined through her body languidly like smoke haze. The tenderness and delicacy of the simple union of their lips left her shaky and she nestled into him, holding him closer.

When they finally pulled away, Declan kept his arms loosely around her. She slowly opened her eyes. They gleamed. But they asked him questions as well. 'Let's go in,' he said, his voice rough with emotion. His fingers slid down her arm, dragging through hers, and they made their way inside. 'Make yourself comfortable,' he said. 'Something to drink?'

'No, I'm fine, thanks.' Emma curled herself into the corner of the soft, cushiony settee.

Declan looked about him and then, because anything else would have seemed ridiculous, he parked beside her, stretching his arms along the back. He looked a question at her as much as to say, *Well, let's hear it.*

Very aware of him beside her, Emma bit gently at her bottom lip. He seemed ill at ease, although he was pretending not to. There was definitely an air of vulnerability about him. 'About what happened at the hospital—'

'When you all but cut me dead.'

She made a little gesture with her hand. 'None of this has been easy from the start, Declan. You landed on me out of nowhere. Took me over—'

'On the contrary. We agreed on a course of action for the practice.'

Her mind a whirlpool of jumbled thoughts and emotions, Emma said starkly, 'I just wonder if you'll stay, Declan.'

'That's not a decision for now.' His voice tightened and there was a long pause. 'You don't trust me at all, do you, Emma?'

'It's the circumstances we're in I don't trust. I see how frustrated you get with the shortcomings of working in a rural practice. Friday night with Agnes, for instance.'

'Guilty as charged.' His mouth pulled down. 'But that's nothing to do with my personal relationship with you.'

Emma's heart was pounding, uncertainty spreading to every part of her body. 'It has everything to do with it, Declan.' She blinked rapidly. 'If you walk away, then I'll have left myself open to hurt again.'

'Aren't you even willing to try? When we could have something good and true between us?'

She gave a bitter little laugh. 'I thought I had something good and true with Marcus.'

At his growl of dissent, Emma shook her head. 'I know it sounds pathetic but everything just imploded when I saw you and Rachel together. I was seeing Marcus and Bree again and I suppose I overreacted.'

'Just a bit.' Declan looked at her narrowly. 'How well do you know Rachel?'

She seemed surprised at the question. 'Professionally, quite well. Personally, I guess not that well.'

'So you don't know she's facing something of a personal crisis.'

Emma's eyes widened in alarm. 'Is she ill?'

'No. You're aware some time ago Rachel spent several tours of duty with Médicins Sans Frontières?'

'Doctors Without Borders—yes I knew that. She was a theatre nurse. Dad always said she was brilliant.'

Declan lifted a shoulder. 'Apparently, during her time abroad, Rachel had a long-term relationship with one of the surgeons, Ethan O'Rourke. They were planning to marry on their next leave. But it never happened because he was killed in some kind of tribal skirmish. Rachel got out and came home.'

'That's so sad.' Emma's hand went to her heart.

Declan continued, 'It was always Ethan's dream to have a properly equipped OR at the hospital where they worked. Now, it seems, his parents have gathered enough funds and support to make it happen. They want Rachel to go back and oversee its setting-up.'

Several wild thoughts juxtaposed in Emma's head. Her nerves tightened alarmingly. Had Rachel asked Declan to go with her? With his medical background, it would seem a feasible request. The implication struck her as painfully as fists.

'You said there was a problem?'

'Rachel doesn't want to go.'

'So, why did she need to speak to you about it?'

'She wanted an objective opinion.'

'I see…and what did you tell her?'

'I told her to follow her instincts.'

Emma nodded and felt relief sweep through her. 'Rachel's a strong person. She'll stand by whatever she decides. It will be the hospital's loss if she goes, though.'

'Another problem we don't need to solve just now.' Declan gave her a long look. 'Nothing's black and white, Emma. We're all just muddling along. But sometimes you have to take a chance. To trust someone other than yourself.'

'You're talking about us, aren't you?' She had a lump in her throat. 'I want to try—'

'But you're afraid?'

She nodded bleakly.

Oh, Emma…' He made a rough sound in his throat and opened his arms wide.

'Come here…'

On a little broken cry, she scooted up the settee and straight into his arms. They held each other tightly for a very long time, until Declan broke the silence with, 'Feel better now?'

She gave a shaky smile and touched a finger to the smooth skin at his throat where his shirt lay unbuttoned. 'You sound like my doctor.'

'I am your doctor,' he answered softly. 'If you want me to be?'

Her gaze faltered. 'I hate it when we're not friends.'

His fingers, blunt and strong, tipped her chin up gently so that she met his gaze. 'How long can you stay?'

He'd spoken so quietly, his voice so deep it made her shiver. 'Not as long as I'd like to,' she murmured, raising her hands, spreading her fingers to bracket his face. 'We could kiss and make up a bit, though…'

Their mouths sought each other's, then sipped and nipped and she heard a half growl escape from his throat as their kiss deepened. Was there time for what she really wanted? To make love again with him was what she really wanted. Needed.

Instead, she felt Declan pulling back, his fingers moving to twine in her hair at the back. The gentlest pressure brought her head up. His eyes were disturbingly intent as they looked into her face. 'Emma…' His throat worked as he swallowed. 'I want you. But not like this. Hurried and under pressure because you have to go. When we make love again, I want it to be long and leisurely. Slow. Very slow and with all the time in the world afterwards. You understand, don't you?'

'I suppose…' She felt her head drop a little. 'There will *be* a time, won't there?'

'I give you my word,' he said huskily, nudging a strand of her hair sideways, seeking the soft skin at her nape. 'Even if we have to close the surgery and fly the coop to accomplish it.'

'I can just see Moira's face if we did that!'

'I'm not so sure,' he countered with a lazy grin. 'Moira's a canny soul. I think she'd probably give us her tick of approval and reschedule all our appointments.'

On Monday morning, Declan popped his head into Emma's consulting room. 'Good morning.' His mouth tweaked at the corners. 'Sleep well?'

'Fine, thanks.'

'Good.' They exchanged a very private smile. 'Me too. Er...' He lifted a hand and pressed it to the back of his neck. 'Quick team meeting before surgery?'

'Now?'

'Please.'

'OK.' Emma left what she doing and went with him along to the staff kitchen.

'This is just to pull a few things together before the week gets away from us,' Declan explained to the assembled group.

'Before we start, Declan,' Moira said, 'what's the latest on Agnes? They won't tell me anything at the hospital except the standard response.'

'Sorry about that, Moira. I should have got back to you,' Declan apologized. 'Agnes has settled quite nicely. At this stage they don't think they'll have to operate. And I believe some family members from Brisbane arrived yesterday to be with her.'

'Oh, that is good news.' Moira picked up her cup of tea and held it against her chest. 'How long will she be in, do we know?'

'Not sure. I wouldn't think the hospital will be in any hurry to discharge her, though.'

'In that case, I'll send some flowers.'

'Better still, Moira, make the flowers from all of us and charge them to the practice,' Declan said. 'I think the place can stand the cost for one of our senior citizens.'

'That's a nice gesture,' Emma said quietly.

'I'm a nice guy,' Declan joked.

Emma laughed huskily, trying to hide the sudden leap in her pulse as his thigh brushed against hers. 'What else is on the agenda?' she got out quickly before her thoughts became entirely scrambled.

Declan sent her a wry smile. He knew what he'd *like* to be on the agenda. Instead, he snapped to attention. 'Cedric Dutton. I called round to see him, managed a good chat about things. He's OK now about you making a home visit, Libby. Just keep it low-key, hmm?'

The practice nurse made a small grimace. 'In other words, don't be a bossy cow.'

Declan grinned. 'I wouldn't have put it quite so bluntly. But he'll respond better if we all gentle him along. He's also agreed to try and socialize a bit. He thought the card morning at the seniors' club might be a start. He'll need transport, though. Ideas, anyone?'

'I'll have a word with Tiny Carruthers,' Moira said. 'He runs a minibus around to collect the older folk. There are a few with mobility problems. I'm sure he wouldn't mind adding Cedric to his list.'

'*Tiny* Carruthers?' Declan looked a question between the women. 'Is he quite fit himself, then?'

Emma chuckled. 'Perfectly. Tiny is six feet and used to play rugby.'

'I see…' Declan raised an eyebrow.

'He treats the older folk like they're the most important people in the world,' Moira enlarged. 'Cedric will be well looked after.'

'Good.' Declan nodded approval. 'I'll leave that in your capable hands, then, Moira. Now, as you know, I'm invited to the P&C meeting at the school tonight to put our case for the pool to be opened for the seniors' use. I wondered, Moira, whether you'd be free to come with me?'

'Me?' Moira looked flustered. 'What would you need me to do?'

'What you do best.' Declan tipped the older woman a reassuring smile. 'Advocate for the seniors. I can cover the obvious health benefits that participating in physical activity brings. Like helping to strengthen bones and muscles and so reduce the possibility of falls and so on.'

'To say nothing of maintaining folk's independence and social connection,' Moira added, warming to her role. 'And water aerobics is so low-impact and lovely. It's such a shame the pool can't be put to use for the benefit of our older folk.'

'You've convinced me.' Looking pleased, Declan leaned back in his chair and folded his arms.

'Oh, heavens, I fell right into that, didn't I?' Moira looked a bit bemused. 'But I'm happy to do what I can.'

'Would you like me to swing by and give you a lift to the meeting?' Declan asked.

Moira flapped a hand in dismissal. 'You'd have to come in from the cabin and then detour to collect me.'

'Why go home at all after work?' Emma turned to Declan with a sudden idea. 'Stay and have dinner with me and the kids. Then you can leave from here for the meeting.'

He thought about it for one second. 'Thanks. Like me to cook?'

Remembering Friday night when he'd *cooked* for them, Emma felt her body engulfed in heat. But with the children around there'd be none of *that* happening tonight. She didn't know whether to feel glad or sorry. She lifted her gaze to his and for a second their eyes held and they were lost in a hush of silence, a stillness as profound as a mountain top at dawn. 'No need—' Emma blinked, lifting a hand to clutch the unbuttoned collar of her shirt. 'I'll pop a casserole in the slow-cooker at lunch time. If that's all right with you?'

His rather bemused smile began at his lips and moved to his eyes. 'I'll look forward to it. So, Moira—' he snapped back to attention '—I'll collect you and drop you home after the meeting.'

A few more matters regarding the practice were raised and settled.

'You going all right, Jodi?' Declan asked as the meeting broke up and people began standing and clattering their chairs back into place. 'Finding the job OK?'

'I love the work. It's so…interesting.'

'Perhaps you'll rethink your uni course.' Emma laughed. 'Switch to medicine.'

'Don't think so.' Jodi wrinkled her pert nose. 'I love my thoroughbreds too much.'

'I know it's difficult but try to avoid the temptation to scratch,' Emma told her first patient for the day. Shannon Gilmore had recently moved from North Queensland to settle in Bendemere's much cooler climate.

'Pardon me for saying the obvious, Doctor, but you don't have this wretched condition. Some days I could scratch myself to pieces.' The thirty-year-old's bottom lip quivered. 'I don't think the climate here suits me. I wish we'd never had to leave the north. And I don't think it's fair that the wife has to trundle along like so much baggage wherever the husband's job takes him.'

So, they were dealing with much more than her patient's eczema here. Emma's professional instincts sharpened and she prepared for a longer than usual consult. It was obvious Shannon had issues with alienation and resentment and probably sheer loneliness that were all adding to her stress levels and pushing the symptoms of her eczema into overdrive. Her doctor offering half-baked platitudes was not going to help matters. 'It must be difficult when you have your own career to think about,' she commiserated.

'I didn't have a structured career as such. But I had a nice little shop specialising in home décor. And clients willing to pay quite large sums for my expertise. I loved it…'

Emma thought. 'Is there a possibility you could start something like that here?'

Shannon's smile was brittle. 'If I hear that once more, I'll scream. I was living in the *tropics*, selling pieces in beautiful vibrant colours. Here, it's so cold all the time. Who wants to go out and shop? And the days never warm up.'

'Well, they do, actually.' Emma proffered a wry smile. 'But obviously not to the degree you're accustomed to.'

Shannon's shoulders hunched over.

'I understand things seem a bit bleak and insurmountable at the moment,' Emma said gently. 'But if we can't change that immediately, at least let's see what we can do for your eczema, shall we?'

'I didn't mean to come across as so pathetic and needy…' Shannon's little shrug was almost defensive.

Emma decided no follow-up comment was required. Instead, she said, 'First, I think we should consider the type of clothing you're wearing, Shannon. Overheating is a trigger for the eczema to flare up and the skin to start itching.'

'I just can't seem to get warm.' Shannon's fingers plucked at the bulky-knit jumper she was wearing.

'Anything synthetic is probably not a good choice for you at the moment. You'd be better wearing layers of lighter garments so your skin can breathe. Cotton clothing is good. Check out the shops in Toowoomba. You'll find they have a range of wonderful separates. I'm sure you'll find something to suit you. Now, on more practical matters, I imagine you know it's best to avoid soap and detergents?'

Shannon nodded. 'I use a non-perfumed moisturizer and I'm aware of the food allergy factor.'

'And stress,' Emma added gently.

'I guess…'

'You're obviously on the right track with your food.' Emma smiled. 'But you could try increasing your intake of vitamins A, E and C and fish oil supplements can help rebuild the skin. All that will take a little while to kick in so in the meantime I'll give you a script for a steroid cream as a short-term measure. That should get you back on track and don't hesitate to use a cold compress to help things along.'

'Thanks for this.' Shannon took the script and folded it into her bag. 'And for just listening, I guess…'

At the end of the surgery hours Emma popped her head into Declan's room and asked, 'Are you through for the day?'

He looked up from his computer, his eyes softening. 'One

more patient to see.' They exchanged a smile. 'I'll come through when I'm done, OK?'

'Fine. Lauren and I are making an apple crumble for dessert.' She fluttered a two-fingered wave. 'See you.'

Declan still had the smile on his face when he scooted his chair back and got to his feet. Rolling back his shoulders, he stretched. He had a few minutes before his last patient for the day was scheduled. He'd never read so much nor spent so much time on the Net than in the past weeks, he thought a bit ruefully. But there were so many areas where he'd had to refresh his knowledge to function effectively as a family practitioner. But he was getting there. Maybe there was hope for him yet.

CHAPTER TEN

DECLAN walked Moira safely to her door and then returned to his car. The meeting had gone well and he was upbeat about how his suggestions had been taken on board by the committee. It was a good outcome for the seniors. Very good.

Suddenly, he wanted to share his news with Emma. And it wasn't that late. She might still be up. He was only a few minutes from Kingsholme. He could cruise by and see whether her lights were on. Decision made, he started the motor and slid away from the kerb.

When he arrived at Kingsholme, Declan could see one solitary light on at the rear of the house. She was probably in the kitchen. Getting out of the car, he followed the path along the side of the building to the back verandah and mounted the steps. He gave a cursory knock and opened the kitchen door, calling gently, 'Emma? It's me.'

'Declan?' She spun round from the stove and frowned uncertainly. 'I didn't expect you.'

'Hi.' Slightly bemused, he stood with his back to the door and looked at her. She was dressed in polka-dot winter pyjamas, a cuddly dark blue dressing gown and fluffy socks. She looked adorable and he wanted to hold her for ever. 'I wanted to tell you about the meeting.'

She nodded vaguely. 'I've made some hot chocolate. It'll stretch to two.'

'Thanks.' He rubbed his arms briskly, watching as she

tipped the hot milk from the saucepan and filled the two mugs. 'It's cold out there.'

Taking their mugs, they sat at the kitchen table. Declan leaned forward eagerly. 'The committee have agreed to the seniors using the pool. They've even gone a step further and suggested having a huge fundraiser to have it heated.'

'Oh, good.'

'And Moira was impressive—in full flight,' he added with a chuckle. 'The committee didn't know what hit them. Even asked what more they could do for the older folk. I hope something comes of it—' He stopped abruptly. Emma was barely listening. Instead, she was gripping her mug like a lifeline and staring fixedly at the opposite wall. 'Hey…' he said gently, touching her arm to bring her out of her trance-like state. 'Are you all right?'

She looked at him blankly. 'Mum's here.'

A frown touched his eyes. 'Is that a problem?'

'It could be. I haven't told her about you. Only that I have a suitable partner for the practice.'

Declan's frown became more pronounced. 'What are you saying, Emma, that you don't want me to meet her?'

'Of course I want you to meet her!' Her gaze fluttered down and she hesitated. 'But when she hears your name—what if she…?'

'Connects the dots? Emma, we can't be held responsible for what our parents did. We don't even know if they did *anything* untoward. Do we?'

'No…' She swallowed heavily and foolish tears blurred her vision. 'I'd hate for her to be hurt, Declan.'

'Because of us and what we mean to each other? Emma, that's ridiculous.' He took her hands in his and gently chafed them. 'You're imagining wild scenarios that have no basis in fact. I'll meet your mum, OK?' he cajoled softly. 'And we'll go from there.'

She nodded mutely.

'Good.' He gave her fingers an approving squeeze. 'Now, drink your nightcap. It'll help you sleep.' Declan looked thoughtful as he lifted his own mug and took several deep mouthfuls of the hot chocolate. 'When did your mother arrive?'

'Just after you'd left for the meeting. She flew up today from Melbourne and hired a car at the Brisbane airport. She said she wanted to surprise me.'

Well, she'd certainly done that. Declan finished his drink. 'Is she just here for some family time or—'

'No,' Emma cut in and shook her head. 'There's an auction at one of the heritage homes in Toowoomba tomorrow. She's interested in bidding for a couple of paintings for her gallery. But I imagine she won't stay long. She'll want to get back to her business. We didn't have a chance to talk much. She was tired after the drive so she more or less had a shower and went off to bed.'

'I'll come in early, then.' Declan made up his mind. 'That way, I can at least meet her before she heads off about her day.'

Emma resisted the urge to lean closer and rest her head on his shoulder. Just. 'That might be best. I guess…'

'Emma, we can't keep walking on eggshells about this. Let's just take things as they come.'

'I'm sure you're right.' She drummed up her best and brightest smile.

He glanced at his watch. 'I should go and let you get some sleep.'

'And you as well.' She walked with him to the door. 'See you in the morning,' she said.

Declan cupped her face with both hands. 'I'll be here *early*.'

She gave a nod of understanding and agreement.

'It'll be all right, Emma.' His mouth brushed against hers. 'Trust me.'

The following morning, Emma felt the nerves in her stomach churning endlessly. She'd fed the children and now they'd gone to get dressed for school while she organized their lunches. Earlier, she'd heard her mother's alarm so she'd probably be up and dressed by now… Was Declan on his way in from the cabin? Oh, Lord…

'Morning, darling.'

'Oh—hi, Mum.' Emma's heart rate quickened as her mother came into the kitchen. 'Sleep all right?'

'Seemed a bit odd to be back in Andrew's and my old bedroom. But I slept well. I like the makeover, by the way.'

'It seemed time.' Emma was guarded. 'Now, what about some breakfast?'

'Just toast, thanks. Do you have leaf green tea?'

'China canister there on the shelf. Help yourself. I'll just finish packing the kids' lunches.' Emma's mouth flicked into a quick smile. 'You look lovely, by the way.' Dressed in her beautifully tailored black trousers and jacket, her mother looked Melbourne *chic* all the way. 'Your boots are *gorgeous*.'

'And comfortable. I expect to be doing a bit of running around today.'

Emma watched as her mother slid bread into the toaster. 'Are you after anything else beside the paintings?'

'The Kingsley estate was vast. There are some extremely delicate tapestries I might go after—if the price is right,' she added with a wry smile.

True to his word, Declan arrived early at Kingsholme. He unloaded his medical case in his consulting room and then made his way through to the living quarters. He heard muted conversation from the vicinity of the kitchen and guessed the voices belonged to Emma and her mother. His heart did a quick tango. He'd pretended to be calm about things for Emma's sake. But he was far from it. Mrs Armitage's reaction could ruin everything he and Emma had found. He hoped with all that was in him it wouldn't come to that.

Reaching the kitchen, he paused and then leant against the doorframe and poked his head in. Emma's mother was standing against the bench of cupboards, a delicate teacup in her hands. At least he supposed it was her mother. She looked like an older version of her daughter. Declan's gaze flicked discreetly and quickly over the slender-framed woman. She oozed style and sophistication in her dress and *very* good gold jewellery decorated her throat and hands. Hell, he hoped he'd measure up. He cleared his throat. 'Good morning.'

'Declan!' Her heart thumping, Emma turned, holding Lauren's lunch box like a shield against her chest. 'Come in. Um—this is my mother. Mum—' she smiled, her voice a bit breathless, earnest with her own need for things to go well '—this is Declan O'Malley, my practice partner.'

Emma's mother turned with a graceful movement and replaced her cup on its saucer and then held out her hand. 'Declan. How very nice to meet you.'

'Mrs Armitage.' Declan's handshake was firm. 'It's good to meet you too.'

'Oh, please. Call me Roz.' The older woman smiled. 'You've an early start this morning?'

'Most mornings,' Declan replied. 'But we don't mind, do we, Emma?' His wide-open gaze seemed natural and frank but it was telling Emma so much more. First hurdle over. It will be all right.

'It's like most jobs, I guess,' Emma said, getting into the spirit of the conversation. 'You get into a rhythm of sorts.'

Declan looked hopefully around the kitchen. 'Any tea going, guys?'

'I've just made a pot if you like green tea?' Roz offered.

'Sounds just the ticket,' Declan said diplomatically, even though he would have preferred Emma's strong brew first thing. As he poured himself a cup, he set out to be sociable. 'Emma tells me you have a busy day ahead, Roz.'

'Yes, and I should get going.' Emma's mother glanced at her watch. 'The paintings I want to bid for are up first thing. I shouldn't be too late home, though, darling,' she told Emma. 'Penny and Clive Bailleau are driving in from Munbilla and we're meeting up for lunch. After that, I'm pretty much done.'

'Oh, I'm glad you're seeing friends,' Emma said warmly. 'Give Penny and Clive my best.'

'I'll do that.' Roz rinsed her cup and placed it in the drainer.

Turning, she plucked a section of paper towel and dried her hands. 'And I thought I might pick up a treat for the children,' she said in a confidential undertone. 'What are they into?'

'Oh, that's so nice of you, Mum.' Emma's heart warmed.

Roz flapped a hand in dismissal. 'They've had a hard time, from what you said. And I'd like to do it anyway.'

'OK—' Emma thought for a second. 'Well, Lauren likes to read and she's keen to learn to ride, although she knows practically nothing about horses. Not sure about Joel...'

'He's mad about soccer,' Declan chimed in with a grin. 'At the moment, he's kicking a clapped-out piece of leather around the yard. I had it on my list to get him a decent soccer ball but now I'll leave it in your capable hands, Roz.'

'So—' Roz Armitage held up two crossed fingers '—the book shop and the sports shop, right? Now, I really must be on my way.'

'Take care on the roads.' Emma gave her mother a quick hug.

'And you two have a good day,' Roz said in reply and wrinkled her nose. 'If that's possible.'

'It is, Roz,' Declan quirked his mouth and drawled, 'even in medicine.'

Two hours later, Declan realized the rashness of that statement.

They had an emergency situation at the hospital. Students from a girls' school in Toowoomba were being brought in with suspected food poisoning. 'Apparently they're here in Bendemere on a school camp,' Moira told the doctors as they came together for a quick briefing. 'Both our ambulances have gone out and the teachers will bring the rest in the school bus.'

'The rest!' Declan's head pulled back. 'How many are we expecting?'

'Maybe in excess of ten?' Moira made a small grimace. 'They're from the upper grades, thirteen and upwards.'

'So at least we can expect some degree of cooperation and sensible answers,' he commented ruefully.

'Nursing backup might be a bit thin on the ground at the hospital,' Emma said. 'No doubt Rachel will call in casuals but apparently a few of the regular nurses are off with winter ills. Perhaps Libby could fill in and come with us?'

Declan nodded. 'Good idea. And Moira, do what you have to do to reorganize our patient list, please.'

'Anyone who is just waiting for repeats of their scripts could perhaps come back tomorrow,' Emma added. 'Whatever, we'll leave things in your capable hands.'

'Do we have any idea of the expected ETA?' Declan asked as they pulled in to the hospital car park.

'They won't be long,' Emma said. 'Camp Kookaburra is only about ten kilometres out.'

From the back seat of the car, Libby pondered, 'I wonder what they ate?'

Declan snorted. 'Something dodgy for breakfast, if they've all gone down so quickly.'

Within minutes the ambulances arrived, followed by the school bus.

Emma could see at once that the students were quite ill, some of them pale and sweaty. They were going to take some sorting out, that was certain.

Declan grimaced. 'Bang goes the rest of our morning surgery list.'

'Rural doctoring,' Emma reminded him.

'Got it.' Declan lifted a finger, acknowledging her point.

Talitha looked goggle-eyed at the volume of patients. 'We'll run out of cubicles! Where will we put them all?'

'We'll put some of them out on the verandah ward.' Rachel was in full flight in charge. 'And Tally, run and get bags or basins, please. They're bound to be still vomiting.'

Tally ran.

'Right, guys,' Declan came in authoritatively, 'Let's get some triage going, shall we?'

'Sorry I'm late.' Casual nurse Irene McCosker, fiftyish, arrived slightly breathless, still adjusting the belt on her uniform trousers. 'Jeff's off sick so I had to shoo the customers out and close the shop,' she explained.

Emma smiled at the older woman. 'Thanks so much for coming in at short notice, Irene. Perhaps, where you can, would you start taking names, please? And liaise with the accompanying teachers about letting the parents know. That would be a great help.'

'Certainly, Dr Armitage.' Irene looked pleased to be given responsibility.

'We should see the kids on stretchers first,' Emma said quietly to Declan. 'Would you like to team with Rachel? Then Libby and I can work together.'

His brow furrowed for a second. 'If you're sure?'

She nodded. 'Absolutely.' He'd said it was all about trust and so far he hadn't let her down.

Accompanied by Rachel, Declan went into the first cubicle. Their patient looked pale and clammy. Bending over the stretcher, Declan asked, 'What's your name, sweetheart?'

'Bronte Pearce.'

'And how old are you, Bronte?'

'Sixteen.'

'And when did you start feeling ill?'

'Soon after breakfast—' The youngster rocked her head restlessly from side to side and moaned softly.

'It'll be all right, honey.' Rachel smoothed the girl's long dark fringe away from her forehead. 'We'll get you feeling better soon.'

'Bronte,' Declan came in gently, 'I just need to feel your tummy.' His mouth compressed as he palpated. 'Right.' He stepped back and drew the sheet up. 'That's fine. Have you had any diarrhoea?'

'Some. Oh—help…' Her plea came out on a moan.

Noticing her patient's sudden pallor, Rachel reached for a

basin and helped her sit up. Then, exhausted from the bout of vomiting, Bronte fell back on the pillows. She blocked a tear with the palm of her hand. 'I feel awful,' she sniffed. 'And my little sister Sasha is so ill. She's only thirteen and she started her periods just yesterday…'

'It's OK, sweetie. Don't worry.' Rachel squeezed Bronte's hand. 'She'll be well looked after.'

'Someone's head should roll for this.' Grim-faced, Declan scribbled instructions on the chart. 'Put up ten milligrams of maxolon stat, please, Rachel. That should settle her tummy.'

'Lomotil for the diarrhoea?'

Declan nodded. 'Let's start with two orally and cut back to one after each bowel movement.' He frowned. 'She's dehydrating. I'd like her on four per cent glucose and one-fifth normal saline IV. Sips of water only. Could you take her blood sugar levels as well, please? Anything below three, I need to know. And, while you're doing that,' he added, replacing the chart, 'I'll just have a quick word with Emma.'

Declan found Emma in the next cubicle and beckoned her aside. 'Have you treated a child by the name of Sasha Pearce yet?'

'I've just sent her to the ward,' Emma confirmed. 'She was seriously dehydrated. She'll need to stay on a drip for some time yet. I'm recommending we keep her overnight.'

'How was she generally?'

'As you'd expect—scared and miserable. Is there a problem?' Emma queried.

'I've just seen her older sister, Bronte. She was concerned.'

And so are you, Emma decided. Declan really cared about these kids and that thought warmed her through and through. 'Tally's taken Sasha under her wing, Declan. Trust me, she'll be fine.'

'OK, thanks. I'll just relay that to Bronte.' He hesitated. 'Poor kid was pretty upset about her little sister's predicament.'

'The women's business?' Emma shot him a look as old as time. 'All taken care of.'

'Great. Thanks.' He swished back the curtains and disappeared.

They went on assessing and treating their juvenile patients for the next couple of hours, answering questions from anxious parents as they trickled in to check on their offspring. Several of the students appeared quite poorly and had to be admitted for observation but the majority were treated and allowed to go home.

'Did you get any joy from the Health Department?' Emma asked later, as they made their way out of the hospital to the car park.

'They've promised urgent action,' Declan said. 'Obviously, whatever they find will be sent for analysis. In the meantime, the camp has been cut short. Most of the kids will be home in their own beds by tonight.'

Moira had refused to overload the lists so the afternoon surgery finished in reasonable time. After his last patient had left, Declan went along to Emma's consulting room. He knocked and poked his head in. 'All done for the day?'

'Mmm.' She waved him in and swung off her chair as if her feet had wings. 'Hi…' She met his gaze, an almost shy smile playing over her lips. And Declan knew he'd crack wide open if he didn't kiss her.

He held out his arms and she flew into them, wrapping herself tightly around him and turning her face up for his kiss.

'Emma…' A gravelly sigh dragged itself up from the depths of his chest and his mouth took hers as if he were dying of thirst.

She shifted against him, each tiny movement a subtle invitation for him to hold her more tightly, more intimately.

And he did.

Heat exploded in him and he gave a strangled groan, her soft pleas driving him closer to the edge. For a split second he considered letting his natural instincts run wild and making love with her here in her office. To be inside her, to feel her legs wrapped round him, hear the sweet sounds of her climax…

But only for a second. Suddenly, the compulsion took flight. Somehow it seemed tacky and not worthy of her—of them.

But how he ached for her.

He found just enough control to break the kiss. 'Emma…' He pressed his forehead to hers. 'We have to slow down.'

'Yes, I know…' Her voice shook. 'But I wish—'

'Wish we didn't?' He gave a hard laugh. 'Opportunities are a bit unworkable at the moment.' He released her, then slid his hands down her arms to mesh her fingers with his. 'Our time will come,' he promised huskily.

'I suppose…yes.' She hung her head a little. 'Can you at least stay for dinner?'

'Nice thought, but no.' He leaned forward, brushing her mouth with his lips. 'You should have some quality time with your mother. Somehow, I think it's what you both need.'

She smiled unwillingly. 'Guru is your middle name now, is it?'

'Christopher, actually.' They looked at each other for a long moment and suddenly her eyes clouded. Declan shook his head. 'You're not still worrying about all that stuff regarding our respective parents, are you, Emma?'

'Perhaps a bit.'

He frowned. 'Why, for crying out loud? Roz was clearly very at ease when I met her.'

'I wonder—' Emma bit her lips together and hesitated. 'I mean—I hope Dad didn't deceive her. That would be too awful.'

'Emma, Emma.' Declan pulled her in close again, his patience clearly under strain. 'For your own sake, you have to let this go. None of it matters now. You do see that, don't you?'

'Yes, you're right. None of it matters.' Well, one part of her believed that. The logical, clear-thinking part. But underneath there was still a tiny doubt, niggling away like a bothersome pebble in a shoe.

But clearly Declan wanted to close the page, to put the discussion to rest once and for all. Deep down, she knew it was the best option. And yet… 'You're right,' she said again, as if she really meant it. 'None of it matters now.'

'Tell me again how you and Dad met.'

The children had long gone to bed and Emma and Roz, both dressed in their nightwear, were sitting in front of the fire. 'Darling, I've already told you several times, as I recall,' Roz said mildly.

'But not since I was about fourteen.' Emma filled their tiny glasses with a peach-flavoured liqueur. 'Now Dad's gone, it would be nice to hear it again,' Emma pleaded. 'And from the beginning, please.'

Roz gave a resigned kind of smile. 'We were both at Uni. I was doing fine arts. Andrew was doing medicine. I guess it was unlikely we would meet up at all, both doing very different disciplines. But there was a move on to close the crèche at the university.'

'Why?' Emma asked, more than a little interested.

'Oh, someone in a high place got a bee in his bonnet that babies and young children had no business being on campus.' Roz lifted a shoulder. 'Independently, both Andrew and I had read the flyers that were asking for numbers to rally to protest against the decision. And we both went along.'

'So you met waving banners.' Emma smiled, her chin parked on her upturned hand.

'Something like that.' Roz took a sip of her liqueur. 'As I remember, we were pretty outraged. We linked up and formed a committee and in time the idea to close the crèche was vetoed. In those days, most of the students who used the crèche were single mums. They really needed the facility.'

'So, you and Dad must have had very strong feelings about child welfare,' Emma pressed.

'We did.' Roz nodded her ash-blonde head. 'In fact, when the director at the crèche called for volunteers occasionally, we both went and helped out with the little ones. We both loved kids,' she added quietly.

'And yet you only had me.'

Roz responded to the question in her daughter's eyes with a tiny shrug of her shoulders. 'I didn't enjoy being pregnant,' she confessed. 'Andrew understood. But we delighted in you when you were born, Emma. So much.' She frowned a bit. 'You never felt...*unloved*, did you?'

'No, of course not.' Even as she said the words Emma felt the painful lurch in her heart. But, knowing what she did now, had that been the reason her father had drifted towards Anne O'Malley? A young widow with her little brood? He must have felt so *needed*. Would it be going too far to say even *fulfilled*? She swallowed deeply. 'Were you and Dad always happy together?'

'Yes, we were.' There was no hesitation in Roz's reply. 'It wasn't easy being married to a doctor, Emma. It took me a long time to realize the demands of Andrew's job. His patients always came first. I thought he was busy enough when he was at the Prince Alfred, but then, when he was offered tenure at John Bosco's, he got even busier. He was always very involved with his interns.' Roz gave a faintly wry smile. 'I guess in a way they became like his own kids.'

They were quiet for a while and then Emma said carefully, 'I sometimes wondered why you went off to Melbourne to open your gallery and left Dad here.'

'Yes...I suppose you did.' Roz sighed, slightly daunted by the need for explanation. 'Your dad thoroughly approved, you know, Emma. In fact, he suggested it. I'd put my own career on hold when we came here to Kingsholme. But I knew how much it meant to your father.'

'You never really settled here, though, did you?'

Roz laughed shortly. 'And I thought I hid it so well. It was different, that's all. I made a life, formed a few good friendships. I was managing. But suddenly, out of the blue, Andrew suggested the gallery idea. You'd returned to the practice.

Dad was quite sure you'd found your niche in rural medicine. And he was so proud to have you as his practice partner.'

'Yes, he told me that.' Emma looked down at her hands. 'But he missed *you*, Mum.'

'We missed one another,' Roz said patiently. 'But all along he'd planned to join me in Melbourne as soon as he'd found someone to replace him at Kingsholme. Someone he was sure would work well with you. Someone he could trust. He wanted to have it all lined up before he told you. Unfortunately, it didn't work out quite like that…'

'No…' Tears blurred Emma's vision and she reached for her mother's hand.

They stayed like that for some minutes more, both with a new sense of calm and acceptance. 'We should have talked like this a long time ago,' Emma said.

'My fault.' Roz looked a little sad. 'I had to grieve for Andrew on my own. He meant the world to me…'

Emma searched her mother's face. 'We should have grieved together.'

'Yes, I see that now. I do love you, darling.'

The reassurance flooded into Emma like warm sunshine parting a cloudy sky. 'I love you too, Mum.'

'Mum's under the impression Dad was still looking for a suitable practice partner for me when he died,' Emma told Declan the next day. They were sitting over a cuppa after surgery had finished.

'Maybe that's for the best,' Declan said. 'But *we* know Andrew tried his best to make sure both your and Roz's futures were assured when he was out of the picture.'

Emma gave a tiny shrug. 'Yes.'

Declan's jaw worked for a minute. 'If only I'd been able to fly out at the time Andrew first called me, instead of being banged up in a hospital rehab unit—'

'But you did come, Declan. You came as soon as you could. And Dad's wishes were fulfilled.'

'Did Roz get home all right?' he asked, changing the tenor of the conversation subtly.

'Yes. She rang about an hour ago. And you were right.' Emma felt a mix of emotions tumble around inside her. 'Mum and I did need to talk.' She stopped and bit down on her bottom lip. 'I think I've matched up all the pieces now.' And, if there was one small piece that still refused to go exactly where she wanted it to, well, so be it.

He smiled. 'I'm glad. By the way, I had some other news today about the Jones family. Carolyn has gone on holiday and Adam was discharged from hospital. For the present, he's staying with Tracey at the shelter.'

'Well, I guess that's progress of a sort.'

'I think we can assume that.' Declan moved restively in his chair. 'Just means you'll have Lauren and Joel for a bit longer, I guess.' And longer still until they could make love again…

CHAPTER ELEVEN

A WEEK later and the staff were on their lunch break before the afternoon clinic.

'Bendemere is hosting the schools' annual sports day tomorrow,' Emma said.

Declan looked up from his reading. 'Is it a big event?'

'All the schools from the neighbouring districts compete.' Jodi dipped into her mug of soup. 'It's a big deal. I was sports captain both years Bendemere won,' she added modestly.

'So, you want the day off tomorrow to go strut your stuff, do you?' Declan teased.

Jodi wrinkled her nose at him. 'I work at the supermarket tomorrow,' she reminded him.

'Lauren's race isn't until eleven.' Emma gave a tentative look around the faces. 'And, as she doesn't have her mum to cheer her on, I thought I might try to get across to the sports ground.'

'I'll cover your list,' Declan offered promptly. 'In fact, I might try to get along for Lauren's race myself. How are tomorrow's lists looking, Moira?'

'Fairly light,' Moira said. 'Most folk will be at the sports day.'

Declan lifted a hand and rubbed the back of his neck. 'Nev can't make it?'

'My guess is he would have used up all his family leave,' Moira said. 'I doubt he'd want to ask for a day off to go to his grandchildren's sports day.'

Emma looked at Declan. 'So, it's agreed I'll go?'

'No question.' Declan leaned back in his chair and folded his arms. 'What about Joel's events?'

'He's involved only in team events. I think he's more concerned about the food on the day,' Emma ended with a chuckle. Then she sobered. 'But I think it would make Lauren feel special if I was there for her.'

'Yes, it would,' Declan said softly. He wanted to lean forward and kiss her on the lips and tell her what a great job she was doing as a stand-in parent. Instead, he restrained himself and went back to his reading.

At a few minutes to eleven the next day, Emma took her place among the parents and supporters who were rapidly filling every space along the sides of the running track.

'Which one is your kiddie?' a friendly lady who looked like someone's nanna asked as she made room for Emma beside her.

'Over there.' Emma smiled, pointing to Lauren, her little face fierce in concentration as the children began to line up. 'Her mum can't be here so I'm standing in,' she felt compelled to add.

'That's my granddaughter, Taylor, beside her,' the older woman said.

She's at least a head taller than Lauren, Emma thought, her heart dropping. She'd been hoping like mad for Lauren to win. Even a small victory like winning a race would be magic for the child.

Emma felt strung tight, waiting for the starter's whistle to sound. So focused was she that it was a moment before she registered the tap on her shoulder. Spinning round, she took a quick breath of surprise. 'Declan! How did you manage to get here?'

'Easy.' He grinned. 'I booted the patients out of the waiting room and told them to come back tomorrow.'

Emma rolled her eyes.

'Moira and I juggled things. Several agreed to an after-hours consult. I'll see them.' Moving closer, he rested his hand on Emma's shoulder. 'Am I here in time for Lauren's race?'

'They're lining up now.' Emma flicked a hand. 'Lauren seems like a little sprite next to some of the others.'

'I bet you she's a pint-size rocket.' Declan increased the pressure on his hold. 'Look! They're off!' he yelled. 'Go, Lauren!'

The race, it seemed, took only seconds—seconds when they cheered themselves hoarse. Running like the wind, pace for pace with her rival, Lauren finally pulled out a burst of speed from somewhere within her slender little body and took the lead, sprinting over the finishing line just centimetres in front of her rival.

'She won! Lauren won!' Unable to contain her excitement, Emma grabbed at Declan and he whirled her around until she was breathless.

'Come on—' He grabbed her hand and together they began moving towards the finish line.

'Lauren!' Emma shrieked. 'Honey, over here!'

'Wait—' Declan hauled Emma to a halt beside him. 'Look…' he said with something like disbelief in his voice.

Emma looked. 'Oh, my goodness,' she whispered and took a shaky breath. 'It's Tracey… Oh, Declan!' she exclaimed softly. 'Lauren's wish has come true. She so wanted Tracey to be here to watch her run.'

'Lauren's got her mum back,' he rejoined quietly, and their eyes linked in understanding.

Together they watched as Lauren threw herself into her mother's arms. It was the hug of a lifetime. A hug that went on and on, mother and child clinging together and looking as though they never wanted to be parted ever again.

Declan squeezed Emma's hand. 'Are we going over to say hello?'

'Maybe we should. Unless…do you think we'd be intruding?'

'No, I don't,' Declan said and he smiled. 'Come on.'

Lauren's little face lit up when she saw Emma. 'I won!' she said and her thousand-watt smile said it all.

'You did.' Emma held out her arms. 'Well done, sweetheart. You ran like the wind.'

Lauren allowed Emma a brief fierce hug and then she slipped back to her mother's side, tucking her skinny little arm through Tracey's very possessively.

Emma felt something crack inside her. Was it a feeling of loss? she wondered. But that was silly. She was never going to have Lauren indefinitely. She was back with her mother now and that was how it should be. But how she was going to miss that sweet child.

'Hello, Tracey.' Declan stuck out his hand. 'This is a real turn-up.' He grinned. 'You look great, by the way.'

'Thanks.' Tracey looked shyly between the two doctors. 'Marcella from the shelter drove me over. She's got Adam with her.'

'That's wonderful,' Emma said warmly. 'I'm so glad you managed to get here.'

Tracey held her daughter's hand tightly. 'I wouldn't have missed it. I would have got here somehow.'

'Are you back home with us now, Mum?' Lauren's big brown eyes asked the question neither Declan nor Emma had felt able to.

'Yes, baby, I am,' Tracey said softly and bent to press a kiss on her daughter's fair head. 'We'll all be back at Granddad's tonight.'

'You're going to miss them.' Practical as always, Moira was helping Emma pack up the children's clothes for their return home.

Emma blinked a bit, popping a pair of Lauren's jeans into the suitcase. 'Their place is with their mother now she's well. I was just the stopgap until things got back to normal.'

Moira kept folding. 'This house was made for children.'

'And maybe one day it will have some here permanently.' Ignoring Moira's not too subtle implication, Emma forced lightness into her voice. Already a gnawing kind of emptiness was beginning to surround her. But she'd get over it. She had to. 'Oh, Moira—hang on a tick before you close the case. I've something for Lauren. I'll just get it.' She came back with a jumper in the softest, purest wool. It was a happy poppy-red colour with a chain of daisies embroidered around the neckline.

'That's…lovely,' Moira said, but with a note of disquiet in her voice. 'But Emma, should you be spending so much money on the child?'

'It's a gift, nothing more, nothing less.' Emma folded the jumper neatly between some layers of tissue paper and placed it on top of the rest of the clothes. 'I thought Lauren might like to wear it when she goes riding. I want her to keep up her lessons.'

Moira sniffed. 'And who's paying for those riding lessons? You?'

Emma replaced the lid of the suitcase and zipped it shut. 'With respect, Moira, that's my business. Jodi and I have come to an arrangement.'

'You're just like your father.' Moira shook her head. 'Your heart overrules common sense sometimes. Let's just hope Tracey doesn't mess things up for those children again,' she added darkly.

'She won't.' Emma was firm. 'People have worked very hard with her and she's responded. For once, it's been a good outcome.'

'You're going to be at a loose end tonight.' It was late on the same day and Declan was grabbing a coffee before heading out to a house call.

'I suppose I will.' Emma looked up from giving the kitchen bench a quick tidy. 'Got any solutions?'

'I might.' Placing his mug carefully back on the counter top, he half turned to look at her. 'Come home with me.'

There was a moment's loaded silence. Emma blinked uncertainly and she realized what he was saying. She'd been thinking only about the children's departure and how it would affect her. She'd completely forgotten that, with their going, her life was her own again. Her options were suddenly wide open. 'I hadn't thought—'

'Well, I have.' He looked at his watch. 'I'm about to do this house call, then I'll see the three after-hours patients. Should be through by six-thirty. Put a few things together, hmm? And something for work tomorrow.'

'All right.' She smiled, swallowing back a throatful of emotions. 'I'll be ready.'

She hadn't been in his bedroom before.

It was almost spartan with a king-sized bed, books on the bedside table, family photos in a fold-out frame, a set of weights in the corner. And why was she even noticing?

Declan put her bag on the end table. 'Do you want to hang anything?'

'Um—yes, please.' Emma slipped past him to hang her work clothes in the wardrobe. She tried to swallow. Her mouth had become so dry and her heart, with a mind of its own, had gravitated to her throat. It seemed ages since they'd been lovers. Perhaps she'd imagined more than the reality. Could they possibly recapture what they'd found together? And, if they couldn't—what then?

'Emma…'

'Declan, what if…?'

He shook his head, drawing her down to sit on the edge of the bed. He stared at her for a moment. Then, lifting his hands, he cupped her face. 'Emma, do you trust me?'

The catch in his voice told her everything she needed to hear. 'Yes.'

'Oh, heavens! Look at the time!' Emma sprang upright and then leaned down to tug Declan awake. 'Declan, get up! We've only minutes to get to the surgery!'

He groaned. 'What's the hurry? They can't start without us.'

'But it'll look odd if we straggle in late. *And together*.'

'As if we care.' He reached up and pulled her back under the covers. 'I want to tell the world we're together.'

'Oh…' Emma felt her lips sigh apart. 'Really?'

He pulled her closer, nuzzling her throat, behind her ear, then her throat again. 'Yes, really. What about you, Emma? Want to shout it to the tree tops?'

'It's all so new,' she offered, hardly knowing what her answer should be but tucking further into his closeness. His body felt deliciously warm, hard, expectant. Wonderful. All for her. 'Yes, oh, yes,' she said at last and turned her face to meet his mouth.

They tasted each other, taking it slowly, each press of their lips renewing their sense of wonder and delight. Emma closed her eyes and let it happen, letting her tongue tease him and her breath sigh over his face. She ran her hands along his torso, up the lightly tanned curve of his neck and into the dark, soft strands of his hair.

And she didn't let herself think for one second that this commitment was anything but right. Right and perfect.

She opened her mouth wider on his, letting herself drown in his kiss, flinging her doubts into the air like a handful of sand in the wind.

Emma drifted through the morning surgery in a cocoon of dreamy recollection as memories of their lovemaking rolled over her. She felt as though someone had poured liquid sunshine over her bones. She was in love. In love with the most wonderful man in the world.

When, only seconds later, Declan rapped on the door and stuck his head in, she started up out of her reverie, snapping back to reality when he said starkly, 'We have the worst kind of emergency, Emma. Jodi's had a fall at the stables. It looks bad.'

'Oh, my God!' Emma's hand went to her mouth. 'How bad?'

He shook his head. 'Let's get out there. Every second counts.'

Declan looked strained as he took the emergency kit from Libby. 'Keep the hospital in the loop, please, Libs.' The nurse merely nodded.

Moira hovered, her face pale with shock. 'I know you want to come with us, Moira,' Declan said gently. 'But—'

'I'd be in the way.' Her mouth trembled. 'Take care of her, Declan. She's the dearest thing on earth to me.'

Emma wrapped an arm quickly around Moira's shoulders. 'We'll let you know the minute we have some details,' she promised.

'Do you have any more details about the accident?' Emma asked.

'Not much. Jodi was riding track with several others. Apparently, the horses were flat out in a time trial. The lead horse stumbled. Jodi was immediately behind.'

Emma sucked in her breath on a grimace. It would be a domino effect, resulting in a wild mix of riders, horses, limbs and bodies.

'Jodi's parents?' Declan's question took on the practicalities of the situation.

'Last I heard, they're away on holiday up north somewhere. She was staying with Moira.'

'Siblings?'

'One brother at Uni in Brisbane. Final year engineering.' Worst scenarios curled in a knot in Emma's stomach. Jodi's family would have to be summoned immediately.

When they arrived at the stables, they were out of the car and running. Jodi's cries of distress were endless. Heartbreaking. Emma ran faster.

Sarah McGinty was waiting. 'I tried to make her more comfortable,' she said. 'But I didn't dare move her. Patrick and James are away at the yearling sales. There's just me here.' She tightened her arms across her middle as if she was in pain herself. 'None of this should have happened…'

Emma placed a quick hand of sympathy on Sarah's forearm and squeezed.

The doctors worked seamlessly as a team, checking first

for any head or spinal injury. 'Stay with us, Jodi,' Declan said gently. He slipped the oxygen mask into place. 'We'll have you feeling better soon.'

And pigs might fly, he added silently, grimly.

Emma was doing her best to insert an IV. She shook her head.

'Problem?' Declan snapped.

'Veins thready and constricted. OK,' she said with relief. 'I've got it. Normal saline going in now. What pain relief do you want?'

'Spleen seems OK. We can give morphine. Let's make it five milligrams, please. Anti-emetic ten. Both IV.'

'Jodi, sweetheart, we're giving you something for the pain now.' Emma injected the drugs quickly. 'All done.'

'Thanks. I need to assess what's going on with her legs.'

Emma knew what had to be done. Grabbing the scissors from the emergency pack, she slit Jodi's jodhpurs from ankle to thigh, peeling back the layers of material. She bit hard on her bottom lip at what lay revealed. Bone was protruding from Jodi's thigh.

'Compound fracture to the right femur.' Declan was clinically calm. 'I'd guess the horse in its fright has kicked out and caught her legs.' His fingers ran gently along her shins. 'Multiple fractures to left tib and fib so both legs compromised. Let's get a doughnut dressing over that exposed bone, please, and we'll splint both legs together for the transfer to the ambulance.'

'For the best possible care, I think we should chopper her straight through to the Royal Brisbane.' Emma's tone was unequivocal. 'She's going to need hours of surgery and follow-up rehab.' She drew out her mobile phone. 'I'll put a call into CareFlight. Ask them to meet us at the hospital. By the time they get here, we should have Jodi stable enough to go.'

Two of the town's ambulance crew who had arrived barely minutes behind the doctors moved in with the stretcher. Nick Turner, the senior officer, looked stricken. 'I've known young Jodi all her life…'

Declan's mouth drew in. This was no time to start hand-wringing. Their patient needed to be in the care of a surgeon and fast. 'What's the situation with the other riders, Nick?'

'There were two lads. Both managed to roll out of the way of the horses. They're a bit shaken. No obvious injuries and we've checked their neuro obs.' He shook his head. 'Poor little Jodi was caught in the middle of the scrum. Blasted animals…'

Emma closed off her mobile. 'The base can't give us an ETA on the chopper. It's presently evacuating injured from a motor pile-up on the Warrego Highway.'

Declan's expletive was muted. 'What now?'

Emma bit her lips together. Declan's face spoke volumes.

'We could take her by ambulance to Toowoomba and try and get backup transport from there,' Nick said without much conviction. 'The road's still a bit dodgy in places from the storm but if we're careful…'

Declan shook his head. 'We can't put Jodi through that.'

'Then we'll wait on the chopper,' Emma said doggedly.

Declan's jaw tightened. God only knew what Jodi's circulation would be doing by the time the air ambulance got to them. And they were wasting precious seconds messing about here. Jodi's cry of distress sent a chill around the gathering.

'I'll check again with CareFlight.' Emma pulled out her mobile.

'Hold it,' Declan said clearly. 'I'll do the surgery here.'

Emma's eyes flew wide in alarm. Did Declan realize what he was suggesting? Surely he was placing their patient's life at risk if he didn't know for certain whether he had the stamina to complete the operation? Should she try to intervene and stop him? 'Declan—'

In an abrupt movement, he drew her aside. 'I need you to back me on this, Emma. It'll be a far better outcome for Jodi if she can have the surgery done here.'

But would it be the best outcome for *him*? Operating before he was ready could undo all the progress, both physically and emotionally, that he'd made. And she knew if she dug her toes in and refused to back him, he'd respect their professional partnership and stand aside and wait for the chopper. But what of Jodi? Poor little injured Jodi. The wait would be terrible. For all of them.

'Emma, listen…' he said, his jaw working. 'I can do this.'

Emma closed her eyes, praying for courage, because this was the hardest decision she'd ever had to make in her life. Her heart pounded. She thought of her father and what he'd want her to do. He'd tell her to trust her instincts. She closed her eyes for one second and then snapped them open. 'As long as you're sure, I'll back you.'

'Thank you.' Declan already had his mobile phone in his hand. He punched a logged-in number and waited to be connected. 'Rachel? Declan. We're still at the stables. The chopper's a no-show. We're bringing Jodi in now. I'll do the surgery. I'll have to pin and plate so I'll need all orthopaedic trays sterilized and ready.'

'Word of the RTA is all over the TV news,' Rachel said. 'I've gone ahead and anticipated your request.'

'Brilliant—thanks.' Declan felt a huge weight begin to slide from his shoulders. They could do this. 'What nursing backup can we manage?'

'Well, I'll scrub, of course, and I've got Dot here. She's theatre-savvy, even if she doesn't get much practice these days.'

'Oliver Shackelton lined up to gas for us?'

'There we might have a slight problem.' Rachel sounded cautious. 'I called Oliver. He's had flu, and he's feeling too rocky to be in Theatre.'

'So, we don't have an anaesthetist?' Declan just resisted thumping his fist against his forehead in frustration. What options did he have now to safely go ahead with Jodi's surgery? 'Just give me a second here, Rachel.'

Beside him, Emma got the gist of the conversation and wondered what unkind fate had singled her out today. She felt as though her professional integrity had been pushed to the limits. It wasn't fair. Emotion, real and powerful, churned inside her. Could she take this last step that would enable Declan to operate? Could she afford not to? When did it become obligation to speak up? Was it safer to just stand aside and wait?

In her heart, she knew the decision had already been made for her.

'Declan?'

Her fleeting touch in the small of his back had his gaze swivelling in her direction. He shrugged. 'Looks like we're stuffed,' he said flatly. 'Oliver can't help.'

'But perhaps I can.' She looked unflinchingly at him. 'I did my elective in anaesthesiology. I could probably manage. But it will be a long op. I'll need Oliver's input on dosage for longer-acting drugs. But if you think the whole thing's too risky, I want you to pull out now.'

Declan shook his head. In his mind there were no doubts left and only three words to be said. 'We'll go ahead.'

Emma could hardly believe how smoothly their little hospital was coping with the emergency. She was still basking in a sense of pride as she finished scrubbing. The sound of a door swishing open sent her turning away from the basin and, by the time Declan had begun scrubbing beside her, she was drying her hands and asking sharply, 'You OK?'

'Yep.' He sent her an abrupt look from under his brows and grinned. 'Glad I had that extra X-ray equipment installed, though.'

'Even though we'll be paying for it for the rest of our lives.'

'Oh, tut, Emma. We've managed so far, haven't we?'

She had to admit they had. And she knew they were batting light conversation around because to get too serious now would be more than either of them could cope with. The decision to operate here had been made. They just had to make sure they gave it their all.

'See you in there.' She turned and left the annexe and crossed to the theatre. Rachel had prepared the anaesthetic trolley perfectly and Emma felt a rush of adrenalin she hadn't experienced for the longest time.

She'd do a brilliant job for Jodi.

They all would.

The surgery took almost seven hours. Hours when Emma felt her skills were being tested mercilessly. Even though the monitors indicated Jodi was handling the anaesthetic well, Emma knew she couldn't afford to relax her vigilance for a second. Time after time she raised her eyes to meet Declan's, wanting reassurance, wanting anything to tell her they'd done the right thing. *I'm fine*, his look said, and he gave her the merest nod.

'Thanks, team. Fantastic effort.' Declan inserted the last suture in Jodi's shin. He dressed the site with care and signalled for Emma to reverse the anaesthetic. 'How's our girl looking, Emma?'

'She's looking good,' Emma said.

'That's what I like to hear.' Above his mask, Declan's eyes crinkled with tired humour. 'OK, guys, would you mind finishing up here?' He stepped back from the operating table, working his shoulders briefly. 'I don't want to keep Moira waiting for news any longer than necessary.'

'I'm sure we don't mind at all.' Emma paused and then added barely audibly, 'That was a fine piece of surgery, Declan.'

Declan's eyes met hers and held. 'You made it easy, Dr Armitage.' With that, he turned on his heel and left the theatre.

Declan answered the clamouring of his aching back with a long hot shower. The whole day had begun to take on a surreal quality. The adrenalin rush he'd felt at the beginning of the operation had disappeared, leaving him flat. He didn't dwell on it. Instead, he dressed quickly and went to meet Emma at the nurses' station.

At his approach, Emma looked up and smiled. She had a

lot to smile about. Jodi was in Recovery and doing well. 'Apparently, there's some dinner for us in the canteen. Betty's made us her special Turkish lamb casserole,' she said.

He raised his brows in mock awe. 'We'd better have second helpings, then.'

'Did you get all your follow-up done?'

'I reassured Moira and left a few post-op instructions with the night sister. Jodi should be stable enough to make the transfer to the Royal late tomorrow. Her parents are flying back in the morning. They'll make their base in Brisbane for the next few days and see their daughter settled in.'

Emma nodded. She had a dozen questions for him, about him, but none she could ask. Not yet. And maybe she wouldn't have to ask them at all. Maybe, without her prompting, Declan would simply tell her what she wanted to know. Had to know.

They ate hungrily.

'Not half bad,' Declan said, finishing his meal and placing his cutlery neatly together on his dinner plate.

'And so sweet of Betty to have made it especially for us.' Emma sent him a half-smile. 'Word's got round pretty quickly that big things happened here today.'

'Is that so?'

Emma stood up. 'Cup of tea?'

'Sounds good.' He turned away as his mobile phone rang.

Emma placed their cups of tea on a tray, added some rosemary shortbread she'd raided from the nurses' cookie jar and began making her way back to their table. It was late and they were the only ones left in the hospital canteen. Although he hadn't said it, Declan must be feeling the strain of the day, she thought. The charcoal shadows around his eyes were a dead giveaway.

Well, they'd be home soon. She'd hold him all night, smooth away the tensions, pleasure herself with the hardness of his body and the careless male beauty of his nakedness. They'd made love only this morning but it already felt like a year ago.

Her breath felt fluttery.

'Drink up and we'll make tracks.' Declan's brow furrowed. 'I'll drop you home and then take off. I need to wind down a bit and I want to make a call to Scotland. Have a chat to Angus Menzies at St Mary's about today. Debrief, I guess.'

Why couldn't he debrief with *her*? A look of disbelief scorched Emma's gaze. Hell, she'd been there with him at the cutting edge. It was only because of her compliance that he'd been able to go ahead and perform the surgery at all. She couldn't believe he wouldn't want them to spend the night together. 'You could do all that from Kingsholme.'

Of course he could. But he knew that would mean Emma would want him, *expect* him, to stay the night. To make love with her. How could he tell her he doubted if he was physically capable? The hours spent in surgery had left him with a burning pain in his lower back, his legs feeling as if he'd run a marathon. It was too soon to know if it would be an ongoing problem for him. But hell, what if it was? He gathered the strands of his tattered pride, raising an eyebrow at her. 'I've got a bit to sort out. You know how it is.'

No, she didn't know at all. Her confidence in their newfound commitment dropped to the floor. And stayed there like an unwanted garment that didn't fit. Lifting a hand, she brushed an imaginary crumb from her bottom lip. 'I'm ready when you are, then.'

They made their way in silence to his car. When they arrived at Kingsholme, Declan walked her to the door. 'I thought we could meet up at the hospital in the morning. See Jodi together. Around eightish? Is that all right with you?'

'Fine.' Emma shrugged. 'I hope you get your debrief.'

'Mmm.' He leant and placed a swift little kiss on her mouth and then stepped back. 'Thanks for today,' he said abruptly then walked away.

The house felt cold and unlived-in. Emma shivered. She went from room to room, switching on the lights. She could have a fire. But why bother? The empty feeling inside her was terrible.

What was going on with Declan? Physically, he appeared to have coped with the long stint in the OR. But he hadn't enlightened her about how he was feeling. Surely she deserved more than the cursory thanks he'd offered? Unless—Emma felt a river of alarm run down her spine. Was he intending to walk away now he had his career back? He'd said she had to trust him, but just now her trust was wearing very thin. Gossamer-thin and fragile.

The next morning, there was no sign of Declan when Emma arrived at the hospital. She decided to go and visit Jodi without him. He'd made the arrangements. It was up to him to keep them. Or let her know if he couldn't for some reason.

She found Jodi sitting up in bed, looking pale. Well, that was to be expected. The youngster had undergone major surgery. 'Hi, sweetie.' Emma pulled up a chair and sat down. 'How are you feeling?'

'I've been better.' Jodi pulled a sad little clown's face. 'I *so* cannot believe what happened.'

'They call them accidents, honey. All said and done, you were very fortunate.'

Jodi made a sound of disgust in her throat. 'The guys got off scot-free.'

'Except for getting the fright of their lives—and I think Mr McGinty will have a few hard words to say to them,' Emma predicted soberly.

Hell. Declan dragged a pair of jeans and a long-sleeved sweatshirt out of the pile of clean laundry and dressed hurriedly. How on earth could he have slept in? He hadn't heard the alarm. Well, what did he expect? He'd spent most of night wide awake before sleep had finally claimed him around 4:00 a.m.

And he hadn't solved anything. He still felt caught in a sea of confusion. He felt bad about how he'd handled things with Emma last night. Or not handled them. With hindsight, he knew he should have told her how physically exhausted he'd felt. She would have understood. But then that would have opened another can of worms—should he have operated at all?

Now he was facing an even worse scenario. By the way he felt this morning—would he ever be able to operate again? Grabbing his jacket, phone and car keys, he stepped out into the chilly morning.

He wasn't surprised to see Emma's little four-by-four in the parking lot when he arrived at the hospital. He shook his head. She was always so reliable, did things by the book. Except for yesterday. His mouth twisted grimly. He knew that backing him to do the surgery had been a huge call for her. Right outside her comfort zone.

Entering the hospital, he flung a greeting at the nurse on duty at the station and made his way along the corridor to Jodi's room. Taking a deep controlling breath, he knocked and entered.

'Morning.' Both women looked up. Emma held his gaze for a second, then looked pointedly away. He winced inwardly. She was cheesed off with him and he didn't blame her. He picked up Jodi's chart and studied it. 'How's our star patient this morning?'

Jodi managed a half smile. 'I'm still here. I guess that's a plus.'

'A pretty big plus from where I'm standing.' Declan raised his dark head. 'And I dare say Emma feels the same. How's the pain this morning, Jodi?'

'Still hurts a bit.'

A lot, Declan interpreted, going on the night report. 'I'll up your pain relief. That should help.'

'Nan says I have to go to Royal Brisbane. Is that really necessary?'

''Fraid so.' Declan replaced the patient chart and pocketed his pen. 'We don't have the facilities to nurse you here, Jodi. Besides, you're going to need some specialized rehab to get your legs back in working order.'

Emma squeezed Jodi's hand. 'You're young and fit, Jodi. You'll be back with us before you know it.'

'And what *about* my legs?' Jodi's voice wobbled. 'How badly hurt were they? Will I be able to ride again? Can I have the truth, please…?'

Emma glanced at Declan, then snatched her gaze away as if it hurt her eyes. 'They're probably questions for your surgeon,' she said and held Jodi's hand tightly.

'I won't keep the truth from you, Jodi.' Declan slipped seamlessly into a role he knew so well. Dealing with the anxieties of post-surgery patients. 'Your legs were pretty badly knocked about.' At Jodi's little gasp of dismay, he lifted a staying hand and went on, 'But I've done this kind of operation dozens of times. You're back together.' He smiled then. 'And almost as good as new.'

'Oh—' Jodi gave a little mew of relief.

'If you work hard with your physio,' Declan promised, 'your fitness will return quite quickly.'

'And my legs… Will...will they look…gross?'

'Of course they won't!' Emma looked appalled. 'I won't regale you with the clinical details of the operation, but Declan did an amazing job. You'll find there'll be hardly any scarring at all.'

Jodi sent them a watery smile. 'Thanks.' She leaned back on her pillows, her look braver than before. 'And what about my job at the surgery?'

'Well, I don't know about that.' Declan rubbed his jaw as if considering a weighty problem. 'What do you think, Emma?'

Emma did her best to join in the light-heartedness for Jodi's sake. 'Oh, I think we can muddle along until you can come back to us, sweetheart.' She got to her feet. 'Now, we'll leave you in peace.'

'Nan said she'd be in a bit later on.' Jodi blocked a yawn. 'Are you both coming in to see me off on the chopper?'

'Wouldn't want to be anywhere else, would we?' Emma

placed a gentle hand on Jodi's shoulder. 'I'll check with the nurses' station about the ETA of the CareFlight chopper.' She fluttered a wave in Jodi's direction and made her way to the door. Declan followed closely behind.

Emma waited until they were outside the hospital before she asked, 'You do intend being here to see Jodi safely off, don't you, Declan?'

He shoved his hands into the back pockets of his jeans. 'I...need to talk to you about that. Could we go somewhere for a coffee?'

Emma sent him a speaking look. 'You mean you'll actually make time for me?'

He hunched his shoulders and scrubbed at a pebble with the toe of his shoe.

'Emma, this is very hard,' he said. And she could see in the strained expression in his face how much he meant it.

'It doesn't have to be, does it?' she countered, her throat tight. 'You could just talk to me.'

'I can't—not yet. A lot's happened over the last twenty-four hours. I need to find my own way through this. Please understand.'

Was he saying he couldn't share his thoughts with her? Or was it something deeper? Her mouth drooped. Whatever it was, she knew she couldn't push him any further. She glanced at her watch. 'Rina Kennedy is reopening the garden centre today. I promised I'd go along. They've incorporated a food court in the refurbishment. We could get a coffee there.'

'Fine,' he agreed quickly. 'I'll follow you.'

The garden centre was already buzzing. Quashing her immediate problems, Emma looked around her. The townsfolk had come out in droves to support the Kennedys. And it was looking lovely. Very upmarket.

Declan touched her arm. 'This looks like the coffee shop through here. Shall we get a table?'

Emma nodded, the well of emotion rising in her throat

threatening to choke her. When they were seated, she picked up the menu and made a pretence of studying it. 'Well, this is different,' she joked thinly. 'Fancy a wattle seed tea?'

Declan's mouth twisted in the parody of a smile. 'I'll stick to coffee, thanks. But don't let me stop you. What about some raisin toast to go with it?'

'I'll have a friand, I think.' She turned to catch the eye of the waitress and blinked. 'Oh, my goodness—there's Tracey! She must work here.' She was looking wonderful in her pristine white T-shirt and black pants covered by a dark green apron with the little shamrock embroidered on the front. Her hair was pulled neatly back and her smile was wide and welcoming as she approached their table.

They exchanged greetings and Tracey said, beaming, 'I've got a job here.'

'Congratulations,' Declan said warmly.

'From me as well,' Emma added. 'You're a star, Tracey.'

'I got the job off my own bat too,' Tracey said proudly. 'Mrs Kennedy is going to teach me the nursery side of things and I can do some college courses in Toowoomba and learn how to propagate plants and stuff.'

'That's brilliant.' Declan raised dark brows. 'I'm impressed.'

'Well, I've you to thank really, Dr O'Malley.' Tracey blushed. 'I mean you believed in me…'

Declan shook his head. 'You did all the hard work, Tracey.'

'Maybe…' She bit her lip. 'And Dr Armitage—you looked after my kids…' She stopped, embarrassed.

'It was a pleasure, Tracey.' Emma blinked a bit. 'They're wonderful kids. Are they here today?'

'Heck, no.' Tracey rolled her eyes. 'They're with Nev.'

'So, life is looking pretty good, then?' Declan asked.

Tracey nodded. 'And, best of all, I've been placed on the Defence Department's housing list. The kids and I should get our own place pretty soon. We'll be together again and Carolyn will get some peace at last. Anyway…' she huffed an embarrassed laugh and took out her order book '...what can I get you?'

There was an awkward silence after Tracey had gone.

'So, did you manage your debrief?' Emma's question had a sharp edge to it.

His look was guarded and cool. 'After a fashion.'

'Look, could we stop talking in riddles?' Emma threw caution to the winds and said what was uppermost on her mind. 'It hurt that you didn't want us to be together last night. What am I supposed to think now, Declan?'

'I hardly know what to think myself, Emma,' he said baldly. 'Yesterday changed everything.'

'You mean it's given you options you didn't have before, don't you?'

Declan's face was tightly drawn. 'I don't know yet. That's something I have to find out.'

The silence between them lengthened and became thicker.

'I need to ask a favour of you, Emma,' he said at last.

Her heart pounded uncomfortably. 'What do you need?'

'I need to be in Melbourne for a couple of days. I'll get a flight today from Brisbane and I should be back for surgery on Tuesday. If you could cover my patient list on Monday, I'd be grateful.'

She was hardly surprised at his request. It wasn't as though she hadn't conducted surgery countless times before on her own. It was obvious he was going to Melbourne to sort out what options were open to him. Maybe even get a new job operating now he knew he could. Well, she hoped he got what he wanted. He certainly didn't want *her*. She took a deep breath and pressed her palms down hard on the table. 'Go and do what you have to do, Declan. I'll manage.'

CHAPTER TWELVE

'MOIRA, streamline the patient lists as much as you can, please,' Emma said on Monday morning to the practice manager. 'I'm covering for Declan today.'

'Where *is* Declan?' Moira raised a questioning brow.

'Melbourne,' Emma said economically.

'He has family in Melbourne, doesn't he?'

'Yes.' Emma shrugged. And Declan was known there, had a network of professional contacts there. No doubt felt at home there. Enough to draw him back?

Her nerves tightened alarmingly. If he knew he could resume his chosen discipline, what on earth could entice him to stay in Bendemere?

The thought was painful. Almost impossible to bear. But Emma brought her fair head up determinedly. 'Don't worry about morning tea, Moira. I'll work straight through to lunch.'

Declan waited in the foyer of the lovely old building that contained within its hallowed architecture the professional rooms of the city's leading specialist doctors.

No one knew he was in Melbourne. No one apart from Emma and Matthew Levingston, one of Australia's top spinal consultants, who had agreed to see him first thing this morning as a professional favour. He hadn't wanted to tell his sisters he was in town. There would be too many questions—questions he didn't have answers to.

The lift arrived and Declan stepped inside. Even though he'd had only tea and toast for breakfast, it was sitting uneasily in his stomach. Breathing out a jagged breath, he pressed the button for the third floor.

Dr Levingston's receptionist, Jill Carter, was middle-aged and pleasant, her smile professionally in place as Declan approached the counter.

'Declan O'Malley.' His voice was clipped, strained. 'I have an appointment this morning.'

'Yes, Dr O'Malley. Dr Levingston is expecting you. Take a seat for a moment. He shouldn't be long.'

'Thanks.' Declan hesitated. 'Would you know if my notes arrived from Scotland? They were coming from St Mary's in Edinburgh.'

'Faxed through during the weekend. Doctor has them now.'

Declan nodded, relieved. That was the first hurdle over, then. He crossed to where a row of comfortable chairs were arranged along the wall and lowered himself into one of the cushioned seats. He stretched out his legs and looked at his watch for the umpteenth time. It was barely eight o'clock.

It seemed only seconds later when a side door opened and the consultant poked his head out. 'Declan. Come through, mate.'

The two men shook hands warmly. 'Thanks for seeing me at such short notice, Matt,' Declan said.

'Happy to do it.' The consultant's mouth twisted into a wry grin. 'Have to look after our own, don't we? Now, could I organize coffee?'

Declan's stomach protested. 'No—no, thanks. I'm fine.'

'Right, let's put you through your paces, then.'

Matthew's examination was painstaking, his questions, and Declan imagined there were a thousand of them, probing. 'OK,' he said finally. 'That's it for now. Anything you want clarified?'

'The residual pain I experienced after I'd been in Theatre?'

'Pretty normal. It would have helped if you'd been able to ease yourself back into work rather than go for a seven-hour marathon straight away,' he suggested dryly.

'I was faced with an emergency,' Declan said. 'Not much choice there.'

'Probably not.' Matthew's mouth pursed thoughtfully. 'You can get dressed now, Declan. Come back out when you're ready and we'll have a chat. It's looking good, by the way,' he added before pulling back the screen and returning to his desk.

Declan felt one layer of trepidation roll off him. One step at a time, though. That was all it could be until he knew…

'You appear to have healed particularly well,' said Matthew. 'Your spine is in good order.' He amplified the statement with technical language because he rightly guessed Declan would want the clinical assessment. 'Now, all that said, I'd like you to have an MRI before I can give you definitive answers.'

Declan gave a resigned grin. 'I was afraid you'd stick me with one of those.'

'You betcha. But, with the new technology, they're less onerous than they used to be.' Matthew picked up his phone and spoke briefly to his receptionist. 'Do the best you can,' he ended. 'Thanks.' He clipped the phone back on its cradle. 'There's normally a bit of a wait on these. How soon do you need to be back at your practice?'

In an instant Declan was transported back to Kingsholme, visualizing Emma beavering away through the morning's list, her fair head bent over the patients' notes. She probably hadn't had a moment to think of him. But he'd had the whole of the weekend to think of her. And she was filling his heart to overflowing. But his feelings were laced with vulnerability. Such vulnerability. He wasn't sure of her or her feelings for him. 'My partner is holding the fort but I'd like to get back as soon as possible.'

Matthew nodded, his hand reaching out as his phone pad lit discreetly. He leaned back in his chair, holding the receiver loosely and listened. 'OK, thanks, Jill. Excellent. We're in luck,' he said, replacing the handset. 'The imaging centre has a cancellation. How does ten-thirty sound?'

Although he wasn't particularly looking forward to the procedure, Declan nodded gratefully. 'Sounds good. Which centre do you use?'

'The new state-of-the-art set-up in St Kilda. Jill will give you the address. Then I'll need to see you again and discuss things.' Matthew pulled his diary open and studied it. 'I'm not in Theatre today so I could see you, let's see—around four this afternoon?' he suggested, sending a quizzical glance across his desk.

'I'll be here.' The two men stood and shook hands again.

'A word of advice, Declan,' Matthew said as he saw his patient out. 'Don't spend the day sweating about outcomes. I'll see you back here at four.'

Outside the building, Declan took a moment to get his bearings. He hardly remembered getting here this morning, so totally preoccupied as he'd been with the weight of his medical appointment. Now, he felt better, freer. The worst was over. His fitness hadn't lapsed and, whatever the outcome of the MRI, he knew now he could make a life for himself in medicine, even if it couldn't be permanently in the operating theatre. He'd enjoyed being a family practitioner more than he'd ever thought he would.

The feeling of optimism startled him, refreshed him. God, it felt good just be out in the world again, in a city he loved.

Suddenly he longed to share his news with someone who cared. He grimaced. Emma was out of the question. He had a lot of making up to do before he could expect her to listen to him. Both his sisters would be at work. Hailing a passing cab, he got in and gave the St Kilda address of the imaging centre. Then it came to him. There *was* someone he could talk to.

At the airport, Declan prowled past the ticketing booth yet again. He'd been waiting on standby for his flight to Brisbane. Several flights had been called but each time he'd missed out on a seat. Another flight was about to depart and he *had* to get on board if he was to have any chance of seeing Emma tonight.

He almost missed his name when it was called. Finally. Thank God. He looped his carry-on bag over his shoulder and strode swiftly down the covered walkway to the waiting aircraft.

Emma sat on the sofa in a kind of twilight daze. Earlier, she'd been for a run and on her return she'd showered and dressed in her track pants and fleecy top. She supposed she should go to bed but she knew she'd never sleep. She'd had one brief text message from Declan telling her he'd be back some time tonight. She wondered how late his flight had got in.

She should have swallowed her pride and texted back and insisted he stay the night in Brisbane. With the possibility of a fog always present, driving up that mountain road at night was fraught with risks.

When the knock sounded on the back door, she lifted her head sharply towards the sound, her heart swooping. Swallowing back a little cry of anguish, she half-ran, half-walked to the door. Reaching for the latch, she yanked it open.

Seeing him there, smiling, expectant, in one piece, when she'd envisaged all kinds of calamities, she felt suddenly overwhelmed by anger. 'What time do you call this, Declan? It's after midnight!'

The amber in her eyes glittered like fiery embers. She was beautiful and he suddenly realized he couldn't wait a moment longer to tell her how he felt about her. Feeling he was opening up his chest and showing her his heart, he said, 'I love you, Emma. I'm never letting you go.'

'Ooh—' Emma felt all the breath leave her body, a great jumble of emotions tumble around inside her. Was she dreaming? She stood frozen, love, hope and joy colliding in a great ball in her chest.

'Emma?' His eyes clouded. 'I'm freezing to death here. Did you hear what I said?'

She gave a frenzied little nod and found her voice. 'Come inside then, you crazy man.' She drew him inside to the warmth of the lounge room. And turned to him, eyes over-bright. 'You must have been mad driving up the range at this time of night.'

'I must have been.' His eyes glinted and he reached for her and pulled her hard against him. 'Mad for the sight of you,' he said hoarsely. 'Do you love me too?'

Emma took a deep breath, feeling overwhelmed suddenly by recent events. 'Of course I love you.'

'Oh, thank God,' he whispered. 'Thank *you*,' he echoed, pressing kisses all over her face. 'I never want to be away from you again.'

They were words she'd longed to hear. But she wasn't letting him off the hook just yet. 'You owe me an explanation, Declan. I've been going slowly crazy wondering where your head was at for these past couple of days. Did I do something wrong—say something wrong?'

'No! It wasn't you—it was me. After Jodi's surgery, I was so preoccupied with my own problems, I wasn't thinking straight.'

'We *should* have debriefed,' she insisted. 'I needed it as much as you.'

'Yes, you did. I honestly didn't realize.' He frowned down into her face. 'I wasn't feeling all that great after Jodi's surgery,' he confessed, his voice a bit scratchy. 'But I didn't want to burden you. I'd pushed you to support me and I was afraid my career might be completely over—that you'd be forever lumbered with a practice partner—and a lover—who couldn't pull his weight…'

'Oh, my God—Declan!' Emma shook her head as if she couldn't believe his thought processes.

'I know, I know,' he admitted ruefully. 'It all sounds a bit pathetic and over-reactive now.'

'Shh.' She placed her fingers on his lips. 'It was a big deal for you. I should have understood that. I guess I was a bit selfish.'

'You're the least selfish person I know,' he countered.

Emma curled her fingers up around his neck. 'Are you terribly tired—or could we talk?'

The curve of her bottom through the soft stuff of her track pants felt good tucked into his palms and he shook his head. 'I'll never be too tired for you, Emma.'

They stoked up the fire and fell on to the sofa in a tight tangle of arms and legs, her cheek pressed against his chest so that she could hear the steady rhythm of his heart. 'So—' she paused and reached up to touch his face, stroking the dark shadows around his eyes with gentle fingers '—what did you do in Melbourne?'

His brain fizzed with technical information but he kept it simple, telling her about his medical appointments but leaving nothing out.

'And what did Dr Levingston say when you went back to see him?' She almost held her breath for his answer.

'That I'm fully recovered.' He looked suddenly youthful, eager. 'I can operate again without fearing I'll fall over.'

'Oh, Declan!' Emma's pulse trebled before she could put the brakes on. 'I'm so happy for you,' she said, but thinking also what this new state of affairs could mean to them personally, to their practice, if he wanted to leave… 'It's going to change things here, isn't it?'

'Only if it's what we both want.' He looked down at her, his face unsmiling, deep in concentration. 'I had plenty of time to think while I was waiting for a flight home. I came up with a couple of possibilities.'

'OK…' Emma felt a hard-edged little lump that lodged somewhere in her chest. 'Tell me.'

'Well, we could leave things as they are,' he said slowly. 'I'm sure I could schedule enough orthopaedic work in Toowoomba to keep my hand in, as well as pulling my weight here in the practice.'

Emma looked doubtful. 'Would that be fulfilling enough for you, though?'

'Yes,' he said without hesitation. 'If that's what you want too. I've learned a lot here. Being a doctor in a rural practice carries clout, enables you to get things done for people. Good things. Necessary things. It's a great feeling.'

Oh, she was so glad he felt like that. 'That's what I think too.'

He smiled. 'Yes. I knew that.'

'And we could open up the OR here and do basic procedures, like Dad did,' Emma expanded. 'Rachel's staying, by the way. I talked to her yesterday.'

'That's good. She's needed here.'

Emma noticed he'd gone quiet. He looked tired, she thought. And a little strained. It made her love him more. Made her want to smooth out those lines around his eyes and mouth with her fingers, and with her lips… They'd get to that. Later. 'What was the other possibility you came up with, then?'

'Ah!' There was life in his face again. 'I thought we could lease out the practice for a year and go and live in Melbourne.'

'Melbourne?' This was right out of left field. Emma wriggled upright. 'What would we do there?'

'I could go back to the OR full-time, be part of a surgical team again.'

'I see.' A tiny frown came to rest between her brows. 'And what would I do?'

'You, my love, could get a place in an anaesthetist training programme, upgrade your skills so you could be my gas woman when we come back to Kingsholme.'

She chuckled. 'Your gas woman? I like the sound of it, though. But would I get into a programme? I imagine places are at a premium.'

'I know a few faces,' he said modestly. 'And I imagine if you used your dad's name in the right places, doors would open.'

Emma digested all that. The idea appealed to her. Quite a lot, actually. 'I think I'd really, really like to do that,' she said quietly. 'But we'd need to get someone of calibre for Kingsholme.'

'We would. If we offered a year's tenure, we'd be sure to get quality applicants.'

'And we *will* come back to Kingsholme eventually, won't we?'

'Of course we will,' he promised. 'We'd want to raise our kids here, wouldn't we?'

'Oh, yes… I'd love to fill the house with our children.' He looked startled and she wrinkled her nose and compromised, 'With two or three, then.'

'That's manageable.' He sliced her a grin and then sobered. 'You've been bowed down under tremendous pressure for a long time now, Emma. A year away will be good for you to do something for yourself, be a student again.'

She rolled her eyes at him. 'I'll probably end up with some pedantic authoritarian boss who'll yell at me.'

'Yell back.' Declan ran the tip of his finger down her straight little nose. 'You're a fully qualified doctor, not some poor intern struggling for approval.'

'Mmm.' She settled herself more comfortably in his arms. 'It's pretty exciting to think we could do something like this, isn't it, Declan?'

'I think so.' He paused and rested his chin on the top of her head. 'I had lunch with Roz while I was in Melbourne.'

Emma twisted to look at him. 'You had lunch with my mother! Why?'

'I was at a loose end. Felt the need for family but Erinn and Katie were at work. Then I thought of your mum and it just seemed to fit. If I couldn't have you with me, then I had the next best thing. Roz was brilliant. We got on like a house on fire. We talked about you a lot.'

'Did you tell her why you were in Melbourne?'

'Yes. She was sympathetic, practical. Talked me up. I also told her I was in love with you.'

'You did?' Emma laughed. 'What did she say?'

'Said she'd gathered how things were between us when she stayed here recently. She approves, by the way.'

Emma gave him a quick intense glance. He'd taken her breath away.

'And she gave me something for you as well,' Declan said. 'A photo album she thought you'd like to have. It's in the car.'

'Oh, Lord,' Emma groaned. 'Not nude baby shots—please?'

His head went back in a laugh. 'One or two. But mostly they're of you and your parents from when you were tiny until your teens. Your parents had a happy marriage, Emma. You can't fake the kind of warmth I saw in those snapshots.'

'I'd come to that conclusion myself,' she said softly, drawing closer to him. 'But it was sweet of Mum to send the album.' And put her last remaining fears to rest. Emma wanted to say it but her heart was so full she couldn't find the words and anyway he didn't give her time.

'Will you marry me, Emma?'

The words were bliss to her ears. She hesitated and then said, 'Yes, Declan, I'll marry you. But not yet.'

His dark brows shot up in question.

'I want us to do some old-fashioned courting first.'

He reached out and brought her chin up gently, and his eyes when they looked into hers were lit with devilment. 'You want me to *court* you?'

'Yes, please.'

'Like with flowers and presents and…love notes?'

'All of those.'

'And dinners out?'

She looked dreamily at him. 'And dinners in.'

'I can do that.' He kissed her very sweetly, very tenderly. 'And when I've done everything to your satisfaction, you'll become my bride?'

'Yes, Declan…' Her voice broke on a whisper as she looked up at him and saw the soft sheen of love in his eyes. 'Then I'll become your bride.'